TWO WORLDS, ONE LOVE

"I love you," I whispered as, pulling Shadow's head down, I kissed him—gently at first, then with greater intensity.

I was not prepared for his quick response. With a sudden rush of passion, he crushed me close, covering my face and neck with kisses that seared my skin.

A quick flame of desire sparked in the deepest core of my being, and what had started as a game now turned abruptly serious. Shadow's dark eyes burned with a fierce inner fire as he began to stroke my quivering flesh in places he had never dared touch before.

My breathing grew rapid, and I began to tremble with delight and longing, confused by a jumbled tide of emotions I had never known or dreamed of. Shadow's breathing was also erratic, and when I grasped the lithe muscles in his arms, I was surprised to find he, too, was trembling.

Abruptly, he drew away. "No, Hannah," he murmured in a ragged voice.

"What's wrong?" I cried, stung by his rejection. "You want me. I know you do!"

He did not deny it, and I was suddenly drunk with the power I had over him. Taking his hand, I laid it over my fiercely beating heart.

"I love you," I whispered fervently. "I want to be your woman, your wife."

With an animal-like cry of defeat, Shadow wrapped his arms around me. His kisses, long and hard, were filled with passion and desire and I knew I had won. He would not turn back now. . . .

RECKLESS HEART

Madeline Baker

LEISURE BOOKS  NEW YORK CITY

A LEISURE BOOK

Published by

Dorchester Publishing Co., Inc.
6 East 39th Street
New York, NY 10016

Printed in the United States of America

Chapter 1
1868 - 1871

I was nine years old the first time I saw the Cheyenne warrior who would one day be known as Two Hawks Flying. Of course, he wasn't a warrior that day near the old river crossing—just a boy a few years older than I. And since he had yet to earn his proud warrior's name, he still was called by the name his mother had given him at birth: Shadow.

I had been gathering wildflowers that lazy Sunday afternoon. Overhead, the sky was a vivid azure blue, so bright and clear it almost hurt your eyes to look at it. The grass was thick and green, wondrously cool beneath my bare feet. Birds warbled high in the treetops, their cheerful melodies occasionally interrupted by the fierce screech of a blue jay, or the wild raucous cawing of a crow.

Lacy ferns of emerald green, and flowers in pastel colors grew abundantly in the rich black earth. Bright yellow butterflies flitted lightly from one aromatic blossom to another, while the gentle hum of winged insects made soft music in the air.

A pine tree forest bordered this side of the river, and as I skipped along my favorite path into its sun-dappled heart, I pretended the forest was an enchanted fairyland and I was the fairy queen. The fat brown frog croaking on the riverbank was a handsome prince under an evil spell, and the masked raccoon washing its hands was a wicked witch in disguise. The distant snow-capped mountains were really a crystal palace filled with riches.

Humming softly, I penetrated deeper into the woods, my footsteps muffled by the thick layer of pine needles that carpeted the forest floor. At every turn a new bunch of daisies or a mustard yellow dandelion tempted me on, until I had wandered much further than I had intended.

It wasn't until I glanced up and saw the big old boulder rearing up at the end of the forest path that I realized just how far from home I had roamed. It was an unusual hunk of rock, gray in color and shaped like the head of a jack rabbit with its ears laid back. I had been warned time and time again never to venture past it. Stretching beyond Rabbit's Head Rock lay a vast sea of yellow grass, in many places taller than I was. Somewhere out there lived the Cheyenne. And beyond the Cheyenne, the Sioux.

I was about to turn and head for home when I caught sight of a dazzling red flower, the likes of which I had never seen, shining like a beacon in a yellow sea. I glanced thoughtfully at my bouquet of pale-colored flowers, and it seemed to cry out for a bright splash of color. Surely it wouldn't hurt if I went just a few feet out past the old rock! It would take less than no time at all to run out, grab the flower, and run back. And so, knowing I'd never be happy until I possessed that gorgeous crimson bloom, I darted across the few yards of dusty ground that separated the forest from the grassland and quickly, but carefully, picked the coveted red bud.

Smiling happily, I placed it in my bedraggled bouquet. It added just the right touch, and as I glanced around, hoping to find another, I heard a horse blow softly behind me.

Startled, I whirled around and felt a quick surge of fear as I found myself staring up at a half-naked savage mounted on a prancing bald-faced bay mare. My carefully picked bouquet cascaded from my hands in a profusion of color as every lurid tale of redskin treachery tumbled through my mind: grisly tales of trappers who had been skinned alive, pioneers who had been covered with honey and staked out over ant hills, women and children carried off by painted warriors, never to be seen again.

Horrible visions of being tortured and scalped flooded my mind, and my knees went weak as I imagined my father finding my mutilated body lying face down in a pool of blood. Why had I come out here? I had been warned to stay close to home. Why, oh why, hadn't I listened to Pa?

The Indian was looking at me strangely, as if I were some kind of rare oddity. Somewhat surprised that he hadn't killed me immediately, or even made so much as a threatening gesture in my direction, I decided to take what might be my first, and last, opportunity to study a 'wild' Indian up close. And as I took a good long look at him, I realized he was not a warrior at all. Relief gushed through me like water through a sieve.

"You scared me!" I accused, suddenly angry because he had frightened me so. "What's the big idea, creeping up on a body like that? What are you doing sneaking around on our land, anyway?"

"I am not sneaking around," he replied haughtily and in surprisingly good English. "I am hunting old Pte."

I didn't know who old Pte was, and in an effort to hide my ignorance, I said rather imperiously, "Well, you've no business hunting on our property."

"This is not your property," he remarked coldly. One brown-skinned hand went out in a broad gesture that encompassed all of Bear Valley and our homestead as well. "This is the land of the Tsitsitsas. And it is you who are trespassing."

"I am not!" I retorted indignantly.

"Warriors do not argue with little girls," he said scornfully.

"You're no warrior!" I cried, stung by his arrogance and by his obvious disdain for my sex. "You're just a little boy!"

A boy he might have been, but he was not little. Even then Shadow was tall and well-proportioned, with the promise of great strength in his broad shoulders and long muscular legs. His hair was long and straight, blue-black in the harsh sunlight, but unadorned as he had not yet counted coup or killed an enemy in battle. His dark eyes were like twin chips of obsidian, glinting with anger because I had dared call him a child.

Feeling suddenly contrite, I turned on my

11

sweetest smile and asked if he would like a cookie.

"What is cookie?" he asked suspiciously.

"Well, really!" I declared, pulling a small bandana-wrapped parcel from my pocket. "Don't you know anything? This is a cookie."

Stunned by his ignorance of the finer things in life, I handed him one of my mother's delicious, melt-in-your-mouth oatmeal cookies.

Shadow took the proffered treat like it was some kind of deadly poison, sniffed it like a cat inspecting a questionable piece of meat, and then popped the whole thing into his mouth.

"Good," he allowed grudgingly. "You have more?"

Well, my mother had sent me off with a dozen cookies, and Shadow wolfed down ten of them in less than a minute.

"I guess your mother doesn't ever make cookies," I remarked dryly, grinning as he licked the last crumbs from his finger tips.

"I have no mother," he replied flatly, and his dark eyes warned me not to feel sorry for him.

An uncomfortable silence fell between us after that and while I was trying to think of something cheerful to talk about, a brisk wind blew down out of the mountains, sighing mournfully as it rattled the leaves on the trees. A second gust caused the tall yellow grass to bend as if in supplication to its power. In minutes, scattered powder puff clouds veiled the setting sun, and I realized with dismay that it soon would be dark and that I had a long cold walk ahead of me.

"I must go," I announced abruptly. "Pa will skin me alive if I don't get home before nightfall."

"You have a long way to go," Shadow remarked. It was not a question but a statement of fact, causing me to wonder, briefly, how he knew where I lived. But I had other more important things to worry about, so I said, "Yes...Well, good-bye," and set off down the mossy trail that led to the river, my carefully collected bouquet completely forgotten.

The path I had taken through the woods earlier that day was the quickest way home, but I was afraid of the woods at night. So I hurried down the long narrow trail that ran along the river, knowing I'd never make it home before dark and already feeling Pa's angry hand on my backside.

I had gone only a few yards when hoof-beats rumbled behind me. Glancing over my shoulder, I saw Shadow bearing down on me, and I gasped with fear. He had decided to kill me after all!

13

Really scared now, I cast about for a place to hide, but it was too late. Petrified with fright, I mumbled a hurried prayer as he reined up alongside me. He looked disgusted by my fear as he plucked me from the ground as easily as I had plucked that desired red flower.

Plopping me down in front of him, he said gravely, "I would not want to see such a skinny girl-child skinned alive," and kneed the bay mare into a gallop.

It was exhilarating, racing along the dusty river road. The wind's icy fingers tangled my hair and stung my eyes, but I only laughed and begged Shadow to go faster.

We were careening around a sharp bend in the road when a white-tailed deer bounded across our path. With a war whoop that sent shivers down my spine, Shadow steered his mount after the frightened doe, but the bay mare was no match for the deer's agile speed. With a flick of its tail, it leaped gracefully over a bramble bush and disappeared from sight.

Minutes later, Shadow deposited me at my front door and rode away without a word.

Our place wasn't much to look at in those days, just a three-room log cabin on a dozen acres of newly plowed ground, but it was solid and well-built. Pa had seen to that. A split-rail fence housed our stock: four cows and a yearling calf, two draft horses, Pa's Tennessee Walker, and my old mare Nellie. A pig and a litter of curly-tailed piglets lived in a separate pen behind the outhouse. Six Rhode Island Reds scratched in the dirt near the wood pile, clucking and cooing as they searched for worms and bugs.

Gently rolling hills, lush with grass this time of year, rose behind our house. Wild roses grew on either side of the front door, and crisp white curtains fluttered at the front windows. I thought our place was perfect!

It caused quite a stir when I told my folks an Indian boy had brought me home. Pa bawled me out 'til he was blue in the face. Had I gone mad? Had I taken leave of my senses? Didn't I realize I might have been kidnapped? Or killed? Or worse?

"What could be worse than getting killed?" I asked innocently, and Pa's color changed from blue to red as he mumbled something unintelligible under his breath and stomped out of the house.

Strangely, my mother didn't seem too worried. She even smiled, pleased, when I told her how Shadow had gobbled down ten of her cookies and would likely have polished off ten more if I'd had them.

"I'm glad you found a friend, dear," Mother said, caressing my cheek in that special way that told me louder then words that I was loved.

Let me tell you about my folks. My father is a big man—not just tall, but big, with arms like trees and shoulders as wide as our barn door. Pa's name is Samuel Obediah Kincaid, but Mother calls him Curly on account of his hair is curly brown. I think Pa would take a stick to anyone else who dared call him Curly, but he kind of glows when Mother says it. Pa has long sideburns, blue eyes, and a red moustache. Bright red! And let me tell you, he has a temper to match that moustache! But he never stays mad for long.

My mother is beautiful—not just pretty, but beautiful inside and out. She has clear ivory skin that refuses to tan even in the hottest weather, lovely chestnut hair usually worn in a severe bun at the nape of her neck, and the warmest gray eyes in the world. Even her name is beautiful: Katherine Mary Kincaid. I never heard my mother raise her voice in anger or an unkind word pass her lips. If ever there was an angel, it was my mother. Pa says I'll look just like her when I grow up, except for my red hair. My eyes are the same quiet shade of gray, though they lack that special something that makes Mother's shine. Once, when I asked her how she got that sparkle in her eyes, she smiled mysteriously and said Pa put it there. When I asked how, she blushed prettily and told me I'd understand when I was older. I have mother's ivory skin, too, only mine tans to a deep golden brown in the summer.

I never knew two people so right for each other or so much in love. Pa told me once that he met Mother on Thursday, courted her on Friday, kissed her on Saturday, and married her on Sunday. Mother insists things didn't happen quite that fast. Almost, but not quite.

The day after I met Shadow, I took Pa's old fishing pole and rode Nellie down to the river. Mother had mentioned she would like some fish for dinner, and I was determined to catch her some. Pa usually did the fishing, but he was busy planting and I knew he wouldn't have time. Grimacing a little, I baited the hook with a fat red worm, tossed my line into the water, and then sat back to wait. I guess I'd been there drowning worms for almost an hour when I decided to give up. I was pulling in my line when a familiar voice said, "You would have better luck from this side of the river."

"How do you know?" I asked sulkily.

"Because the fish cannot see your

reflection from over here."

"My reflection? What difference does that make?"

"Try it and see," Shadow suggested.

Frowning, I rode Nellie across the river, skewered a fresh worm, and dropped my line into the still, blue-green water. In minutes I had a bite.

Crowing with delight, I reeled in a good-sized trout. In less than twenty minutes I had three fat fish.

When I offered Shadow my thanks, he just shrugged and said, "If you are going to fish, you might as well do it right."

I saw a lot of Shadow after that. Sometimes we met down at the river crossing, but more often than not he showed up at the house. I tried to tell myself he liked my company but honesty forced me to admit it was Mother he really came to see. Not having a mother of his own, I could understand why he was so taken with mine. Sometimes it made me jealous, the way she fussed over him. She spoiled him with cookies and praise and lots of special attention, and Shadow lapped it up like a starving kitten devouring a bowl of fresh cream. Still, I was glad for his company. There were no other families in the valley and I'd been kind of lonesome for someone to play with. Of course, Shadow never really played. He thought 'girl things' were foolish and a waste of time and refused to do anything he considered silly or undignified—which was practically everything I wanted to do.

So he taught me how to read trail signs instead, and how to find my way home at night by using the stars. He taught me how to skin a deer, too, and then showed me how to tan the hide. First, the skin was staked out on the ground. Then all bits of flesh were removed with a buffalo leg bone. Next the hair was removed—unless you were going to use the hide for a robe, in which case it was left on for added warmth. Next, brains and liver mixed with melted fat were worked into the skin. After that, the skin was soaked in water. Later, the excess liquid was stripped out with a long stone blade and the skin was hung up to dry. Lastly, the skin was worked and pounded until it was soft as velvet.

Personally, I thought the whole process was disgusting, though I didn't say so for fear of incurring Shadow's scorn. But then I disgraced myself forever in his eyes the day he ate the raw heart of a buffalo calf—and I threw up all over him.

With the coming of winter, the Cheyenne moved south. Shadow's absence left a void in my life—one that could not be filled. I was lonely again and spent most of my time reading in front of the fireplace, losing myself in stories of pirates and treasure and ill-fated lovers.

Shadow came with the spring, bringing gifts for us all—a bone-handled hunting knife for Pa, an intricately woven Indian blanket for Mother, a headband beaded in black and yellow for me. That year Shadow instructed me in the fine art of distinguishing one set of animal tracks from another. He also taught me how to recognize the print of a Cheyenne moccasin from that of a Sioux. He began teaching me his tribe's spoken tongue as well as sign language, which was the universal language of the plains, enabling warriors from different tribes to communicate with each other.

One afternoon he told me how wolves mark their hunting grounds by urinating on the rocks and trees, then further astonished me by declaring that if a warrior made water across the entrance to a cave, no wolf would dare enter!

Of course, Shadow was learning, too. His English became less stilted with everyday use, and he picked up some American expressions as well as a handful of cuss words from Pa. But Mother was his best teacher. I remember she was quite upset the first time

Shadow had dinner with us and ate the mashed potatoes with his fingers! Right then and there she insisted he learn American table manners. And when she discovered he could not read or write, out came pen, ink, paper, and my old McGuffey's reader.

Shadow proved to have a quick mind and he rapidly mastered the art of reading and writing the English language. Reading especially appealed to him and he read everything in sight: labels on tin cans, old newspapers, my books, a volume of Shakespeare (which neither of us understood), my mother's cookbooks, and Pa's mail order catalog.

But his favorite book was the Bible, and he read it through twice!

"The white man respects nothing," he remarked one night after reading the 27th Chapter of Matthew, which is an account of the crucifixion of Jesus. "Not only does he kill the buffalo, and the Indian, and his own white brothers, but his God as well!"

Shadow openly adored my mother. He frequently brought her gifts: a pair of soft doeskin moccasins, an exquisite necklace of turquoise and silver, a set of delicately carved wooden combs for her hair. I was sure Shadow would have walked barefoot over flaming coals if my Mother asked him to, so you can imagine my surprise the day she asked him to please fetch some water from the well and he refused.

I stared at him in open-mouthed astonishment. He swelled up like a toad and coolly informed us that such menial tasks as hauling water, gathering firewood, curing hides, sewing, weaving, food preparation and child care were squaw work, and that a warrior NEVER did squaw work when there was a woman around. He further informed us that he thought it quite strange that my father worked in the fields when he had two healthy females in his lodge.

"Well, we do things a little differently here," Mother explained calmly, completely unruffled by his arrogant outburst.

But I noticed she never again asked Shadow to do any chore he considered 'squaw work.' When I asked why, she said it was all right to teach Shadow to read and write, and even show him how civilized people behaved at the dinner table, but that it was wrong to interfere with his customs and beliefs. She went on to explain, somewhat sadly, that Shadow would one day be a warrior and would find it hard to live as a Cheyenne if he acquired too many American habits.

Pa was less than enthusiastic about Shadow's frequent presence in our home, though he made the best of it because of Mother. Often, after Shadow had ridden off for home, Pa would go around mumbling about taking a viper to our bosom—whatever that meant.

"Dammit, Mary," I overheard him say one night, "that half-naked savage is gonna be a warrior before too long, and Hannah's gonna be a young woman!"

"Yes, Curly, I suppose so," Mother agreed serenely.

Pa pounded the table with one ham-like fist. "Don't be deliberately obtuse, Katherine Mary Kincaid," he growled. "You know what I mean."

"Don't be absurd," Mother chided gently. "Hannah isn't going to run off with him."

I gasped in astonishment. Was that what was worrying Pa? Me running away with Shadow? I ducked out of my hiding place and ran outside where I burst into gales of laughter. Me and Shadow! Now that was funny! Even though I was only eleven going on twelve, I already knew the kind of man I wanted to marry. He would be tall and handsome and rich and we would live on a big ranch somewhere in Bear Valley and raise blooded horses. We'd have lots of kids and travel to New York, and I'd buy lots of pretty dresses—all silk and satin and lace—and we'd go to the theatre and dine in a fancy restaurant with velvet chairs and crystal chandeliers. And we'd ride in a fine carriage pulled by a team of matched black stallions. . . .

Oh, I had a lot of ambitious dreams for a girl on the shy side of twelve, and you can be sure there wasn't a half-naked arrogant Indian boy in any of them!

When Shadow turned fourteen, he began the rigorous training boys undergo to become full-fledged Cheyenne warriors, and we saw him less and less.

By the time I was twelve and Shadow was going on sixteen, his visits to our place had ceased altogether. I missed him more than I would admit, but I think my mother missed him most of all.

Chapter 2
1872 - 1874

The summer I turned thirteen we got some neighbors down the road apiece. Pa said, sourly, that Bear Valley was getting crowded, but I think he was as glad of their company as Mother and I were. It was a good feeling, knowing we were no longer the only white people in our part of the country.

Our new neighbors, Ed and Claire Berdeen, had two sons: Joshua, 16, and Orin, 14. They were mighty handsome boys, both tall, blond, and blue-eyed, with easy-going ways and nice manners. The boys and I had a good time that summer. Once our morning chores were done we were usually free until evening, and we spent our time horseback riding and picnicking and swimming. Often, we went walking in the woods down by the river crossing. Josh and Orin spent a lot of time wrestling each other and generally showing off by climbing trees and jumping over rocks, each trying to outdo the other for my benefit. Naturally, I loved being the center of attention, but then, what girl doesn't?

Of course, I did some showing off of my own. Weren't they surprised to learn that I could turn out a decent loaf of bread, make jam, and bake a deep-dish apple pie just as good as their mother's! But my culinary talents didn't astound them nearly as much as my tracking ability. I'll never forget the day we went hunting together. I bet Josh and Orin that I could find a deer quicker than they could—and did it, too. And didn't their mouths drop to their knees when I not only killed the buck with one well-placed shot, but skinned it out, too!

It was fun asking them to do ridiculous things, just to see if they would do them to please me. Like the time I saw a bear cub and asked Joshua to fetch it for me.

"Don't be silly," Joshua said scowling. "You can't take that cub home."

"I don't want to take it home," I countered petulantly. "I just want to hold it awhile. It's cute."

"I'll get it for you, Hannah," Orin offered, and with a Rebel yell that would have made the South proud, he dashed off toward the unsuspecting cub. Scooping the furry little creature up in one hand, he trotted back toward us, looking right pleased with himself.

He'd only gone a short distance when a mighty roar thundered behind him and the cub's mother came charging out of a thicket, jaws agape, sharp yellow teeth stained crimson with berry juice. Lordy, was that old sow mad!

"Orin, run!" I screamed.

For a moment, he seemed frozen to the ground as he saw the enraged animal rocketing toward him, and I screamed again, certain he was going to be torn to shreds right before our eyes.

"Drop the cub, you fool!" Josh hollered. "Hannah, run for home!"

The next few moments were mighty tense, let me tell you. I ran toward the river, casting anxious glances over my shoulder to see how Orin and Joshua were making out. Orin had dropped the cub and was running hellbent for leather down the path after me with Josh hot on his heels. The old sow streaked past her cub like a runaway locomotive and for a long, heart-stopping moment it looked like she wouldn't halt until she'd caught us. But then the cub whimpered sort of sad-like, and that big old bear turned in mid-flight, graceful as a ballet dancer, and trotted back to her baby.

I ran until I couldn't run anymore, then sank down on the grassy riverbank, gasping for air. Now that the danger was past, it was funny and I began to laugh.

"Oh, Orin," I giggled. "You should have seen your face when that fat old sow reared up in the bushes."

"Pretty funny, huh?" he asked good-naturedly. "Would you have cried if she'd caught me and ripped me to pieces?"

"You know I would have," I said. "Why, I'd have cried buckets every night!"

"See, Josh, it's me she's crazy about," Orin boasted. Falling to one knee, he grabbed my hands and said, with mock gravity, "Hannah, thou art fairest of all the fair. For one smile from thy ruby lips, I would climb the highest mountain, swim the deepest river, defend thee to the death, but please, please, don't bid me fetch any more bear cubs!"

Josh scowled as I burst into laughter. Always the serious one, Josh was. I'm afraid Orin and I sorely tried his patience with our endless clowning and joking.

Rising, I found a long thin reed and tapped Orin lightly, once on each shoulder.

"For services rendered, I dub thee Sir Orin the Brave. Arise, Sir Knight."

Looking properly humble, Orin rose to his feet and bowed from the waist. "Might I be so bold as to beg a favor?"

"Perhaps," I allowed with queenly grace. "What is thy wish?"

"A kiss from she who holds my heart," Orin responded gallantly. "One kiss from that maid whose name brings joy to my soul, beauty to my eyes, and a song to my lips."

"Well spoken, Sir Knight. Claim thy favor."

Eyes twinkling, Orin took me in his arms, bent me back, and kissed me soundly on the mouth.

We parted, laughing, to find that Joshua was gone.

Joshua rode over the next morning alone and asked if I would go riding with him. Since my chores were done, Mother said I could go—as long as we were home before dark. Josh threw a saddle on Nellie and helped me mount. One thing about Josh, he always treated me like a lady.

Side by side, we rode down to the river crossing. We weren't supposed to cross the river but I was tired of riding the same old trails and I urged Nellie down the bank. That old mare sure hated getting her feet wet! She picked her way across that shallow stretch of water as if she were walking through a nest of snakes.

As soon as we reached the opposite bank, I gave her a solid thwack on the rump. Startled, Nellie lined out in a dead run.

"Hannah, stop!" Josh yelled.

"Catch us if you can!" I hollered over my shoulder, and lashed Nellie with the reins.

It wasn't much of a race. Nellie was no fit match for Joshua's big black gelding, and he caught up with us in practically no time at all.

"You little fool!" he scolded angrily. "Don't you know better than to run off like that? This side of the river is Indian territory, remember?"

"Oh, Josh, stop being such a worry wart. The Indians aren't going to bother us. They never have."

Joshua did not look convinced, and his eyes darted nervously from side to side as he said, "Well, we'd better be heading home just the same."

"You're worse than an old woman," I snapped irritably. "Now, stop worrying. There probably isn't an Indian within twenty miles."

"Oh, yeah?" he muttered drily, pointing over my shoulder. "What do you call those?"

Turning, I felt my confidence quickly crumble as a number of warriors trotted over a low ridge toward us.

"Oh my," I murmured. "Indians! Lets get out of here!"

"I don't think running is such a good idea just now," Josh said. He was suddenly calm, now that we were facing real danger. "Better just sit tight."

In minutes, we were surrounded by a dozen armed young braves, all dressed alike in deerskin clouts and beaded moccasins. Three of the warriors had deer carcasses slung over their ponies, and I breathed a sigh of relief. Thank goodness they were only a hunting party and not a war party as I had feared.

One of them—the leader, I supposed— quickly searched Josh for weapons. He looked mildly disgusted when all he found was an old Barlow knife. "What shall we do with these paleface dogs?" he asked.

"Let us take their horses," said one brave, casting an envious eye at Joshua's fine black gelding.

"Let us take their scalps," suggested another, and I pulled away as he ran a long brown finger through my hair.

"Let us kill the boy and take the girl," a third remarked. "She will make a fine slave."

"You talk big for untried warriors!" I blurted, trying to cover my apprehension with bravado. "Why don't you just go home to your mothers where you belong?"

I knew it was the wrong thing to say the minute the words were out of my mouth, but there was no way to call them back. The leader's black eyes flashed with anger and wounded pride. Scowling, he hefted his lance as I berated myself for my quick tongue. The Indians were mad now—perhaps mad enough to kill Josh. What better way, after all, to prove they were warriors than to spill the blood of a white man?

The other braves leaned forward expectantly, ebony eyes glinting, as they waited for their leader to uphold their honor. Joshua's face went deathly pale as the leader drew back his arm to hurl his lance.

Just then a second group of Indians arrived on the scene.

"What is going on here?" one of them demanded, and I nearly fell off my horse with relief.

It was Shadow! Seventeen now, and a head taller than any of the other braves, he sat proudly astride a tall roan stallion. There was neither warmth or recognition in his gaze when he glanced my way, yet my heart began to pound inside my breast, and I felt my cheeks grow hot.

"It is no business of yours," the leader of the first group retorted.

"We are hunting meat, not scalps,"

Shadow countered evenly. "Let the white eyes go in peace."

"No. They are my prisoners. It is for me to decide if they live or die."

"Hear me, Running Buffalo," Shadow said in a hard tone. "I know this girl, and I will not see her hurt. Or her friend, either."

The two warriors glared at each other for several taut moments. For a brief time it looked like they might fight it out, but then Running Buffalo's eyes wavered before Shadow's steely gaze, and he lowered his lance. Sullen-faced, Running Buffalo gave his mount a savage kick and raced away toward the mountains.

"Go home, Hannah," Shadow said, in English. "Do not cross the river again."

Before I could thank him for his help, he signaled his warriors to follow and galloped after Running Buffalo.

"Whew! That was close," Josh exclaimed, wiping the sweat from his brow. "Who was that Indian, anyway? How did he know your name?"

"Oh, that's Shadow," I replied nonchalantly. "He's an old friend. Come on, let's go home."

"What do you mean, an old friend?" Josh demanded. "Where'd you ever meet an Indian?"

"Why, Joshua Lee Berdeen, I do believe you're jealous."

"Of a savage?" Josh scoffed. "Don't be ridiculous!"

"Well, you certainly sound jealous to me," I insisted sweetly. "And it's none of your business where I met Shadow. But, if you must know, I met him out at Rabbit's Head Rock years ago. He's a very nice boy."

"Nice!" Josh exploded. "Hannah Kincaid, have you taken leave of your senses? Nice! What would your folks say?"

"Oh, they know all about him," I replied airily. "Shadow used to come to our house all the time."

Joshua's mouth fell open, and he looked so funny I couldn't help laughing. "For goodness sakes, Josh, don't look so shocked. Indians are people, too, you know."

"That's not a very popular notion, Hannah," Josh said testily.

"Well, it's true just the same," I retorted sharply. "And I would think you would be a little more tolerant, seeing as how an Indian just saved your scalp!"

Josh scowled at me, and we rode the rest of the way home in silence. I don't know what thoughts were running through Josh's mind as we crossed the river, but all I could think of was Shadow. How tall he'd grown. How handsome he was. And how wildly magnificent he looked on that prancing roan stallion.

I bid Joshua a hasty farewell at the door and hurried into the house, bursting to tell my folks, especially Mother, how Shadow had saved Joshua's life.

Mother didn't seem the least bit surprised that Shadow had come to our rescue, but Pa's brows gathered in a frown as he remarked, dourly, "Just give him a year or two, and he'll be as eager to take our scalps as the rest of the red bastards."

"Curly, shame on you!" Mother scolded gently. "Shadow will always be our friend."

"I hope you're right, Mary," Pa muttered under his breath. "I just hope you're right."

In the spring of 1873 five families moved into the north end of Bear Valley, and suddenly we were up to our ears in people. The population jumped from seven to thirty-six, and Mother started talking about building a church and a schoolhouse, now that we had enough people to make such an undertaking worthwhile. There were rumors circulating that Custer had discovered gold in the Black Hills, and Pa predicted sourly that once news of a gold strike got out, we'd be swamped with folks looking to get rich quick.

And Pa was right.

Prospectors swarmed into the Dakotas,

utterly disregarding the treaty rights of the Indians. Naturally, this upset the Indians, and we began to hear about Sioux and Cheyenne raids on white settlements further west.

With more and more people flocking westward, Pa started talking about turning our farm into a trading post. Joshua allowed as how he thought that a trading post was a prime idea, since we were near the river, and even offered to help Pa start building if he was of a mind to.

And that's just what they did. Orin and his pa and our other neighbors pitched in, and by late summer our farm had been transformed into a kind of fort. The split-rail fence was gone, replaced by stout log walls with lookout towers at each corner. Our corral was enlarged, and our barn spruced up. Our cabin underwent some changes, too. Pa and the men added a second floor, and we moved our living quarters upstairs, leaving the main floor free for the store.

With the building done, Pa and Josh went off to Steel's Crossing—the only town within a hundred and fifty miles—and stocked up on dry goods and seed and harness and whatever else they could find. By the spring of '74 we were in business.

The Tabors were our first official customers. They came marching in one sunlit morning, herding their six kids like sheep. Jed Tabor was a short little man with a face like a cherub and a tongue like a serpent. Martha Tabor towered over her husband by a good six inches, but Jed Tabor was the undisputed boss of the family. When he was present, Martha and her brood maintained a respectful silence.

The other families came, too. Some out of need; some out of curiosity.

The Henrys were five of a kind: pale of face, pale of hair, pale of personality. I never heard any of them laugh out loud. Muriel Henry rarely came to the Fort—as our trading post came to be called—and hardly spoke two words when she did. Pa said they were proud folks fallen on hard times and didn't know how to adjust to their changed lifestyle. Perhaps he was right, but I never cottoned to any of them.

The Greens were as volatile as the Henrys were quiet. Loud and colorful, they were outspoken about everything—especially Indians.

"The sooner the Army wipes out the red devils, the sooner the west will be fit for decent folks," Saul Green opined, and his wife, Ida, heartily concurred.

Their five kids, all boys, were unruly and impolite and into everything, especially the candy jar we kept on the end of the counter near the cash register. I thoroughly disliked the whole bunch.

John and Florence Sanders were nice people. They had only one child, a darling little girl about six years old. Blond and blue-eyed, Kathy Sanders was the most adorable child I had ever seen. John Sanders openly adored both his wife and daughter, and I think most of the women in the valley were a little envious of Florence Sanders. At parties, while the other men clustered together to talk about crops and Indians and such, John Sanders stayed with Florence, plying her with punch and cookies, treating her as if she were his sweetheart instead of his wife of ten years. Once, when I caught them kissing on the front porch, John Sanders actually blushed, but Florence Sanders just smiled.

Carolyn and Seth Walker were from the South. They were refined, genteel people and added a touch of old world charm to our rough valley ways. They had two sets of twins: girls, aged seven, and boys, aged nine. They also had the only piano in the territory, so we had most of our parties at their house.

Carolyn was a gracious hostess, knowing instinctively how to make her guests feel right at home. Excepting my mother, I think Carolyn Walker was the prettiest woman in the valley. She had a flawless complexion, rich brown hair, and the most expressive lavender-colored eyes imaginable. I used to listen, spellbound, while she talked about life in the South.

"Oh, but it was grand," she'd say. "The air was so sweet with the scent of magnolias and honeysuckle, you could gain five pounds just breathing in! There were parties and barbecues and balls every week. Hannah, you have no idea. Life was so relaxed, so pleasant. Why, I can remember when my biggest problem was what hat to wear! And, I declare, I had more dresses than a body could wear in a year. And the men. . . Hannah, they were all so charming and well-mannered. So. . .so gallant. Not like the crude ruffians you meet out here.

"But then the war came and turned our world upside down. Seth went, of course. Those were terrible years. Sherman burned our plantation to the ground, and everything in it. I went to Atlanta to stay with my sister and my mother until the war was over. When Seth came home, we started to rebuild Shady Oaks, but his heart wasn't in it, and we decided to start over somewhere else, where there were no unhappy memories."

She sighed as she glanced at her surroundings, and I thought how pitiful their little cabin and crude furnishings must appear when compared to the spacious home she had once known. But then she smiled and said, "Always remember, Hannah, that pretty clothes and big houses don't always bring happiness. It's having a man to love, and one who loves you—*that* makes a woman's life worthwhile."

Our neighbors weren't our only customers. We served prospectors, trappers and traders, and men whose pasts would not bear close inspection. You could always pick out the men who were on the dodge. There was a wary look in their eyes, and they never turned their backs on you, not for a minute. They were a rough lot, and Pa always sent me upstairs when he saw one of them coming.

Later that summer we had a real honest-to-goodness shoot-out right in our front yard. I was out back hanging up a load of wash when I heard someone come riding hell-for-leather into the Fort. Peering around the side of the house, I saw a dusty, tough-looking young man pull up at the hitch rack. He had no more than stepped from the saddle when a second, equally dusty, gent came pounding through the gates mounted on a lathered pony. The second man dismounted before his horse even came to a halt. It was then that I saw the U.S. Marshal's badge pinned to his shirtfront.

Unaware of my presence, the two men stared at each other across six feet of barren ground.

"I'm taking you back, Cory," the Marshal said in a hard tone. "On your horse, or tied across your saddle—makes no difference to me."

Cory's eyes were wild and scared, but the hand hovering over his gun butt was rock steady.

"I ain't goin' back!" he shouted, and grabbed for his Colt.

There was a double explosion as both men drew and fired, the reports echoing like thunder. When the smoke cleared, Cory lay dead on the ground, a slightly surprised look on his face. Blood trickled from a neat hole in his chest, just left of center.

I had never seen a dead man before and I felt suddenly sick to my stomach as I ran past the lawman and into the house.

Later, I learned that the dead man had cold-bloodedly killed three men and a young girl while escaping from jail in Steel's Crossing.

Luckily, most of our days passed in a quieter fashion.

By the time I was fifteen, Joshua and Orin were both courting me in earnest. I might have been flattered if I hadn't been the only white girl their age within a hundred miles. Mrs. Berdeen and my mother had become good friends and made no secret of the fact that they both hoped I'd decide to marry one of the Berdeen boys. I think my folks, especially Pa, favored Joshua, for he was older than Orin and a lot more mature. Personally, I preferred Orin. He had a dazzling smile and a wonderful way with words. Nights, when we sat on the porch holding hands, he'd tell me I was prettier than all the flowers in the world, and sometimes he'd whisper poetry in my ear while he nuzzled my neck.

Josh liked to hold hands, too, but he rarely told me the things a young girl likes to hear. Instead, he told me his plans for the future—how he'd like to build up a spread of his own and raise cattle and horses and a couple of kids and help turn our part of the country into a civilized place to live. Which was all well and good, I suppose, but not particularly romantic. Sometimes it sounded like he was running for public office instead of wooing his sweetheart!

Orin and Joshua both asked Pa for my

hand in marriage, but Pa said they'd have to ask again when I was sixteen, and that when the time came, the decision would have to be mine, not his.

And so the days passed. I did my chores and studied my lessons and helped Pa in the store on weekends. Evenings, I learned how to do needlework and how to cook something besides apple pie, dreaming of the day when I'd have a home of my own and a man to do for. Nights, when I lay in bed, I'd try to imagine what it would be like to be married. I'd close my eyes and try to conjure up a picture of myself as a married woman—tending my own children, or sleeping in my husband's arms, the way I supposed Mother slept in Pa's. Strangely, every time I saw myself in my husband's arms, he had black hair and dark eyes! When I mentioned it to Mother, she just laughed and said maybe a tall, dark stranger was going to ride into my life and sweep me off my feet.

Pa laughed, too, but said I had as much chance of marrying a dark eyed man as I had of marrying a prince—unless the Berdeen boys decided to dye their hair, or another family with grown boys moved into the valley before I turned sixteen.

So the days passed, tranquil as a summer sky, and I dismissed my notions of a raven-haired husband as meaningless and foolish and set my mind to deciding between Orin and Joshua.

Chapter 3
1871 - 1874

Becoming a full-fledged warrior of the Cheyenne nation was not an easy task. There was much to learn: how to read the tracks of man and beast; how to interpret the signs of earth and sky; how to take an enemy scalp; how to count coup; how to locate food and water while traveling across the trackless plain; how to make and repair weapons. There were endless tests of courage and skill, as well as dances and rituals and sacred songs to learn and understand. One must go alone to a high place and pray to Maiyun for a vision, for a man without a vision could never hope to be a great warrior. One must endure the agony and ecstacy of the Sun Dance, that most sacred of all Indian rituals.

At sixteen, Shadow was ready to seek his

vision. Ordinarily, a boy set out on his vision quest at the age of fourteen. But because Shadow had been spending so much time with the Kincaids, the medicine man had advised him to wait. One did not seek help from the gods unless one's heart was wholly in tune with the Great Spirit. And one could not be completely in harmony with Maiyun when one was busily learning the ways of the white man. So spoke Elk Dreamer, the medicine man.

But Shadow was ready now. And so, according to tribal custom, he went first to counsel with Elk Dreamer. Upon receiving the shaman's instructions, he proceeded to the sweat lodge to purify his body for the coming ordeal, accompanied by his father and the medicine man. Naked, they sat in a small circle inside the sweat lodge. Elk Dreamer sang the sacred songs and chants while Shadow's father poured cold water over the hot rocks piled in the center of the lodge. Great clouds of steam filled the tiny brush hut, and as the sweat poured from his body, Shadow emptied his mind of all thoughts, all desires, all wordly ambition, and silently prayed that the Great Spirit would grant him a vision.

Time passed slowly. The words of the sacred chants ran together in his mind. Enveloped by a curious sense of weightlessness, he closed his eyes, content as one unborn in its mother's womb.

After what seemed like hours, Elk Dreamer indicated it was time to leave the sweat lodge. Rising, the three men rushed outside and plunged naked into the icy stream that gurgled behind the camp.

Shadow gasped as the frigid water closed over him. For a moment he was numb and unable to move. His breath seemed frozen in his lungs, and he wondered fleetingly if he would drown. But then an unexpected rush of strength surged through his limbs, filling every fiber of his being with a wild exhilaration, making him feel more alive, more aware, than ever before.

Early the following morning, clad only in clout and moccasins, Shadow climbed the high hill that rose in rocky splendor behind the village. It was not an easy climb, and it took him several hours to reach the top. At the summit, he squatted on his heels and stared down at the village. When he'd caught his breath, he pulled a small leather pouch from his clout and reverently offered a pinch of tobacco to the four directions, to earth and sky, chanting softly all the while. That done, he stretched out on the barren ground, arms raised, and cried to Maiyun for a sign.

Time passed slowly. He grew thirsty. His

belly rumbled for food. Night came, and shivering with cold, he slept fitfully and woke with the rising of the sun.

The second day passed as the first.

The third also. His tongue grew fat in his mouth, and hunger was a constant ache in his belly. His voice sounded weak in his ears as he offered the last of his tobacco to the four directions, to Man Above and Mother Earth. Lying on his back, arms outstretched, he beseeched the Gods for help, but only endless silence and the sun's hot rays answered his cries.

The fourth day. Waking, he did not rise but stared at the horizon, watching in awe as the sun climbed over the mountains, painting the gray sky canvas with slashes of color, until the heavens were alive with all the brilliant hues of the rainbow.

"Perhaps it is a sign," he thought dully. "Perhaps, on this, my last day, a vision will come." How could he face his father if it did not?

Summoning the last of his strength, he raised his arms skyward and lifted his voice in mighty supplication.

"Hear me, Man Above, father of all life! Hear me, and grant me a vision, lest I perish!"

For the space of three heartbeats a great stillness hung over the hilltop, as if the very earth were holding its breath. Then a wild rushing noise filled Shadow's ears and as he stared upward at the sun, it seemed suddenly to be falling toward him. In terror, he pressed himself against the damp ground, fearing certain destruction. Suddenly the sun split in half and out of the middle flew two red-tailed hawks. In perfect unison, they soared through the air, wheeling and diving, moving with timeless grace, until they hovered above Shadow's head.

"Be brave," the male hawk cried in a loud voice. "Be brave, and I will always be with you. You shall be swift as the hawk, wise as the owl."

"Be strong," the female admonished in a loud voice. "Be strong, and I will always be with you. You shall be smart as the hawk, mighty as the eagle."

With a rush of powerful wings, the two hawks soared upward and disappeared into the sun.

The sky was streaked with flame when Shadow found the strength to rise. Walking slowly, like an old man, he made his way to the edge of the summit and there, lying in one of his moccasin prints, he found two feathers and a small red stone. Reverently, he touched the feathers and the stone, then placed them in his tobacco pouch. Later, they would go into a medicine bag to be worn around his neck.

Elk Dreamer was mightily impressed with Shadow's vision and that night there was feasting and dancing as the entire tribe turned out to welcome a new warrior into its midst. Shadow, the boy, was dead, and in his place was born Two Hawks Flying, the warrior.

Many things happened in the next few years. Two Hawks Flying killed his first enemy, a Pawnee brave scouting for some white buffalo hunters. He scalped his first white man, a prospector searching for gold in violation of the treaty which promised the Sioux and the Cheyenne ownership of the Black Hills for "as long as grass shall grow and water flow." He counted coup on a dozen enemies, both red and white.

To the Indians, war was a game. They did not fight to annihilate one another as the whites did, but to gain honor among the tribe. Any man could kill another from a distance. There was no honor in that. But to touch an armed foe with the tip of your bow or a coup stick—now there was courage! And if you then killed him and scalped him and took his horse and weapons—ah! That was a major coup, one that would be told over and over around the campfires. And if that man was a chief, so much the better!

At the age of seventeen, Two Hawks Flying was heralded as a mighty warrior, brave in battle, wise beyond his years. By the time he was eighteen, he had earned enough coup feathers to make an impressive warbonnet. Only his father, Black Owl, had a finer one. When he rode into battle, Red Wind's flank carried the print of a man's hand, indicating his rider had killed at least one enemy in hand to hand combat.

Having thus established himself as a warrior, Two Hawks Flying began to think about taking a wife. There was not a family in the village that would not have been pleased to have him as a son-in-law, and he knew, with a touch of pride, that he could have his pick of the maidens. But it was Elk Dreamer's youngest daughter, Bright Star, that finally caught his eye. Tall and willowy she was, with a warm smile, a merry laugh, and a way of swaying her hips that made him shaky inside. Virtue and chastity were highly prized among the Cheyenne, and though he longed to hold Bright Star in his arms and his loins ached to possess her as a man possesses a woman, he admired her only from afar.

He might have spoken to Black Owl about a go-between, might have asked Bright Star to run away with him if, for some reason, her parents refused to let them wed. Might have done a hundred foolish things if he had not ridden down to the river crossing one warm mid-summer day and seen Hannah walking in the woods with two young men.

Just the sight of her took Shadow's breath away. She was dressed in a simple cotton frock that showed off her slim waist and young breasts to perfection. Her hair, bright and red as a new flame, fell in soft waves around the loveliest face Man Above had ever created. Her laughter was low, sensual, and she moved with the light easy grace of a young doe.

Hidden from their sight in the trees across the river, Two Hawks Flying watched Hannah and the two paleface boys cavort like three untamed puppies, and he knew, deep in his heart, that he would never be satisfied with Bright Star or with any other woman, red or white.

Thereafter, Shadow waited often at the river crossing hoping to catch Hannah alone, but always the two wasicuns were with her, laughing and flirting as they tried to please her. Doing some quick mental arithmetic, Two Hawks Flying figured Hannah was fifteen. Still too young for marriage, according to the whites, and so he went off to the Cheyenne winter camp, certain she would still be a maiden when he returned in the spring. Certain that, when he returned, he would make her his.

Bright Star was understandably puzzled by Shadow's abrupt lack of interest, as was Black Owl, though neither the girl nor Shadow's father spoke of it.

The winter was thankfully short that year, and when he returned to Bear Valley, Two Hawks Flying was determined to see Hannah alone, even if he had to kill both her admirers to accomplish it. But first he would fulfill his promise to participate in the Sun Dance.

Every summer the Cheyenne met on the plains to give thanks to the Great Spirit for His blessings in the year past, and to ask for His continued help in the year to come. The celebration lasted twelve days.

The first four days were given to feasting and dancing, as all the various bands of the Cheyenne nation came together to participate in their most sacred ritual. There were foot races and horse races, wrestling matches, and contests of all kinds. Mothers showed off their young and renewed old acquaintances. Maidens donned their finest apparel and paraded through the camp, pointedly ignoring the young men. And the young men strutted about in their feathers and paint and elaborately decorated buckskin shirts, pretending to ignore the maidens. The children ran wild and free, getting into everything as they laughed and played to their heart's content, while the old warriors sat in the sun, baking their bones as they spoke of the shining times before the coming of the white man.

They spoke of Red Cloud and how he had forced the whites to surrender the Bloody Bozeman Trail, and how he and his warriors drove the soldiers from Fort Phil Kearney and then burned it to the ground. They spoke of Black Kettle and Sand Creek. You couldn't trust the whites, they said bitterly. Sand Creek was proof of that.

The second four days those who had volunteered to participate in the Sun Dance were taken aside and given instruction from the tribal holy men. By taking part in the dance, by willingly enduring the physical pain involved, the dancers were seeking the blessings of the Great Spirit, not only for themselves individually but for the entire tribe as well.

The last four days were sacred. On the first of these sacred days Thunder Running was sent out to find a cottonwood tree to be used as the Sun Dance pole. Not just any tree would do. The Sun Dance pole must be straight and strong and notched at the top.

When Thunder Running found just the right tree, he would mark it with red paint and return to the village.

On the second sacred day, the virtuous women of the tribe went out to find the sacred tree. Three times they looked. And three times they failed to find it. But the fourth time they spied the tree and hastened back to the village with the good news. Rejoicing, all who were able formed a ceremonial procession and followed the women back to the chosen tree. Upon reaching the site, four warriors counted coup on the tree. Then, one by one, the virtuous women took turns chopping down the selected cottonwood. The woman considered to be the most virtuous was given the honor of delivering the final blow, and Two Hawks Flying could not help feel a touch of pride when Bright Star was chosen for that honor.

The third sacred day the trunk of the cottonwood was painted four different colors, representing the four corners of the earth. Cutouts of a male buffalo and a male Indian, both with highly exaggerated genital organs, were placed in the fork of the tree, and then the tree was placed in position. After that, all the able-bodied warriors did a war dance around the pole, shooting arrows at the cutouts.

At dawn of the final sacred day, the tribal

medicine men rose to greet the sun with special prayers and songs. And then the dancers were prepared for their ordeal. Two Hawks Flying stood with clenched fists, eyes raised to the sun, as Elk Dreamer inserted two skewers through the flesh of his chest, just above the nipples. Long rawhide sinews were suspended from the top of the Sun Dance pole and attached to the skewers in his chest. Then he was hauled upward and left hanging in mid-air, until the weight of his body ripped the skewers from his flesh and he fell to the ground. The pain was tremendous, worse than he had anticipated, and when it grew unbearable, he blew on the eagle bone whistle Elk Dreamer had given him, calling upon Man Above to help him endure his agony.

Below him, other warriors danced around the Sun Dance pole. Skewers had been inserted high in their backs and attached to the skewers were sinews tied to heavy buffalo skulls, and as they danced, they dragged the heavy skulls behind them. Other participants had skewers inserted into their chests with sinews attached to the Sun Dance pole, and as they blew their whistles, they rocked back on their heels, pulling against the thongs to increase the pain. A lone woman stood among the warriors. Her sacrifice had been bits of flesh cut from her arms. It was the only way women were allowed to participate in the ritual.

In one corner, four old men beat a sacred drum and chanted ancient songs and prayers to the Cheyenne gods. Their fervent supplications were accompanied by the intermittent shrill notes of the dancers' whistles.

For a time, Two Hawks Flying watched the participants dancing below him, their steps in time with the drum. But as time dragged on, he forgot about his fellow sufferers, forgot everything but his own agony as the pain in his chest spread downward to every part of his body.

Floating on a red sea of pain, he stared into the sun as he blew his whistle.

"Hear me, Man Above. Accept my offering."

The steady beat of the ceremonial drum throbbed like the heartbeat of his people, keeping time with the cadence of pain pounding through him. Again and again he blew his whistle, voicing his anguish in its high-pitched wail.

"Hear me, Man Above. Give me strength."

The sun beat down on his face and chest. Sweat mingled with the blood oozing from his pierced flesh. His mouth felt dry and his body jerked convulsively as his agony increased. Lost in a world of pain, he summoned his waning strength and blew his whistle one last time.

"Hear me, Man Above, lest I perish."

The words were a prayer in his heart, a desperate cry for relief, and his answer came in a mighty rushing of wings as two red-tailed hawks swept out of the bright blaze of the sun. Side by side, wings touching, they hovered near his head.

"Be brave," the male hawk cried. "Be brave, and you shall be a mighty war leader among the people."

"Be strong," the female hawk cried. "Be strong, and everything you desire shall be yours."

Everything you desire. . . Hannah's image flashed across his mind. Then, with a mighty rush of powerful wings, the hawks were gone.

With their going, a merciful darkness dropped over Two Hawks Flying.

When he regained consciousness, he was in his father's lodge. Moments later, New Leaf, one of his father's wives, came in to treat his wounds.

Later, she fed him spoonfuls of thick venison stew flavored with sage and wild onions.

And then he slept.

Chapter 4
1875

My sixteenth birthday. I woke early that morning, even before Pa. Dressing quickly in an old blue gingham frock, I tiptoed down the stairs and out of the house. Whistling up Old Nellie, I swung a blanket over her sagging back and climbed aboard.

It was a beautiful clear morning as I reined Nellie toward the river, wanting some time to be alone with my thoughts and maybe take a swim if the water wasn't too dreadfully cold. All around me birds were singing hymns to the new day, while here and there bushy-tailed gray squirrels chattered as I rode by.

Near the river, a big four-point buck darted gracefully from sight, tail waving in the wind. I dismounted beneath a stand of lacy cottonwoods, smiling with the sheer joy of being young and alive on such a glorious day. Tethering Nellie to a stout sapling, I couldn't help laughing out loud as she quickly buried her nose in the rich grass that covered the riverbank like a thick green carpet.

Stepping out of my clothes, I tested the tranquil water with my big toe. Then, taking a deep breath, I plunged into the river, gasping as the chill water closed over me. I swam briskly for ten minutes or so before making my way ashore. Shivering a little, I stood naked on the riverbank, letting the sun bake me dry before I slipped back into my dress.

Feeling alive and refreshed, I stretched out on the thick spongy sod and stared up at the bold blue sky. Lying there, I decided that I would marry Joshua. True, I liked Orin best and was flattered by his flowery compliments and winning smile, but Mother was right. Josh would make the best husband. And what he lacked in romance and pretty speeches, he more than made up for in sincerity and ambition.

Frowning, I plucked a dandelion and twirled it between my fingers. I had thought to feel a sense of happiness, or at least relief, once I made a choice between Josh and Orin. Instead, I felt oddly dissatisfied, even though I was certain I had made the right decision.

Disgruntled, I tossed the dandelion aside. Contemplating the vast blue dome of sky again, I knew that I wouldn't be happy with Orin, either. The truth of the matter was, I just didn't love either one of the Berdeen boys, not the way my mother loved my father. Oh, I was fond of Joshua, and I was fond of Orin, too. But my affection was that of a sister for a brother—nothing more. The longer I thought about it, the more I realized I had decided to marry Joshua simply because everyone expected it.

With a sigh, I plopped over on my stomach and gazed across the river at the distant mountains. Now that I had decided not to marry either of the Berdeen boys, who would I marry? Single young men were mighty rare in our part of the country. Most of the men moving West already had a wife. And children, too. Perhaps I should marry Joshua after all. Perhaps, in time, I would grow to love him. Perhaps. . . .

A sudden rustling in the tall grass stilled my thoughts. Nellie let out a long nervous whinny. I sat up, suddenly conscious of being alone and far from home as I wondered who, or what, was lurking in the thicket behind me. Apprehensively I glanced over my shoulder and spied the cause of Nellie's unrest: an Indian brave mounted on a tall, red roan stallion.

It was Shadow, fully grown, and even more handsome than I remembered. Clad only in moccasins and the briefest of deerskin clouts, he was the closest thing to a completely naked man I had ever seen. I could not tear my eyes away. His legs were long and well-muscled by years of riding bareback; his belly was hard and flat, ridged with muscle; his shoulders broad. Two livid scars marred his bronze chest, proof that he had participated in the sacred ritual of the Sun Dance. A third scar zigzagged down his right shoulder, and I wondered fleetingly if the wound had been inflicted by the enemy warrior he had killed to earn the eagle feather that adorned his long black hair.

Like a bird hypnotized by a snake, I could not tear my gaze away from him. I could only stare, awed by his proud carriage, mesmerized by his savage yet utterly fascinating appearance. Was this the same boy who had eaten at our table and shared our laughter only a few short years ago? The same boy who had taught me to warble like a thrush and coo like a dove? A raw, animal-like power radiated from him, causing my heart to pound with such force I was certain he could hear it. Orin, with his foolish poetry and shy stolen kisses, had never caused my pulse to race so or brought such a warm flush to my cheeks.

A quiet word brought the stallion to within a few feet of where I sat, spellbound. Shadow slid easily to the ground beside me, causing me to tremble, though I could not have said why.

There was just the hint of a twinkle in his eye as he said, gravely, "Did you bring any cookies today, Hannah?"

"N...no," I stammered, unaccountably pleased by the way he murmured my name.

There was a hint of mischief in his dark-eyed gaze, and a sudden suspicion slid into my mind, prompting me to ask how long he had been watching me.

"Since you first rode up," he admitted, suppressing a smile, and I blushed with the knowledge that he had seen me swimming in the river, and drying, naked, on the bank afterwards.

"You have grown well," Shadow remarked casually, and my cheeks burned with embarrassment, for there was no mistaking his meaning or the way his eyes glowed with the memory. And yet, perversely, I was pleased that he had seen me and found me attractive.

"So have you," I murmured shyly. And indeed he had. The promise of his youth had been fulfilled, and he was tall and strong. Powerful muscles rippled in the sunlight as he stretched out beside me.

"I am called Two Hawks Flying now," he said proudly, and I knew that he was indeed a full-fledged warrior of the Cheyenne nation. I wondered what he had seen in his vision and what charms he carried in the small medicine pouch he wore around his neck. Pa said such things were foolish and heathen, but I couldn't see that Shadow's medicine bag was any different from the crucifix Mrs. Walker wore on a chain around her neck.

"How did you know I'd be here today?" I asked curiously, for I hadn't been to the river in over a week.

"I did not," he answered quietly. "I have been coming here every day for a month, hoping to catch you alone."

Every day for a month, I thought to myself. Imagine that. I was about to ask why, but one look into his dark eyes told me everything I needed to know.

We sat and stared at each other for a long time after that, neither of us able to think of anything to say—content, somehow, just to sit quietly close. All my life I had heard people say, contemptuously, that Indians smelled like shit and rancid grease. Yet Shadow—I never did learn to call him Two Hawks Flying—did not smell the least bit offensive. Rather, he smelled of woodsmoke and pine, of traildust and deerskin.

When I remarked on this, he said that the Indians bathed every day, summer and winter, even when they had to break through ice-bound rivers to do so. He added with a faint grin that the Indians thought white people smelled bad.

"Really?" I asked, surprised. "Do I smell bad to you?"

Shadow shook his head. "No, Hannah. You smell fresh and clean, like a spring day along the river, when all the flowers are in bloom."

"Thank you," I murmured. It was the loveliest compliment I had ever received.

Sometime later, Shadow rose gracefully to his feet. He moved with the quick easy strength of a mountain cat, his actions smooth and sure, and I felt a tingle of excitement just watching him. I knew now what was lacking in my relationship with Josh and Orin. It was the peculiar knot of wanting that made my senses reel and my heart pound like a wild thing. I had never had any real desire to have Josh or Orin hold me or kiss me, but I was suddenly filled with longing for the touch of Shadow's arms around me and the touch of his lips on mine. My cheeks burned hot with my unladylike thoughts, and I turned away.

A short whistle brought the roan to Shadow's side, and he swung effortlessly aboard the stud's bare back.

"Will you be here tomorrow, Hannah?" Shadow asked, and I knew with crystal clarity that my whole future hinged on my reply.

A dozen reasons why I should refuse to meet Shadow ran quickly through my mind. Joshua wouldn't like it. People would talk if they found out I was secretly meeting an Indian. My reputation would be ruined. He was red and I was white and we were worlds apart. I was practically engaged to another man. Pa wouldn't approve. . . .

Oh, there were a hundred reasons why I should have said no, but they all seemed shallow and unimportant as Shadow gazed down at me, waiting for my reply.

"I'll be here," I said, experiencing a sweet sense of joy and peace as I spoke the words.

I floated in a world all my own the rest of that day. My feet went lightly from task to task, and I couldn't seem to stop smiling or singing.

That evening Joshua and his family came over to celebrate my birthday. Mother had baked a beautiful cake for the occasion, decorated with pink icing and candles. There was singing and dancing and gaily wrapped presents, but I wasn't really there. Oh, I danced and flirted with Josh and Orin and made all the proper replies, but all the while I was remembering Shadow and how wonderfully exciting it had been just to sit beside him. His very nearness had made me feel vital and alive, as if I were looking at the world through new eyes.

I remembered how his dark eyes had moved over me from head to heel in a lingering glance that was as warm and intimate as a caress. I had read the open admiration and desire in that bold stare, and when, at last, the party was over and I was alone in my room, I went to the mirror and took a critical look at myself.

My hair fell in soft waves around my face, and my skin was a smooth golden tan. I had a nice figure—nothing men would rave about, but my breasts were high and firm, and my legs were long and shapely. My waist was trim, my hips well-rounded and not too big. And if my nose was a trifle too small and my mouth a little too wide, well, there was nothing I could do about that.

"Why, I'm pretty," I mused aloud to my reflection. Or maybe I only felt pretty because of the way Shadow had looked at me.

It seemed the night would never end, and

when the first faint gray light bloomed in the East, I was already saddling Nellie. When I reached the river, Shadow was already there, waiting for me. Chill as the morning was, he was clad in just a clout and fringed buckskin leggings, and I knew I had never seen a more handsome, virile man in my life. Heart pounding like a drum, I slid from the saddle and went straight into Shadow's waiting arms.

"Hannah," he whispered huskily, and as his strong arms enfolded me, I knew I would never be happy with Josh or Orin or any other man save the tall dark warrior who held me fast.

"Kiss me," I begged shamelessly, and when he seemed uncertain, I pulled his head down and pressed my lips to his.

It was like touching a match to gunpowder. I felt the explosions right down to my toes, and when we parted, I saw that Shadow had felt it, too. How can I describe the wondrous feeling that rushed through me, that warm soft glow that started at the innermost core of my being and permeated every fiber of my body and soul? It was a feeling of joy and happiness, of peace and security, and yet it was more than that. It was like. . .like having your fondest dream become reality, and finding that reality was even sweeter than the dream.

We went for a long walk that day, our hearts and hands touching as we strolled through the verdant countryside. Never had the sky been so blue, the air so sweet. Never had the world seemed quite as wonderful as it did that lovely summer morning.

"Who is the yellow-haired wasichu who rides often to your lodge?" Shadow asked after awhile.

"Oh, that's Josh Berdeen," I answered airily. "He wants to marry me."

"Do your parents approve?"

"Oh, yes. They like Josh very much."

Shadow came to an abrupt halt and swung me around so that we stood face to face. His eyes were fathomless pools of darkness as he asked, flatly, "Do you?"

"Oh, he's all right, I guess," I replied with a shrug.

"Are you going to marry him?"

"Do you think I should?" I asked coquettishly.

I suppose I was trying to spark Shadow's jealousy with my reply, but all it evoked was an angry scowl as he said, fiercely, "Do not play your silly woman's games with me, Hannah. I am not one of your pale-faced admirers."

"I'm sorry," I apologized, properly contrite. "Of course I shan't marry him. Not now."

69

All too soon it was time for me to return home. Joshua was there, waiting for me, when I arrived. He looked quite nice in his Sunday best, with his long blond hair slicked back, and his boots polished to a high sheen. Like the gentleman he was, he helped me dismount, opening the door for me when we went into the house. I knew what he had come to say and wished heartily that there was some way to avoid it. But of course there wasn't, so I took a deep breath and sat down on the sofa, my hands folded demurely in my lap.

"Would you care for some cider, Josh?" I asked, hoping to delay the inevitable. "Or a slice of Mother's blackberry pie?"

"No, Hannah," Josh replied, coming right to the point. "What I'd like is for you to marry me."

"Joshua, I. . . ."

"Oh, I know you aren't crazy in love with me like I am with you," he interrupted in a rush, "but I'll make you a good husband, Hannah. I. . .Damn it, I'm not good at flowery speeches like Orin, but you must know how I feel. Say yes, Hannah, and I'll live and die for you."

It was the most impassioned speech Josh had ever made. His blue eyes pleaded with me to accept, but another man held my heart. A man with piercing black eyes and skin like fine copper. Shadow.

Looking down at my hands, I said as gently as I could, "I'm sorry, Josh. I can't."

"Is it Orin?" he demanded jealousy.

"No."

"Hannah. . ."

"Please, Josh, don't make this any harder than it has to be."

"Very well," he said heavily. "But if you ever change your mind, I'll be waiting. I love you, Hannah Kincaid. I'll always love you."

My folks were terribly disappointed when I told them I had turned Joshua down. Both had been eagerly anticipating our marriage. Pa had planned to take Josh on as a full partner in the store after we were married, and Mother was happily looking forward to being a grandmother. Unable to have any more children of her own after I was born, she was counting on me to give her dozens of grandchildren.

Still, disappointed as they were, they accepted my decision without a lot of fuss, and for that I was grateful.

Two new families moved into the valley in August, but I was so preoccupied with Shadow and the love blossoming between us that I paid little attention to them. One bit of news that did catch my attention concerned

Orin. It seemed he was courting Lucinda Bailey, another recent arrival. Paul Brown was also courting her. In fact, all the valley boys seemed to be spending a lot of time at the Bailey place. And who could blame them! Lucinda was a tall, statuesque brunette with ivory skin and emerald eyes. If I hadn't been so in love with Shadow, I might have been jealous of the attention she got. Truth be told, I suppose, deep down, I was a little jealous of the way Orin followed her around. But only a little. Joshua, alone, seemed immune to her charms. He still came to see me now and then, and though he never again mentioned marriage, I knew he was hoping I'd reconsider and say yes.

But I had no time for Joshua. My thoughts and hopes and dreams were centered around Shadow. Waking or sleeping, I could think of nothing else. Our love blossomed like the gaily-colored flowers that brightened the hills and valleys, permeating the warm summer air with a delightful fragrance that seemed to be for us alone. Our kisses grew longer and more fervent, and it delightful fragrance and more fervent, and it became increasingly difficult to say good-bye. Sometimes Shadow trembled with desire as he stroked my hair or caressed my willing flesh, and I ached to satisfy his hunger, even as I longed to satisfy my growing curiosity about the intimate relationship between a man and a woman.

Often, I thought how wonderful it would be if we were married. We could build a little house a few miles down the valley and raise cattle or horses. Or maybe Shadow could work in the store with Pa—though I wasn't sure that would be such a good idea. I dreamed of having children and hoped our first child would be a boy with thick black hair and dark eyes. Perhaps one day we'd go East and tour the cities there. I'd never gotten over my yearning to dress in fine clothes and go to the theatre. Oh, it would be such fun, I thought, and then giggled out loud as I tried to imagine Shadow in a coat and tie. Somehow, I couldn't picture him in evening clothes and the harder I tried, the sillier it seemed.

But I had no trouble imagining myself as his wife. None at all. And so the warm summer days went by on running feet, and my heart swelled with love and a growing hope that one day soon Shadow would ask me to be his bride.

Chapter 5

The warrior sat atop a high bluff, his face set in a deep scowl as he watched a half-dozen hunters decimate a herd of buffalo. Fifty of the huge curly-haired beasts had fallen, kicking and bleeding, before the herd caught the scent of blood and stampeded, thundering across the sunlit prairie like an angry brown sea. Hides were selling for three dollars apiece in the East, and the plains were crawling with buffalo hunters who took the great shaggy hides and the tongues and left tons of meat to rot in the merciless Dakota sun. Their Big Fifties made short work of bringing down the buffalo. One hunter, accompanied by a band of professional skinners, claimed to have killed 1500 animals in a single week.

Predictably, the tribes were growing increasingly hostile as their main food supply was callously slaughtered and left for the wolves and the buzzards. Again and again, hunters had been ambushed and killed, but still they came. And as the great herds dwindled, tribes that had known nothing but prosperity found themselves starving and forced to settle on the reservation.

Lost in thought, Two Hawks Flying reined his big red stallion toward the river crossing. If the whites did not give heed to the treaties—and when had they ever?—there was going to be war on the plains. The Indians could not survive without the buffalo. Virtually everything the red man used, ate, or wore, came from old Pte. The people covered themselves and their lodgepoles with Pte's hide, made rope from his hair, cooking vessels from his paunch, spoons and rattles from his horn, glue from his hooves, jerky and pemmican from his rich red flesh.

But the buffalo hunters were not the only whites swarming over the country. There were others that came scratching in the Black Hills for yellow iron. Still others came with their cattle and their families, crowding the Indians off their land, scaring away the deer and the elk, fencing the grassland, churning up the soil with their plows.

Troubled by his thoughts, Two Hawks Flying pulled Red Wind to a halt and sat staring towards Bear Valley. Not long ago there had been only one cabin in the valley. Now there were more than could be counted on two hands.

The young warriors were talking more and more about wiping the settlers out.

"Kill them now," the angry young men argued around the campfire. "Why wait until their numbers grow larger?"

They spoke words of wisdom, Two Hawks Flying mused ruefully. And yet, because he loved a white girl, he spoke for peace.

So far, there had been no bloodshed in the valley, although Snake and a handful of hot-headed young warriors had burned down a squatter's shack the week before and run off the white man's cattle and horses.

But that was mild compared to the carnage that would surely take place if the whites continued to violate the treaties. Once the young men got a taste for blood, there would be no holding them back. What real warrior would be content to sit at home when there were honors to be won on the field of battle, when there were white scalps for the taking?

Once the fighting started, not even the combined efforts of Black Owl and Elk

Dreamer would be strong enough to maintain peace.

Two Hawks Flying sighed heavily. War was inevitable, he thought gloomily, and when it came, it would totally destroy his relationship with Hannah. Once the fighting started, it would be red against white, with no quarter given on either side.

Even now, he knew the Kincaid family would be severely criticized by their neighbors, perhaps shunned entirely, if it was known that Hannah was seeing an Indian on the sly. It would be best if they stopped seeing each other altogether, he mused, but even as he considered it, he was nudging Red Wind with his heels.

Like a moth to a flame, he was drawn toward the river crossing. And Hannah's waiting arms.

Chapter 6

"Why won't you come?" I asked for the tenth time. "Mother would love to see you—you know she would."

"And your father?" Shadow asked drily.

I shrugged. "Pa won't care," I answered, and the lie tasted flat in my mouth. The truth was, I didn't know how Pa would behave. He never had liked Shadow, but then, Pa just didn't like Indians. Of course, he had a good reason. His parents, a sister, and two brothers had all been killed by Blackfoot Indians when Pa was just a little boy. Pa had been left for dead and would surely have died of starvation and exposure if a kind-hearted old mountain man hadn't happened along the next day and found Pa wandering around the charred ruins of their wagon. The mountain man had raised Pa until Pa was sixteen, and then Pa had set off on his own.

"Please come," I begged, and Shadow finally, reluctantly, gave in.

Mother gave me quite a probing look when I told her Shadow was coming for dinner that night. However, she asked surprisingly few questions and readily agreed to speak to Pa about being on his good behavior. I smiled all day as I rushed about tidying up the house, dusting and mopping and polishing until every room sparkled from floor to ceiling. That evening I took an extra long bath, then slipped into a becoming green dress and tied my hair back with a matching ribbon. Humming softly, I twirled before the mirror, pleased with my appearance.

Pa was in the parlor, pouring over some mail order catalog and muttering about the high cost of something or other, when I entered the room.

"Evening, Pa," I said cheerfully.

"Evening," he grunted. Then, looking up, he frowned as he said, suspiciously, "You'd think somebody special was coming to call, instead of just an old playmate."

"Oh, Pa!" I chided, and hurried into the kitchen to help Mother set the table before

Pa could ask any questions I didn't want to answer.

Shadow arrived on the stroke of six, and as I saw him enter the room, my heart began to pound. He was dressed in a shirt of bleached doeskin, heavily fringed along the arms and exquisitely decorated with dyed porcupine quills. His thick black hair hung loose down his back, adorned with a single white eagle feather. Tall and straight and proud, he shook my father's hand, kissed my mother's cheek, and smiled at me.

"Well, dinner is ready," Mother said cheerfully. "I hope you're all hungry."

Mother outdid herself that night. She served up chicken and feather-light dumplings, succulent baked ham, fresh picked peas, and hot biscuits dripping with butter and honey. And for dessert she had deep dish apple pie. And oatmeal cookies.

Shadow and I grinned at each other as he reached for one of Mother's cookies, and Mother grinned, too, as she asked, teasingly, "Can you still eat ten in less than a minute?"

"I do not know," Shadow replied soberly. "But I am willing to try."

We all laughed at that, even Pa.

After dinner, the men retired to the parlor while Mother and I cleared the table. It made me nervous to leave them alone together, and I wondered uneasily how they would get along. Pa had been quiet during dinner, leaving me to wonder if they would just sit and glare at each other.

Abruptly, Pa cleared his throat and I frowned as I heard him say, "Well, Shadow, do you think there will be any more trouble this year?"

"Yes," Shadow answered flatly. "There is going to be a lot of trouble if the whites do not stay off our land."

"I'm afraid it won't be your land much longer," Pa replied bluntly. "Tales of gold and grass and fertile soil will draw people West like shit draws flies."

"I think you are right," Shadow agreed. "But know this. My people will not give up their hunting grounds without a fight. We have lived here for hundreds of years. We are not afraid to fight for what is ours. And we are not afraid to die. And we will fight to the death before we surrender!"

"Likely!" Pa snapped, and in my mind's eye I could see them glowering at each other, bristling like two dogs over a bone.

There was a taut silence. Then Shadow said, "Because your family has been good to me in the past, I will tell you something. I think, if you are smart, you will take your wife and your daughter and get out of this part of the country before it is too late. Crazy Horse and Sitting Bull and the other chiefs are talking war. Sitting Bull is making big medicine in the Sacred Hills. The young warriors among the Tsi-Tsi-Tsas and the Lakotas are eager to join him."

"Yes, they've already been out practicing up," Pa acknowledged flatly. "The Henrys were burned out last week, their cattle and horses run off."

"It was a warning," Shadow said. "No one was killed this time. The next family may not be so lucky." Shadow's voice dropped as he said, earnestly, "Take your family away from here before it is too late."

Pa snorted. "This land is mine as much as anybody's! I worked it, and I sweated over it, and I'll not leave it. No, by damn, I won't!"

For the second time that night a heavy silence fell between the two men. Even in the kitchen, I could feel the tension between them. Worried, I cast an anxious glance in Mother's direction. She smiled reassuringly as she removed her apron, picked up the coffee pot, and glided into the parlor.

"Coffee, anyone?" she asked brightly, and tactfully steered the conversation into more pleasant channels.

Shadow left soon afterward, and Pa stomped off to bed, leaving Mother and I to finish up in the kitchen. Mother looked preoccupied and increasingly worried as she washed the last cup and drained the water from the sink. Then, with a sigh, she looked me right in the eye and said, "All right, Hannah. Tell me everything."

"Why, whatever to you mean?" I asked innocently.

"You know perfectly well what I mean, Hannah Kincaid," she said sternly. "How long have you and Shadow been meeting on the sly?"

My mouth popped open in astonishment. How had she known?

I had difficulty speaking past the lump in my throat. "Since my birthday," I confessed, and Mother frowned as she dropped her apron over the back of a chair and took me firmly by the hand.

"I think we had better have a talk, dear," she said, and led me to the sofa. I sat beside her, not meeting her eyes.

Still holding my hand, Mother sat quietly for a moment, studying my face. Then, in her dear sweet voice, she said, "Hannah, you know how fond I am of Shadow. I couldn't love him more if he were my own flesh and blood, but Hannah dear, he is an Indian. And even though he speaks English almost as well as you do, and even though he seems just like one of the family when he's here, he isn't one of us and never will be."

I couldn't believe my ears. She sounded

just like Pa! I felt as if I had been betrayed. I had been so certain she would be happy for me—happy for Shadow—because we were in love. In the back of my mind, I had been counting on her support, counting on her to make Pa see things my way. And now this.

Impatiently, I said, "Oh, Mother, you don't understand. I..."

"But I do understand, child. That's just the trouble. You and Shadow haven't done anything we need to worry about, have you?"

I felt my cheeks flame as I realized what she was implying, and said, rather indignantly, "Mother, really!"

"Don't look so shocked, Hannah. I know what goes on between a boy and a girl."

"We haven't done anything wrong," I said sullenly. "Honest."

"I believe you, dear," Mother said, squeezing my hand. "And I think it would be best for all concerned if you end it now, before it goes too far."

"I can't. I love him more than anything in the world."

"I know, child," Mother said sympathetically. "I can see it in your eyes. But it will never work."

"We'll make it work!" I cried passionately. "I love him with all my heart, and he loves me."

"Sometimes love isn't enough, Hannah," Mother remarked quietly. "Where will you live? Here, in the valley? I don't think so. Our neighbors would never accept him."

"Then we'll live with the Cheyenne."

"Do you think you would be happy there, living with strangers—knowing you would never belong?"

"I don't know."

"Perhaps you should think about it carefully before you rush into something you may regret. I doubt if Shadow's people would accept you any more readily than folks here would cotton to Shadow. And in the meantime, it will only get worse. You heard what Shadow said to your father. If war comes, it won't be safe for Shadow to show his face anywhere near the trading post. And it won't be safe for you to leave the protection of these walls, either."

Tears of despair and frustration welled in my eyes. Jerking my hand from Mother's, I walked over to the window and stood staring out into the darkness. Out there, somewhere beyond the trees and across the river, was the man I loved. What difference did it make that he was an Indian? If I didn't care about the color of his skin, why should anyone else? No one would care if he were Dutch or French.

"Hannah, perhaps if you gave Joshua

another chance. . . ?"

"Joshua!" I exclaimed. "You must be kidding."

"He loves you. He would make you a fine husband."

"Never! If I can't marry Shadow, I won't marry at all!"

"Has he asked you?"

"No," I admitted miserably. Mother had touched a sore spot that time. I had been waiting—hoping Shadow would propose, but he never did. Maybe I was wrong. Maybe he didn't love me as much as I loved him. Maybe he didn't love me at all. He had never said so.

Resolutely, I put such thoughts from my mind. He did love me. I knew he did. His eyes and his kisses could not lie.

"I doubt if he will," Mother said gently. "Shadow is a realist even if you are not. He knows it would never work."

"It would work, if everybody would just leave us alone."

"Hannah, marriage is hard enough when two people share the same background and the same beliefs. Without a common heritage, it's almost sure to fail."

"Oh, leave me alone!" I cried petulantly, and ran from the room, blinded by my tears. Why couldn't she understand how I felt? Distraught, I slammed my bedroom door and threw myself across my bed. Burying my face in my pillow, I cried until my throat was raw and my eyes swollen. And still the tears came, until, exhausted and discouraged, I fell asleep. Only to toss and turn all night long.

I woke before dawn and left the house. Outside, the air was cold and clear and still. A thin blanket of sparkling frost covered the ground, and my breath came out in little clouds of white vapor.

Nellie humped her back and flattened her ears when I laid the cold saddle pad in place, stubbornly refusing to budge when I climbed onto the saddle. Even my horse is against me, I thought angrily, and pounded her sides with my heels. Finally, with a soulful look at the cozy barn, she broke into a shambling trot.

In spite of my heavy coat and wool scarf, I was shivering and my teeth were chattering when I reached the river crossing. Shadow was there, waiting for me, and I saw that he had spent the night beneath 'our' tree, wrapped in a furry brown buffalo robe.

"You have been crying," he observed as I dismounted. "Was it bad after I left?"

"No," I lied.

"Hannah, you are as easy to read as the stars in the sky," he chided gently. "I told you it would be better if I stayed away."

"Please don't scold me," I begged. "I've had enough of that to last a lifetime."

"You're cold," Shadow observed quietly. "Come, let me warm you."

And so saying, he spread my coat beneath our tree, sat me down beside him, and drew his buffalo robe around our shoulders. It was very cozy, bundled in the heavy robe, and I lifted my face for his kiss, desperately needing to feel the strength of his arms around me and feel the reassuring warmth of his lips on mine. As always, his touch left me breathless and yearning for more. But he held me away from him, and I raised troubled eyes to study his face.

"What's wrong?" I asked tremulously.

"Hannah, you must persuade your father to leave the valley. There is going to be war, if not this year then the next."

"What has that to do with us?"

"Everything. When my people fight, I must fight with them, and I do not want to fight you or your parents. I would not like to see any of you killed."

The thought that we might be killed had never entered my mind. War, and talk of war, had always seemed vague and far off, something that only happened to other people, in other parts of the country. Even when the Henrys had been burned out, it hadn't affected me personally. No one had been hurt, and I didn't know them anyway, not really. They were just a placid, middle-aged couple with three tow-headed kids who had come into the trading post now and then.

"Maybe there won't be any war," I suggested hopefully. "And even if there is, surely your people won't harm us. They never have before."

"This is not like before," Shadow said gravely. "The buffalo hunters are killing the buffalo for their hides and leaving the meat to rot in the sun. My people cannot live without the buffalo. This summer, ten new families moved into the southern end of the valley. Soon there will be ten more, and then ten more. The hunters are bad enough, but the settlers are worse. They come with their families and their cattle and fence the land. We must stop them now, while we can."

We must stop them now, while we can. The words sent a shiver down my spine, and yet I knew what he meant. The valley was growing every day. Counting the ten new families Shadow had mentioned, there were now seventeen families in Bear Valley. We had a church now, and a school. Charlotte Brown, Paul's mother, was a bona fide school teacher. Charlie Bailey, Lucinda's father, was talking about building a hotel next year. And Frank Fitch was making plans to open a saloon, though there was some doubt that the ladies in the valley would allow it.

Yes, we were growing. There was no doubt about it. I could understand why the Indians were concerned.

Troubled, I glanced up at Shadow and found myself wondering, guiltily, if he had ridden with the Indians who had burned out the Henry family. Unable to help myself, I stared at the lone white eagle feather in Shadow's hair and found myself wondering if the enemy he had killed to earn that feather had been red or white.

"He was a Pawnee," Shadow murmured, reading my thoughts, and I could not hide my relief.

His dark eyes held mine for a long time before he said, quietly, "I think it would be better for both of us if we did not meet again. It will only lead to trouble and unhappiness for all concerned."

"Oh, you sound just like my mother!" I wailed unhappily.

"She is a wise woman, Hannah. Perhaps you should listen to her advice."

"I wish I were an Indian girl," I muttered sulkily, and Shadow granted me one of his rare smiles.

"Things would certainly be less complicated," he allowed.

"How would you court me, if I were an Indian girl?" I asked. "Is it romantic?"

"I suppose so," he said with a shrug. "I never gave it much thought."

"Well, think about it," I insisted. "Would you bring me flowers and take me picnicking in the woods?"

"Not quite. When a Cheyenne warrior is interested in a girl, he makes himself a flute, usually in the shape of a bird. Sometimes he paints it with the likeness of a horse, because horses are believed to be ardent lovers and hard to resist. At night, the warrior plays his flute outside the girl's lodge. The notes are sweet and low, and every flute has its own sound. Sometimes the warrior follows his girl to the river, or waits for her there, hoping to catch her alone."

"That sounds romantic," I said, and smiled as I remembered that Shadow and I often met by a river, as we did now.

"I suppose, but the warrior rarely manages to see his sweetheart alone. Indian mothers keep a close eye on their daughters, especially when they know some warrior is after them."

"How do you find time to be alone, then?"

"In the evening, the maidens stand outside their lodges, each wrapped in a big red blanket. If a girl is interested in a particular warrior, she holds the blanket open when he walks by, inviting him to join her. When they are standing very close, the girl covers them both with the robe."

"That doesn't sound very private," I remarked skeptically.

"It isn't," Shadow allowed. "But we have very few pregnant brides."

"Very funny," I retorted, punching him on the arm. "Suppose they decide to get married. What then?"

"The warrior's father would send a go-between to speak to the girl's family. If her family approves the match, the warrior leaves a number of horses outside the girl's lodge, preferably stolen horses, not only as a token of his affection but to prove to her family that he can provide for a wife."

"Stolen horses!" I exclaimed. "How awful!"

"Horse stealing is viewed a little differently among my people," Shadow explained with a grin. "I know it is a hanging offense among the whites, but to the Tsitsitsas it is an art. It can be a lot of fun, too. Anyway, if the horses are accepted, the girl's mother sets the date for the wedding."

"Does the bride wear white?"

"Usually."

"Is there a big ceremony with music and dancing?"

"No. On the day of the wedding, the bride is placed on a blanket and carried to the lodge of her future father-in-law and left there. Most couples live with the husband's family until they collect enough skins for a lodge of their own."

"Hmmm. . . Shadow, if I were an Indian girl, would you bring my father horses?"

"I would offer your father my entire herd," Shadow replied solemnly. "But you are not an Indian girl, and I think your father would gladly see you dead before he would let you go away with me."

"Then I'll run away!" I cried passionately.

"No, Hannah."

I had known he would say that. Shadow was a proud and honorable man, and I knew he would not let me disobey my father nor take me away unless my father consented. And Pa would never consent.

Still, Shadow wanted me. I knew he did, and the sliver of an idea started in my mind as I pressed myself shamelessly against him.

"Why didn't you go home last night?" I asked, caressing his cheek with my fingers.

"Because I had a feeling you would need me this morning," he answered ruefully.

"You always seem to know what I'm thinking, or what I'm going to do," I said, pouting a little. "It isn't fair."

"I know what you're thinking now, too," Shadow remarked with a wry grin. "And it isn't going to work."

"Don't you want me?" I murmured. Boldly, I pressed my breasts against Shadow's naked chest.

"Hannah, listen to me. . ."

"I love you," I whispered as, pulling his head down, I kissed him—gently at first, then with greater intensity.

I was not prepared for Shadow's quick response. With a sudden rush of passion, he crushed me close, covering my face and neck with kisses that seared my skin.

A quick flame of desire sparked in the deepest core of my being, and what had started as a game now turned abruptly serious. Shadow's dark eyes burned with a fierce inner fire as he began to stroke my quivering flesh in places he had never dared touch before.

My breathing grew rapid, and I began to tremble with delight and longing, confused by a jumbled tide of emotions I had never known or dreamed of.

Shadow's breathing was also erratic, and when I grasped the lithe muscles in his arms, I was surprised to find he, too, was trembling.

Abruptly, he drew away. "No, Hannah," he murmured in a ragged voice.

"What's wrong?" I cried, stung by his rejection. "You want me. I know you do!"

He did not deny it, and I was suddenly drunk with the power I had over him. Taking his hand, I laid it over my fiercely beating heart.

"I love you," I whispered fervently. "I want to be your woman, your wife."

"Hannah, please," he groaned. "I am not made of iron."

"Prove it," I challenged, and pressed myself wantonly against him a second time.

With an animal-like cry of defeat, Shadow wrapped his arms around me, squeezing me so tight I thought my ribs would break. His kisses, long and hard, were filled with passion and desire and I knew I had won. He would not turn back now.

And then he was rising over me, and I gasped aloud at the visible sign of his aroused desire.

I had never seen a naked man before, and a sudden fear cooled my passion so that I lay rigid beneath him.

"No," I said, trying to push him away. "No, don't."

But it was too late, and I shivered uncontrollably as Shadow thrust into me. A sharp pain caused me to cry out, and Shadow groaned low in his throat as he shuddered to a halt.

"You hurt me!" I accused. "No one ever told me it would hurt."

"It will never hurt again," he promised, and then he was moving deep inside me, evoking sensations and feelings that I had never imagined.

Once I opened my eyes, and I marveled that the earth had not changed, that the sky was still blue and the grass green, for it seemed as though the whole world should be enflamed with the glorious passion that forged Shadow's flesh and mine into one being.

With a sigh, I closed my eyes and drew Shadow closer, until there was nothing in all the world but the two of us, bound together by our love.

I would have been content to lie in Shadow's arms forever, and I dared not speak, for fear of breaking the magical spell between us.

Shadow sighed as he sat up, as if he, too, were reluctant to end the peaceful silence between us.

"I am sorry, Hannah," he murmured.

"Don't be. I'm not."

Shadow's dark eyes held a faint hint of merry laughter as he said, with mock resignation, "I suppose I shall have to marry you now. That was your intent, wasn't it? To tempt me into marriage with your irresistable woman's body?"

"Yes," I admitted happily, and hurled myself into his outstretched arms.

"Do you think it was fair, to tempt me with such sweetness that I could not refuse?"

"All is fair in love and war," I said with a shrug.

Shadow's mouth turned down in a wry grin. "I will come for you tomorrow," he promised.

I couldn't stop smiling as I slipped into my clothes. We were going to be married. Nothing could stop us now.

Jubilant, I lifted my face for one more kiss. " 'Til tomorrow," I whispered, and rode hard for home, aware of Shadow's eyes on my back until I was out of sight.

Chapter 7

Monday was not a good day. I rose early and packed my clothes, wanting to be ready to leave the minute Shadow came for me.

I looked around my room as I closed my valise. It was a nice room. The walls were whitewashed. Blue curtains hung at the window, and a matching spread covered the bed. A tall mahogany chest of drawers stood against one wall.

It would be strange, living in a hide lodge instead of a house. I wondered what the Indians did for closets, and how I would manage to cook a whole meal over a firepit instead of on a wood stove.

Yawning, I stared out the window. I had spent a sleepless night, wondering what my mother's reaction was going to be when I told her I was going to marry Shadow with or without her blessing. I knew what my father's reaction would be, and I was dreading it. But nothing they could say or do would dissuade me. I was Shadow's woman now, and nothing could change that.

Noon came and went, and still there was no sign of Shadow. Mother fixed my favorite meal—roast beef and potato salad—but I had no appetite and merely picked at my food. Pa muttered under his breath about good food going to waste, but Mother didn't say a word, merely pursed her lips and looked worried.

Shortly after lunch, Joshua rode up and insisted I go walking with him. I didn't want to leave the trading post, but I couldn't think of a plausible reason to refuse, so I went. I knew my mother was smiling happily as we left the house together.

As we walked down the path to the river, I could not help but compare Joshua with Shadow. Joshua came off a poor second, I'm afraid. Oh, he was tall and handsome, and a nice boy, but he lacked that elusive animal-like magnetism that had first drawn me to Shadow. Josh was lean and fit, but Shadow was more so. Where Josh was shy and a bit reserved, Shadow exuded strength and self-confidence.

There was just no comparison between the

two, and when Joshua begged me to please reconsider his marriage proposal, I said 'no' bluntly, hoping to close the subject once and for all.

"There's someone else, isn't there," Josh demanded, shoving his hands into his pockets.

"Yes," I admitted, wishing he would just shut up and go home.

"It's Orin, isn't it?"

"For goodness sakes, Josh, it isn't Orin. I've told you that a hundred times. It's Shadow!"

I clapped my hand over my mouth, horrified to realize what I had let slip.

"Shadow!" Joshua exclaimed. "You mean that Injun kid?"

"He's not a kid any more," I retorted. "He's a man full grown. And I love him."

"I don't believe it," Josh said, shaking his head. "You've got to be kidding."

"Well, I'm not. Now please go home and leave me alone."

"Does your father know? I can't believe he'd approve of your carrying on with a red-ass nigger."

"Of course he doesn't know," I muttered, wishing I had kept my big mouth shut. "You won't tell him? Promise?"

"I won't tell. But you had better think this over careful before you go off and do something you'll likely regret. I...I love you, Hannah. I guess you know I'll always be here if you need me."

"Thank you, Josh," I said sincerely, and liked him better at that moment than I ever had before.

"Come on—I'll walk you back to the post. It's not safe for you to be out here alone."

"Don't be silly," I scoffed. "I've been coming down here alone since I was a little girl."

Joshua's blue eyes were dark with worry as he said, urgently, "You mustn't go out alone anymore, Hannah. Haven't you heard? John Sanders was killed last night on his way home from the Tabor place and his little girl was kidnapped."

"I didn't know," I said tremulously. "Who did it?"

"Cheyennes, of course," he answered bitterly. "A dozen or so—judging by the arrows they pulled out of his body."

"Poor Mrs. Sanders," I murmured. "Kathy was their only child. She'll be all alone, now."

My thoughts were glum as we walked back to the trading post. A family burned out. A man killed. A child kidnapped. I couldn't believe it. The Indians had never bothered us before. Not really. Oh, they'd stolen some stock now and then, but that was about all.

I wondered suddenly just how close the Cheyenne village was. For some reason I'd always imagined it to be miles and miles away because we rarely saw any Indians around the trading post. Occasionally a hunting party passed within sight of our place, and we caught a brief glimpse of dark brown bodies and feathers as they rode by on their spotted ponies, lance tips glinting brightly in the sunlight. They had seemed colorful and exciting from a distance but now, with news of John Sanders' death, they loomed ugly and menacing.

With a start, I realized I knew practically nothing about Indians. I had no idea how they lived, or what they believed in, or what they did for fun, if anything. And while I was at it, I had to admit, if reluctantly, that I knew very little about Shadow; only that he was 19 or 20 and that his mother had died when he was very young. Oh, but I knew he loved me and I loved him, and what else mattered, anyway?

When we reached the trading post, I bid Josh good-bye and went to my room to wait for Shadow. Looking out my window, I found myself thinking of John Sanders. Why had the Indians killed him? I remembered the night I had caught Mr. and Mrs. Sanders kissing on the porch, and the way Mr. Sanders liked to carry Kathy on his shoulder, pretending she was a princess. Depressed by my thoughts, I went downstairs to help Pa in the store. It was a busy time of day, and waiting on customers kept my mind off Mr. Sanders' death. Every time the door opened, I expected it to be Shadow. But he didn't come that day.

The funeral was the next day. Everybody in the valley turned out, dressed in their best, for John Sanders had been liked and respected by one and all. It was a somber group that stood at the grave site—the first grave in Bear Valley. The Indian attack had left everyone a little nervous, and I noticed the men were all carrying rifles and the women kept their children close at hand.

Since we had no preacher, Pa read over the grave, using the 23rd Psalm and John, chapter 11, for his text. Many of the women wept as Pa read, "I am the resurrection and the life, he that believeth in me, though he were dead, yet shall he live. . . ."

Florence Sanders stood beside my mother, her face white as paper, her eyes blank. She never shed a tear, nor spoke a word. I don't think she even knew what was going on.

When the services were over, Mrs. Sanders went home with the Walkers.

Shadow did not come that day, either.

* * *

Wednesday morning a half-dozen grim-faced men rode into the trading post, led by Saul Green and Jed Tabor.

"Mornin', Sam," Mr. Green said curtly.

"Mornin'," Pa replied. "What brings you men out so early?"

"We're going after them redskins," Saul declared vehemently. "We don't aim to let John's death go unavenged."

"That's right," Jed Tabor agreed. "We're going after the bastards. Show 'em they can't go around killing a white man and stealing his youngun!"

"Yeah," Charlie Bailey chimed in. "If we let them get away with this kind of thing now, it will only get worse later."

"I hate to admit it," Seth Walker said glumly, "but I think they're right. Are you with us, Sam?"

"I don't know," Pa replied thoughtfully. "Just what are you aimin' to do?"

"Get Kathy back," Saul Green answered confidently. "And wipe out as many of those Godless savages as we can in the process."

"Hmmm. How many men you figure to take with you?"

"Every man in the valley," Saul answered firmly.

"That'd be sixteen men," Pa murmured. "Eighteen counting Josh and Orin."

"That's right."

"Just what are you leading up to, Kincaid?" Ted Tabor demanded.

"Just this. We don't have one experienced Indian fighter in the whole valley. And there's no way eighteen farmers can hope to ride into an angry Cheyenne village and rescue one little girl. No way in the world. And while you're out getting yourselves killed, who's gonna stay behind and protect your women?"

The men stirred uncomfortably as the truth of Pa's words struck home.

"I know a little about Injuns," Pa went on. "They ain't likely to hurt Kathy none. Injuns set a store on kids. Any kids. Likely some couple lost a child of their own and the husband took Kathy to perk up his wife."

"Then why didn't they steal an Injun kid?" Charlie Bailey muttered.

"I don't know," Pa said with an impatient shrug. "Likely they would have if they hadn't run across John and Kathy first. But that's neither here nor there. Reasons don't matter now. What does matter is that you'll all be committing suicide if you ride against the Cheyenne."

There was a lot of mumbling and grumbling and cursing while the men talked it over. They finally allowed as how Pa was right, but Ted Tabor and Saul Green were still spoiling for a fight when they rode off.

Things were quiet the rest of the day. Time and time again I found myself at the window, hoping to see Shadow striding through the gate. Later that afternoon I walked outside the stockade, longing to see the man I loved riding up the path from the river.

But he didn't come that day either.

I hadn't said a word about going off with Shadow, but my folks both knew he was the cause of my unhappiness. Mother's eyes were worried when she looked at me, and after asking if there was anything she could do, and receiving a negative reply, she left me alone to work it out by myself.

Pa suspected I'd had a fight with Shadow and he put his arm around me and said, gruffly, that it was for the best.

Thursday came, but Shadow did not.

I couldn't sleep that night. Plagued by nagging doubts and nameless fears, I lay awake, wondering why Shadow had changed his mind. Had he lost interest in me, now that I had so freely given him my most precious gift? Had he ever really loved me? He had never said so—not in words, anyway. Had my unexpected passion disgusted him? Or had he decided Mother was right after all, and that we were better off apart?

With a sigh, I faced the fact that Shadow was not coming for me. Something, or someone, had changed his mind about marrying me. I was sorry now that I had seduced him. Not because I had lost my virginity, but because my body desperately craved fulfillment. I yearned for the touch of Shadow's flesh against my own, for the harsh rasp of his breath against my cheek, for the melding of our two spirits into one being.

Restless and unhappy, I crept silently down the stairs and went outside. I shivered as I stepped into the yard. A hint of the coming winter chilled the air, and I drew my wrapper tight around me as I walked to and fro across the moon-dappled ground. Shadow had mentioned that his people were preparing to move south for the winter, and I wondered if they had gone yet. And if he had gone with them.

I knew so little about Indian ways. I wondered how Shadow spent his days. And nights. I wondered, painfully, if he had an Indian girl in the village. Was he, even now, serenading her with a flute shaped like a dove? Or, worse yet, cuddling with her beneath a big red courting blanket. The thought filled me with such a sense of loneliness that I could hardly bear it, and I thrust the image from my mind. However, no sooner had I done so than another even more insidious fear sprouted into being, and I found myself wondering if Shadow had been one of the Indians responsible for the death of John Sanders. I had grown up on stories of Indian treachery. Knowing Shadow, loving him, I could not believe they were true, and yet with so many tales of butchery and mayhem, some had to be based on fact.

I could not imagine Shadow killing and scalping a helpless white man just because of the color of his skin. And yet John Sanders was dead. I had seen his body. And I had seen the arrows that had killed him. And they were Cheyenne arrows.

Florence Sanders was staying with the Walker family. I had seen her just the day before when Mother and I went over for a visit, but Florence Sanders never even knew we were there. Stony-faced, she sat in a straight-backed chair staring out the window, one of her huband's shirts clutched tightly to her breast. She never said a word. Not one word.

"She hasn't eaten a bite since John was killed," Carolyn Walker told us. "Nor slept either. She just sits there, staring out the window. I don't know what will become of her, poor thing."

There had been something eerie about the

way Florence Sanders just sat there, her face completely void of expression, her eyes staring vacantly at the empty land. I had been glad to leave.

Head aching with troublesome thoughts, I turned to go back to the house when one of Pa's redbone hounds rushed out from under the porch. Straight as an arrow, he ran toward the stockade gate and began scratching at the gate and whining low in his throat.

In less than a minute, all the dogs were howling. Their cries sent a shiver down my spine, and I was suddenly conscious of being alone in the yard. My imagination, always vivid, began to conjure up all kinds of danger lurking in the dark. I knew most of my fears were groundless, but the threat of Indian attack was real. The death of John Sanders had proven that.

Just then, Pa's favorite hound began to bark shrilly.

Sixty seconds later Pa was standing beside me, his big old buffalo gun cradled in one hirsute arm. A sharp word from Pa silenced the dogs. Thrusting the heavy rifle into my arms, he scooted up the ladder to the look-out tower, then quickly scrambled down again. Lifting the heavy cross-bar from the gates, Pa hurried outside.

Puzzled by my father's peculiar behavior,

I followed him out of the yard, only to come to an abrupt halt when I saw the copper-hued body sprawled in the dust, and the big roan stallion standing patiently beside it. Shadow!

"Pa," I whispered hoarsely, my hands shaking as much as my voice. "Pa, is he. . . ?" I could not say the word, could not take my eyes from the inert, bloodied form of the man I loved and yearned to marry.

"No, he isn't dead," Pa said curtly. "Not yet." Scowling, he lifted Shadow as if he weighed no more than a child and carried him into the house.

Inside the stockade, I struggled to drop the heavy cross-bar back into place. Then, burdened by Pa's rifle, I hurried into the house.

Mother was waiting for us next to the big pot-bellied stove that stood in the middle of the store. One look at Pa's burden set her in motion. She quickly swept a display of ladies hats to the floor, then covered the counter top with a clean white sheet.

As gently as he had ever placed me in my own bed when I was a child, Pa now lay Shadow on the counter top. Face grim, he put a pot of water on to boil while Mother began tearing an old sheet into long strips for bandages.

"Curly, what happened?" Mother asked.

Laying the bandages aside, she added salt to the water warming on the stove.

"I can't say for sure," Pa answered gruffly. "But it looks like he's been pistol whipped, and then dragged across half the valley."

"And knifed," Mother added, glancing down at Shadow's right leg. "Hannah, you'd best put that rifle down and light another lamp. Curly, fetch some whiskey, and my sewing kit."

Wordlessly, Pa and I hastened to do Mother's bidding. Minutes later the three of us were gathered around Shadow's inert form. I bit down on my lower lip to keep from crying out as I got a good look at him. He had been horribly beaten. His nose was bloody. Both of his eyes were black and swollen shut. His buckskin shirt hung in shreds, and there was blood and dirt crusted all over the front of him. But worst of all was the hideous gash along the outside of his right leg. It had been slashed from thigh to ankle. In some places, his leg had been cut to the bone. But for all the blood, Mother said no major muscles or ligaments or veins, thank God, had been severed.

"Well, we'd best begin," Mother said, and taking a deep breath, she began to clean the ghastly wound in Shadow's leg with the strips of cloth that had been boiling in the salt water.

Shadow groaned and began to thrash about as the hot cloths touched his mutilated flesh, and I cringed to think of the awful pain he was suffering.

"Curly, hold him down!" Mother exclaimed as Shadow endeavored to rise, and Pa draped one big hand over Shadow's left ankle, and the other on Shadow's right shoulder. But such precautions proved unnecessary, for Shadow ceased struggling the minute he heard my mother's voice.

"That you, Mary?" he asked hoarsely.

"Yes, dear, it's me."

"Hannah?"

"I'm here. Lie quietly now."

"My eyes. . . ."

"Swollen shut," Mother told him. "But don't worry. Everything's going to be fine."

"Who's holding me down?"

"I am," Pa acknowledged gruffly. "Mary's gonna sew up your leg."

"Let me go," Shadow rasped, and, surprisingly Pa did just that.

Mother was threading a small needle with silk thread, and I felt suddenly nauseous as I imagined that gleaming bit of silver weaving in and out of Shadow's torn flesh.

"Lie still now," Mother admonished softly, and after dipping both needle and thread in whiskey, she began to sew the raw edges of

Shadow's skin together with neat even stitches, just as if she were mending a rip in one of Pa's cotton shirts.

Choking back my tears, I held Shadow's hand. Great drops of sweat beaded across his brow, and I carefully wiped them away, wondering as I did so how he managed to endure such awful pain without screaming.

The room grew very quiet, with only the muted swish of silk thread piercing tender flesh, the soft sputtering of the oil lamp, and Shadow's labored breathing to mar the stillness. He was so pale, his pulse so erratic, I knew he was going to die, and that a part of me would die with him.

Distraught, I glanced up at my mother. Her face was quiet and serene, the gray eyes calm and untroubled. Somehow, the sight of my mother's peaceful countenance dispelled my fears. Surely, if anyone could save Shadow, my mother could! I had seen her work miracles before. Often, as a child, I had brought injured animals home for her to nurse. She had never failed me.

I glanced at my father, standing beside my mother, ready to give whatever assistance he could, and I felt a quick surge of love for them both. With a pang, I realized that I wouldn't see much of my folks once I married Shadow and the thought brought tears to my eyes, for I loved them both dearly. But I loved Shadow more.

After what seemed like hours, Mother put her needle aside. Head cocked, she turned a critical eye to her handiwork, then nodded as if she were pleased with the results. Then, with the worst wound taken care of, she began to sponge the dried blood from Shadow's face and chest.

He shuddered convulsively each time she touched him. It was no easy task, painstakingly picking the dirt and debris from the multitude of scrapes and lacerations that criss-crossed his bronze torso. When, at last, the cuts were thoroughly clean and all the dead flesh had been cut away, Mother applied salve to the wounds, then covered Shadow with a sheet.

Through it all, I wasn't much help. Numb with anxiety and fatigue, I could only stand beside Shadow, clutching his hand to my breast.

It was nearing dawn when Mother announced, wearily, that she had done all she could. "It's in the Lord's hands now," she said. "Curly, you'd best scoot upstairs and get that extra cot. It wouldn't do for him to roll off that counter and bust those stitches open."

Minutes later, Shadow was settled on a cot in the corner, and when he was tucked in to

Mother's satisfaction, she took Pa's hand and started upstairs.

"Come along, Hannah," Pa called. "I think we could all use some sleep."

"I'll be up later," I said. "I want to sit with Shadow for awhile."

My folks exchanged a look I could not read, then Mother sighed, "Very well, dear. Call if you need us."

And they went upstairs to bed.

"Hannah."

I flew to Shadow's side. "What's wrong?"

"Water. . ."

"Of course." I quickly poured him a glass of water from a pitcher, spilling a good deal in my haste. He must have sensed my distress, for after quenching his thirst, he whispered hoarsely, "Don't fret, Hannah," and then sleep claimed him.

As the sun rose over the stockade walls, I prayed as I had never prayed before—prayed that the awful gash in Shadow's leg would not fester and that he would recover quickly. I sat by his side all that day, feeding him spoonfuls of Mother's rich beef broth when he was awake. That night he burned with fever. I refused to leave his side, dozing when he was quiet, waking immediately whenever he called for water, or whispered my name.

About midnight, Mother came downstairs to try and persuade me to go to bed, but I stubbornly refused. Though no one had said the words aloud, I knew there was a chance Shadow might die and I intended to spend every minute by his side. While she was there, Mother examined Shadow's leg. One area just above his knee was edged with faint red streaks. Ignorant as I was of such things, I knew that was not a good sign.

Mother's face was grave as she took me aside. "It looks bad, Hannah," she said quietly. "If it begins to swell, it'll have to come off."

Horrified by such a thought, I could only nod that I understood.

"Try and get some sleep, dear," Mother suggested, and offered me a comforting pat on the shoulder before she went back to bed.

Heavy-hearted, I took my place at Shadow's side, wondering how my mother could talk so calmly about cutting off Shadow's leg.

"Hannah?"

"I'm here, darling."

Shadow took my hand in his, and his eyes, open now but still badly swollen, burned into mine as he said, hoarsely, "Don't let them cut off my leg. Promise me."

"It might not be necessary," I hedged.

"Hannah, promise me!"

"Please, Shadow, don't ask such a thing. If your leg gets infected, it'll have to come off or the poison will spread and you'll die."

Somehow, Shadow pulled himself to a sitting position and took my face in his hands. His eyes were bright pools of pain and his hands were hot and trembled with fever as he said, "Hannah, promise me. A warrior needs two good legs, and if I cannot live and hunt and fight as a whole man, I would rather be dead!"

"Very well, I promise," I murmured, and felt hot tears scald my eyes.

With a sigh, Shadow sank back on the cot.

"Can I get you anything?" I asked, wishing I could do something, anything, to ease his pain.

"No. Hannah. . ."

"Sleep now," I said. "Everything will be all right. I know it will."

"Hannah," he whispered. "Come lie with me."

"I shouldn't," I said, but I was stretching out beside him as I spoke, being careful not to bump him or jar the bed lest I add to his suffering.

As his arm drew me close, I buried my face in his shoulder to hide my tears. His hand caressed my hair and I thought anew how I loved his touch, how I only felt complete when he was near me, and I whispered, "Oh,

Shadow, I was so afraid you'd changed your mind."

"You know better than that," he chided gently. "I would have been here early Monday morning, but when I got up that day the warriors were talking of war. Some of the young hotheads had killed a white man and taken his daughter the night before and they were eager for more blood. Crippled Calf and Snake were urging the young men to fight again, to drive the settlers from our hunting grounds now, before Ghost Face covers the plains. All that day and far into the night the warriors smoked and counseled —some arguing for war, some suggesting we wait for spring, hoping perhaps that a hard winter would wipe the settlers out. But the final decision was for war.

"The next day there was dancing. My father and I and a few of the older chiefs tried to persuade the young men to wait, to see if perhaps the Army would drive the settlers out. I'm afraid we were not very convincing. My people have no faith in the Army or their treaties, which are broken before the ink is dry on the paper.

"The following day the warriors purified themselves for battle, and still I stayed, hoping to discourage them. But their blood was up and they were determined to fight. When I knew I could not stop them, I rode out early the next morning, intending to warn your father.

"I had just crossed the river when six white men surrounded me. Before I could speak, the leader threw a rope over me and pulled me off Red Wind. For a while they took turns dragging me behind their horses, and when they tired of that, they pistol-whipped me."

Shadow paused, and when he spoke again, his voice was bitter. "One man didn't have a gun and when the leader offered him one, he waved it aside. 'Crippled redskins don't last long,' he laughed, and they held me down while he cut me.

"I passed out then, and I guess they must have left me for dead. Anyway, when I came to, it was dark and Red Wind was standing over me. At my command, he went to his knees and I grabbed his mane and pulled my-self onto his back. We were almost at the gates of the trading post when I passed out again. The next thing I remember is hearing your mother's voice."

"The little white girl," I said. "Is she all right?"

"Yes. Do not worry about her, Hannah. No harm will come to her."

Talking so long had tired him, and he fell asleep in my arms. My heart ached to see him in pain, and I lay awake for a long time, wondering which men had treated the man I loved so abominably. Certainly, it had been men from the valley. Men I knew. None of the settlers struck me as the kind of people who would wantonly destroy another human being and yet, even as the thought crossed my mind, I recalled hearing Jed Tabor opine just last week that Injuns weren't human. Seth Walker and Saul Green had been in the store that day and they had both agreed, loudly, that 'Injuns weren't nothing but heathen savages, not fit to live with decent white folks.'

Did everyone feel that way but me?

Chapter 8

Shadow was worse in the morning. He trembled convulsively with chills and fever, and there was a look of quiet desperation in his eyes as he drew me close and whispered, "Remember your promise," in a voice weak with pain and fatigue.

"I remember," I assured him. "Here, drink this broth."

Holding back my tears, I fed him the good beef broth Mother had made the night before, praying it would infuse him with strength, willing it to work a miracle and restore him to good health. It grieved me to see him in pain, to know he was suffering and there was nothing I could do to help.

Mother came downstairs as Shadow swallowed the last mouthful.

"How's our patient this morning?" she

asked cheerfully, laying a slim ivory hand on Shadow's brow. "Feeling any better?"

"About the same," Shadow rasped, and Mother nodded as she lifted the sheet and checked the dressing on his leg. "Hannah tells me the little Sanders girl is with your people."

"With the Sioux," Shadow explained. "Some of Sitting Bull's young men were staying with us when the girl was taken. One of them had a mother who was grieving for a child that had died of a white man's disease. He traded his war pony for the girl."

"Now Kathy's mother is grieving," my mother remarked softly, her voice quietly accusing. "We'll need to change that dressing later," she went on in a kinder tone. "Come, Hannah, I need your help upstairs."

"I'll be up in a few minutes," I answered.

"Right now, Hannah," Mother said sharply, and swept out of the room.

Startled by my mother's abrupt tone, I hurried up the stairs. Pa was in the kitchen, staring into a cup of coffee. I guess I knew, when he refused to meet my eyes, what he was going to say. But that didn't make it any easier to hear.

"The leg has got to come off," Pa said bluntly. "The wound's infected and the poison's spreading. If we wait much longer, it'll be too late to save him."

"You can't do it, Pa. I promised Shadow I wouldn't let you cut off his leg."

"Then he's a dead man!" Pa snapped. "Is that what you want?"

"No, Pa," I said miserably. "But it's what Shadow wants."

Exasperated, Pa swore and turned to Mother for help, and at that moment I loved my father more than ever before. I knew how he felt about Indians, knew he would fight me every inch of the way when I told him I was going to marry Shadow, but right now Pa was on my side because he was a fine man, a decent human being who couldn't stand idly by and watch another man die needlessly.

"Perhaps we should go down and talk to Shadow," Mother suggested.

And we did. Pa told Shadow just what he had told me, in the same forthright, no-nonsense tone. And when Shadow said no, Mother then tried to make him change his mind, but to no avail.

"Dammit, Shadow!" Pa bellowed. "That leg has got to come off, and *now*, whether you like it or not. I won't sit on my hands and let a man die in my house if I can stop it!"

"Then I will leave your house," Shadow retorted, and before anyone could stop him, he was off the cot and heading for the door.

Where he got the strength, I'll never know, but he didn't get too far before his injured leg collapsed beneath him and he fell to the floor. Shadow's face went gray, and he groaned as fresh slivers of pain shot through him.

Pa cussed under his breath as he went to help Shadow to his feet, but Shadow refused his help. "If I cannot walk out of here, I will crawl," he rasped, and stubbornly began to do just that. Sweat poured down his face as he slowly dragged himself across the rough wooden floor.

Distraught, I rushed to Shadow's side. "Please let Pa do what has to be done," I begged. "Please, Shadow. For me!"

"No."

"If we only had a doctor," Mother said. She made a gesture of helplessness. "If only I knew a little more about such things..."

Shadow's slow progress across the room had come to a halt. He sat with his back against the wall, too weak to go any further, too stubborn to accept help. There were tight lines of pain around his mouth, and his breathing was harsh, as if each breath was an effort.

"Elk Dreamer," he rasped. "Take me to Elk Dreamer."

"Who's that?" I asked, feeling a surge of hope.

"Medicine man."

"You shouldn't be moved," Mother said. "Besides, it would probably be faster for him to come here. Will he come here?"

"I do not know."

"He'll come," Pa said curtly. Grabbing his rifle from the rack above the door, he started outside.

"No, Kincaid," Shadow called after him. "The warriors will kill you on sight."

"Then I'll go," I said resolutely.

"No, Hannah!" Mother said quickly. "I'll not permit it. Shadow, tell her it's too dangerous."

"I'm not afraid," I countered. "Anyway, I'm the only one here who speaks the language."

"Curly, tell her she can't go!"

"She will be in no danger from my people," Shadow said. "The warriors will not harm a lone woman."

"It's settled then," I announced in a firm tone. "I'm going."

My folks were not happy with my decision, but they accepted it because there was really no other alternative. Shadow could not sit on a horse. And he was in no condition to be moved, not even on a litter, so taking him to Elk Dreamer was out of the question. And even if we could move him on a litter, it would take too long. At least a day—perhaps

125

two. And I was desperately afraid that we didn't have two days.

"How will I find the village?" I asked.

"Take Red Wind. He will go home if you give him his head."

With everything decided, Pa went to help Shadow back to bed. But Shadow would not accept help, not even from me. Summoning strength from some deep inner reserve, he pulled himself to his feet and then, with his teeth clenched against the pain and sweat pouring down his face, he made his way back to the cot.

Ten minutes later I was dressed and ready to go. While I was putting on my heavy coat, I heard Shadow beg Pa to quit the territory before it was too late, before the scattered Indian raids mushroomed into all-out warfare.

Pa's face got that stubborn 'this is my land, too' expression, but before he could form a reply, the door to the trading post banged open, and Joshua Berdeen staggered into the room. He was covered with dirt and blood. His shirt was ripped down one side, and there was a bullet hole in the crown of his hat.

Startled by his battered appearance, I exclaimed, "Josh, what happened? Are you all right?"

"Indians," Josh mumbled thickly. "They

burned us out just after dawn. Killed my folks. Orin, too."

Orin—dead! I remembered how we had laughed and played together in our childhood days, how he had whispered poetry in my ear and made me feel like I was the most wonderful girl in the world. And now he was dead; his cheerful laughter forever stilled.

For a moment we could only stare at Josh, too stunned to speak. I saw Pa glance anxiously at Mother and me. Hate for the Indians burned like a deadly flame in my father's eyes. Unconsciously, he picked up the rifle propped against the counter, and his knuckles went white around the stock.

Expelling a long breath, Pa asked Josh if the Indians were headed our way.

Joshua shook his head. "No. I killed their chief in the last charge, and they ran for home."

"Hannah, put the kettle on," Mother said. "Joshua, sit down. You're hurt."

"It's nothing," Josh murmured absently. "Just a flesh wound."

But Mother was in no mood for argument. "It needs looking after just the same," she insisted. "Hannah, fetch the scissors."

I felt Joshua's eyes following me as I moved across the room and then, suddenly, he was darting past me, his gun drawn, his eyes wild.

"Joshua!"

My father's voice stopped Josh dead in his tracks. But the gun aimed at Shadow's chest was rock steady, and Josh's blue eyes continued to burn with implacable hatred.

"Let me kill him!" Josh pleaded. "Please let me kill the red son of a bitch!"

"Joshua, put that gun away. Now!"

"I can't," Josh replied. His voice was ragged with hate and grief. "You weren't there. . .you didn't see them! You didn't see Orin, dying slow from an arrow in his guts. You didn't see my Pa lying in the yard shot to pieces. You didn't see my Ma. . ." Racking sobs tore at his throat, and his voice dropped to a hoarse whisper. "My Ma. . .they slit her throat. . ."

A terrible silence filled the room as Joshua's voice trailed off. His face was twisted with pain. His finger went white around the trigger.

Shadow's expression remained impassive, and I wondered what he was thinking and why he wasn't afraid when death was staring him in the face.

Mother stood pale and silent, her lips moving in a silent prayer. Claire Berdeen had been my mother's dearest friend. Once they had hoped Josh and I would wed.

"I got no love for Indians," Pa said stonily. "You know that, Josh. But it wasn't

128

Shadow who killed your folks."

"Injuns is Injuns," Josh retorted bitterly.

"Joshua, put that gun down. Now!" Pa did not raise his voice, but his hard tone carried the ring of authority, and Josh swore under his breath as he shoved the big old Colt back into the waistband of his pants. The tension drained out of the room as he sank down onto a chair by the stove and buried his face in his hands.

"I'm sorry about your folks, Josh," Mother said compassionately. "We all are. You know you're more than welcome to stay here."

Joshua's head snapped up. He shot Shadow a venomous glance as he said, "No, thanks, Mrs. Kincaid. If you folks will lend me a horse and some grub, I'll be on my way."

"Where to, Josh?" I asked.

"I can't fight the whole Indian nation by myself," he said gruffly, "so I'm gonna join up with the Cavalry."

"Joshua. . ."

"Don't try to stop me, Mrs. Kincaid. There's gonna be war on the plains, and I mean to be right in the middle of the hottest spot—killing Injuns!"

It was nearing one o'clock by the time I left the trading post. By then, Mother had bandaged Josh's wound, and I had packed him some food. Pa had given him a horse and a change of clothes and a few dollars to tide him over 'til he reached Fort Lincoln. Josh gave me a light kiss on the cheek, then rode out of the stockade without a backward glance. I felt a sudden sadness as I realized I'd probably never see him again. Even though I had spurned his proposal, he was still my friend, a part of my childhood.

With a sigh, I swung aboard Red Wind's bare back. He was twice the size of Nellie and I had to stand on a box to mount, hoping, as I did so, that he was as gentle as my old mare. Patting his short, muscular neck, I shook out the reins and Red Wind stepped out briskly, as if he knew just how terribly important our mission was.

Not knowing how far we had to go, or if there were any water holes between here and the Cheyenne village, I let the big steed drink his fill at the river crossing. It was peaceful, there by the river. Waiting for Red Wind to finish, I happened to glance down at the ground. My heart skipped a beat as I saw a single white eagle feather lying crumpled in the grass, and next to it an ugly brown stain. It was blood, I thought. Shadow's blood. He had taught me well in the days we had played together, and I read the signs easily. There, only a few feet to my left, marked the place where he'd been roped and pulled from his horse. The turf was chewed up by running hooves—shod hooves—and I followed the tracks with my eyes until they disappeared in the rock-strewn flats that fell away from the river. My mouth was dry as I reined Red Wind around. The trail was harder to follow on the rocky ground, but not impossible—not when you'd been trained by a Cheyenne warrior.

Bits of buckskin and an occasional trace of bloody dirt showed where they had dragged Shadow back and forth across the rough terrain, and I flinched as I imagined the sharp stones tearing his shirt to shreds and gouging his flesh. The last rider had dragged Shadow back to the edge of the grass. Signs of a scuffle and traces of blood-soaked ground marked the spot, and in my mind's eye I could see the violent struggle that must have taken place as Shadow fought back, trying in vain to escape the six white men that held him down and then beat him with their guns and fists.

I could not comprehend such wanton cruelty. I had never hated anyone in my life, but I was hating now, fiercely—hating not only the white men who had assaulted Shadow, but the Indians who had murdered the Berdeens, and all the other intolerant people in the world as well.

I was wasting time, too. Clucking to the stallion, I urged him down the bank and across the river. Once we cleared the woods, Red Wind lengthened his stride and the miles flew by until, away in the distance, I saw the conical hide lodges of the Northern Cheyenne.

Apprehensive—now that I was so close—I reined the stallion to a walk and then to a halt, as the courage I had flaunted at home deserted me and fear took its place. Indians! Perhaps the very Indians that had killed the Berdeens. The same ones that had killed John Sanders and kidnapped Kathy. The same ones that had burned the Henrys out. I remembered the first day Shadow had brought me home, remembered my father's words: "Don't you realize you might have been killed? Or worse?" And my innocent reply: "What could be worse than being killed?"

Well, I was older now, and I knew there were many things worse than death. There was hunger and pain and remorse. And surely death was a blessing compared to end-less suffering, or the needless loss of a loved one. Wouldn't I rather be dead than live without Shadow?

Red Wind pulled impatiently against the reins, as if to remind me we had urgent business ahead. With an effort, I put my morbid thoughts aside and thought of Shadow. He was in pain, might be dying, and I was the only one who could help him. Squaring my shoulders, I touched Red Wind's lathered flanks with my heels and the stallion moved out smartly, proud neck arched, ears pricked forward. He was a magnificent animal. Though we had come a long way in a short time, he moved tirelessly, his stride still long and powerful, his gait as smooth as a rocking chair. Shadow had told me once that it took months of patient training to produce a war horse like Red Wind. Indian men set a great store by their fighting horses, knowing that, in the heat of battle, the loyalty and stamina of their mounts often meant the difference between life and death. Prized horses like Red Wind were never turned out with the herd but were tethered in front of the warrior's lodge, always handy in case of emergency. It was considered a great coup, Shadow said, to sneak into an enemy camp late at night and steal such a horse.

Red Wind snorted and shook his head, ears twitching nervously from side to side, as we rode through a narrow swath of trees. Abruptly, two warriors materialized out of nowhere, and I screamed as they grabbed the stallion's bridle. Too frightened to speak, I sat stiffly, trying to hide my fear, as they led us into the village.

My first impression of the Indian camp was one of noise and confusion. Countless dogs barked and snarled at our approach. Half-naked children with straight black hair and shiny black eyes chased each other around the lodges, whooping shrilly as they darted in and out of the lanes. There was the soft cooing of a mother nursing her papoose, and the happy clatter of squaws as they stirred huge iron pots filled with strong-smelling soup. I saw long racks of meat drying in the sun, and an old woman beating the dust from a buffalo robe. I saw several hides stretched between cottonwood poles, and others pegged on the ground. Beyond the village proper a horse race was in progress.

There was a sudden hush as we entered the village, and I felt every eye swing in my direction as the two warriors leading Red Wind halted before one of the largest and most elaborately decorated tepees.

The Indian on my left gestured at the lodge. "This is the lodge of Two Hawks Flying," he said in Cheyenne, prompting me to wonder how he knew I was interested in this particular lodge, but then I realized they had recognized Shadow's horse.

"Thank you," I mumbled, and was about to dismount when a tall warrior wrapped in a red blanket emerged from the lodge. I knew immediately that this was Shadow's father. He had the same hawk-like nose, the same stubborn set to his mouth. Through eyes as black and fathomless as those of his son, he examined me from head to heel.

"You must be Hannah," he said at last, and when I nodded, he remarked tonelessly, "You've brought bad news, daughter. Come inside and we will talk."

The interior of the lodge was dim and cool. It reeked of woodsmoke and grease, of hides and tobacco, of sage, and other alien smells I could not identify. There was a firepit directly before the doorway, with a willow backrest on the far side of the pit. Clay pots and woven baskets of all sizes and shapes hung from the lodge poles. Two women were seated on a blanket to the left of the doorway. One was sewing porcupine quills on a pair of exquisitely wrought moccasins; the other was braiding a red ribbon into her long black hair.

"My wives, Fawn and New Leaf," Shadow's father said, nodding briefly in their direction. "I am Black Owl." He dropped gracefully to the ground, indicating I should sit beside him. "Will you eat?" he asked politely.

"No," I replied, puzzled that he should offer me food when he had guessed I carried bad news. Later, I would learn that Cheyenne hospitality required it. Had I been a man, he would also have offered me his pipe.

With the amenities disposed of, Black Owl said, "You bring me news of Two Hawks Flying. I would hear it now."

Haltingly, in English and Cheyenne, I related the story Shadow had told me, ending with Shadow's request for Elk Dreamer.

"It is good you came," Black Owl said tersely. "Come, we will get Elk Dreamer and be on our way."

Black Owl did not wait for my reply. Rising, he strode briskly out of the tepee, calling orders as he crossed the village, and ducked into a huge lodge decorated with golden suns and crescent moons and brightly-colored comets. Moments later he emerged from the lodge, followed by the skinniest, ugliest man, red or white, I had ever seen.

Elk Dreamer must have been a hundred years old if he was a day, I thought, amazed that a man so bent and frail could get around under his own power. He was dressed in a knee-length shirt of bleached doeskin, fringed leggings, clout, and moccasins. A necklace of bearclaws hung from his neck. His hair hung over his shoulders in two long gray braids, tied at the ends with bits of fur. His face was gaunt, the skin the color of an old saddle left too long in the sun and rain. Only his eyes had escaped the ravages of age. They were as bright and alert as those of a child.

Just then a youth of perhaps thirteen appeared leading three horses, and I watched in open-mouthed astonishment as Elk Dreamer swung aboard a big roman-nosed sorrel with all the grace and agility of a much younger man. Shadow's father mounted a skittish gray stallion, leaving a dainty chestnut mare for me.

We rode out of the village single file with Black Owl in the lead and the old medicine man bringing up the rear. Once clear of the village, Black Owl put his stallion into a mile-eating lope, a pace the hardy Indian ponies could maintain for long distances without tiring. We stopped only once on the long ride back to the trading post, and then only for a few minutes.

We reached home just as the sun was sinking over the horizon. I was off my winded little mare and running into the house before the weary chestnut came to a halt. Breathless, I flew to Shadow's side, then felt myself go cold all over as I saw how pale he was, how labored his breathing.

"He's unconscious," Mother said softly, and I felt her arms go around me as she added, "I'm afraid we've waited too long, Hannah."

"No!" I screamed. "No! No!" and buried my head in her bosom as I had when I was a child.

A polite cough at the door drew Mother's attention, and she left me to greet Elk Dreamer and Black Owl. Shadow's father spoke English, and as I sank to my knees beside Shadow's bed, I could hear Mother explaining about Shadow's leg.

Feeling as if my heart would break, I took Shadow's hand in mine. It was hot and dry. "Oh, Shadow, please don't die," I whispered brokenly. "Please don't leave me."

"Hannah?" His voice was weak and seemed to come from far away.

"Yes, I'm here. I've brought your father and Elk Dreamer. Hang on, darling. Please hang on."

Still clutching Shadow's hand, I rose to my feet as Elk Dreamer approached the cot. Gently, the old medicine man removed the sheet from Shadow's leg and unwrapped the bandages. Shadow flinched as Elk Dreamer ran a gnarled but steady hand down the length of the wounded leg. Nodding to himself, Elk Dreamer sniffed the wound, muttering something I did not understand. Squaring his thin shoulders, he said, in halting English, "Women leave lodge."

"Not. . .Hannah," Shadow rasped.

Black Owl and Elk Dreamer exchanged disapproving looks, then Elk Dreamer shrugged. "Squaw go," he insisted, and Mother went upstairs.

Elk Dreamer had brought a rawhide bag into the house with him, and he rummaged around inside it for a few minutes before producing a long, thin Mexican dagger and an assortment of square packets wrapped in leaves and doeskin.

While Elk Dreamer laid out his medicines, Black Owl spoke to Shadow, encouraging him to be brave, offering him gentle words and comfort and affection. I was strangely moved when Black Owl caressed Shadow's cheek, much as Shadow had caressed mine in days past. Elk Dreamer was ready then, and Black Owl's face was suddenly wiped clean of emotion as he took hold of Shadow's leg and held it immobile in his strong brown hands. Shadow had objected when Pa held him down but he accepted his father's restraining hand without complaint. With a quick sure motion, Elk Dreamer thrust the dagger into the swollen mass of discolored flesh just above Shadow's right knee. Shadow squeezed my hand and his face went dead white as dark red blood and greenish-yellow pus spurted from the wound. Chanting softly, Elk Dreamer pressed gently but firmly on the infected area, forcing more and more poison from the angry wound until, at last, only bright red blood oozed from the incision. Shadow endured the medicine man's ministrations in tight-lipped silence, and I marveled anew that he could endure such torture without a sound. Only the pressure of his hand clasping mine and the rivers of sweat coursing down his face indicated the depths of his suffering.

Elk Dreamer let the wound drain for perhaps another 30 seconds. Then, satisfied that all the poison was gone, he sprinkled a fine white powder over Shadow's leg from thigh to ankle, chanting all the while in a minor key. A yellow substance was sprinkled over the white, followed by more chanting and the rhythmic shaking of an elkhorn rattle. Lastly, the wizened old man wrapped Shadow's leg in soft brown leaves, and over this he laid a strip of softly tanned deer hide.

"Need plenty robes," Elk Dreamer demanded, and I hurried to the back of the store and pulled three gray wool blankets from the shelf. Elk Dreamer nodded as he took the blankets and covered Shadow.

"Make sweat," he explained. "Cleanse

body. Break fever. By morning he will be dead or healed."

And with that comforting bit of news, he gathered up his herbs and the dagger and went to sit on the floor at the foot of Shadow's bed. For a moment, he sat with his head bowed and then, ever so softly, he began to chant—a strangely compelling tune that sent shivers down my spine. Over and over again he repeated the same words, and though I could not quite make out the words, I knew Elk Dreamer was praying to Maiyun, the Great Spirit of the Cheyenne, to spare Shadow's life. After perhaps five minutes, Elk Dreamer pulled a red stone bowl from his pack, sprinkled some sacred pollen and herbs into the bowl, and offered it reverently to the four corners of the earth. Soon a pungent aroma wafted through the air, making me think of berries and burning sage.

I turned to ask Black Owl what was in the bowl but he was nowhere in sight. A movement caught my eye and glancing outside, I saw a tall dark figure standing alone in the moonlight, arms upraised, head lifted toward heaven. It was Black Owl, supplicating the Cheyenne gods for his son's life.

Shadow tossed and turned all night long, mumbling wildly as he refought old battles. Occasionally he called my name, and at such times I would squeeze his hand and whisper that I loved him. Sometimes chills wracked his body and he shook uncontrollably. At other times, sweat poured from his body, almost faster than I could wipe it away. About midnight, Elk Dreamer gave him something to drink, and Shadow fell into a deep sleep. I guess I fell asleep, too, because the next thing I knew it was morning and I was in my own bed.

The house was as still as death. Fearing the worst, I raced downstairs. And almost fainted with relief when I saw Shadow sitting up in bed, drinking a cup of coffee.

It was a miracle, I thought—nothing less. Wanting to express my gratitude, I looked around for Elk Dreamer.

"They've gone," Shadow said. "My father wanted to take me home, but your mother talked him out of it."

"I'm glad."

"Hannah."

Just the way he said my name thrilled me with delight and I went into his arms readily, hungering for his kiss, eager for the touch of his hands in my hair and on my face. I wished, shamelessly, that we were alone in the house so that he could make love to me again. I could tell by Shadow's expression that he was thinking the same thing, and the thought warmed me clear to my toes.

"I love you," I said, wanting to laugh and cry at the same time. "Oh, I love you so much!"

"Show me."

"As soon as you're well," I promised.

"Another kiss at least—to hurry my recovery."

Willingly, I pressed my lips to his, loving the taste and the touch of his mouth on mine.

The sound of approaching footsteps shortened our embrace, and I moved out of Shadow's arms as my mother entered the room.

"You two are looking rather well this morning," she noted with a grin.

"Yes. Where's Pa?" I asked, suddenly realizing that I hadn't seen him that morning, or the night before.

"Your father rode out yesterday to have a look at the Berdeen place," Mother said. There was a thin edge of worry in her voice. "He said he was going to stop by the Tabor place, too. And probably the Walker's. Likely he spent the night with one of them."

"Of course," I agreed. The Tabors and the Walkers lived close to the Berdeens, and it was just like Pa to ride out and make certain they were all right. Knowing Pa, I was sure he'd take time to stop and warn the rest of our neighbors that the Indians were on the warpath.

Shortly, Mother went upstairs to fix breakfast, and I went out to feed the stock. Nellie whinnied at me as I forked her some hay, and I spent a few quiet moments scratching her ears before I returned to the house.

Mother was unusually quiet during breakfast. Neither of us ate much. Afterward, I suggested she rest while I did the dishes, but she sent me downstairs to sit with Shadow, saying she wanted to be alone for awhile, and I knew she wanted to pray for Pa's safe return.

Shadow was asleep when I got downstairs. I sat in the chair beside his cot and studied his face. How handsome he was! And how I loved him!

Mother joined me about an hour later. An uneasy stillness settled over the house as we waited for Pa to come home, neither of us daring to speak the ugly thought that nagged at the corners of our minds, somehow afraid that speaking the words would make them so. Mother sat by the front window, mending one of Pa's shirts, a faraway look in her lovely gray eyes. Seeing her there like that reminded me of Florence Sanders, and I shivered with sudden apprehension as I mumbled a prayer for my father's safe return.

Restless, I tidied up the storeroom and

stocked the shelves. Later that afternoon several families rode in to pick up supplies. It seemed strange to be waiting on customers when Shadow was hurt and Pa's whereabouts were unknown.

I questioned each family that entered the store and felt more and more relieved as, one after another, they said they had seen Pa earlier in the day.

I sold one box of ammunition after another to anxious homesteaders who had taken Pa's warning to heart. Several of the men made nasty remarks about Shadow's presence in the far corner of the room. A few said they would not come again as long as we were harboring "that redskin killer" under our roof.

Elias Walt, one of the valley's newest residents, suggested getting a "little necktie party together to show those red-ass niggers how white folks treat murdering savages!"

When Elias Walt left the store, I gave Shadow one of Pa's pistols—just in case Mr. Walt decided to put his words into action.

Ida Green asked my mother flat out how she could tolerate a dirty, no-good Injun in her house. "Have you forgotten those savages burned down the Henry place and killed poor John Sanders?" Mrs. Green demanded. "Not to mention that poor little child they kidnapped. Really, Mary, I think you're carrying Christian charity a little too far!"

"This is my home," Mother replied quietly. "And my Bible says nothing about basing hospitality on the color of a man's skin." Mother's eyes bored into Ida Green's as she added, softly, "Shadow would not be here now if our men had exercised a little honest Christian tolerance."

"Well!" Mrs. Green exclaimed indignantly, and flounced out of the store, skirts swishing.

It was going on evening when Pa rode in. With him were Hobie Brown and four of Hobie's five sons. Conspicuously absent were Hobie's wife, Charlotte, and his eldest son, Adam. I was about to ask their whereabouts when a harsh look from Mother stilled my tongue, and I went upstairs to set the table for dinner instead. Pa and the Browns were covered with dust and grime, and Mother quickly warmed some water for them to wash in while I put dinner on the table. It was a quiet, strained meal with nobody saying much. When it was over, Pa offered Hobie and his boys the makings of a drink, and then the Browns went out to bed down in the barn, since our house wasn't large enough to accommodate them.

Later, my folks and I went downstairs. I

took Shadow a tray with his dinner on it and sat beside him while he ate. Mother moved about the store, a troubled look on her face, while Pa locked up and counted the day's receipts.

"Are they dead?" Mother asked at last, and we all knew who she meant.

Pa nodded. "Charlotte died easy. Adam wasn't so lucky. But we gave a good account of ourselves, and that's what saved us. The Indians retreated to talk it over, and we made a break for it. We were damn lucky to get away alive."

"Their place?"

"Burned to the ground." Pa threw a hard look in Shadow's direction. "Where will it end?" he demanded. "Three homesteads have been destroyed. Six people killed. Seventeen, counting the Indians we did for today. A child has been kidnapped. Dammit, Shadow, when will it end?"

"When your people are driven from our land," Shadow replied evenly, "or when the last Indian lies dead on the plains. My father, and his father, and his father before him lived and hunted in these hills. As far back as the oldest warrior can recall, the Cheyenne have lived and died here. We will not give up the land where our ancestors are buried. Our brothers, the Sioux, will not give up the sacred Pa Sapa, the Black Hills. We will fight and win, or we will fight and die. But we will fight!"

"And will you fight against us?" Pa asked angrily. "Will you kill those who have helped you?" He glanced over at me. "Will you kill those who love you?"

"I do not know," Shadow replied honestly. "But this I do know. There will be no more fighting until spring comes again. Tomorrow the Cheyenne will leave for their winter camp. But when the grass is new, and the ponies are fat, my people will fight again." Shadow's black eyes, which could melt my heart with their warmth, were cold and flat as he said to Pa, "I have asked you before. Now I am begging you. Take Hannah and Mary and leave the land of the Cheyenne before it is too late."

"No," Pa replied firmly, as I had known he would. "We'll stay and fight it out. There's seventeen families in the valley now; seventeen families just as determined to stick as I am. Come spring, we'll fight for what's ours."

"You're a fool," Shadow murmured, and Pa's head jerked back as if he'd been slapped. Only a word from Mother kept him from doing something rash, and he turned on his heels and stomped up the stairs, his face as dark as the night sky.

"Don't stay up too late, Hannah," Mother said, and she looked suddenly old and tired as she followed Pa up to bed.

Chapter 9
Winter 1875 - Spring 1876

The letter was lying on his pillow, written in his bold hand.

"Hannah, your father and I will be at each other's throats if I stay longer, so I have gone south to join my people. My heart lies heavy within me, for your father is as proud as the Cheyenne, and just as stubborn, and I know he will not leave the valley. I hope, when spring comes, that the hot-blooded young warriors will have cooled off and the battle I fear will not come. If it does, I must fight alongside my people."

It was signed Two Hawks Flying. How strange that name sounded as I said it aloud. Two Hawks Flying. I had never thought of Shadow by that name, and it tasted alien in my mouth. It was a proud name, a warrior's name, and I knew that when he used it to sign his letter, he was telling me that he had cut his ties with my family and with me. He was no longer Shadow, the boy I had played with and loved and yearned to marry, but Two Hawks Flying, the Cheyenne warrior, bound to his people by a sense of pride and honor that was stronger than his love for me. A great sadness settled over my heart, for I knew I could have no part in the path he had chosen.

And so winter came. The wind screamed through the wooded hills, stripping the last leaves from the trees until they stood barren and forlorn. Dark clouds shrouded the sky, as heavy and gray as the pain in my heart. I had never felt so alone. Lying in my bed at night, I listened to the coyotes baying at the moon and their bittersweet cries were like the echo of my own tears. I watched, listlessly, as heavy rains pelted the ground, until the trading post stood like an island in a sea of brown slush. The first snowfall came, turning the drab world into a shimmering wonderland of pristine white, but I saw no beauty in it. Christmas came and went, and I found neither joy nor hope in that most wonderful of all days. Likewise the new year, 1876.

Mother left me to myself, knowing I needed to be alone. It was enough for me to know she was there, ready to talk when I felt the need, ready to counsel and comfort when the hurt was gone. Pa, too, respected my grief. I doubt either of them knew how much I loved Shadow, or that I had planned to run off with him. I know Mother thought I was merely infatuated with him and nursed a secret hope that I would soon come to my senses and marry Joshua, though she never voiced her thoughts.

In late January the sun came out, and though it was bitingly cold, it was good to have dry weather and sunshine, if only for a few days. I turned Nellie out of the barn, and she cavorted around the yard like a young colt, slipping and sliding in the mud. But even her ridiculous antics failed to cheer me.

Days later a detachment of cavalry pulled into the trading post, the first soldiers we'd seen since we moved into the valley. One of them, an old trooper named MacIntosh, had a letter for me. It was from Joshua. He was stationed at Fort Lincoln under Major Reno. Josh briefly described the daily life of a trooper—roll call, mess call, stable call, close-order drill—the endless training that took a green recruit and fashioned him into a crack trooper. The tone of his letter brightened as he mentioned his idol: George Armstrong Custer, the 'boy general.' Even in our remote part of the territory we knew about Custer.

Though graduated last in the West Point class of 1861, his daring bravado and love of fighting gained him quick promotions during the Civil War, and he had attained the rank of Major General by brevet at the age of twenty-five. When the war was over, his rank was reduced to Lieutenant Colonel and he was sent to Fort Riley, Kansas, where he gained great aclaim as an Indian fighter. Now he was at Fort Lincoln preparing to ride against the Sioux, determined to bring them to their knees once and for all.

He was a dashing and romantic figure, and as I read Joshua's glowing description of Custer, I wondered which picture correctly portrayed the man with the long yellow hair: the one Josh painted of a brave soldier and valiant fighter, or the one Shadow had drawn for me one afternoon down at the river crossing—that of a strutting, arrogant, glory-hunting murderer who had massacred a sleeping village of Cheyenne in the valley of the Washita.

Josh went on to say that word had gone out to all the Plains tribes in December, admonishing them to surrender immediately and report to the reservations by January 31st or be considered as hostiles and treated accordingly. Josh went on to say that in view of the bitter weather and the short notice, it was doubtful if the tribes would comply, and that there'd likely be war at last. He said that latrine rumor had it that the Army was tired of fighting the Sioux and had decided to wipe them out once and for all; that, come spring, a major campaign was sure to be mounted against the Sioux in the Black Hills. . . .

I laid Joshua's letter aside. The Sioux and the Cheyenne were allies, and a cold hand closed over my heart as I recalled Shadow's words:

"Our brothers, the Sioux, will not give up the sacred Pa Sappa, the Black Hills. We will fight and win, or we will fight and die. But we will fight!"

Troubled, I picked up Joshua's letter and read the last few lines:

"Tell your pa it might be wise to pull out of the valley as soon as the snow thaws. There's talk of a lot of unrest among the Northern Cheyenne. Our scouts report that Black Owl is thinking of joining Sitting Bull."

As I put Joshua's letter away, I thought of the things he'd said, and of the things Shadow had said, and it seemed to me that sooner or later the two men I cared for most beside my own father were destined to meet somewhere in the Black Hills. I wondered which, if either, would survive, and knew I would be condemned by everyone in the valley if they knew it was Shadow I prayed for most of all.

Hobie Brown and his sons stayed with us through the winter, and we were glad to have them. Hobie's oldest boy, John, was a skilled hunter and trapper and managed, somehow, to keep meat on our table through that long miserable winter. Benjamin was a natural artist, and we wiled away many a night watching him sketch scenes of local wildlife that were so real you wanted to reach out and touch them. I especially liked his drawing of a red-tailed hawk, for it reminded me of Shadow. Paul played the banjo and brightened many a long dark night with his music. David, the youngest, was a born clown. He kept us laughing with silly stories and funny poems that didn't make a lick of sense. They didn't rhyme, either, but that didn't matter.

It was David that became my dearest friend. We talked often of books we'd read, of faraway places with exotic names and curious customs. He never asked why I was so sad, but one night he took my hand in his and said, simply, "Hannah, if you ever want to talk about it, I'm here to listen."

It was David's unfailing cheerfulness that

reached through the layers of my unhappiness and made me smile again; David made life worthwhile.

Spring came at last. One day it was cold and bleak, gray as Nellie's hide, and the next morning the sun was shining, the sky was a clear unblemished blue, and the snow was melting. Business picked up at the post. Mother's flowers bloomed. Hobie Brown and his boys started talking about rebuilding their place, and Pa offered to lend them whatever tools and supplies they needed to get started. Paul Brown proposed to Lucinda Bailey and they set the date for late June.

David and I spent long hours together walking in the woods along the river's edge, glad to be out of the stockade walls. We were picnicking there one sunny afternoon when David asked me to marry him. I wanted to accept, for I was very fond of David, but I just couldn't bring myself to say yes. Much as I liked David, much as I enjoyed his company and his unfailing ability to make me laugh, I didn't love him and never would.

"I can't, David," I said sadly. "I'm sorry, but I just can't."

"Hey, don't look so glum about it," David responded cheerfully. "I'm the one who's being rejected, not you."

"Oh, David, can't you ever be serious?"

"Don't know—never tried."

"I'm glad. Can we still be friends?"

"Couldn't we be kissing cousins instead?" he queried impishly, and I laughed as he claimed a kiss.

The better I got to know David, the sorrier I was that I couldn't love him, for we were well-suited for each other in both age and temperament. I began to think that should he propose again, I might accept, for I was terribly lonely for someone to love. And perhaps it was wiser to marry a man you didn't love after all. Perhaps, in the long run, it was better never to love at all, for only those you loved could hurt you. And I was determined never to be hurt again.

I thought often of Shadow, though I had forgotten his predictions of war. The troubles of last year seemed far away. Everyone in the valley was busy. The men spent their days planting and plowing, while the women were all happily engaged in preparing for Lucinda's wedding. Mother was altering Mrs. Bailey's wedding gown for Lucinda, and one day I slipped it on, curious to see how I'd look as a bride.

Staring at my reflection in the big mirror downstairs, I pinned the veil in place and imagined myself standing before the preacher with Shadow at my side.

"Beautiful! Just beautiful!" came a voice

behind me. Startled out of my daydream, I turned to find David smiling at me.

"You'll make a lovely bride one day," he said huskily. "I hope whoever you marry will realize what a prize he's getting."

"Oh, David," I murmured, blushing before the frank admiration in his eyes.

He might have tried to kiss me then, and I might have let him, if Mother had not come in looking for Pa.

Later that day Jed Tabor, Saul Green, and Elias Walt rode into the trading post, bragging about how they had captured a couple of Indian kids skulking around the Tabor place.

"They won't be stealin' no more of my stock!" Jed Tabor boasted. "No, sir!"

"Nor anyone else's," Saul Green added, slapping his thigh with delight.

"How's that?" Pa asked suspiciously.

"Cause we strung 'em up, that's why!" Elias Walt chortled and burst out laughing like he'd just told the year's best joke.

"Strung 'em up!" Pa growled. "I thought you said they were just kids."

"Nits make lice," Jed Tabor said curtly. "If we kill the bastards while they're young, we won't have to fight 'em later."

"You're a fool, Jed," Pa muttered. "You're all fools."

"You turning into an Injun lover, Sam?" Elias Walt asked gruffly.

"Don't be a bigger fool than you already are," Pa warned sharply. "I got no love for the Indians, but I've got no desire to fight them, either, and if what you boys have done today doesn't start an all-out Injun war, we'll be damn lucky!"

After that, it seemed we heard stories of raids and killings every day. Some German settlers located at the south end of the valley were massacred. A Sioux village was attacked by the Army, with heavy casualties on both sides. A wagon train was wiped out by a mixed band of Sioux and Cheyenne. The Walkers, upset by the increased Indian activity, pulled up stakes and left for Oregon. They never made it.

Near the end of April the Indian raids came to an abrupt halt, and when a whole week went by without a single incident, David and I rode up into the hills behind the trading post for a picnic. It was good to be out in the open, out of the stockade walls. Below us, the valley lay bathed in golden sunlight. The river made a narrow swath of blue against the valley floor. A thin thread of blue-gray smoke spiraled from the chimney of the trading post.

Lifting my eyes, I gazed into the distance,

the sandwich in my hand forgotten. Far away, beyond the mountains, lay Custer and Joshua and Fort Lincoln. And Shadow. Why did his memory still have the power to hurt me? Why didn't time erase his image from my mind? All I had to do was close my eyes and Shadow's swarthy countenance appeared, every detail in sharp focus, undimmed by time or distance.

David was a nice looking young man. He had thick sandy-brown hair, kindly brown eyes, and a warm, loving smile. He was bright and clever; he was generous and good-natured. Why couldn't I love him? Why did I continue to long for a man who put loyalty to his people before his love for me? Oh, how I longed for Shadow to hold me and love me. Why didn't David's kisses make my heart sing with joy? Why didn't the touch of his hands fill my soul with sweet agony?

Shadow. Long black hair, skin like rich copper, eyes black as a midnight sky. Why couldn't I forget him and marry David, who loved me and wanted me?

With a sigh, I put my sandwich back in the picnic basket and faced David. "I'm not very good company today, am I?"

"Well, now that you mention it, I have had more sociable companions," David allowed. "But none as pretty. You know, Hannah, it might help if you talked about it."

"There's nothing to talk about," I said, shaking my head. "Really."

And there wasn't. Shadow was gone, and all my tears would not bring him back. In the meantime, I had a man who loved me and wanted to marry me, and I knew that I would be a darn fool to let him get away.

I was about to tell David I would marry him if he still wanted me when a faraway speck of movement caught my eye. In minutes, the speck became a long dark line snaking along the crest of the next hill. Before my mind could accept what my eyes were seeing, David grabbed me around the waist and thrust me onto Nellie's back.

"Ride, Hannah!" he shouted, swinging aboard his own mount. "Ride hard!"

I kicked Nellie and she broke into a shambling trot, and then into a gallop as David lashed her rump with his quirt. Behind us, a shrill undulating war whoop rang out as the ever-nearing war party gave chase.

The sound of that horrendous, blood-curdling cry spooked my old mare, and she lined out in a dead run, her ears flat. Neck and neck, David and I flew down the hill towards the trading post. Each time Nellie began to lag behind, I dug my heels into her ribs, praying she wouldn't stumble or step into a hole.

Never had home seemed so far away. Glancing over my shoulder, I saw that the Indians were gaining on us. Their faces, streaked with paint, were hideous and unreal, like something from a nightmare.

We were almost home when Nellie stumbled. My heart dropped into my stomach as I sawed on the reins. I cried, "Oh, God, help me!" then sobbed with relief as Nellie scrambled to her feet and began running again.

Her gray coat was yellow with foamy lather, her heart pumping like a bellows, when we finally reached the safety of the stockade walls.

"Indians!" David hollered. Leaping from his horse, he closed the heavy gates and dropped the crossbar in place.

Pa and Hobie Brown burst out of the house, checking their weapons as they ran. Hobie's boys were right behind him. Pa threw David a rifle and a box of shells, and the men clamored up the ladder to the catwalk that ran around the fortress walls. I heard Pa holler, "Make every shot count!" as the men spread out.

I led Nellie and David's gelding into the corral and turned them loose, then raced into the house and grabbed a rifle from the rack. Picking up a box of .44 cartridges, I scooted up the ladder and took a place beside Pa.

"Get on down from here," Pa said curtly. "Go back to the house and stay with your mother."

"Mother's coming, too," I said. "Look."

Pa frowned as he saw Mother climbing the ladder, laden with a rifle, bandages, and three canteens of water.

"Damnit, Mary, this ain't no place for you or Hannah," Pa scolded, but Mother silenced him with a wave of her hand.

"Don't be silly, Sam Kincaid," she scolded right back. "This is our home, too, and we aim to fight right here beside you."

Pa got that stubborn look in his eye, but there was no time for further argument. The Indians reached the stockade in a rush of noise and dust and the battle was on. We were outnumbered ten to one, but we had the high ground, so to speak, and the protection of the stockade's stout wooden walls. The Indians, not armed with guns, unleashed their deadly arrows as rapidly as we levered our rifles. For what seemed an eternity there was nothing in all the world but the feathered hum of bowstrings, the hiss of arrows, and the echoing roar or our rifles.

Dust and powdersmoke choked the air, clogging my nose and throat, making my eyes water. I fired the rifle until the barrel grew hot in my hands, feeling sick to my stomach each time one of my shots struck home. And even as I fired into the Indian ranks, I prayed with all my heart that Shadow was not down there—that none of the feathered, screaming, paint-streaked warriors was the man I loved.

Funny—I knew Shadow was an Indian, knew he lived and behaved the same as the rest of his tribe, and yet I could not imagine him painted for war. I could not visualize his handsome face twisted with implaccable hatred, his dark eyes wild with the lust for blood, his mouth drawn back in a savage grin.

And yet I knew he had killed a man. A Pawnee. He had said as much, and the feather in his hair gave credence to his words.

There was a brief lull in the battle as the Indians pulled out of range to regroup, and I found myself searching their ranks for a tall warrior astride a roan stallion. Abruptly, I tore my eyes away. If he was down there, I didn't want to know.

I glanced around the catwalk, grinning as I saw my mother wiping dust and perspiration from her face. I had never seen her with her face dirty before or her hair uncombed.

Beside me, Pa was staring hard at the brave nearest the stockade wall and when I asked him what was wrong, he said, "That's

Jed Tabor's palomino mare. I'd recognize her anywhere."

"Looks like it," I agreed. So the Tabors had been hit, too. There was always a chance, of course, that the Indian had stolen the horse from the Tabor corral, but I knew it was a mighty slim chance and that, more likely, Jed Tabor and his family were dead.

Further down the line, I saw David. He threw me a crooked grin and waved, and I waved back. Hobie Brown and his four sons were good shots, and the ground beneath their part of the stockade wall was littered with the bodies of more than a dozen Indians.

Only one of the Indians wasn't dead. Slowly, he sat up, shaking his head as if to clear it. He had been hit twice, once in the leg and once in the side. Bracing his hands against the stockade, he slowly gained his feet.

We were all watching him now, including the Indians. The injured warrior must have felt our gaze, for he turned and glanced up at us. His dark eyes glittered with hate and contempt as he pushed away from the wall and started to walk boldly toward his comrades.

He had gone only a few feet when his wounded leg buckled, and he fell to the ground. Paul Brown raised his rifle and sighted down the barrel, the Indian his target, but he hesitated to pull the trigger as one of the Indians out of range broke away from the group.

With a wild cry, the warrior raced his horse toward his stricken companion. Dropping to the side of his paint pony, he reached out to grasp the fallen warrior's upraised arm.

It was a brave act, but one that cost him his life. Simultaneously, two shots rang out as Paul Brown and his brother, Benjamin, killed the two Indians.

It seemed cruel, to kill a man who was trying to rescue a friend. And yet I knew Paul and Benjamin were just trying to even the odds against us.

"Hell of a shot," Pa murmured.

And then the Indians charged us a second time, and there was no more time for talk.

For awhile we held our own, and I prayed the Indians would get discouraged and retreat. But then the tide began to turn as half a dozen braves pulled out of the battle and began lobbing fire arrows over the stockade walls. Others found a log and began ramming the gates, while their companions kept up a steady stream of covering fire, forcing us to keep our heads down or risk getting them blown off.

When it looked like the gates were about to

give way, Pa hollered for us to retreat to the house. It was, I knew, the only logical place to hole up. There were only two windows upstairs, both too small for a grown man to crawl through, so we wouldn't have to worry about them sneaking in on us, and there was no back door.

Pa and Hobie were the last to leave the catwalk. They were running for the house when the gates collapsed and a horde of screaming Indians poured into the stockade. Hobie cussed as an arrow caught him in the back, and I felt my heart skip a beat as I saw my father stop, whirl around, and spray a murderous stream of bullets toward the charging warriors.

Paul and Benjamin immediately laid down a hail of covering fire while Pa scooped Hobie up in his arms and sprinted for the house. David slammed the door shut and shot the bolt home as soon as Pa crossed the treshold.

While Mother looked after Hobie, the rest of us manned the windows. Pa and I took one of the front ones, David and John the other, leaving Benjamin and Paul to cover the single window in the rear of the house.

Once we gained the safety of the trading post, the Indians ignored us. A few warriors caught up our animals and drove them outside the stockade, while others disappeared from sight around the corner of the house, presumably toward the barn and the smoke-house.

I felt a great sadness when I saw one of the braves leading Nellie away. She had been mine ever since I was a little girl, had been my first friend—my only friend before I met Shadow.

But there was no time for memories, no time for regret. The Indians were firing again, circling the house as they looked for a way to break in. There were footsteps on the roof, and Mother quickly lit a fire in the fireplace to discourage any brave who might be thinking of dropping through the chimney.

Time lost all meaning. The past and the future ceased to exist; there was only the horror of now. Bullets and arrows whistled through the air like angry hornets, and I cringed, frightened by the confusion and the noise and the sudden realization that I was going to die a horrible death. Our house, which only moments before had seemed like a haven of refuge in a world gone mad, had become a death trap. There was no way out, no way we could possibly escape.

Across the way, John Brown screamed and fell forward. A torrent of blood gushed from a bullet hole in his throat. David's face contorted with rage and grief when he saw his brother fall, and he began to fire recklessly, wasting precious ammunition as he hosed off a dozen rounds.

"David!" I yelled. "David, get down!"

But my warning fell on deaf ears. A bullet exploded in David's face and he toppled over backwards, his body awash in a sea of bright crimson.

"David," I whimpered, and turned away as Pa ran over to the now unguarded window and fired point blank into the paint-daubed face of a howling Sioux warrior. Vomit rose in my throat, thick and hot and vile, and I could not choke it back. Retching violently, I doubled over, and as I did, I felt a warm rush of air sweep past my head. Behind me, Mother cried out in pain, and then there was a terrible silence as all firing suddenly ceased.

As if from far away I heard Pa whisper Mother's name, heard him curse the Indians and his own hard-headed stubborness—and I knew that my mother was dead. The realization hit me with such force that for a moment I was numb, unable to move or think. Tears of grief welled in my eyes as I stared blankly out the window into the smoke-filled yard.

A lone Indian had ridden into the stockade, and I surmised that it was his unexpected arrival that had brought the shooting to a halt. The stranger's face and chest were hideously streaked with broad slashes of vermillion. A single white eagle feather adorned his waist-length black hair. A black wolfskin clout covered his loins; moccasins beaded in red and black hugged his feet. For a moment he sat unmoving, his narrowed eyes sweeping the yard, the burning barn, and the house in one long glance.

He dismounted with the lithe easy grace of a panther as a stocky Sioux warrior wearing an elaborate warbonnet called to him. The two warriors conferred for some time, and although I could not hear their words, I could tell by their gestures that they were arguing and that we were the source of their disagreement.

After several minutes, Warbonnet gave a shrug of resignation, and the lone warrior strode toward us, unfurling a square of white cloth pulled from inside his clout.

About twenty feet from the house he stopped and called out, "Sam Kincaid, can you hear me?"

My knees went weak as the warrior's voice penetrated my mind. Unable to believe my ears, I leaned out the window for a closer look, whispering his name as I recognized the face beneath the hideous red paint.

"Shadow."

"I hear you," Pa hollered. "Speak your piece and then say your prayers, cause you're dead where you stand."

"Don't be a fool, Kincaid."

"You're the fool, redskin," Pa retorted, levering a round into the breech of his Winchester. "I cut you down, that's one less guteater to kill later."

"I am not fighting you," Shadow replied evenly. "I am not carrying a weapon."

Pa studied Shadow thoughtfully for a few moments before he said, "What is it you want?"

"You and the others have no chance of getting out of here alive," Shadow said dispassionately. "The Sioux can burn you out or starve you out. You agree?"

"Maybe," Pa allowed grudgingly. "What are you getting at?"

"I cannot save you, Sam, or the other men, but the Sioux chief, Tall Cloud, is willing to let me take Hannah and Mary and ride out of here."

"Mary's dead," Pa said hoarsely, and the pain of my mother's death tore through me again. She had been so gentle, so kind and loving; it was inconceivable to me that she should die so violently and leave me bereft.

"I am sorry, Kincaid. She was a good woman."

There was a long pause, and then Pa said, "How'd you know Hobie and his boys were here?"

"I have been watching your place for the last two weeks, waiting for something like this to happen."

Pa laughed bitterly. "How come the Sioux beat the Cheyenne to the punch?"

"My people have gone to Montana to meet Sitting Bull and Crazy Horse. Tall Cloud and his warriors are headed that way, too."

Pa let out a sigh that seemed to come all the way from his toes. "So it's started, huh?"

"I warned you, Kincaid. You should have listened. There is going to be a big battle between your people and mine, one that will make all the others look like child's play. I do not know where or when, but I know it is coming."

"Your people will lose," Pa said tonelessly. "Unless you can figure out a way to unite all the tribes, the Army will rub you out one by one."

"I think you speak wisdom," Shadow remarked. "The good times are gone. The whites will not rest until they have killed every Indian on the plains or confined them on reservations. Myself, I would rather be dead than penned up like the white man's cattle. But enough of this. We are wasting time. Let me take Hannah out of here before Tall Cloud changes his mind."

I saw the struggle in Pa's eyes as his hatred and distrust of Shadow and all Indians crumbled beneath his love and concern for me. Shadow had once remarked that he thought Pa would see me dead before he'd let me run off with an Indian, and I had agreed. But we were both wrong, for Pa pulled me to my feet and said, gruffly, "Go with him, Hannah."

"I can't leave you, Pa!" I protested. "I won't!"

"You've got to go, Hannah. Shadow's right. We haven't got a snowball's chance in hell of getting out of here alive. Now go on, get out of here while you can."

"Pa!" I sobbed, throwing my arms around his neck.

"There's no time for tears, Hannah," he said sadly. His big, work-worn hands patted my back. "No time for long good-byes. Give me a kiss now, like a good girl."

His cheek was cool beneath my trembling lips, rough with the stubble of a day's growth of beard.

"She's coming out, Shadow," Pa called gruffly.

And then, with gentle determination, my

father pushed me out the door.

"I will take good care of her, Kincaid," Shadow promised.

"Thanks," Pa murmured.

Blinded by my tears, I stumbled out into the yard. I heard Pa close the door behind me, and the sound was like a death knell in my ears.

I would have fallen then but for Shadow. Wordlessly, he grabbed me by the arm, steered me to where Red Wind stood patiently, helped me mount—and I hated him! I hated him because my Mother and David were dead. Hated him because my father and the others were going to be killed, and he couldn't do anything about it. Hated him because he was an Indian.

And even as I hated him, I loved him.

With ease, he swung up behind me and walked Red Wind out of the stockade. I could feel his arm tighten around me as we approached the gates, and I realized he was not as calm as he looked.

Glancing over my shoulder, I saw the Indians watching us. A few of the warriors were stroking their rifles, and I knew suddenly why Shadow was so tense. I could almost feel their anger and hatred as he carried me out of harm's way. I knew it would only take one small hostile move to ignite that hate into action.

I was holding my breath when we cleared the stockade gates and reached the cover of the trees outside.

We had gone only a short distance when he reined Red Wind to a halt. Dismounting, Shadow retrieved his weapons—bow, arrows, knife, and rifle—from behind a large boulder.

He was swinging aboard Red Wind when the first gunshot sounded behind us, quickly followed by a heavy barrage of rifle fire as the Indians renewed their attack against the trading post. Sensing my distress, Shadow put the stallion into a gallop and held him there until the sound of gunfire was no longer discernable above the quick tattoo of Red Wind's pounding hooves. We were across the river and well into the trees on the other side before Shadow reined the lathered stallion to an easy canter.

We rode without saying a word, with only the sound of hoofbeats and the whisper of the rising wind to break the awkward silence between us. I shed bitter tears for the loss of my family, glad that I had not looked at Mother's body, glad that I would always remember my parents as they had been in life and not in the still, eerie pose of death. I remembered the sweet patience of my dear mother as she taught me to read and write, remembered her serene beauty as she knelt at my bedside while I dutifully recited my childhood prayers. And Pa...Like all little girls, I had once planned to marry my father when I grew up. I'd thought him the most perfect, wonderful man in the whole world, and he had never done anything to tarnish that image.

At dusk, Shadow reined the stallion to a halt in a fragrant grove of juniper that grew along a shallow underground spring. Dismounting, he spread his buffalo robe on the ground and gazed at me speculatively as I slid from Red Wind's back and dropped onto the blanket.

"I am sorry, Hannah," he murmured compassionately. And kneeling before me, he held out his arms.

I knew then that I had a decision to make. Shadow had promised my father to take care of me, and I knew he would keep his word. I also knew that if I asked, Shadow would take me to Steel's Crossing. Pa had friends there who would take me in.

I stared hard at Shadow. He had not moved a muscle. He still knelt before me, arms outstretched, face impassive, and for the first time since I had fallen in love with him, I saw him not just as a man but as an Indian. The hideous red paint on his face, the eagle feather in his long black hair, the wolfskin clout that covered his loins—all bespoke Cheyenne blood, Cheyenne ways.

How could I spend the rest of my life with this man, this stranger? How could I ever forget that he was Indian, and that it was an Indian who had killed my mother, an Indian who might even now be taking my father's scalp?

I thought of John Sanders, of Florence, and Kathy. I thought of all the people in our little valley who were now dead because of Indian hatred and Indian vengeance.

I gazed deep into Shadow's eyes, but I saw nothing there—no trace of love to persuade me—and I knew this was a decision I had to make entirely on my own. Only Shadow's outstretched arms betrayed his inner feelings.

For endless seconds, I did not move. My parents were dead, killed by Indians. My friends, everyone I had ever known, had been killed by Indians, and hate for the whole red race churned in my breast. But wrestling with that hatred was my love for Shadow, for love him I did. And I knew that no matter what happened, my love would remain unchanged. Our people might turn the sun-kissed grassland red with blood in their efforts to slaughter each other, but I knew our love for each other would survive.

With a sigh, I went into Shadow's waiting arms, and he held me close while I cried again, deep wracking sobs that tore at my throat and scalded my eyes. And yet, even as I wept, I felt a curious sense of warmth and peace steal over me, a wondrous feeling of contentment that permeated my soul whenever Shadow took me in his arms.

I cried until I was empty inside and Shadow held me all the while, lovingly stroking my hair and comforting me with his gentle touch and reassuring presence.

That night there were no words spoken between us, no promises of undying devotion and loyalty. There was only the silent communication of Shadow's heart speaking to mine, and mine answering. And from that night on Shadow was not an Indian, and I was not white. We were simply a man and woman desperately in love.

Chapter 10
1876

When I awakened, it was morning, and I was alone. Frightened, I sprang to my feet, only to go weak with relief when I saw Red Wind grazing peacefully nearby. A warrior might desert his woman, I mused drily, but never his prized war horse. Shadow would be back, I thought, and then he was striding toward me, a young deer slung over his shoulder.

"Breakfast," he remarked as he began skinning the buck. "When we reach the Cheyenne, you will have to do the skinning and the butchering and the cooking," he reminded me.

"I remember," I said. "A warrior never does squaw work when there's a woman nearby."

"Right," Shadow said, grinning. "I am only making an exception this time because

I am too hungry to wait while you butcher the meat. As I recall, you usually did it with your eyes closed."

"I'll get better," I promised. And all at once I realized what I was saying. And where we were going. I could not help but feel apprehensive at the thought of living with Indians. What if my mother had been right? What if Shadow's people would not accept me? Much as I loved Shadow, I had no desire to live as an outcast among alien people, scorned and mocked because I was the enemy.

"How far is it to the Cheyenne?" I asked tremulously.

"Three or four days from here. Do not worry, Hannah," he said, reading my mind as he always did. "My people will welcome you as warmly as your mother once welcomed me. And they will love you because I do, if for no other reason."

It was the first time he had ever said he loved me. The words filled my heart with a warm glow, and all my doubts vanished as I threw myself into his arms. Shamelessly, I removed his buckskin shirt, boldly running my hands over his broad shoulders and chest, wondering at the hard strength he possessed.

Shadow stretched out on the ground, grinning with pleasure as my hands roamed his flesh. I laughed aloud as a sudden telltale bulge appeared beneath his loincloth. When he reached for me, I rolled away.

Gaining my feet, I ran from him, anticipating the thrill of the chase and the joy of surrender. But when I looked over my shoulder, Shadow was still stretched out on the grass, arms folded behind his head.

Pouting, I walked toward him, stopping out of reach of his long arms.

"Come here, woman," he called softly. "I have something to show you."

"No."

Shadow's eyes danced merrily. "You have started something," he mused, glancing at the bulge swelling under his clout, "and now you must finish it."

"Then you come to me."

"Hannah. . ."

Smiling seductively, I began to undress, until I stood naked before him. The sun was warm on my skin, but not as hot as the desire in Shadow's eyes.

With a wordless cry, he bounded to his feet, grabbed me around the waist and fell to the ground, carrying me with him.

We wrestled playfully beneath the bright blue sky, and then, like wild things, we made love there in the tall grass. I rejoiced in Shadow's touch, purring like a kitten as his powerful hands gently stroked my eager flesh. I murmured his name as our two bodies became one, and we soared high above the earth in heavenly ecstasy, everything else forgotten in the magic of our love.

It was much later, after a quick breakfast of venison and berries, that we broke camp. While I smothered the fire, Shadow wrapped the remaining choice cuts of meat in the deerhide and draped it over Red Wind's withers.

That done, he swung aboard the horse, sheathed his rifle, gave me a hand up, and we were on our way.

It was an eerie feeling, riding over the vast rolling plains, just the two of us. We might have been Adam and Eve in the Garden of Eden, for the only other living creatures we saw were animals—buffalo and deer and once, far in the distance, a grizzly scratching itself against a tree. We never lacked for food or water, for Shadow knew every waterhole and was a skilled hunter with rifle or bow.

The morning of the fourth day I spied what appeared to be a long black snake undulating across the plains. As we drew nearer, I saw that it was a tribe of Indians on the move.

"The Tsi-tsi-tsas," Shadow exclaimed, urging Red Wind into a lope.

Tsi-tsi-tsas, I had learned, meant "those related to us—our people." The Dakotas called Shadow's people the Sha-Ye-Nas, meaning people of alien speech. It was the Dakota name the whites picked up, pronouncing it Cheyenne.

An Indian village on the move was a colorful sight. The warriors rode at the head of the column. Dressed in their finest robes and feathers and mounted on their best ponies, they were a magnificently wild, proud, and fearsome sight.

Young braves dashed up and down the line, hanging precariously over the necks of their fleet ponies as they showed off for the maidens.

The pack animals and travois ponies came next, laden with camp gear, lodge covers and poles, blankets, cooking utensils, extra weapons, robes, dried meat and pemmican, and whatever else the Indians owned. Children and squaws walked among the animals, while the very young and the very old shared seats on the travois ponies.

And behind all this came the Indian pony herd which must have numbered in the thousands, churning up great clouds of dust and noise as they squealed and kicked, lashing out at the dogs that ran barking and snapping between their legs.

I had never seen so many animals and Indians in one place at one time, and it was a sight I never forgot. They were a wild, free people, and I knew, intuitively, that they would never be happy tucked away on a reservation, that the Army would never subdue them without a fight.

I recognized Shadow's father, Black Owl, riding at the head of the long, winding column. He was mounted on a flashy spotted stallion. Red Wind snorted and laid his ears back as Shadow drew rein alongside Black Owl's mount, and for a taut moment I thought the two studs would fight, but soft commands from their riders brought both animals quickly under control.

Black Owl smiled fondly at Shadow, and they clasped hands. After exchanging a few words with his father, Shadow dropped back to where the women were, and the next thing I knew I was walking between Fawn and New Leaf, trying to choke back my indignation at being forced to walk while Shadow rode in comfort with the warriors.

I had much to learn!

That night I discovered that the squaws did not eat until after the warriors were satisfied, and that they were expected to keep silent if their husbands were entertaining guests. I also learned that the women always prepared more food than was necessary, and that it was considered an insult to refuse an invitation to sit down and eat.

Indeed, I learned a good many things in the days that followed, primarily that Shadow had told me the truth when he said the women did all the menial tasks. Menial tasks included gathering the wood, washing everything that needed washing, including his war horse, cooking, sewing, mending, erecting and dismantling the lodge, tanning hides, drawing water, raising the children, butchering the meat, and a dozen other, equally distasteful chores.

Though Shadow and I had not been formally wed according to Cheyenne custom, it was assumed that I was his woman. As such, I was expected to do all the things a squaw did for her man—which was practically everything! And what did the warriors do while the women were breaking their backs? Why, they spent their time parading around in their finest feathers, smoking, visiting, and gambling.

Daily, small hunting parties rode away from the main body of the caravan to locate meat for the tribe. It was the only work I saw the warriors do, and I wondered if the other women resented the apparently carefree life of the men as much as I did.

By the end of the second day, my feet were

swollen and sore. New Leaf, Black Owl's first wife, gave me a pair of her moccasins. They were ever so much easier to walk in than my own shoes, and so much more comfortable that I vowed then and there never to wear shoes again. Fawn was also generous. Seeing how awkward and cumbersome my long skirt and petticoats were, she gave me a lovely doeskin dress beaded and fringed in the manner of the Cheyenne. It, too, was a great improvement over what I was accustomed to wearing, though I felt somewhat naked without my petticoats and chemise.

Dressed in my new Indian garb, and with my long hair hanging in twin braids down my back, I began to feel as though I'd been born in a lodge myself!

Speaking of lodges, since Shadow and I had neither skins nor poles with which to make one of our own, we moved in with his father. Black Owl and his wives treated me with unfailing kindness and respect, and I soon grew to love them dearly. Black Owl's wives were years apart in both age and temperament.

New Leaf was about forty, with a wide, expressive face and a tendency toward plumpness. I assumed she and Black Owl had been married for years and years and was surprised to learn they'd been married less than five years. In that time, she had borne him two sons. Both had died before they learned to walk. Her eyes were always sad, even when she smiled. New Leaf was quiet and soft-spoken, but she had a quick mind. Often, late at night when Fawn was asleep and the lodge quiet, I overheard Black Owl discussing tribal affairs with her.

Fawn was quite young, no more than sixteen or seventeen. Much too young, I thought, to be married to a man close to fifty! She had married Black Owl only a month ago and seemed quite pleased with her husband, even though she had to share him with New Leaf, which I thought was not only shocking but downright immoral. However, after I'd been with the Cheyenne awhile, I noticed several of the warriors had more than one wife. Plenty Beaver had three. Elk Dreamer, the decrepit old medicine man, had four!

Being close in age, Fawn and I soon became good friends. She was a changeable creature, her moods shifting rapidly from merriment to anger. I often saw Black Owl scowl at her, as if he were trying to decide whether to scold her or hug her. When Fawn and I were better acquainted, I asked her if she really liked being a second wife.

"Why should I not like it?" she asked. "Black Owl is a brave warrior and a good hunter. We always have meat in our lodge.

And the work is not so hard when there are two to do it."

Well, sharing the work seemed like a good idea—I hadn't thought of that—but sharing your husband? I thought that was going too far, but of course I didn't say so. After all, it was none of my business.

When I'd matured enough to put my prejudices aside, I realized there was nothing sordid about a warrior having two wives. It was, in fact, a practical solution to a major problem. Women far outnumbered the men, and a warrior often married an old squaw or a widow merely to provide her with food and shelter and protection.

Living five in a lodge offered very little privacy, and I was deeply touched when Shadow's family purposefully stayed out of their home an hour or so each day so that Shadow and I might have some time alone. How I cherished those moments we shared under the buffalo robes—kissing and touching until I knew every inch of Shadow's powerful, lean body as well as I knew my own. What joy, what bliss—to lie in his arms, to feel his mouth on mine, to know he loved me as I loved him.

As we traveled, I frequently caught one of the maidens staring at me. She was a lovely young thing, tall and slender, with thick black hair that fell to her waist and luminous black eyes. When I smiled at her, thinking perhaps she wanted to be friends, she scowled and turned away. Puzzled by her attitude, I asked Fawn who she was.

"Oh, that's Bright Star," Fawn said airily. "Two Hawks Flying used to play his flute outside her lodge. Everyone expected them to marry, but he suddenly lost interest in her and began spending much time away from the village."

I felt my cheeks flush as Fawn threw me a knowing look. Mumbling some inane excuse, I dropped back to walk with New Leaf. I experienced a curious stab of jealousy as I thought of Shadow courting Bright Star. I wondered if she had invited him inside her blanket and if he had held her close.

Curious as to our destination, I asked New Leaf where we were going and learned that the Cheyenne were headed for the Rosebud River to join their Sioux allies led by Sitting Bull and Crazy Horse. We passed through miles and miles of beautiful country along the way, and I began to understand why the whites coveted this land, and why the Plains Indians were so determined to hold on to it. The grass was tall and thick, waving ahead of us in an endless sea. Scattered stands of timber bordered crystal clear rivers and cascading waterfalls. There were groves of cottonwoods and box elders, chokecherries and wild plums. Game abounded. We saw white-tail deer and antelope, bears, wolves, rabbits, foxes, coyotes, eagles, elks, hawks, and more. I marveled at a great herd of shaggy brown buffalo that covered the prairie like an enormous furry blanket. Shadow remarked, bitterly, that the really big herds were gone, slaughtered by the whites. He told me how, years ago, the northern herd had been so big it took a warrior three hours just to ride around it. I found that hard to believe, yet I could tell by his expression and tone of voice that he was telling me the truth, and I began to understand why the Indians hated the white man.

I learned a lot about the Cheyenne on that journey. I learned, for instance, that Cheyenne children were taught from infancy not to cry, lest, in time of war, their childish wails alert the enemy. To my amazement, I found that Indian children were rarely spanked or reprimanded and that most lessons were taught the hard way—by experience. Boys, especially, were indulged, and their childish pranks were either ignored or viewed with amusement.

When I mentioned this to Shadow, he shrugged and said, "The life of a warrior is often short. Sometimes he is killed in his first battle. My people understand this, and as long as the young boys adhere to tribal laws and do not offend their elders, they are allowed to do pretty much as they please until they are fourteen. Then they must begin to take on the responsibilities of being a man and a warrior."

I discovered, with some surprise, that when a Cheyenne girl had her first menstrual period it was cause for rejoicing. The girl's mother told the father, and the father spread the word throughout the tribe, often giving away a favorite horse to celebrate the fact that his daughter was now of marriagable age. A special ceremony accompanied a girl's first period. During this ceremony, she was bathed and then painted red. For a time, she would sit quietly before a fire in her lodge while sweet grass and white sage and cedar needles burned in the firepit to purify her body. Then, wrapped in a fine robe, she was taken to the menstrual hut where she remained in the company of her grandmother for four days, receiving instructions about her future role as a Cheyenne woman. I learned that from then on she would be thus isolated for four days whenever her time came. It was the only Cheyenne custom I disliked.

I was also amazed to learn that Shadow's father, Black Owl, who was considered to be the head chief of the tribe, had no real power or authority over the Indians. The people would follow him only as long as he led them wisely. If he spoke for peace, and others wanted war, those in favor of war chose a leader and went out to fight. If a warrior wanted to steal some horses from the Crows, he would announce his intent, and any warrior who wanted to go along was free to go. If a man didn't feel like fighting that day, he stayed home and no one thought the less of him.

The most comforting discovery I made was that, red or white, male or female, people were pretty much the same. Every nation was composed of good people, and those not quite so good, and the Cheyenne were no exception. There were Indians who were outgoing and friendly, and others who were reserved and always a little aloof, even among their own relatives. There were some I liked immediately, and some I thoroughly disliked. There were shy ones and braggarts, those who were unfailingly kind, and those who seemed a little lacking in charity. And there were a few who stood out for one reason or another—like Plenty Beaver, who drank too much. And Snow Flower, who was a shrew. Or Black Lance, a handsome warrior, but one so lazy the tribe took to calling him Always Lying Down.

And then there was Three Ponies. Three Ponies was a chronic gambler. One night he lost everything he owned, including his

lodge, to Beaver Tail. When Three Ponies'
wife heard about it, she threw him out—lock,
stock, and barrel—screeching at the top of
her lungs that Beaver Tail could have Three
Ponies, too, but that the lodge was hers, not
her husband's, and could not be gambled
away. Three Ponies was properly contrite
the next morning but his wife refused to take
him back. As was her right, she burned her
lodge and went to live with her sister and
brother-in-law.

The children of the Cheyenne were adorable.
The very young ones ran naked and carefree
through the camp, playing the games children
play the world over. The little girls played with
dolls; the little boys played tag or wrestled in
the dirt, growling like young puppies. The
children stared at me with unabashed curiosity, fascinated by my long red hair and light
eyes. Sometimes one or two would gather
enough courage to give me a shy smile.

Later, when they got to know me better, I
always had two or three of them following
me around, pestering me with questions
about the white eyes.

One little cherub, Rising Dawn, was my
especial favorite. She loved to hear how I
met Shadow at Rabbit's Head Rock when I
was a little girl about her age, and how I
threw up all over him the day he ate that raw
buffalo heart.

Rising Dawn thought Shadow was the most wonderful warrior alive, and told me, in confidence, that she hoped to be his number two wife when she was old enough to marry —if it was all right with me.

Sometimes, watching Rising Dawn and Shadow together, I would pretend that she was our daughter. There were many babies in camp, and I longed to have one of my own to love and cuddle.

Rising Dawn was full of boundless energy. Some days she appeared at our lodge with the sun, eager to help me prepare Shadow's morning meal. She helped me straighten the lodge and gather wood and look for berries and roots. I loved her company and her merry laughter as we made our way across the plains. New Leaf nicknamed her 'the little wife' because she was always in our lodge helping with the work.

I spent a lot of time studying the Indian boys in the days that followed, and as I watched them engage in their activities, I grew to understand Shadow a little better. Indian boys were given weapons at an early age. At first they shot at targets fastened to trees. Later, as they grew older and their skill increased, they were given bigger bows, and they went after rabbits and deer, then buffalo. And finally after man, the most dangerous game of all.

Indian boys did not cry when they were hurt. They did not show grief when they were sad, except in the privacy of their lodge or within the circle of family and close friends. A true warrior was brave and fearless. He spoke always with a straight tongue. He provided his lodge with meat, defended the tribe against all enemies, and showed unfailing respect to his elders.

Dishonesty, adultery, murder, cowardice— these were looked upon with loathing and were severely punished. A woman who was unfaithful to her husband had her nose cut off—a permanent symbol of her infidelity.

Pride came early to a Cheyenne male: pride of race, pride of family, pride in his physical prowess. The dead he held in reverence and respect, rarely, if ever, speaking their name.

A warrior respected a man's right to be different, too. The most startling example of this was manifested in a tall slender Cheyenne man known as Bull Cow. Bull Cow was not a warrior. He dressed and acted like a woman, and Shadow said that was his right. There was no disgust in his voice when he spoke of Bull Cow—no derision, only a touch of pity.

I had heard it said among the whites that the Indians never laughed and had no sense of humor. I found this to be totally untrue. The Cheyenne loved a good joke, whether on themselves or someone else. They loved stories, too, and often the whole village would gather around while one of the old men spun a fascinating tale. Sometimes they told stories of great warriors or great battles; sometimes they told the history of the Cheyenne nation, and sometimes they related how Maiyun had created the earth. No matter what the subject, I noticed both children and adults listening with awe.

I learned that the Cheyenne religion was closely bound up in their daily lives. Man Above was the Supreme God, the creator of all life. The Indians believed that everything possessed its own spirit. Trees, animals, rocks, the tall grass, the rushing water, the earth itself—all were endowed with life and were thus revered. No animal was ever killed unless its meat was needed for food or its hide for clothing or shelter. Also, the Cheyenne believed that life was made up of circles—the earth, the sun, the moon—and that there was a center to the earth and that all things were in balance. Thus, they built their lodges in a circle and laid their villages out in circles. Some surmised that because the whites built square houses, they didn't know where the center of the earth was, and that was why they were such peculiar people. The Cheyenne did not try to change their world but lived in harmony with it, content to live where the Great Spirit had placed them. Too bad, I thought ruefully, that my people did not feel the same way.

It was the first of May when we reached the Sioux camp located at the Big Bend of the Rosebud River. How can I describe it? It stretched for miles and miles—a panorama of lodges and milling horse herds and Indians of all sizes and ages and colors, from pale copper to dark bronze. And even as we arrived, others were coming in. Minneconjou, Sans Arc, Arapahoe, Blackfoot Sioux, Hunkpapa, Santee, Oglala, other bands of Cheyenne. The word of Sitting Bull had gone out to all the tribes: "It is war. Come to the Rosebud."

And they came in droves!

Shadow's tribe pitched their lodges alongside a contingent of Arapahoe, and the warriors were soon caught up in the general air of excitement and anticipation that permeated the valley. If the whites wanted war, they would get war. Everywhere I looked I saw men working on their weapons, either repairing old ones or fashioning new ones, sharpening lance tips and arrowheads. War ponies stood ready outside each warrior's lodge: pintos, grays, blacks, chestnuts, bays, duns, roans, buckskins. I remarked on the absence of white or cream-colored horses, and Shadow explained they were rarely used by warriors because they made too good a target at night and were too easily spotted from a distance.

For the first time since we had joined up with Shadow's people, I felt alien. Around me were thousands of Indians, all with but one thought in mind: Kill the white eyes! Drive them from the land! They spoke of victory as if it had already been accomplished. As I puzzled over their optimism, I learned that at the last Sun Dance Sitting Bull, the great Hunkpapa medicine man, had made a flesh offering of a hundred pieces of his skin to Wakan Tanka and in return had received a vision in which hundreds of American horse soldiers fell dead at his feet.

Later that day I saw Sitting Bull, known as Tatanka Yotanka among his own people. I learned he had once been called Jumping Badger, but after showing great courage in a raid against the Crows when he was but a boy of fourteen, he had been given his father's name. Though Sitting Bull was no longer an active warrior, he was still the leader of the Hunkpapa, revered and respected by all the Sioux tribes. He had a typical Indian face—broad and flat with narrow eyes, a wide thin mouth, and a large nose. I did not find him particularly impressive, until I heard him speak. He was a great orator.

That same day I saw Crazy Horse, the esteemed war chief of the Oglala Bad Face. Here was a man! Slender of face and frame and of medium height, he was yet a commanding figure and, except for Shadow, easily the most handsome man I had ever seen. There was an air of quiet dignity about Crazy Horse that demanded respect, and he was held in high regard by every tribe on the Plains. Of all the chiefs present—and there were many, including Gall, who seemed to be third in command—none received quite the same degree of hero worship as Crazy Horse.

Days passed and Indians continued to pour into the war camp until it looked as if every Indian from the Atlantic to the Pacific was gathered along the banks of the Rosebud River.

It was during one of those warm summer days that Shadow came to me, a grave look in his deep black eyes.

"What is it?" I asked anxiously. "Is something wrong?"

"Yes," he said. "Very wrong."

"What's wrong?" I asked hoarsely. A dozen dreadful thoughts crowded my mind. The soldiers had found us. Someone had died. He didn't love me any more. . . .

"We have not been properly married,

Hannah," Shadow said. "I want you to be my wife. Will you marry me according to Cheyenne custom?"

Relief washed over me in great waves. "Marry you," I breathed. "Oh, yes, yes, yes!"

As we kissed, I felt as if a two-ton rock had been lifted from my shoulders. I had thought of Shadow as my husband ever since the day he carried me away from the trading post, and yet I had longed for a ceremony of some kind to bind us together. Deep down, I had felt guilty because we were living together out of wedlock.

"I have spoken to Elk Dreamer," Shadow said, his voice warm against my ear. "He has agreed to perform the ceremony, if it is all right with you. It will not be the usual wedding ceremony, since we have been living together for a long time. But it will show everyone that you are mine, and a part of my family."

The next evening, just after sunset, Shadow and I stood together before Elk Dreamer, surrounded by all the Cheyenne people. I wore a doeskin dress that had been bleached white and tanned to a softness like velvet. It had been a gift from Fawn, and was, in fact, the dress she had worn when she married Black Owl. Foot-long fringe dangled from the sleeves; hundreds of tiny blue beads decorated the bodice. New Leaf had stayed up the night before to make me a pair of moccasins. They were beautiful, as intricately designed and crafted as any evening slippers I had ever seen. My hair fell free about my shoulders, adorned with a single white rose.

Shadow stood straight and tall beside me, looking more handsome than I had ever seen him. He wore a white buckskin shirt that was open at the throat, white leggings heavy with fringe, and white moccasins. A single white eagle feather was tied in his waist-length black hair.

Elk Dreamer raised his right hand for silence. "This is a special day for our people," he began. "One of our warriors has chosen a woman to share his life. Though she is not of our blood, her heart is good for our people. From this day forward, she will be one of us." Pausing, Elk Dreamer drew his knife. Taking Shadow's right hand, he made a shallow cut in his palm, and then did the same to my right hand. Caught up in the beauty of the moment, I did not feel the pain.

Taking our hands in his, Elk Dreamer pressed them together, palm to palm. "Now their blood is mixing, and they are one. From this time forward, all pain will be divided, all joy will be doubled." Elk Dreamer smiled at us as he released our hands. "Go now, my children, and may the Great Spirit bless you with many sons and daughters."

I felt my cheeks grow hot as Shadow took my hand and led me away from the crowd. Black Owl, Fawn, and New Leaf had found other quarters for the night so Shadow and I could have the lodge to ourselves.

I felt suddenly shy as Shadow dropped the lodge flap into place, shutting out the rest of the world.

"Hannah. . ."

His voice, so full of love, made my heart race with longing. Married, I thought. Married, at last. I was trembling as he came toward me.

His hands gently untied the lacings that held the front of my dress closed, and then he was caressing my breasts. There was fire in his touch, and we were suddenly clumsy in our haste to be together.

Shadow's voice whispered in my ear, speaking words of love in English and Cheyenne, and I responded to his touch and his voice as never before, giving all I had to give, and receiving that and more in return.

I knew a deep sense of contentment as Shadow possessed me that night. I was his, really his, forever. And he was mine. I would not have thought our love could grow any sweeter, but that simple ceremony in the wilds of the Dakota plains took something already wonderful and made it perfect.

Chapter 11

Living with the Indians, being one of them, I soon learned the women didn't spend all their time cooking and sewing and tanning smelly hides. The Cheyenne women loved to play games, and they often met beside the river to toss a ball back and forth or play tag. A popular game was played with dice made from bones or beaver teeth. Points were scored according to what design came up on the dice, and counting sticks were used to keep score. The Cheyenne women loved to gamble almost as much as the men, and they wagered ribbons or beaded chokers or blankets. Games, like almost every other aspect of Plains life, were accompanied by songs. Sometimes the songs had no words or meaning but were simply feelings put to music. I was amazed at the number and variety of songs employed by the Indians; there were ceremonial songs, war songs, powwow songs, lullabies, romantic melodies, love songs, prayer songs, and funeral dirges.

Fawn was an excellent gambler. For a girl who so freely vented her emotions, she had a wonderful poker face. Another popular game was an Indian version of 'button, button, who's got the button?' The women played this game with two small stones—one marked, one plain. One player concealed the stones in her hands; the other player tried to guess which hand held the unmarked stone. Fawn was marvelous at this game.

Running contests were also a favorite with the women and girls. Fawn was fleet of foot, and she won more races than she lost. I was too shy to join in the games and races at first, but Fawn and New Leaf kept after me until I finally agreed to enter one. I knew I didn't have a chance of winning, since Fawn was in the race, too.

Several of the men were present that day, Shadow and Black Owl among them. Black Owl bet Shadow that Fawn would win and put up a fine bay mare against one of Red Wind's colts.

Elk Dreamer started the race, and Fawn bounded into the lead. I ran close on her heels, excited by the contest and eager to win for Shadow. I could hear the other girls behind me and the spectators hooting for their favorites, but I was more determined than ever to win. I kept my eyes on Fawn's back, all my energy concentrated on passing her, and at the very end, I pulled ahead.

I had never expected to win, and I couldn't help shouting for joy as I crossed the finish line first. Then, winded, I sank to the ground, one hand pressed against my aching side.

Fawn dropped down beside me, grinning hugely. "Congratulations, my sister," she panted. "You run like a mountain lion."

Shadow was beaming when we returned to the starting line. I fairly glowed as he put his arm around me and gave me a squeeze.

"I did not know my son had married the wind," Black Owl said with a wry grin. "My ignorance has cost me a fine horse."

"I was very lucky," I said modestly, and then started to laugh.

"I think we will run again tomorrow," Fawn said, grinning at me. "We will see how lucky you really are. I will wager my fine black shawl against the hide you are tanning that you cannot beat me twice."

"Done," I said, and we went off to prepare the evening meal.

The match race was set for the following morning, and practically the whole tribe was there for the big event. Fawn looked determined, and I was terribly nervous.

Again, Elk Dreamer started the race. As usual, Fawn bounded into the lead, but this time she stayed there, and all I ever saw was her back and a pair of swift brown legs. I ran as fast as I could, but I could not catch that will-o-the-wisp, and she crossed the finish line a full two yards ahead of me.

I was happy in the days that followed. I was no longer an outsider, an alien, but one of the people and accepted as such. Now that I was also a wife, there was a stronger bond between Fawn and New Leaf and myself. When we were alone, the three of us often remarked on the strange ways of men. Sometimes they were like children, wanting to be spoiled and pampered, angry if they didn't get their own way. I had noticed that about other men, but never about Shadow. He never acted childish or immature. Always, he was in command of himself. Never had I known anyone so self-assured, so certain of who he was and where he belonged. It gave him a kind of serenity that few men, or women, ever achieved.

I adored my husband. He was so kind to me, so unfailingly thoughtful of my wants and needs. Daily, I thanked God that I had found such a man.

Shadow came back from a war council late one night and told me that the battle promised by Sitting Bull was not far off. Two Yankonai scouts had brought word that Yellow Hair was coming from Fort Lincoln and that 'Three Stars' Crook was riding north from Fort Fetterman, Wyoming. 'Red Nose' Gibbon was on his way, too, having put together a sizeable column from the troops stationed at Forts Ellis and Shaw. And they were all headed our way. Hoping to catch the Indians between them, they were determined to wipe out Sitting Bull and Crazy Horse and their men and force the rest to surrender.

The news caused me great anxiety. Mention of Custer brought Joshua Berdeen to mind, for I knew he would be riding into battle with the Seventh. But mostly I worried about Shadow. And about myself. What would happen to me if Shadow were killed in battle? Would his family still view me as a daughter, or would I become the enemy, to be hated and destroyed?

These and other troublesome thoughts were in my mind one evening as I wandered down to the river in search of a secluded place to bathe.

It was the first time I had gone off by myself, but I felt safe knowing that only the Cheyenne and their allies were in the vicinity. No man, red or white, could possibly penetrate this far into the Bighorn Valley without being seen by one of the many sentries who patrolled the area.

Slipping out of my doeskin dress, I waded into the cool water. For a time I floated lazily on my back, staring up at the darkening sky. Shadow was at yet another war council, and I wondered what was being said and where it would all end. It seemed like all I had heard about for years was war, war, war, and I wondered if there would ever be peace on the plains and if Shadow and I would ever be able to settle down and raise a family.

With a sigh, I waded ashore for the soap I had left on the river bank. It was soap I had made myself. New Leaf had shown me how to find and mix the necessary ingredients. I had learned a great many things in the short time I had been with the Indians, and I was constantly amazed at their knowledge and resourcefulness.

A faint breeze wafted across the land, and I washed quickly, not wanting to be alone away from the camp now that night had fallen. I was stepping from the water when I saw a dark form coming forward. At first I thought it was Shadow, and I started to call a greeting, then bit back the words as I saw that the man was too short and stocky to be the man I loved.

Fear struck at my heart, for no honorable man would accost a woman while she was bathing. Grabbing my dress, I ducked behind a bush, my pulse racing as my ears strained for the sound of his footsteps.

When I heard nothing, I told myself it was just a warrior looking for a place to relieve himself and not someone looking to do me harm. "I've got to get a hold on my imagination," I mused, chuckling with relief. "I'll be seeing flying elephants next!"

Weak with gratitude, I was about to step into my dress when rough hands grabbed me from behind, closing around my throat and mouth as the warrior dragged me away from the river toward a stand of trees some twenty yards away. All my struggles were in vain as he wrestled me to the ground. I winced with pain as his weight fell over me, grinding my naked flesh into the dirt.

When I tried to scream, he stuffed a dirty cloth into my mouth, then sat back on his haunches, a satisfied expression glittering in his eyes.

I recognized the warrior now. His name was Laughing Wolf, and I had seen him watching me ever since we arrived in the valley.

Certain he meant to rape me, I fought with all my might as he pulled a length of rawhide from his belt and began to lash my wrists and ankles together.

Subdued, I lay panting on the ground, my eyes wide with terror as he drew a knife from inside one knee-high moccasin and laid the blade against the base of my neck.

Laughing Wolf spoke to me then in a language I did not understand. But I understood the look in his wild black eyes, and I cringed with impotent fear and horror as he drew the blade between my breasts.

The knife did not cut very deep—only enough to draw blood, blood that felt very hot against my clammy flesh.

Still speaking to me, he drew the knife slowly downward across my belly. I shook my head violently, silently pleading with him to stop, but he only laughed a soundless laugh and raked the blade across my left thigh.

I was trembling convulsively now. Helpless tears rolled down my cheeks as the knife moved slowly over my quivering flesh, leaving tiny rivers of blood in its wake. He was going to kill me by inches. I knew that now, and there was nothing I could do.

I watched, mesmerized, as he placed the blade under my left breast, and gasped with pain and fear as, with agonizing slowness, he pulled the blade around my breast until it was outlined with blood.

And now Laughing Wolf paused, the blade raised high overhead. I stared at that blade in grim fascination. My blood dripped from the crude weapon, falling in tiny scarlet droplets upon the ground. The wind stung the many cuts on my body, yet I knew the pain was insignificant compared to what was to come.

As Laughing Wolf slowly dropped his arm, I began to pound my head against the ground, hoping I could knock myself unconscious and so avoid the awful agony that was coming. Lights were dancing in front of my eyes when a wild animal-like cry rent the stillness. Glancing over my shoulder, I saw Shadow emerge from the darkness, his mouth open in a feral snarl of rage, a knife in his hand.

Laughing Wolf was scrambling to his feet when Shadow lunged at him, and the two warriors hit the earth with a dull thud. They rolled over and over, grappling wildly, before they sprang to their feet to stand facing each other. Warily, they began circling, their bodies slightly bent at the waist, knives thrust forward.

Suddenly they came together in a rush of metal against metal, and when they parted, both men were bleeding. Again and again they closed and parted, and each time there were new wounds.

Far off in the distance I could hear music and laughter as the Indians danced and sang around their campfires. But here, on this lonely stretch of ground, there was only the harsh ring of knife striking knife, and the labored breathing of the two men who were engaged in a battle to the death.

Shadow and Laughing Wolf were evenly matched in size and strength, and I thought the battle would last forever as, time and again, they sought for an opening in one another's defenses and found none.

Both men were weary now and bleeding profusely from a multitude of minor wounds. The end, when it came, came quickly, as Laughing Wolf charged Shadow in a desperate lunge.

To my horror, Shadow made no move to avoid Laughing Wolf's charge except to turn sideways as Laughing Wolf's knife came down, sinking to the hilt high in Shadow's left shoulder. Too late, Laughing Wolf realized his mistake, but before he could withdraw his knife and strike again, Shadow's blade had ripped into his belly.

Laughing Wolf cried out in pain and frustrated rage as Shadow twisted the knife upward. Then, hands pressed over the gaping wound in his belly, the warrior fell to the ground, dead.

Shadow came slowly toward me, his face

dark with pain. Kneeling beside me, he freed my hands and legs and removed the gag from my mouth.

"Are you all right?" he rasped.

"Yes," I answered, all thought of my own fear and pain forgotten as I removed my headband and pressed it against Shadow's bleeding shoulder. "Hurry, lets get back to the lodge. You're badly hurt."

He did not argue. I dressed quickly, and we started back to the camp, Shadow leaning against me for support.

When Shadow was safely inside Black Owl's lodge, I summoned Elk Dreamer, then stood with Fawn and New Leaf while the aged medicine man dressed Shadow's wound and purified the lodge against evil spirits.

"Why?" I asked later. "Why did Laughing Wolf want to kill me? I never did anything to him."

"There will always be white men who hate Indians," Shadow said matter-of-factly. "And red men who will hate whites. Other than that, I have no answer for you."

"I can't help being white," I muttered.

"Do not dwell on it, Hannah. It is over and best forgotten."

It was late the next night when we learned the reason for Laughing Wolf's attack. Some weeks earlier, his wife had been captured and tortured by three white men. He had

214

brooded over her death ever since, haunted by vivid images of her mutilated body. In desperation, he had gone to the medicine man of his tribe and been advised that only by capturing and torturing a white woman would he be free of his bad dreams.

"His family is deeply ashamed that he chose to take his vengeance on you," Shadow said. "For as my woman, you are one of us and not to be harmed."

"You must tell them I bear them no ill will," I said, feeling suddenly sorry for Laughing Wolf. "Tell them I understand what it is like to lose loved ones."

"You have a good spirit, Hannah," Shadow said, caressing my cheek. "Your words will help to ease their shame."

Somehow, knowing why Laughing Wolf had attacked me made it seem less frightening.

There were many war councils in the days that followed. Some lasted far into the night, for each warrior was permitted to speak his mind. In mid-May runners brought word that Three Stars had arrived and was camped up on the Tongue River, apparently unaware of the fact that the Indians knew of his presence. The scouts opined that Crook planned a surprise attack on the village early the following morning.

With that in mind, Crazy Horse decided to carry the battle to Crook. I begged Shadow not to go, but of course he went anyway. A warrior did not remain at home because his woman was afraid he might be killed.

I bit back my tears as he walked out of the lodge and swung aboard Red Wind's bare back. Shadow was clad only in clout and moccasins, as were the other warriors. I had puzzled over their scanty attire until Shadow remarked that if a man was wounded, it was better if the bullet or arrow passed cleanly through flesh rather than take bits of cloth with it. The familiar lone eagle feather was missing from his hair that morning, and in its place he wore a magnificent warbonnet that trailed halfway down his back. Each feather represented an enemy killed, a coup counted, or a brave deed, and I marvelled that he had accumulated so many. His face and chest were streaked with broad slashes of scarlet.

Shadow sat staring down at me for several moments before he wheeled the big stud around and rode off to join the other warriors.

I stared in surprise as Laughing Turtle rode by mounted on a frisky paint pony. He was far too old for battle and yet there he was, resplendent in a deerskin clout and feathered bonnet twice as long as Shadow's.

He carried no weapons, only a coup stick trimmed in black. Curious, I sought New Leaf for an explanation.

"He has set his face toward death," she explained, as if it were the most natural thing in the world. "His wives and children are dead, his body filled with pain, and so he has decided to go out to meet death as a warrior. He is a brave man. It is fitting that he die as a warrior."

Minutes later Crazy Horse rode into view. Dressed all in black and mounted on a sleek black stallion, the Sioux war chief took his place at the head of the war party. Raising his rifle high overhead, he shouted,

"Hopo! Let's go!"

An answering cry rose from the assembled warriors and then, amid scattered war cries and a cloud of yellow dust, they were gone.

The day passed slowly. I could not eat or sleep or think. I could only sit staring northward, wondering. Had the battle started? Were the Indians winning? Did I want them to win? Was Shadow all right? Around me, squaws carried on as usual, busily engaged in their endless tasks, but I noticed their talk was low and reserved, their normally cheerful voices subdued.

Warriors too old for battle sat in the sun, thrilling the young boys with old war stories, stoking the fires of their hatred with tales of white treachery, like the massacre at Sand Creek. There was fire in their eyes as they told how Colonel John Chivington, a former Methodist minister turned soldier, had cut a bloody path through a peaceful Cheyenne village back in 1864. Ignoring both the stars and stripes and the white flag flying over Chief Black Kettle's lodge, Chivington and his men laid waste to the village, butchering five hundred Indian men, women, and children, including Chief White Antelope.

They talked of Custer, and their voices crackled with emotion as they related how Custer and eight hundred soldiers massacred a sleeping village of Cheyenne at the Washita while the company band played "Garry Owens," and how, after he killed the Indians, Custer ordered all the lodges burned and slaughtered nine hundred Indian ponies. Black Kettle, who had escaped death at Sand Creek, was not so lucky at the Washita.

"Hear and remember," said an old warrior. "The white man is not to be trusted. He speaks with a double tongue. His words are like a two-edged blade, and his heart is not good. He will offer you peace with one hand and cut you to pieces with the other."

Just after dusk a sweat-stained scout rode into camp on a lathered pony. Crook had been defeated! Gall and Crazy Horse and

Two Hawks Flying had led the Sioux and Cheyenne to victory.

There was immediate rejoicing in the camp. The warriors were on their way home. This announcement stirred the squaws into brisk activity. Fires were freshened. Unwary dogs found their way into cook pots mounted on tripods. Boiled puppy was an Indian favorite. Great haunches of venison and choice slabs of buffalo hump and tongue were brought out and hung on spits over low fires. Soon the whole valley was redolent with the aroma of woodsmoke and roasting meat.

With my fears for Shadow's safety allayed, I was suddenly famished and filled with nervous energy. Eager for something to do, I went to help New Leaf prepare dinner. I was stirring a big pot of venison stew flavored with sage and wild onions when the victorious war party rode into camp, shouting exultantly as they waved their rifles and lances high in the air. Eager to see Shadow, I ran with the rest of the women to greet the men, trying not to notice the fresh scalps dangling from the manes and tails of the Indian ponies or hanging from the belts of the warriors.

Shadow saw me standing a little apart from the other women, and he rode toward me. As he drew near, I let my eyes travel over him. Though he was covered with sweat and grime, he seemed to be unhurt, and I breathed a sigh of relief as he slid to the ground and took me in his arms.

"Hannah. . ."

"Oh, Shadow, I was so worried, so afraid. . ."

"I am unhurt."

"I know. But you might have been killed."

Shadow took my chin in his hand and lifted my face to meet his. "You must not worry every time I ride to battle," he said gravely. "It is a thing you must accept. Our lives are in the hands of the Great Spirit, and all your tears and foolish womanly worries will not change what is to be."

"I cannot help worrying," I retorted. "I cannot help being afraid that you'll be killed, and I'll be left alone."

"You will not be alone. My father will care for you if anything happens to me. My people will not abandon you if I am killed. You are one of us now and always will be."

"I know. But I could not bear to live without you. Please don't fight the next time."

"I am a warrior. Do not ask me to be less than what I am."

"I'm sorry," I said, ashamed. "Forgive me."

"There is nothing to forgive."

Unmindful of watching eyes, I laid my head against Shadow's chest and wept. I wanted him to give in to my wishes, to stay home from the next battle, and yet, perversely, I was glad that he refused, glad that he would not give in to my fears. Oh, but it was hard, sometimes, to love a man! But how wonderful to love a man like Shadow.

There was a victory celebration that night that lasted until dawn. I wore the dress I had been married in and basked in the love I read in my husband's eyes.

Crazy Horse praised his warriors, saying they were the best fighting men in all the land. And with a victory like the one they had seen this day, who could doubt it?

Sitting Bull spoke also, his words deep and powerful as he promised another victory in the days ahead. For there could be no doubt that soon, very soon, Custer would come.

There was singing and dancing and feasting that night. The Indian voices filled the air as they sang of victory and brave deeds. I danced with the women and then with Shadow in the married peoples dance, and it seemed we danced on air.

Later, there were rousing tales of the battle itself, of coup counted and enemies slain. One of the warriors related how Two Hawks Flying had saved Short Elks life by riding into the midst of the enemy ranks and slaying three bluecoats with his bow before hauling Short Elk up behind him and carrying him to safety. One of the most stirring exploits was told by Chief Comes-In-Sight, of the Cheyenne. In word and sign and dance he told how he had repeatedly charged the soldiers, counting many coup on the enemy, until his horse was shot down.

"I was preparing my death song," he said, "when I saw my sister, Buffalo Calf Road Woman, riding down the hill. With great courage, she rode straight toward the soldiers, ignoring the bullets whining about her like angry hornets. 'Ho, brother, it is a good day to die!' she cried, and when she slowed her lathered mount, I vaulted up behind her and we rode to safety. Hear me, warriors, with women like this to bear our children, we have nothing to fear!"

A great cheer went up from the women, and when the shouts of aclaim died away, Fawn told me Buffalo Calf Road Woman had earned the right to wear an eagle feather in her hair as a symbol of her courage. It was a great honor, Fawn said, that few women ever achieve.

There were proud words spoken for Laughing Turtle, too, for he had died bravely in battle, counting many coup before he was struck down.

I, too, was caught up in the fevered excitement of victory, though my happiness was due solely to the fact that Shadow had come through the battle alive and unscathed. Later that night, when the camp was quiet, some of my joy ebbed as I realized there would likely be many other battles. For the first time I let myself think of the men, red and white, that lay dead on the field of battle. I thought of John Sanders, of the Tabors and the Walkers, of Hobie Brown and his family, of my own dear parents. All dead because the Indians and the whites could not live together in peace. It was sad, I thought, that there wasn't room for everyone when there was so much land.

In the morning I learned that Sitting Bull had pulled up stakes and left for the Greasy Grass and that General George Crook had quit the Rosebud. Once again the Indians struck their lodges. A holiday air prevailed as we journeyed toward the rendevous with Sitting Bull. Runners brought word that 'Yellow Hair' Custer, General Alfred 'Star' Terry, and Colonel John 'Red Nose' Gibbon were moving against us, but the Indians were almost unconcerned. "We beat them at the Rosebud," the warriors boasted, "and we will beat them again."

We traveled at a leisurely pace. The grass was high enough, in some places, to brush the bottom of a tall pony's belly. Cottonwoods and willows, bright with new growth, flanked the waterholes. Birch, aspen, and oak grew heavy on the hillsides. And far in the distance were the beautiful Big Horn Mountains of Montana.

Once, looking back over the long caravan, I was reminded of the children of Israel fleeing Egypt. Like the Israelites, the Indian horde was carrying everything it owned, and the column must have been seven or eight miles long: a noisy, dusty parade of men, women, children, dogs, and horses. I could not begin to guess how many Indians there were, but Shadow estimated at least eight thousand, probably more. Of that number, roughly four thousand were warriors of fighting age.

It was nearing the end of June when we arrived at the war camp. New Leaf and Fawn immediately began setting up the lodge while I prepared the afternoon meal. We had eaten both lunch and dinner before the last stragglers reached the village.

Scouts rode in and out of camp continually, keeping an eye out for soldiers. Many councils were held, and the little boys were constantly wide-eyed as they spied on the great chiefs: Tatanka Yotanka, Hump, American Horse, Gall, Crazy Horse, Two Hawks Flying—these were names to stir the imagination and swell the heart.

One afternoon Shadow and I went for a walk along the river. We had to walk quite a distance to find a place that was not populated by people, horses, or dogs. Hand in hand, we strolled along, happy to be together on such a lovely summer afternoon.

We were laughing over the antics of a family of beavers when we heard a rustling in the brush behind us. Suddenly wary, Shadow thrust me behind him as he turned and drew his knife.

Motioning for me to stay where I was, he padded noiselessly forward and peered cautiously into the shrubbery.

Fearing attack by some enemy or predatory beast, I was puzzled when Shadow called me to him.

"Look," he whispered.

Following his pointing finger, I stared into the thicket and uttered a soft cry of delight at what I saw, for there, not three feet away, lay a chestnut mare in the midst of delivering a late foal.

Fascinated, I watched as two dainty feet slid into view, followed by a delicate nose and well-shaped head.

Another few minutes and the foal was free of the mare and breathing on its own. The mare whickered to her baby; then, lurching to her feet, she began to lick its damp spotted hide.

We watched, smiling, as the little filly struggled to stand on long, wobbly legs and silently applauded as she nuzzled her dam's side, sucking greedily at the mare's swollen teats.

"She's darling, isn't she?" I murmured. "So small, so perfect."

Shadow nodded, his midnight eyes as full of wonder as my own. "New life is always beautiful," he said, squeezing my hand. "Perhaps, one day, we will create a little one of our own."

"It is my wish, too," I said, and lifted my face for his kiss.

We had been camped at the Greasy Grass for three or four days when word came by scout that Yellow Hair was coming! This announcement was met with high excitement. Crazy Horse immediately called for a council of war. All the chiefs of all the tribes attended this important meeting, including Shadow, who, I learned with some surprise, was the war chief for our band of Cheyenne.

The Indian camp was strangely subdued that night. Warriors made last minute preparations for battle, checking weapons and war horses. Some purified themselves in the sweat lodge, supplicating their individual gods for an Indian victory. Some warriors did not lie with their women prior to battle, believing that sexual intercourse drained the power from a man. Others spent long hours making love to their wives, hoping to leave a new life behind in case they were killed in battle.

Shadow and I lay close that night, and as he made love to me, I prayed to all the gods, red and white, entreating them to watch over my man when he rode into battle.

The next day, June 25, 1876, the warriors went out to meet Yellow Hair.

The result of that battle is history. The Army's original plan had been for Terry, Gibbon, and Custer to meet along the banks of the Yellowstone River. Terry would then go off with Gibbon to outflank the Indians on the north, while Custer and the Seventh would take up a position to the south of the Indian camp. At the proper time, the two forces would come together, hopefully crushing the Indians between them.

But Custer was too recklessly impatient for battle to wait for Terry and Gibbon. There were honors to be won, medals to be garnered, and so he rode boldly toward the Greasy Grass—two days early.

For reasons known only to himself, Custer split his forces into three squadrons and then, badly outnumbered, was massacred with the two hundred twenty-five men in his immediate command. Thousands of warriors swarmed like locusts down the valley of the Little Big Horn, pinning Custer and his troopers against the hills.

In his haste to confront the hostiles, Custer had left several Gatling guns behind, and I can almost hear him cussing that decision as he and his squadron retreated up a rocky slope, losing men every step of the way. For once the Indians fought like the whites. All thought of counting coup or accumulating personal honors were forgotten as they stormed through Custer's diminishing ranks like a giant red scythe, cutting down everything in its path. The battle, which began at four o'clock, lasted less than an hour. When it was over, every white man was dead.

It was a sad day for the Custer family, for riding with the General that fateful afternoon were his brothers, Tom and Boston, his nephew, Armstrong Reed, and his brother-in-law, Lieutenant Calhoun.

Following the battle, many of the bodies were scalped, many more were savagely mutilated by the Indian women, but the body of General George Armstrong Custer was left untouched. There was a great deal of speculation about this. Some said Custer killed himself, an act considered cowardly by the Indians, and that they refused to touch his body because of it. But I believe, with others, that despite his other faults, Custer fought bravely to the end and that the Indians left him his scalp as a token of their respect.

Captain Frederick Benteen and Major Marcus Reno, the two officers left in command of the remainder of Custer's split forces, also engaged in heavy fighting that day. Between them, they suffered severe losses, though nothing as utterly devastating as the fate that had befallen Custer and his men.

It was a great day for the Indian. Sitting Bull's prophecy had been fulfilled, and there was a rousing celebration in the Indian encampment that night. Drunk on victory, the warriors danced and sang and shouted praises to Tashunka Witko and Tatanka Yotanka. In later years, the whites would give Sitting Bull the credit for the Indian victory, but it was Crazy Horse who won the day, planned the attack and put it into action.

While the Indians were celebrating the greatest victory they had ever known, the remnants of the Seventh, under Benteen and Reno, huddled on a bluff across from the Little Big Horn. Exhausted, plagued by a relentless thirst, the men of the Seventh dug in to await the charge they knew would come with the dawn.

Shadow and I left the celebration early. Alone in the lodge, we lay close beneath the buffalo robes. I tried not to think of the morrow or dwell on the fact that Shadow might be killed, that this might be the last night I would spend in the warm circle of his arms and feel his mouth crushing mine.

I knew the same thoughts were running through Shadow's mind, and our lovemaking, which had started off as a gentle exchange of affection, became more and more intense, more fervent, until, at last, every other thought was burned from my mind.

At dawn, the Indians launched several concentrated attacks against the beleaguered soldiers, but the troopers were well entrenched now, and the Indians gradually drew back as their casualties began to mount.

By midafternoon, the fighting was over. Squaws began dismantling their lodges. Herd boys rounded up the loose ponies. The warriors fired the grass as they prepared to move on.

I had not seen Shadow since he left that morning, and I began to wonder if he had been killed in the last charge against Reno's men. I saw a similar fear mirrored in Black Owl's eyes.

And then Red Wind trotted into camp—riderless, reins trailing. The stallion's right flank was crusted with blood, and when Black Owl ascertained that the horse itself was not wounded, he swung aboard his own pony and rode off to search the battlefield for his son's body. After a few minutes of useless pacing, I climbed aboard Red Wind and headed up the valley, hoping the big red horse would carry me to its master.

And he did.

I found Shadow standing atop a high bluff, a pensive expression on his handsome face. Blood was leaking from a jagged gash in his right side; his leggings were covered with it. He did not seem aware of my presence as I drew rein beside him.

Following his gaze, I saw the cold, unmoving forms of Custer's men scattered below us. Stripped naked, they made an eerie sight in the dusky twilight. Many of the bodies had been scalped. Others had been mutilated with the Cheyenne cut-arm sign or the Sioux cut-throat sign. Ribbons of dried blood made dark stains against their pale, waxy flesh.

A single horse grazed in the distance.

Bits of green paper were scattered everywhere. Later, I learned it was the Cavalry payroll.

"I wonder if we did the right thing," Shadow murmured after awhile.

When I looked puzzled, he said, "The soldiers will be out for revenge now." He made a broad gesture that included the entire, blood-run battlefield. "We have outfought Three Stars and killed Yellow Hair and all his men. Before, the Army sought to kill us because it was their duty. But now..." Shadow shook his head. "Now I think they will ride against us with vengeance in their hearts. I fear they will not rest until they have destroyed us from the face of the earth."

His words, softly spoken, chilled me to the bone. Was he right? Had the Sioux and the Cheyenne and the others sealed their doom by defeating Custer? I did not know, and as I glanced at Shadow and saw the blood still trickling from his side, I did not care. I knew only that Shadow was wounded, and that if he died, I would want to die, too.

"Shadow, you're hurt."

"It is nothing," he assured me. "Just a scratch."

I moved forward on Red Wind, and Shadow swung up behind me, grimacing with pain as he did so.

New Leaf and Fawn had dismantled the lodge by the time we returned to camp. Black Owl rode up shortly thereafter, vastly relieved to see his son alive.

It took me only a few minutes to bandage the nasty gash in Shadow's side and then, without a backward glance, we rode out of the valley of the Greasy Grass toward the headwaters of the Little Bighorn.

Chapter 12

Following the battle at the Little Big Horn, the Indians scattered, each tribe going back to its own hunting grounds. Black Owl and his band returned to Bear Valley, and we spent the rest of the summer there.

How peaceful it was, there in the broad grassy valley. Shadow and I had our own lodge at last, pitched next to that of Black Owl. Often, in the afternoon, I sat outside with Fawn and New Leaf, enjoying their company as we basked in the sunlight. Never idle, we always had a task to occupy our hands, be it sewing or mending, fashioning new moccasins, or making tiny baby things for the child Fawn was expecting in late February. Fawn fairly glowed with excitement and anticipation. And Black Owl could not stop smiling, so pleased was he with the prospect of being a father again.

Hunting was good in the valley that year, and we feasted on juicy red buffalo hump and venison. There were berries and wild plums, as well as wild onions and roots and nuts. I learned to make jerky and pemmican that year. I also learned which herbs were good for seasoning, which were good for medicinal purposes, and which ones were poisonous. Evenings, there were dances for young and old alike.

Sometimes one of the ancient warriors would reminisce about the old days, before the Cheyenne acquired the horse. Things had been different then. Before the arrival of the horse—or the magic dog, as he was sometimes called—the dogs and women had to transport all the camp paraphernalia when the village moved. Warriors could only hunt within a limited range. But the aquisition of the horse changed all that, enabling warriors to range far and wide in search of game. Women were no longer forced to act as beasts of burden when the tribe sought greener pastures. Little wonder that the Cheyenne set such a store by their ponies!

The days ran together, each one better than the last, as my love for Shadow grew and grew. Early one bright sunlit morning, I wandered down to the river in search of wild plums. Some distance from our camp I spied Red Wind grazing beneath a lacy cottonwood tree.

Smiling, I tiptoed forward, careful to keep downwind of the stallion lest he ruin my surprise. Peering through a clump of berry bushes, I felt my breath catch in my throat, for there, standing naked on the shore, stood Shadow—his arms raised toward Heaven, his lips moving in prayer to Man Above. I could not catch all the words, but twice I heard him mention my name. It touched me deeply, knowing he was praying for me.

He stood there for several minutes, and I thought I had never seen anything so beautiful as that tall copper-hued warrior engaged in prayer. Acutely conscious that I was intruding on something very private, I was about to leave when Shadow dropped his arms and dove into the water. He swam beautifully, his strokes long and smooth and powerful as he glided through the blue-green water.

He swam briskly for several moments and then, moving to shallower water, he began to wash. I found it strangely exciting to watch Shadow bathe. His black hair, which hung almost to his waist, glistened in the sunlight; large drops of water rolled down his chest, belly and legs, and I had a sudden urge to run my hands over his smooth flesh, to feel the powerful muscles in his arms ripple beneath my fingertips.

Stepping from my hiding place, I walked toward Shadow. A million butterflies seemed to be fluttering in the pit of my stomach as I stepped out of my dress and joined Shadow in the water.

His skin was warm and wetly sensuous as he took me in his arms and kissed me hungrily. It was the most primitive, exotic feeling, making love there in the cool water near the shore. Like sea nymphs, we came together, seeking the ecstasy that was now familiar and yet always new. . . .

It was a glorious summer. Often, Shadow and I rode to the river crossing to swim or just to be alone.

Once, we rode to the trading post. Tears burned my eyes as we rode to the spot where my home had once stood. There was nothing left now, only an area of blackened ground where the house and barn had been.

Standing there, I relived the awful day when the Indians had attacked our place. I saw David killed again and experienced anew the pain of my mother's death. I heard my Pa's voice, filled with emotion, as he urged me to go with Shadow.

With a sob, I sank down to my knees and let the tears flow. Fragmented images danced across my mind's eye. There was

Orin, running for his life, a bear cub in his arms, while the mother bear chased him. There was Joshua, so blondly handsome, pleading with me to marry him, jealousy accusing me of loving Orin. There was my dear mother, a smile on her lips as she lovingly patted my shoulder. There was Pa, a bulwark of strength in times of sorrow, a happy grin and a hug during good times.

One after the other, all the people I had once known paraded down the corridor of my memory. I saw David smiling at me, his eyes full of love as he made me laugh during that dismal winter when I thought I had lost Shadow forever.

And there was Shadow as a young boy, his dark eyes arrogant and defiant, daring me to feel sorry for him because his mother was dead. How different my life would have turned out if I had not met him that day at Rabbit's Head Rock so long ago.

He stood beside me now while I laid my ghosts to rest. Impassively silent, he let me grieve, and then he took me in his arms. I sighed as I buried my face against his chest, grateful for the comfort of his arms and the love in his eyes.

We never rode to that part of Bear Valley again.

Secure in Shadow's love, happy in the life

we shared, I put all unpleasant memories behind me. I blotted the nightmare of the Custer massacre from my mind, too, and pretended nothing had changed.

But it had.

Custer had been the people's hero and news of his death, and the manner of it, caused great consternation, especially in the east. Irate citizens demanded that the Army do something about the red menace once and for all. As Shadow had predicted, the Army moved against the Indians with a vengeance. Three Stars took the field again. Still deemed the best Indian fighter of them all despite his defeat at the Rosebud, he moved swiftly against the Cheyenne, talking the tribes into surrendering when possible, mercilessly riding them down when all else failed.

Bear Coat Miles traveled to the Yellowstone to talk peace with Sitting Bull. The talks failed miserably; the last one ended in battle.

Word came from Washington that no rations or clothing would be issued to the reservations until all the hostiles had surrendered.

Sitting Bull and hundreds of Sioux fled to Canada.

Crazy Horse was talking about going in.

All the Cheyenne tribes, save for Black

Owl's little band, gave up and went to the reservation.

The day of the Indian was over.

We spent that fall running and fighting and hiding. Army patrols were everywhere, combing the plains for the last, scattered bands of Indians that refused to surrender. Fawn had a miscarriage and nearly died, causing Black Owl much grief.

Late one afternoon the Army overtook us as we were crossing a nasty part of the Yellowstone River. The warriors quickly fell back, forming a defensive line between the Indians and the soldiers while the women and children hastened across the river and ran for cover in the trees beyond.

Shadow had given me a horse, a dark chestnut mare, and I urged her into the water behind Fawn and New Leaf. We were halfway across when I saw Bright Star floating face down in the water. Holding my mare's thick mane, I slipped out of the saddle. Grabbing Bright Star's hair with my free hand, I urged Sunny toward the opposite bank. With an effort, I lifted the unconscious girl into the saddle; then, swinging up behind her, I ran for cover.

We lost a dozen warriors that day and as many women and children. With the coming of night, we somehow managed to elude the soldiers.

We spent the next day nursing our wounded. Bright Star had been shot in the back. New Leaf and I cared for her as best we could, but to no avail. Shadow sat with Bright Star until she died, his face blank, his thoughts obviously turned inward. I did not intrude on his grief, nor did I feel the slightest bit of jealousy when he wept over her body. She had been his childhood sweetheart, a part of his carefree youth. But for me, he might have married her.

But we had little time to mourn our dead. I had never realized how awful it was to be hunted; I had never known such heart-pounding fear, not only for Shadow's life, but for my own. Many of Black Owl's people were killed, women and children as well as men. The soldiers were shooting anything that moved, and I had a recurring nightmare that, despite my red hair, I would be mistaken for an Indian and shot on sight.

And perhaps they would kill me even if they knew I was white, for I was willingly living with hostile Indians. It was a sobering thought.

As usual, Shadow knew what I was thinking, and late one night he asked me if I wanted to return to my own people.

"Of course not," I replied. "I want to be here—with you."

"Are you sure?" he asked quietly. His

dark eyes searched mine for several moments, and in their depths I read his love and concern for my well-being. I knew he would take me to the nearest white settlement if I asked him to; I knew he would risk his own life to see me safely returned to my own people if that was my desire.

"Are you sure?" he repeated when I did not answer. "The Army will not give up this time. They will chase us until we are all dead, or we surrender."

I knew he was right, and for a moment, as I gazed at the Indian lodge and its crude furnishings, I felt a stab of longing for civilization. It would be nice to be able to converse in my own tongue instead of the harsh gutteral language of the Cheyenne. It would be good to see another white face, to be surrounded by my own people, to enjoy the creature comforts that were unknown to the Indians.

My mouth watered for the taste of chocolate and cold milk and coffee. It would be heavenly to soak in a hot bathtub, to sleep on a bed with sheets, to eat at a table, to wear a dress that was not made of skins.

Shadow's eyes had never left my face, and as I met his gaze, I knew where I belonged. Shadow was my life, the only thing that mattered—now and always.

"I want to stay here with you," I said.

"I hope you do not regret it," he said softly, taking me in his arms.

How tenderly he made love to me that night! Gently, carefully, as if I were a precious treasure that might shatter at his touch, he stroked and fondled my breasts and thighs. His kisses were butterfly soft as they rained down on my eyes and mouth, as gently, so gently, he made me his once again.

I was glad when winter came at last. The temperature plummeted overnight. Thunder rolled across the heavens, and great bolts of lightning ripped the darkened skies. Leaden clouds hovered overhead, shutting out the sun by day and the moon by night. The rains came, pummeling the land with fury, turning the rich brown earth to mud and the rivers into great roiling waterways, white with froth. The wind howled down out of the mountains, stripping the last dead leaves from the trees.

And then, at last, the snow came, forcing the army patrols to return to the snug security of their forts to wait out the bad weather.

It was a long winter. Shadow and I spent the icy days and cheerless nights snuggled under the buffalo robes, making the most of the quiet time we had together, knowing the Army would again be in hot pursuit when the snow was gone and the roads were passable.

Winter that year was not only long but extremely harsh. Many of our people had been forced to abandon their lodges, food, and clothing while fleeing the soldiers, and were therefore in desperate need. Those who were able shared what little they had with those who were less fortunate, but soon there was nothing left to share.

Game was practically non-existent, and soon there were no dogs left in camp. What remained of the horse herd dwindled daily as the weaker animals died of the cold or starvation or were killed for food.

Among the Indians, as with everything else in Nature's plan, the very old and the very young suffered the most. Every day a new scaffold rose against the sky as yet another soul was laid to rest. Soon there were more scaffolds than lodges standing in the valley.

Rising Dawn died that winter.

I wept as her father tenderly placed her blanket-wrapped body atop a small burial scaffold. Rising Dawn's favorite doll was laid beside her. A small sack of pemmican was laid at her feet to give her nourishment on her journey to the land of the sky people. A young colt was killed and placed beneath her scaffold so she might ride in comfort to the home of her ancestors. A small container of water came next, so that she would not thirst.

A long keening wail rose on the wind as Rising Dawn's mother and relatives voiced their grief.

I felt bereft in the days that followed. Our lodge seemed empty without Rising Dawn's merry laughter, Often, I turned to speak to her, only to realize anew that she was gone.

Shadow and the other warriors foraged farther and farther afield in an effort to find game. On the day they returned to camp with a young doe, I saw women and children weep with joy. That night, we all slept with full bellies.

But one deer was quickly gone, and hunger stalked our camp again. Black Owl began to talk about going to the reservation when spring broke winter's icy hold on the land. Fawn, never strong again since the loss of her child, was seriously ill, and there was no one to care for her properly now that Elk Dreamer was dead. Perhaps a white doctor could help her.

Shadow did not argue with his father. The will to fight had gone out of the Cheyenne. People were dying every day. The children were hungry and the old ones were tired of fighting. Yes, perhaps going to the reservation was the answer—and when two Army scouts rode into camp early in the spring, promising food and shelter for all if Black Owl and his followers would surrender peaceably, Black Owl agreed to go.

"Perhaps this time the whites will keep their word," Black Owl remarked without conviction. "If not, we will be no worse off than we are now."

"You will no longer be a free man, my father," Shadow said bitterly. "Is that not worse?"

"I am weary of running from the bluecoats," Black Owl replied. "Weary of fighting. Our people must surrender or perish."

"I am sorry to hear you say it, my father," Shadow murmured sadly. "I fear I will never see you again."

"Come with us," Black Owl urged. "You cannot fight the white man alone."

Shadow laughed hollowly. "I am not foolish enough to try. But neither will I surrender my freedom."

Tears stung my eyes as I watched the two warriors embrace for the last time. As always, I was deeply moved by the love and respect they had for one another.

"May you travel in peace, my son," Black Owl said solemnly.

"May the Great Spirit guard your journey

and those you love," Shadow responded, and we left his father's lodge.

An hour later the Cheyenne struck their lodges and left Bear Valley for the last time.

Standing side by side, Shadow and I watched them out of sight.

Chapter 13
Spring - Summer 1877

The snow was gone and the world was new.
The trees were clothed in bright green, and
the hills and valleys were bedecked with
flowers. The rivers ran high and clear, icy to
the touch. Red Wind and my little mare,
Sunny, grew sleek and fat on the rich green
grass that carpeted the plains. Shadow killed
a buffalo, and we stuffed ourselves with
juicy red meat. He was Adam and I was Eve
and there was no evil in the world, only joy
and love and laughter. We frolicked like
happy, carefree children along the river's
grassy banks—swam daily in its chilly
refreshing waters, wrestled like bear cubs,
chased each other through the fragrant
forest, and made love under the warm blue
sky.

But such bliss was too good to last.

I was tanning a deer hide one summer day, humming cheerfully as I worked. Shadow sat nearby, stringing a new bow. As I scraped the last of the meat from the hide, I mentally rehearsed different ways to tell him we were going to have a baby in December. I had not yet settled on the best way to break the news when Shadow suddenly dropped his bow and stood up, eyes narrowed as he stared across the river. Following his gaze, I saw four horsemen riding toward us.

That quickly, Eden was shattered.

"Soldiers?" I asked tremulously, hating the very sound of the word.

"No," Shadow said, and his voice was puzzled. "Indians. Apaches."

Apaches. Here? They were far from home. I felt a prickle of apprehension as the warriors put their mounts across the river. Of all the Indians in the west, the Apache were rumored to be the most savage, the most war-like. Worse, even, than the Comanches.

Shadow picked up his rifle and held it loosely in the crook of his arm as the four braves emerged from the water. They were short, stocky men, with coarse black hair and coppery skin—all dressed alike in cheap cotton shirts, worn buckskin leggings, clouts, red headbands, and tall moccasins.

Only one was armed with a rifle. The rest carried bows and arrows. Four abreast, they drew rein ten feet from where Shadow stood. There was a quiet moment as Shadow and the four Apaches appraised each other. Shadow spoke first, in sign.

"You have ridden far, my brothers. Come, eat with us, and then tell me why you have come to the land of the Tsi-tsi-tsas?"

With a slight nod, the four warriors dismounted. Shadow brought out his pipe, and the five men sat cross-legged in the shade of a tall cottonwood, smoking constantly, while I looked after the Apache horses and then cooked up a pot of venison stew seasoned with sage and wild onions. Like the good Cheyenne squaw I had become, I served the men before I ate, then went back to my deer hide, showing no outward interest in our visitors.

One of the Apaches had a long scar on his left cheek. This warrior spoke English, and he interpreted for the others when necessary. After dinner he explained why they had come.

"Once the Apache were a proud people," he began. "There were no better fighters, no braver warriors in all the land. But then Cochise broke the arrow and made peace with the white eyes. We kept the peace because we loved and respected him. But now Cochise is dead and his son, Tahza, rules in his place. Tahza does his best, but he is not Cochise. Cochise would never have let the white eyes send us to San Carlos...San Carlos," he repeated and made a sound of disgust low in his throat. "On the reservation, the white men give us food and clothing and expect us to be grandmothers to cattle."

He spat into the fire and his eyes blazed with anger. "We are warriors, not women, and we wish to fight! We have no wives, no children. All are dead, killed by the white eyes. We..." indicating his three silent companions, "have heard that Two Hawks Flying is a great war chief among his people. But even a great chief cannot fight alone. If you will lead us, we are ready to fight at your side."

Four pairs of ebony eyes stared hard at Shadow, waiting for his reply.

"It is a fight we cannot hope to win," Shadow responded quietly. "Surely you know that?"

"We know," the scar-faced Apache replied gravely. "But it is better to die in the heat of battle than wet nurse the white man's cattle."

"It is better to die like a man than live like a dog," remarked one of the other braves, and his voice was heavy with bitterness.

"Yes," agreed another. "Death in battle is

251

swift. Far better than slow starvation at San Carlos."

"I will have to think on it," Shadow answered, and I could tell by the tone of his voice that he was deeply moved by their words and their trust.

It was ludicrous to think of five warriors doing battle against the United States Army. I knew it. The Apaches knew it. And Shadow knew it. Even so, I saw his eyes gleam with the desire to fight, and I knew he was excited by the idea.

Shadow and the scar-faced Apache, whose name was Calf Running, stayed up all that night. Lying in my bed, I listened as they spoke wistfully of the old days—those good days before the white man when the red man ruled the plains and the Great Spirit smiled on his children.

"The whites are without number," Calf Running remarked in despair. "If you kill ten, a hundred come in their place. I think...I think their god must be more powerful than all the Indian gods combined."

The next morning three Oglala Sioux rode into our camp. That afternoon a half-dozen Cheyenne drifted in—warriors all, armed and ready to fight to the death beside Two

Hawks Flying, the last fighting chief on the plains.

I had often heard of that mysterious source of Indian communication known as the moccasin telegraph, and now I was seeing it in action. Daily, by twos and threes, warriors rode or walked into our camp. Like wildfire, word had spread to all the tribes that the Cheyenne war chief Two Hawks Flying was not going in, and the hot-blooded young warriors sought him out. They had tried life on the reservation and found it sadly wanting. Rations did not come on time, and when they did come, they were scarce and inferior. The whites would not give the Indians guns so they could hunt fresh meat, and the people were hungry. Dishonest Indian agents sold supplies meant for the tribes and pocketed the money, leaving their charges to get along as best they could. Parents gave what food they had to their children and slowly starved to death. Warriors watched their children die, watched their old people die, watched their wives die, and when they'd had enough, they slipped off the reservation and headed for Bear Valley.

At the end of a month, there were twenty-five warriors camped at the river crossing—Apache, Sioux, Arapahoe, a sprinkling of

Blackfoot and Kiowa. They were men without families, without ties of any kind—men eager to fight the whites who had killed their kin and stolen their land, decimated the great herds of buffalo and penned the Indians up like cattle.

It was ironic, I thought, to see them united against the whites now, when it was too late. How very differently things might have turned out for the Indians if they had only laid their petty ancestral squabbles aside sooner!

Another twenty warriors straggled into camp over the next few days. When Shadow saw that, despite their low number, they were truly determined to fight, he agreed to lead them. And so it was to be war once more.

At first, I fought at Shadow's side. Dressed in deerskin leggings and a fringed doeskin shirt, with my hair tied back and my face painted for war, I was indistinguishable as a woman—at least from a distance.

Our first battle is the only one I clearly remember. All the others blended into a hazy kaleidescope of gunsmoke and noisy confusion.

That first skirmish was against a small cavalry patrol. It was one of the few times when we outnumbered the opposition. I remember I had a good Winchester repeating rifle, and as I was a pretty fair shot, I took aim at the tall Army horses, reluctant to kill the soldiers who were, after all, *my* people.

But my resolve not to kill anyone was quickly swept away when one of the troopers charged straight at me, and I found myself staring into his rifle's awesome black maw. Time seemed to stand still then, and I noticed that the trooper had bright blue eyes and a tiny, heart-shaped scar on his left cheek. He was about my age, perhaps a little older, and I wondered if he was married. . .a father, perhaps. His uniform was dirty, his hands smeared with grime, and I stared, spellbound, at the long brown finger curled around the trigger.

Suddenly time accelerated again, and I knew he was going to kill me unless I killed him first. Woodenly, I squeezed the trigger of my own rifle, then stared with morbid fascination as his shirtfront turned crimson and he toppled from his horse. I had killed a man of my own race. Somehow, it was much worse than fighting the Indians that day they attacked the trading post back in Bear Valley. I saw the dead trooper's face in my dreams for weeks thereafter.

Shadow, always sensitive to my moods, did his best to comfort me. Nights, when we were alone, he talked to me of his youth, telling me amusing stories and tales of his people in an effort to cheer me and obliterate thoughts of the man I had killed.

But it was his touch, the strength of his arms around me, that brought solace to my troubled heart. Only in his embrace did I feel secure. Sometimes it seemed like the whole world had gone mad, and only Shadow, and the love we shared, remained constant and unchanging.

As time passed, the memory of the dead trooper faded, but the horror of the moment was never completely forgotten.

And still the battle between red man and white raged across the plains. No cavalry patrol was safe from our attack. We hit them early in the morning, before dawn, stealing their horses and killing their sentries.

Army supply wagons and civilian wagon trains were our favorite targets. We looted them for guns, ammunition, food, and clothing, and then we destroyed whatever was left. No prisoners were taken, and when I cringed to see women and children injured or killed, I made myself remember the stories I had heard of Sand Creek and the Washita and the hundreds of Indian women and children who had been senselessly slaughtered. It did not make me feel any better, really, and yet it helped me to understand the violent hatred of the Indians.

We harrassed the Army forts, too, lobbing fire arrows over the walls late at night, when the soldiers were asleep and the sentries were sluggish. We never stayed around to fight the aroused troopers. Our arrows were just to remind them we were there—a way to keep them uneasy.

Occasionally, we engaged in a major skirmish with the Army, but such encounters were rare; as soon as the battle turned against us, we broke and ran. Small in number, we could not afford any heavy losses, and so we scattered like leaves in a high wind to meet later at a pre-arranged location.

It was a brutal way of life—always on the run, never able to sleep unafraid for fear of attack. And yet no one complained or spoke of quitting.

It was amazing to me that Shadow ever managed to build a good, closely-knit fighting force out of those warriors, for not only were their religious beliefs different, but so were their fighting techniques. Masters at mounted combat, the Sioux and Cheyenne fought for the sheer love of fighting, willing to face any odds to attain battle honors and personal glory.

The Apache, on the other hand, preferred to fight on foot. They were wizards at camouflage and could disappear into the landscape without a trace. They, too, fought for personal glory, but they rarely provoked a battle unless they were reasonably certain of victory. Before uniting with Shadow and the others, it had been their opinion that only a fool attacked a stronger foe.

But things were different now. They were not fighting for glory or honor or coup feathers; they were fighting for their lives and their freedom.

It was not an easy life, being the only woman in a camp of fifty men. I had thought, with horror, that I would be expected to cook for the entire lot, but Shadow made it clear at the outset that I was his woman alone. In words that were blunt and directly to the point, he warned his men that any warrior who touched me or offended me in any way would answer to him, and that if there were any objections to my presence in their ranks, he would leave and they could find themselves a new chief. It was, I suppose, a tribute to their faith in his leadership ability that no one spoke against his declaration, or seemed to resent the fact that Shadow had a woman when they did not.

When it became obvious that I was pregnant, Shadow refused to let me ride into battle. Secretly, I was glad to stay behind, for I did not like fighting, especially against my own race.

I was often lonely that year, for Shadow and his warriors frequently rode far afield, leaving me at one hideout or another for days at a time.

They returned from one encounter with the Army with their numbers reduced by ten good men. Three others were badly wounded. One of the injured braves was a Cheyenne boy only fifteen or sixteen years old. He had taken a bullet in the belly, low down.

I sat with him for three days while he hovered between life and death. I made him as comfortable as I could, but there was really nothing I could do for him, nothing to give him for the pain except a hand to cling to and the knowledge that he would not die alone.

Sometimes Shadow sat with me. We said little, but his presence was a great comfort to me. He had changed. He was more pensive, more withdrawn, and I knew the weight of leadership and responsibility for his men and for me sat heavy on his shoulders. Each time one of our warriors died, Shadow also seemed to die a little, as if he felt the pain of each man's death.

This night, sitting beside me, there was a great sadness in his face.

"It isn't your fault," I remarked softly. I gestured toward Swift Wind, lying unconscious between us. "He is here because he wanted to be here. They all are. You must not blame yourself every time one of our men dies."

"Who else can I blame? I knew from the beginning that we could not win. That we could never win."

"So did they. It was their choice to be here. No one forced them."

"You speak words of truth and wisdom," Shadow allowed, "but each of our dead lies heavy on my conscience."

"I have often heard your warriors say it is better to die in battle than to surrender without a fight. If this is true, then you have nothing to regret. These men are living, and dying, as they wish. Many more would be dead if someone else was leading them. It is only your good leadership that has kept us all alive this long."

Shadow smiled at me, and the warmth of his glance warmed me through and through. "Thank you, Hannah. You have said the words I needed to hear."

The boy grew steadily worse. I sat with him to the end and wept bitter tears when he died.

Shadow and his warriors were gone again, and I was alone except for one wounded man who had not recovered enough to ride. I kept busy as best I could, tanning hides and sewing things for the baby, which was due around Christmas.

Shadow had been pleased with the news, though worried that he might be far away when the baby came. With more confidence that I felt, I assured him I was quite capable of having the baby alone, if necessary, though the very idea filled me with dread. After all, I said airily, the Indian women had babies in the open all the time. If they could do it, so could I.

He did not mention that I was not an Indian woman, though I was sure I saw the thought flit briefly through his mind.

Now, as I sat in the twilight of a lovely midsummer day, I laid my needle aside and stared into the gathering darkness. Who would have thought, years ago, that I would be living with fifty warriors? Certainly not I. I remembered my dreams of going to the big city, of seeing a stage play and dining in a fine restaurant, of marrying a tall, dark stranger. Well, it didn't look like I'd ever see New York or Chicago, but my girlish dreams of a tall, dark lover had certainly come true! And wasn't I glad. Though I might never wear silks and satins or sup from fine china, and though I might be forever poor in material things, I was rich in Shadow's love and for me that was enough. More than enough!

With a contented sigh, I went to look in on Bear Tree, an Arapahoe warrior who had been shot in the leg the week before. I found him sitting up in the crude lean-to reserved for the injured, awkwardly mending a hole in his warshirt.

"Here, let me do that," I offered, and then, realizing he didn't understand English, I reached for the needle.

And screamed as his hand grasped my wrist in an iron grip. There was no mistaking the lust blazing in the Arapahoe's deep-set black eyes, or his intent as he ripped my dress down the front and began fumbling with his breechcloth. More frightened than I had ever been before, I struggled against the leering warrior with all the strength I possessed, but try as I might, I could not free myself from his iron hand.

Grinning expectantly, Bear Tree flipped me over onto my back and straddled my legs, and I cringed as his exposed manhood brushed my thigh.

"No, please," I sobbed, and when I saw there was no escape, I squeezed my eyes shut and heard myself senselessly babbling, "no, no, no," as the panting warrior lowered himself over me. His breath was hot in my face, and I screamed with terror and revulsion as he forced my legs apart. . . .

"Bear Tree!"

Shadow's quiet voice rent the dusky stillness like a knife. Bear Tree jerked upright as if pulled by a string. Sullen-faced, he rose slowly to his feet and turned to face his chief. Shadow's countenance was terrible to behold, and the Arapahoe warrior trembled visibly before the deadly menace in Shadow's slit-eyed stare.

"Have you anything to say," Shadow asked coldly, and Bear Tree shook his head, knowing that words would not save him.

"So be it," Shadow rasped, and the rifle in his hands breathed fire and smoke, and Bear Tree fell backward, blood spilling freely from a hole in his chest. Once, twice, he twitched convulsively—then lay still.

The gunshot brought the others running, and I covered my nakedness with a blanket as they gathered around the lean-to. The scene that met their eyes was easily read, and they asked no questions.

"Throw that carrion to the wolves," Shadow ordered curtly, and two men moved quickly to obey.

Sensing our need to be alone, the rest of the warriors left the lean-to.

Shadow came to me then. His face was grim as he pulled me to my feet, yet his hands were gentle as they brushed the tears from my eyes.

Taking me in his arms, he asked hoarsely,

263

"Are you all right?"

"Yes," I whispered. "Oh, Shadow, I was so afraid."

His voice was heavy with self-reproach as he said, "I have been a fool to leave you alone. And a bigger fool to keep you here. Tomorrow I will take you back to your own people."

"No!" I cried. "I won't go. You're my people."

"Hannah, be reasonable."

"I won't be reasonable! And I won't let you send me away unless. . .unless you don't want me anymore."

"You know better than that," he murmured, drawing me closer, and I knew I had won.

By late summer there were three separate patrols searching for Shadow and his band of hostiles. There was a price on Shadow's head now—a hundred dollars, dead or alive, preferably dead. Later, the bounty rose to two hundred dollars. And then three.

With discretion being the better part of valor, we quit the broad grassy plains of Dakota and headed for the southwest, home of the Apache. Shadow's warriors had suffered some heavy losses in their last skirmish with the Army, and we were down to less than forty men when we crossed the border into Arizona.

The Apache homeland appeared to be a barren wasteland populated by little more than sand and snakes. Vegetation was scarce, and what there was seemed hostile. Saquaro, catclaw, creosote, prickly pear, ocotilla—everything seemed thorny or spiny. Later, when I saw the desert in bloom, it was like a different world. And as we crossed the country, I discovered there were canyons rich with game and water, green meadows lush with grass, and mountains heavy with timber. But my first impression was one of endless desolation, and I wondered how the Apache had managed to survive so long in such a harsh environment, and why they wanted to hang on to it. I sorely missed the rolling green plains and timbered hills of the Dakotas with the sparkling waterfalls and verdant valleys alive with color.

We had not been in Arizona long when warriors began trickling into our camp, eager to join their wild brothers. Mescalero, Jicarillo, Chiricahua, Coyotero, Mimbreno—they slipped in a few at a time until Shadow's fighting force numbered close to seventy. A handful of these were old warriors, with iron in their hair and the scars of many battles emblazoned on their copper-

hued torsos. But they had fire in their eyes
and a young man's desire to die fightling like
a warrior rather than waste away on the
reservation.

I listened one night as Calf Running and
his Apache brothers reminisced about the
old days, when the Apaches, roaming the
desert highlands, were masters of all they
surveyed. Wide-eyed, I listened to tales of
courage and cunning as they spoke of
Mangas Coloradas, the great chief of the
Warm Springs Apache. His name was Mexican in origin and meant Red Sleeves. When I
asked how he acquired such a name, Calf
Running smiled and explained that the
Mexicans had given it to him long ago
because he liked to dip his hands in the blood
of his victims. But Mangas was dead, shot
down in cold blood at Fort McLean. They
spoke reverently of Cochise, the greatest
Apache leader of them all, and his ten year
battle with the white eyes. But Cochise was
dead, too. They spoke of Gokliya, better
known as Geronimo, who was raising hell
down in Mexico, and of Old Nana, still riding
the war trails though he was well into his
seventies.

I learned a little about Apache religion,
too. They had a story that closely paralleled
the story of the Virgin Mary and Jesus. Only

the names were different. Their virgin was called White Painted Lady and her child, conceived immaculately by the Great Spirit, was called Child of the Waters.

I learned that the Apache would literally starve to death before they would eat fish which, according to their beliefs, was related to the snake and therefore cursed. Another thing I learned about the Apache was that they never said 'thank you.' Instead, they raised their eyes toward heaven, silently acknowledging Usen's hand in all things.

The most peculiar thing of all was the curious relationship between an Apache brave and his mother-in-law. For some reason which I never quite understood, once a man was married, he was forbidden to ever set eyes on his wife's mother!

Shortly after our arrival in Arizona, one of Shadow's scouting parties returned to camp leading three prisoners: two blue-clad troopers and an Apache tracker. These were the first prisoners Shadow's men had ever taken, and the atmosphere in our camp fairly crackled with anticipation as the luckless captives were stripped naked and staked out on the hard, unyielding ground. Calf Running was all for slitting their throats then and there, but the other Apaches wanted to torture the prisoners—especially the Apache tracker, who was considered a traitor.

One of the troopers was little more than a boy, and he began to cry softly as the Indians argued back and forth, some urging a quick death, some holding out for something a little more exciting, like skinning the prisoners alive or staking them out over an ant hill. The smell of fear was strong on the boy, and the warriors laughed with contempt as he pleaded for his life.

The second trooper was older, and judging by the hash marks I'd seen on his uniform shirt, had been in the service for more than fifteen years. His eyes shuttled nervously from the Indians calling for torture to those arguing for a quick death. Sweat rolled freely from his pores, and he began to shiver spasmodically as fear and tension took hold of him.

The Apache tracker paid no heed to the voices rising and falling around him. With a face impassive as a canyon wall, he stared at the dying sun and quietly chanted his death song.

Afraid that the Indians favoring torture were going to win, I went to Shadow and begged him to release the prisoners.

"I cannot," he said evenly. "My warriors must make this decision for themselves.

Many of them have seen their wives shot down in cold blood. They have seen their old people trampled beneath the uncaring hooves of the soldiers' horses. They have seen their little ones slaughtered. I know what is in their hearts, and I must let them take vengeance if they so desire."

And desire it they did. A tall, hatchet-faced warrior known as Black Elk stepped forward, knife in hand. Squatting beside the veteran trooper, he raked the sharp blade across the prisoner's pallied torso. The trooper began to moan as Black Elk's blade went ever deeper, cutting through meat and muscle.

The lust for blood was a tangible force in our camp. Two warriors, chanting softly, suddenly drew their knives and chopped off the prisoner's hands. The prisoner screamed as blood poured from his wounds—a long, agonized scream that ended abruptly as a Blackfoot brave slit his throat.

As one, the warriors turned toward the boy. There was a sudden stench as the prisoner voided his bowels. Eyes wide with fright, the boy rolled his head back and forth and in so doing spotted me. He stared at me for several moments; then, recognizing me as a white woman, he cried, "Lady, help me! For God's sake, do something!"

It was the worst moment of my life.

I felt Shadow's hand on my shoulder. "There is nothing you can do to save the boy," he said quietly. "Neither is there any reason for you to stay and watch him die. No one will think the less of you if you leave."

Wordlessly, I shook my head. I was here of my own free will. I had fought at his side, shared his grief when one of our warriors died. I would share this, too, though it sickened me to watch.

They did not torture the boy long, and when they were through with him, they turned purposefully toward the Apache tracker.

The things they did to him are too horrible to relate. Suffice it to say that when they were through, the prisoner no longer resembled anything human. Through it all, the Apache's black eyes burned with defiance. And only at the very end did he utter a sound, and that was the war cry of his people.

I could not sleep that night. Every time I closed my eyes, I saw the bloody remains of the prisoners. Yet I could not fault Shadow's men for their actions. I knew what they had suffered at the hands of the whites. I knew all about Sand Creek and the Washita, about all the treaties made and broken. Nevertheless, I was glad that Shadow and Calf Running had not taken part.

The bodies were gone the next morning, and only a few scattered bloodstains remained to show there had been violence in our camp. The warriors spoke ill of the two soldiers, saying they had died badly, but they all agreed, if grudgingly, that the Apache tracker had died well for a traitor.

Shadow never made mention of what had happened, but that afternoon he told his men there would be no more prisoners.

In September, seven trail-weary Hunkpapa Sioux joined us. With them they brought sad news. Crazy Horse was dead, killed by soldiers at the Red Cloud Agency. Shadow's men stared at each other in stunned silence. Crazy Horse, Tashunka Witko, the mighty war chief of the Oglala Bad Face band, the heart of the Sioux Nation, was dead at the age of thirty-three.

I was sorry to hear of his death. He had been such a vital, magnetic human being, that it was hard to believe he was dead, hard to imagine that boundless energy forever stilled. But there was no time to mourn his passing.

Early the next morning a small detachment of cavalry rode into our camp, led by a Crow scout and headed by a fresh-faced shavetail who introduced himself as Lieutenant Miles Freeman. His words were brief and to the point. The Grandfather in Washington was willing to let Shadow's warriors return to their respective reservations in peace if Shadow would surrender to General Crook no later than November fifteenth. If they refused, every soldier in the southwest would be mustered against them and they would be hunted down and killed to the last man. It was strong talk, and an angry buzz rose from the listening warriors.

"Kill the bluecoats and send them back to the Grandfather as our answer," Tall Horse said disdainfully.

"Let us take their scalps," Calf Running said eagerly. "I have not taken a scalp in a week."

"Let us stake them out over an ant hill," Black Elk suggested. "That is always entertaining."

"Enough!" Shadow snapped. "They are here under a white flag."

"My parents were shot down under a white flag," Calf Running remarked bitterly.

"Is it your wish to be like the white eyes?" Shadow asked quietly, and Calf Running shook his head and spoke no more.

"You have heard the Grandfather's offer," Shadow said, speaking to his men. "Is it your wish to accept?"

As one, the assembled warriors shouted, "No!"

"You have our answer," Shadow told the lieutenant. "Go now." Shadow's dark eyes bored into those of the Crow scout. "If you ever lead the white man against us, I will cut out your miserable heart and feed it to the coyotes!"

The Crow warrior's face turned ashen. Swallowing hard, he wheeled his pony around, dug in his heels, and raced out of our camp as if pursued by a thousand devils. The soldiers followed, though at a more dignified pace.

The warriors were quiet around the campfire that night, and I wondered if they were having second thoughts about surrendering. But then Calf Running began to speak, and I knew, somehow, that he was speaking for all of them, that each warrior present could have related a similar experience. His voice was low and unemotional, as if he were telling a story about someone else. And as he talked, I saw the other braves nod with sympathy and understanding.

"I was only a boy of twelve when it happened," Calf Running began. "My father had decided to visit his brother, who was camped along the headwaters of the Gila River. My three brothers and their wives traveled with us. I remember it was spring and the desert was in bloom. We were in no hurry and covered only ten or fifteen miles a day before making night camp. We were three days from home when we saw the white men. Our women were afraid, but my father told them not to worry. 'We are not at war,' my father said. 'They will know that when they see we have our wives with us.' His words did not calm my mother's fears, so my father tied a white flag around his lance and told my mother to stop worrying and go about her business.

"When the white men saw our white flag, they tied one around the barrel of a rifle and rode into our camp. My father and brothers went to meet them. And were shot down in cold blood. My mother shoved me under her sleeping robes and bid me stay there. Then, grabbing my father's lance—the one with the white flag fluttering from its tip—she charged the man who killed my father. They shot her many times in the head and chest. They shot my brothers' wives, too, but not until they had violated them many times.

"When it was dark, the white men left. But not until they had scalped the bodies of my family and stolen our horses. I saw it all from my hiding place beneath the robes. That night I buried my family where they had fallen. The next day I followed the white eyes. When I caught up with them, I killed them while they slept, slitting their throats as my father had taught me. And I have killed every white man who has since crossed my path."

The Army was as good as its word. Less than a month later two hundred troopers were riding across the desert with orders to wipe out, once and for all, the Cheyenne chief known as Two Hawks Flying, and all those riding with him. Shadow's scouts were good—the best the Indians had—and we knew the Army's every movement, every order, right down to the one that said they were to stay in the field until Two Hawks Flying was dead or in chains.

In October, we knew we were in trouble. By then, it was obvious that the soldiers dogging our heels were veterans all, seasoned Indian fighters who knew what they were doing and how to do it. They did not make foolish mistakes, nor did they underestimate their quarry. They did not fall for the old tricks that had always worked so well. Our ambushes failed. When they saw a half-dozen Indians ride into view, they did not charge blindly after them as so many had done before.

For the first time, I saw Shadow's warriors begin to worry. Not only did the soldiers have us outnumbered almost three to one, but they were better armed and, with the exception of Red Wind and Calf Running's rangy bay gelding, better mounted. Food, or rather the lack of it, became our biggest concern. With the Army hard on our heels, the warriors had little time to hunt, and we were always hungry.

One night Tall Horse, Two Feathers, and Yellow Deer said they thought they could sneak into the soldier camp and steal some food from the mess wagon. Shadow and Calf Running weighed our need against the risk and decided it was worth a try. Shortly after midnight the three volunteers ghosted out of camp. Unable to sleep, I pulled a buffalo robe around my shoulders and went looking for Shadow.

I found him standing alone near the dying embers of our fire. He looked lonely and sad, there in the darkness, and I knew he was thinking of his father, Black Owl, and of the old days when the Indians ruled the land. I knew he was concerned for my welfare, and that of our unborn child, and for the three warriors who even now would be slipping into the soldiers' camp. Wanting to comfort him, I went to his side and lay my hand on his arm.

Wordlessly, Shadow put his arm around my shoulders. We stood thus for perhaps twenty minutes before Shadow said, "They should have been back by now."

The words were no sooner out of his mouth than three gunshots rattled through the darkness. All around us warriors burst from their sleeping robes, weapons in hand, eyes alert.

A long quarter of an hour went by before Tall Horse returned to camp. He was alone, and the warriors exchanged apprehensive glances as they waited for him to speak.

"There were two bluecoats hiding in the wagon," Tall Horse said when he'd caught his breath. "We did not see them until it was too late. Yellow Deer killed one of them before he was shot. Two Feathers was hit as we jumped from the wagon. Three soldiers pounced on him as he fell. I put my knife into one of them as I ran."

"What of Yellow Deer and Two Feathers?" Shadow demanded. "Are they dead?"

"I don't know," Tall Horse said thickly, then keeled over in a dead faint.

Only then did we see the bullet wound in his back. A closer look showed the bullet had passed cleanly through his body. He was lucky, I thought as I bandaged his wound. A little higher and to the left and he would have been dead.

At dawn, Shadow and Calf Running slipped out of camp. They were gone for what seemed an eternity, and I was a nervous wreck when they finally returned.

Shadow's face was a mask of bitter rage as he said, flatly, "Both are dead. Strung up by their heels like dead meat and slit from groin to navel."

"But they died well," Calf Running added proudly. "Even with their guts hanging out, they died like warriors!"

Chapter 14

The days grew shorter, the nights longer and colder, and still the Army pursued us. In late October I sat alone atop a high bluff while the soldiers and Shadow's warriors engaged in a fierce battle on the desert below. Shadow was easily identifiable by his magnificent warbonnet as he cut in and out among the blue-clad men, loosing arrows as quickly and accurately as the troopers fired their rifles. Guiding Red Wind with the pressure of his knees, he rode down a half-dozen soldiers, killing them all. The air was filled with the bloodcurdling warwhoops of a dozen different tribes, punctuated by the agonized screams of wounded horses and the heart-rending cries of dying men. As the morning progressed, a thick haze of dust and powdersmoke rose in the air, obscuring my vision.

I was leaning forward in the saddle, straining my eyes to see which way the battle was going, when a voice spoke beside me.

"Wal, looky here," twanged the voice. "Jest see what I caught!"

With a start, I glanced around and found myself staring into the leering, pock-marked face of a cavalry trooper.

"I reckon I jest ended the war," he drawled, and before I could think or speak or act, he tied my hands behind my back, looped Sunny's reins over his saddle horn, and led me down the back side of the bluff into the soldiers' camp.

In the distance, I could hear the sounds of battle, and I wondered how much longer the fighting would last and what Shadow would do when he discovered I was gone.

When we reached the Army camp, the trooper pulled me roughly from the saddle and propelled me into a large tent. Inside, a man with iron gray hair, a sweeping gray moustache, and cold grey eyes was seated behind a makeshift desk. He looked up, frowning irritably, as I stumbled into the tent.

"Son of a bitch!" he growled. "I send you out to scout the hills and you turn up with a woman!"

280

"Not jest any woman, Major Kelly," the trooper countered with a sly smile. "The woman of Two Hawks Flying."

The major's eyebrows shot up and his gray eyes brightened with interest. "That right, girl?" he demanded.

I felt my cheeks flame as the major's gaze lingered on my swollen belly. The disgust in his eyes made me mad clear through, and I lifted my chin and said, "Yes, I'm his woman. And proud of it!"

Major Kelly snorted. "Yeah? Well, you won't be so high and mighty when you find yourself behind bars for pussyfootin' around with your country's enemies. Why, I wouldn't be surprised if they tossed you and that brat you're carryin' into the pokey and threw away the key!"

Jail! I could not hide the distress his threat caused me. Would they really send me to jail for living with Shadow? And my baby, too? Oh, but surely they would not subject a child to life in prison!

"Stockton, get this Injun lover out of here," Kelly snapped. "And tell High Horse and Cloud I want to see them on the double."

"Yes, sir!" Stockton acknowledged, and hustled me out of the major's tent and into another, smaller one located at the far end of the camp. With a grin, Stockton tied me to a chair. I cringed as one of his hands groped inside my dress, gasped as he squeezed my breast. His breath was foul as, leaning close to my face, he said, "I'll be back to see ya later, honey." Then, laughing softly, he left me alone.

As soon as he was out of sight, I began to try and free myself, but I could not loosen the ropes one bit. Still, I struggled for a good fifteen minutes before I admitted defeat, and as I sat there in that gloomy tent, I was seized with despair. What would I do if Stockton came back? Oh, but surely he was only trying to frighten me. Surely he wouldn't want to bed me. Merciful heavens, I was big as a house! Surely no man, not even the most depraved, would want to bed a woman pregnant with another man's child!

The minutes dragged by. There was an abrupt silence as the distant sounds of battle came to a halt. The sudden quiet was unsettling. Had the Indians won? Or had they ridden off in defeat, leaving me behind. I went cold all over as I saw myself being handed from one trooper to another, to be used and used again until we reached Fort Apache, and I was thrown into prison.

After what seemed hours, two Pawnee scouts came for me. Wordlessly, they untied my hands and motioned me outside.

"Mount up," one ordered gruffly.

"Where are we going?" I asked, trying to keep any trepidation from creeping into my voice.

"To parley with Two Hawks Flying," came the unexpected, but oh so welcome, reply.

Just the mention of Shadow's name routed my fears. I pulled myself into the saddle, offered no resistance as one of the scouts tied my hands to the pommel while the other took Sunny's reins.

Minutes later we approached the battlefield. Both sides had claimed their dead, but the smell of powdersmoke lay heavy in the air. A dead horse lay in the distance, surrounded by vultures. A white flag fluttered in the rising wind. And next to the flag stood Major Kelly, flanked by a dozen dour-faced troopers, all heavily armed.

I felt my heart quicken as I saw Shadow ride up, followed by Calf Running, Tall Horse, No Wind, Black Elk, and Small Bear. They did not dismount.

When it suited him, Shadow could erase all expression from his face. It was a trait all red men seemed to possess. I called it his Indian face. He was wearing it now, and he gave no sign of recognition when he saw me.

"You see, we have your woman," Major Kelly said curtly. "And we will not hesitate to shoot her for a renegade and a traitor unless you and your warriors surrender immediately."

Shadow glanced briefly in my direction, and for the life of me all I could think of was that I must look a mess. Then he was staring hard at Major Kelly.

"I cannot give you a decision until I counsel with my warriors," he responded tersely in English. "I do not command them as you command your Army. It is for them to decide if we fight, or if we surrender."

Major Kelly looked skeptical until the two Pawnee scouts affirmed Shadow's words. Then, still certain he held the upper hand, he said, coldly, "Very well. You have until dawn tomorrow to give me your decision. If you and your braves have not surrendered by then, your woman will be shot."

Shadow nodded curtly and, without a glance in my direction, pulled Red Wind into a rearing turn and galloped away, followed by his warriors.

Major Kelly swore under his breath. "Stockton, take the woman back to your tent and keep an eye on her. Cloud, you and High Horse keep watch outside. I want to see the rest of you in my quarters immediately."

My mind was in turmoil as Stockton led me away. I told myself the Major had no authority to execute me if Shadow refused to surrender, that he was only bluffing. The words "traitor" and "treason" sounded ugly, and I knew the penalty could very well be death. But not here and now. Major Kelly had no right to determine my fate. I was entitled to a trial before a jury. And yet, who would ever know or care if Kelly had me shot? The soldiers all looked at me with contempt, hating me because I lived with an Indian.

As we approached Stockton's tent, he leaned over and patted my cheek, and suddenly the thought of a firing squad didn't seem so bad. I tried to convince myself that Stockton could not possibly find me attractive, that I had misread the hungry look in his eyes. But I was shaking all over when he lifted me from my horse.

I stared at his tent, thinking I would rather walk into hell than be alone with Stockton. He gave me a little push from behind, and I lurched forward. My legs went weak as he followed me inside and secured the tent flap. I suddenly felt terribly alone and vulnerable, and I knew that if I screamed for help, no one would come. It was a terrible feeling, knowing I was completely at this man's mercy, that he could do whatever he pleased without fear of reprisals.

I swallowed hard as he turned to face me,

and I went cold all over as I realized my worst fears were about to come true.

"Looks like we're gonna be together all night," Stockton drawled, "so you might jest as wal stretch out on thet there bunk and make yourself to home."

"N. . .no, thank you," I stammered. "I'll just sit over there in the chair."

Stockton's face got very ugly very fast. "You'd best do as I say, Injun lover!" he snapped, and backhanded me twice across the mouth.

The threat of another blow and the possibility that he might do something to injure my child prompted me to do as bidden. The springs creaked as I sank down on the thin mattress.

I did not protest when he tied my hands and feet to the cot's frame. Resigned, I lay cold and unmoving as he began to kiss me, his blubbery lips slobbering over my face and neck, wetting the bodice of my dress. His hands squeezed my breasts until they ached and then, grinning like a cat playing with a mouse, he reached under my buckskin skirt. His hands were big and calloused, covered with coarse black hair; his fingernails were broken and dirty, and I shuddered as I felt his filthy hands probe between my thighs.

He was panting now, his face red and

mottled, his yellow eyes aglitter with desire as he shucked his shirt and began fumbling with his belt buckle. Naked, he was even more loathsome. His body was flabby and stark white save for the tangled mass of curly black hair matted on his chest. I thought briefly of Shadow's magnificent physique, all lean and bronze and ridged with muscle. And then there was no more time for thought. There was only fear and revulsion as Stockton lowered himself over me, his breath hot and foul as he began to whisper obscenities in my ear.

Tied hand and foot, I could not resist, but could only pray he would finish quickly and leave me alone.

There was a sudden stab of pain as he thrust into me, and I bit my lips to keep from screaming, but the touch of his hands pawing my flesh and the driving force of his manhood violating my body was more than I could bear. With a strangled sob, I began to retch.

Stockton swore as a rush of hot green vomit spewed from my mouth and dribbled down his neck. Still cursing, he reared up and began to slap me, forehand and back-hand, again and again until my face was numb. He was still hitting me when a dusky shape loomed out of the darkness and dragged him off me.

It was Shadow.

Stockton's face went fish-belly white when he saw the savage hatred glittering in Shadow's cold black eyes and the foot-long knife in his hand. Wild-eyed with fright, the trooper opened his mouth to scream but all that emerged was a hoarse cry of fear. And then Shadow was on him, hacking and stabbing with terrible fury, until what had once been a man was nothing but a grotesque pile of butchered meat.

Shadow's hands looked as if they had been dipped in red dye when he pulled the knife from Stockton's body for the last time. His breath came in short hard gasps, as if he'd been running a great distance, and his eyes blazed like twin coals in hell as he stared at the thing that had been a living breathing human being only moments before.

Feeling my shocked gaze, Shadow looked up. Magically, the enraged killer vanished and the man I loved took his place. He drew a deep breath, held it for stretched seconds before he let it out in a long slow sigh. When I started to speak, he motioned me to silence. Then, after wiping his bloodied hands on the blanket folded across the foot of the bed, he cut me free.

Shadow had gained entrance to the tent by slashing a hole at the rear, and we left by the same way. I grimaced when I saw the bodies of High Horse and Cloud sprawled in the dirt, their throats cut from ear to ear.

And then we were running for cover, and when I could run no further, Shadow carried me the last hundred yards to where Red Wind was waiting. Riding hard, we caught up with the warriors in a shallow gully far to the south of the soldier camp.

Calf Running smiled as he handed me Sunny's reins. "Welcome home, Han-nah," he said cheerfully. His eyes twinkled expectantly as he turned to Shadow and asked, "How many?"

"Three," Shadow answered tersely.

The Apache's grin broadened as he shouted, "Enjuh! Cat-ra-ra ata un Innas yudastcin!" which, roughly translated meant: curses and destruction on all white bastards.

In November it rained. And rained. The ground turned to slush and sucked hungrily at the horses feet as they plodded through it. Great drum rolls of thunder shook the earth, and lightning lanced the darkened skies with scorching fingers of flame. The wind blew continually, its voice low and mournful like the cry of a grieving Cheyenne squaw, or high and shrill like the wail of a tormented soul lost in the bowels of hell. There were teeth in the wind that cut through our clothing like sharp knives, so that we were always cold, always wet. And always hungry. I had been hungry before but never like this. I'd once heard an old mountain man say you weren't really hungry until you were "ready to eat a horse with the hide on." Well, I was hungry enough to eat the hide and the hoofs, too!

I knew the warriors were every bit as cold and hungry as I was, but there were no complaints.

"At least we are free men," Calf Running remarked one miserable night, and that seemed to be the attitude of all the braves.

But I could not help wondering, as I choked down a hunk of cold, half-cooked venison, how life on the reservation could possibly be any worse than slogging through the ankle-deep mud with nothing but a damp buffalo robe to turn away the wind and rain, and nothing to eat but a slice of raw meat. I felt as though I were trapped between two nightmares and I didn't know which was worse—the stark reality of those awful days, or the terrifying dreams that haunted my sleep. Night after night I woke in tears as I relived the unspeakable horror of what had happened in the soldiers' camp. Often I woke screaming as I imagined Stockton's hands exploring my flesh, or felt the weight of his body crushing mine. Again and again I saw Shadow rise up out of nowhere like an avenging angel. Sometimes I woke in a cold sweat, trembling in the dark, as I recalled the awful look of rage and hate on Shadow's face as he repeatedly drove his knife into Stockton's cowering flesh.

For the first time since I'd known Shadow there was a gulf between us, a breach of my own making. I knew Shadow was waiting for me to go to him, but I could not. I felt ugly and dirty and though I washed and washed, I could not wash away the awful memory of that night.

We had not been intimate for a long time, Shadow and I, partly because of my desire to be left alone, and partly because we no longer had any privacy now that our lodge was gone, lost in our last hurried flight from the soldiers.

A week went by. And then another. And then, one cool crisp night when the world was quiet and the midnight sky sparkled with the glow of a million twinkling stars, Shadow took me by the hand and led me away from camp. Under the leafy umbrella of a wind-blown pine, he made love to me as gently and tenderly as ever a man loved a woman. And as his hands touched my flesh, and his whispered words of endearment tickled my ear, all the horror and shame and revulsion I'd felt since that awful night in Stockton's tent melted away.

Afterward, as we lay content in each other's arms, I knew a deep sense of peace and happiness, a warm sense of being back where I belonged. Shadow placed his hand on my belly, chuckled softly as he felt his child's lusty kick, and in that golden moment the war and the soldiers seemed far away. Nothing mattered but the love we shared and the child stirring beneath my heart.

Chapter 15

Despite wind and rain and snow, the soldiers pursued us, relentless as wolves on the scent of a wounded buffalo calf. And now they rode in relays—one group pushing us until their horses tired, then dropping back to rest while the next group took up the chase, and so on. Part of their number always were mounted on rested horses while our ponies grew increasingly weary. Strangely, the troopers seemed to be in no hurry to overtake us, but were content to dog our heels. Shadow conjectured they were hoping to run us into the ground and take us without a fight. If Major Kelly thought that, I mused disdainfully, then Major Kelly was a fool, for Shadow's men would never surrender. Lean as winter-starved lobos, tough as pte's hide, Shadow's warriors would fight to the death. And late one bleak afternoon they proved it.

We were crossing a wind-ravaged meadow up in the high country when Major Kelly caught up with us. Tired and hungry, mounted on gaunt ponies ready to drop, the warriors turned to fight like wolves at bay. Shadow left me in a narrow ravine camouflaged by a tangled mass of dead brush. Huddling there, I heard his exultant battle cry as he joined his warriors.

"Ho, brothers! It is a good day to die!"

And die they did. Outnumbered by soldiers armed with better weapons and mounted on rested horses, the Indians never had a chance. Thirty of them were killed in the first frenetic clash, half that many wounded. And still they fought, bloody but unbowed, until Shadow called a retreat. The Indians scattered like ashes in a high wind, riding hard for the cover of the wooded hills. Unaccountably, Major Kelly did not pursue us. Perhaps he was leary of searching the dense forest; perhaps he was just tired. Who can say?

Shadow and I rode hard until dark, then took shelter in a cutbank arroyo. Like magic, the warriors joined us, materializing like wraiths out of the thick darkness. There was no graze for our horses, nor wood for a fire.

The men shared what water they had with their mounts, then broke out the last of their rations. Before the moon came up, ten of the wounded died.

Later, when the dead were buried and the camp was quiet, Shadow called his braves together. Where there had once been seventy warriors, there were now only thirty. For a moment he stood quietly before them, his dark eyes touching each solemn face.

"You have fought well," he said proudly. "Among all the tribes, there are no finer warriors, none braver than those gathered here this night or lying dead on the field of battle. Tomorrow, the soldiers will attack again. I think we will not be here. I think we will slip away, one by one, while it is dark, and go home."

A quick murmur of dissent rose from the warriors as they realized what Shadow was saying, but Shadow paid them no heed as he went on.

"Our food is gone, our ammunition is low, our ponies are tired. If we split up now, we may yet fight another day. If we stay, I think the soldiers will rub us out."

"Two Hawks Flying is right," Calf Running said loyally. "Let us go home for the winter. In the Season of New Grass we can fight again."

Black Elk rose to his feet. For a long time

he had wanted to take Shadow's place as chief, and now he saw his chance. Head high, he strutted to the center of the group.

"Let us fight now!" he urged. "If Two Hawks Flying has lost his courage, I will lead you!"

"But who will follow?" Calf Running asked contemptuously. "Two Hawks Flying speaks wisdom. We have less than thirty warriors fit to fight. My rifle is empty, and my quiver carries but two arrows." He grinned, thumping his chest with his hand. "I am as brave as the next man, but not so brave that I think I can defeat the bluecoats with two arrows!"

The warriors laughed, but their laughter was tinged with bitterness.

When it was quiet, Shadow said, "It is good to fight, and you have fought hard and long. But we knew in the beginning that this was a fight we could not win. Let it be as I have said. We will leave this place tonight, a few at a time, and when the soldiers come tomorrow, they will find only the wind."

Shadow's nostrils flared as he sniffed the air. "Ghost Face is coming," he predicted, smiling faintly. "By dawn, our tracks will be covered with snow."

There was a moment of silence and though the warriors' faces remained impassive, it seemed to me that the spirit of each man present reached out to touch that of his brother. I felt a lump rise in my throat as I gazed at that quiet group of men. Warriors all, there was a special closeness between them, a bond of love and understanding stronger than words.

There were no spoken farewells.

Abruptly, Tall Horse rose to his feet, saying, "Hopo! Let's go!" And he left the circle, followed by two Sioux warriors.

Others followed in twos and threes, silent as the dark clouds swirling overhead.

Calf Running and the other Chiricahua Apaches were the last to leave. Gravely, Calf Running and Shadow clasped hands.

"It was a good fight, chi-ca-say," Calf Running said, using the Apache words for "my brother." And then he was gone, lost in the night.

I was sorry to see Calf Running go. He was a good man, a brave warrior, and a loyal friend. I knew Shadow would miss him even more than I. They had spent many a long night in quiet conversation, reminiscing over the old days that were forever gone, contemplating the future which loomed bleak and without hope.

And so we were alone again, Shadow and I. With the ease of long practice, I quickly packed our few belongings and loaded them on my horse.

The first snowflakes began to fall as we rode out of the arroyo and headed east.

At dawn, Shadow drew rein beneath a rocky overhang. Behind us, a thick blanket of snow covered the ground, and even before we dismounted, large lacy flakes filled our tracks. Cold and exhausted after our long ride, I spread our robes in the driest spot I could find and then, with my back aching and my stomach rumbling for food, I curled up in my robe and fell asleep.

The sun was high overhead when I awoke to find Shadow sitting beside me. Wordlessly, I rose to my feet, and in a few minutes we were riding again.

The days and nights that followed stretched into one long nightmare of cold and hunger. Our horses suffered, too. They were nothing but skin and bones beneath their shaggy winter coats, and I could not help feeling sorry for them as they pawed through the deep snow for grass that wasn't there. I was hungry all the time, and I wondered how lack of nourishment and rest would affect my unborn child.

Shadow had only three rounds left in his rifle and a handful of arrows for the bow. We ate whatever he could catch: mice, lizards, snakes, and an occasional squirrel if we were lucky. Once, I would have turned away from such disgusting fare, but now I ate it gladly and wished for more.

Like hunted beasts, we fled our pursuers. I wondered, numbly, why they didn't give up. Why couldn't they just go home where they belonged and leave us in peace? We could do no more harm to them now.

In late November, we came upon a solitary cabin set in a small valley. We sat out of sight for over an hour, watching, until Shadow decided the place must be empty, for there was no sign of life. There were no animals in sight, no smoke from the chimney.

We rode slowly down the hillside, dismounted, and trudged through the snow to the front door. Rifle drawn, Shadow pushed the door open and stepped inside. I followed close on his heels, anxious to get out of the wind.

The cabin was not deserted. An old man and woman lay snuggled together on a mattress in a corner of the one room shack. They turned, startled, as I closed the door, and then their faces turned pale as the snow when they saw Shadow and the rifle in his hand.

"Food," Shadow said. "Get some quickly."

"We don't have much," the man said, his rheumy brown eyes focused on the rifle. "Jest a little bacon and some coffee."

"Fix it," Shadow demanded curtly.

The woman scrambled out of the covers, pulling a blanket across her shoulders for warmth. "Don't hurt my man, please," she begged. "He can't do you no harm."

I saw then that the old man had only one arm, and it was badly malformed, the hand twisted into a permanent fist.

I sat on the edge of the hearth, my robe drawn tight against the cold that was only a little less severe inside than out. There was no furniture in the cabin; everything made of wood had been burned, so that only an old stove remained.

Shadow remained standing in the middle of the room, his rifle unwavering, his face impassive.

Fear made the woman clumsy, and she cut her finger as she sliced the bacon and spilled some of the precious coffee as she put it on to boil.

Soon the little cabin was fragrant with the aroma of frying bacon and coffee, and my mouth began to water.

Shadow and I ate ravenously. The couple watched, silent, as we licked the last of the grease from our fingertips. The coffee was bitter, but it was hot, and I sighed with regret as I drained the last drops from my cup.

The taut silence in the shack grew even worse as Shadow jacked a round into the breech of his Winchester.

"Please," the woman begged. "We have done nothing to you." Two large tears rolled down her sunken cheeks.

"Don't beg," the old man told his wife. "Don't you have no pride?"

The old woman turned to me in desperation. "You're a white woman. Please have mercy on us."

"She ain't white!" the old man said with a sneer.

"She is so," argued the old woman. "Look at that red hair."

"Any woman what takes up with a buck is no better than a squaw," the man muttered stubbornly, then quickly shut his mouth as Shadow's face grew dark with anger.

Laying my hand on Shadow's arm, I said, in Cheyenne, "Please ignore his words. He is frightened and doesn't mean what he says."

"He is like all whites, full of hate for anyone who does not have a pale skin."

"Shadow, please. . .No more killing."

"It is no kindness to spare their lives. They deserve to die, and we need the shelter of their house."

"Shadow, no more killing. It is enough."

I rarely argued with him, and he did not like it.

"The baby is due any day," he said in a tight voice. "You cannot have it outside in the snow."

"I will not have it here!"

"Hannah, be reasonable. Think of the baby."

"I am, and I will not have our child born in a house where murder has been done. I will not let our child be the cause of someone's death."

With a sigh, Shadow relented. "Very well. But I insist we spend the night here. You could use a good rest out of the wind."

I couldn't argue with that, nor did I object when Shadow evicted the man from the makeshift bed so I could lay down. The mattress was lumpy, the single sheet dingy, but I didn't care. It was better than the hard cold ground, and I was asleep as soon as my head hit the pillow.

I awoke twelve hours later, feeling greatly refreshed. Shadow had spent the night watching the elderly couple, and he looked bone weary. But when I suggested he get some sleep, he refused, and we left the cabin.

"Thank you," I said.

"It was no kindness to leave them alive," Shadow said. "They will soon starve. Or freeze from the cold. A bullet would have been merciful."

"I could not have them on my conscience. I feel bad enough that we took the last of their food."

"We have all done things we are ashamed of, Hannah. We do what we must to survive."

"There is no honor in stealing from people who are old and weak and defenseless. We should be ashamed."

My words hurt him, and I was immediately contrite. What he had done, he had done for me and our child. "I'm sorry," I murmured. "Forgive me."

"There is nothing to forgive," he said, and we never spoke of it again.

In early December it appeared we had finally lost our pursuers. We rode hard the next few days just to make sure, rising at dawn and traveling 'til dark, stopping now and then to rest the horses. Once, Shadow spotted a deer, but the range was too far for the bow, and he dared not risk a rifle shot that might attract any soldiers in the area to our position. So we rode on.

A few miles later we drew rein at the foot of a snow-covered hillside. I was so tired and achy I could hardly move. For the first time since I had known him, Shadow helped me dismount. Then, shouldering his rifle and leading both horses, he led the way to a small cave cut high in the hillside. It was just large enough for the two of us. Inside, I spread our blankets while Shadow tethered Sunny to an old tree stump. Red Wind would not stray far, and Shadow left the big stud loose to forage as best he could.

I had been bothered by intermittent pains all that day, and I began to wish New Leaf was with us. The baby was due in a few days, and I was afraid. What if something went wrong? What if I had no milk? What if the baby was breech? There were so many things that could go wrong, and I knew so little.

Shadow entered the cave then. As always, he had only to look at my face to know what I was thinking. Murmuring my name, he sat down beside me and took me in his arms. His mere presence routed my fears, and I fell asleep with my head pillowed on his chest.

When I opened my eyes, it was morning, and I was alone. A muffled rifle shot brought me to my feet, my heart in my throat, as I scrambled toward the mouth of the cavern. Had the soldiers found us? Was Shadow dead? Hurt? But no, there he was, riding up the hill toward me, a deer carcass slung over Red Wind's withers.

We had not had anything to eat in two days, and my mouth began to water as I hastily built a small fire in the rear of the cave. I was rummaging in one of the packs for a cook pot when the pain hit. Far worse than any of the others, it tore through me like a dull knife. Choking back a sob, I sank down on my sleeping robe.

"Shadow, hurry," I whispered. "Please hurry. I'm afraid."

Miraculously, he was there. Seeing me, he dropped the carcass and hurried to my side.

"Hannah?"

"It's time," I gasped. "Oh, Shadow, I'm so afraid!"

"Do not be," he said, brushing a wisp of hair from my face. "Everything will be all right."

I nodded weakly, then reached for his hand as another contraction caught me unawares.

Shadow remained at my side all morning, his face drawn with worry as he wiped the sweat from my brow. The contractions came harder and faster as the day wore on, and I squeezed Shadow's hands until they were red and swollen, clinging to him as a drowning man clings to a lifeline.

Sometimes he talked to me of the old days, and I concentrated on every word, trying to focus on what he was saying rather than the pains that seemed to be ripping me apart. He told me of his mother, and how she had died of the white man's spotted sickness when he was only five.

"You are like her, Hannah," he said softly. "Good and kind and beautiful. Our son will be lucky to have you for his mother."

His words warmed my soul. I was the lucky one, I thought. Lucky to have Shadow for my husband and the father of my child.

When my back began to ache, he rubbed it, his hands gently kneading the pain. I felt as if I had been in labor for days, and a new fear took hold of me as all the awful tales of childbirth I had ever heard surfaced within me— tales of women who were in labor for days and days, stories of women who struggled for hours to bring forth a child that was dead, nightmare tales of women who died in childbirth. . . .

Unable to help myself, I began to cry. I was too young to die. I wanted to see my baby, to grow old with Shadow, to feel his arms around me.

Shadow whispered my name as he took me into his arms. Oh, the strength and comfort in his embrace, the magical solace I found as he held me, gently rocking me back and forth as if I were a child myself.

Outside, a light rain began to fall. It was

soon over, and the world was deathly still, as if every living creature were holding its breath. And then, from somewhere in the distance, a horse whinnied. Quick as a cat, Shadow was at the mouth of the cave.

"Major Kelly's scouts have found us, haven't they?" I asked.

"It is not Kelly."

"Not Kelly. Who, then?"

"It is the Seventh," Shadow answered quietly, and then he laughed. "I suspect they have come to get even for Custer. I knew they would never forgive us for that."

"Shadow, you've got to get out of here!" I cried, frantic for his safety. "Go now, before it's too late."

"It is already too late," he replied tonelessly.

Rising, he removed his buckskin shirt. Then, while I watched, he began to paint his face and chest for war. My pains were temporarily forgotten as I watched him apply vermillion paint to his torso, the broad zigzag slashes like ribbons of blood across his flesh. Smaller, similar slashes marked his cheeks.

That done, he reached for his warbonnet. And Shadow, the man, became Two Hawks Flying, the warrior. I knew he was going out to meet the soldiers, that he intended to die fighting like the proud Cheyenne warrior he was, with a weapon in his hand and a last prayer to Man Above on his lips. And though I knew he didn't have a chance in a million if he went out of the cave armed and ready to fight, and though I knew he would surrender if I but asked him to, I could not voice the words.

When he was ready, he took my hand in his, and I felt my heart swell with love for the tall, handsome man kneeling at my side.

"I love you, Hannah," he said quietly. "See that our son grows brave and strong. Never let him forget that he carries the blood of many great Cheyenne warriors in his veins."

"I won't," I promised, choking back a sob as he left the cave without a backward glance.

I heard him call Red Wind, and in my mind's eye I saw Shadow swing aboard the tall stallion with the effortless grace I had always admired. And suddenly I knew I had to see him one last time.

Teeth clenched, I struggled to my knees and crawled to the entrance to the cave. I had to stop twice as pains doubled me in half, but I went determinedly forward.

I was breathing hard when I reached the mouth of the cave. Below, the soldiers were riding toward the hill in neat columns of two. They made a colorful sight, with their hard blue uniforms and the red and white guidon of the Seventh Cavalry fluttering in the afternoon breeze. Riding point were two Pawnee scouts, easily identified by their roached scalplocks. What happened next happened very fast.

Shadow had always harbored a deep hatred for the Indians that scouted for the Army, and in less time than it takes to tell, he threw his rifle to his shoulder and with his last two bullets killed the two Indian scouts.

The dead warriors had no sooner hit the ground than six troopers broke from the others and rode forward at a gallop, firing as they came. Lead whined into the hillside around Shadow, gouging great chunks of dirt from the earth, and my mind screamed for him to run, to hide. But he might have been a statue carved from stone.

And then the soldiers were too close to miss. I saw one of them line his sights on Shadow's chest and I screamed, "Josh, no!" and stumbled out of the cave.

And then I was falling, rolling head over heels down the icy hillside. A terrible pain stabbed through me, followed by a rush of warm water, and I screamed Shadow's name as I felt myself being torn in half. And then I was falling again, falling into a deep black void. My last conscious thought was that I was dying, and I was glad, because I knew Shadow was dead, too.

Chapter 16
Winter 1877 - Spring 1878

Voices. Voices calling my name. Stubbornly, I ignored them, content to drift in the velvety black shroud of darkness that cradled me like loving arms. Beyond the darkness loomed the shadow of death, more welcome than the pain and grief that waited for me in the land of the living. Everyone I had ever loved was dead—my parents, Orin, David, Shadow. Dead, all dead. Waiting for me.

Eager to join them, I burrowed deeper into the soft eternal darkness.

"Hannah. Hannah!"

A different voice summoned me, and I struggled out of the web of death's embrace, crying his name.

"Shadow!"

"I am here."

"Shadow, help me," I begged. "Hold me. Please hold me."

Strong arms encircled me, but they were not Shadow's arms; when I opened my eyes, it was Joshua holding me. Shadow stood a few feet away, his hands bound behind his back. His mouth was bloody where someone had struck him.

"Shadow," I whimpered. "I want Shadow."

As if from far away I heard Joshua say, "Hopkins, turn the redskin loose."

"Captain wouldn't like it," the corporal remarked laconically.

"The Captain ain't here," Joshua retorted succinctly. "And if you don't want to spend the next six months mucking out the tables, you'd best do as you're told!"

Hopkins grumbled something unintelligible under his breath as he untied Shadow's hands, and then Shadow was beside me, his arms closing around me. His dark eyes were sad, and a sudden bolt of fear pierced my soul.

"The baby?" I whispered. "Where's my baby?"

"He is dead, Hannah."

Dead, I thought dully. My son is dead.

But the words had no meaning.

Closing my eyes, I fell asleep in the warm refuge of Shadow's arms.

I spent the next few days in a strange world of light and shadow. Sometimes I drifted on a soft, fluffy cloud—far beyond the reach of pain or sorrow, content to float in timeless space. Sometimes I was flung into the past, and I frolicked through my childhood all over again, joyously caught up in the frivolities of youth, with no cares my mother could not solve with a smile and a kiss and no fears my father could not chase away.

Three days after I lost the baby I opened my eyes to reality and burst into tears. I cried for hours—grieving for the dead child I had never seen, for Shadow who was bound hand and foot and held under heavy guard, and lastly for myself.

Joshua was very kind to me. He'd been a boy when he left Bear Valley, but he was a man now, hardened by the rigors of Army life and by the harsh lessons he'd learned in the field. His hatred for Indians had grown stronger, as had his love for hard liquor and thin black cigars. Young and ambitious, he had risen quickly in the ranks and was already a lieutenant.

Josh spent a good deal of time at my side.

We reminisced about our childhood days in Bear Valley and the fun we had shared. Oh, for those carefree days, I thought wistfully, of golden summer afternoons at the river crossing and quiet nights in the warm shelter of my father's house. How I wished I could fly to my mother's comforting arms once more and have her kiss away my hurt. If only I could lay my troubles on Pa's broad shoulders and listen to his wise words of counsel!

"Hannah?"

Joshua's voice called me to the present.

"What? . . . Oh, I'm sorry, Josh, I must have been daydreaming."

"Remembering the good old days?" he teased.

"Yes," I admitted. "Remember the time Orin and I ran away? I can't remember now where we were going. But I remember you came after us, hollering that your mother's Morgan mare was having her baby. We got so excited, we forgot all about running away."

"I remember," Josh said in a thin voice. "I remember that I was jealous of you even then. Hannah, you can't imagine how surprised I was to see you come tumbling out of that cave. I thought you'd been killed when the Indians burned your father out."

"I was surprised to see you, too," I replied.

"I was sure you'd been killed with Custer."

"A few of us were lucky that day," he remarked bitterly. His eyes probed mine for a long time before he said, in a husky tone, "I still love you, Hannah, as much as I ever did."

"Josh. . ."

"Let me talk," he said, placing his hand over my mouth. "I know you think you're in love with that Cheyenne buck but he's got a short future, and when he's gone, you'll be all alone. I want to take care of you, Hannah. Forever. . .if you'll let me."

I brushed his hand aside. "A short future!" I exclaimed. "What do you mean by that?"

"He's sure to hang when we reach the fort."

Hang! I had supposed they would send Shadow to prison or confine him to some far-away reservation, but hanging! Such a thing had never entered my mind.

Stricken, I whispered, "Oh, no. Josh, please do something."

"There's nothing I can do."

"You can try, can't you?" I snapped. "After all, he saved your life once, remember?"

"I remember," Josh acknowledged grudgingly. "And I remember riding down the valley of the Little Big Horn and seeing

what those damn savages did to Custer, too!
I swore then and there that I'd get even, or
damn well die trying. And when I heard that
your precious Two Hawks Flying was
raising hell from the Dakotas to Arizona, I
went to General Terry and told him how I
felt. Terry'd been in that valley, and he
understood. He let me handpick as many
men as I felt I needed to hunt him down."
Josh laughed bitterly. "And after all my
planning, Kelly nearly beat me to it."

"Major Kelly was a fool," I remarked
contemptuously.

"Yeah," Josh agreed, grinning. "He's gone
back to Fort Grant with his tail tucked between his legs." Joshua's smile broadened.
"What the hell! I got what I wanted, and I
might even get a promotion out of it."

"Josh, you will try to help Shadow, won't
you? Promise me?"

"I'll try," he agreed reluctantly. "But he's
a troublemaker, Hannah, and the Army
wants him out of the way by spring. Permanently out of the way!"

I slept the rest of the day. When I awoke,
it was dinner time. I picked at my food, not
tasting it, more concerned with Shadow's
wellbeing than my own.

Shadow's hands and feet were tightly
bound. And there were several nasty looking

bruises, and a shallow gash on his face where someone had struck him.

Just now, a dour-faced Corporal Hopkins was trying to force a slice of cold meat into Shadow's mouth. When I remarked on this to Joshua, he merely shrugged, saying, "He hasn't eaten a bite in three days, but I reckon he'll give in when he gets hungry enough."

"Three days!" I exclaimed. "He must be starved."

"Well, if he is, it's his own fault. All he has to do is open his mouth."

All he has to do is open his mouth, I thought. Such a little thing, and yet he'd never do it. Not in a million years.

"He'll never accept food from an enemy," I remarked quietly.

"Then he'll go hungry."

"Couldn't you untie his hands for just a little while?"

"No."

"Would it be all right if I fed him?"

Josh did not answer at once; then, with an impatient gesture, he muttered, "Go ahead, if it will make you happy."

Corporal Hopkins looked vastly relieved when I took the plate from his hand and sent him away. Kneeling, I speared a fresh slice of meat and offered it to Shadow, but he made no move to take it, nor did he acknowledge my presence. Back straight, head high, he stared past me as if I wasn't there.

"Shadow," I whispered. "Please eat."

Almost imperceptibly, he shook his head.

"Please," I implored. "Do it for me."

Some of the anger drained out of him, and he said very quietly, "All right, Hannah," and let me feed him.

He must have been starving after three days without food or water, yet he ate slowly, drank sparingly, and finished only half of the meal. It was his pride at work, I thought—that stubborn arrogant pride that was as much a part of him as the color of his skin, pride so strong that he'd remain hungry rather than let Josh and the others see just how hungry he really was.

"How are you, Hannah?" he asked in Cheyenne, then grunted with pain as one of the troopers guarding him jabbed him in the back with the butt of his rifle.

"Speak English, redskin!" the trooper demanded brusquely and raised his rifle again, daring Shadow to disobey.

A cold rage burned in Shadow's eyes but before he could say or do anything, I quickly stepped between him and the trooper and said, "I'm fine, just fine."

Shadow nodded, his dark eyes fathomless, and then Joshua came up beside me, curtailing further conversation. Casting a contemptuous glance at Shadow, Joshua insisted I join him by the fire, and when I seemed reluctant to do so, he took me possessively by the arm and led me away.

The next morning I stood staring down at the little mound of freshly turned earth that marked my son's grave. Tears pricked my eyes as I bid him a silent farewell, and I was sorely tempted to throw myself across his grave and give voice to my sorrow as the Cheyenne women did. I had once thought it barbaric when the squaws slashed their flesh and hacked off their hair to express their grief, but now I understood. And understanding, I would have relished the pain if it would have eased the gnawing ache in my breast.

Some yards beyond, Shadow sat cross-legged on the hard ground, flanked by two heavily armed troopers. I had not been alone with him since the day I lost the baby, and I yearned to speak with him privately and hear his voice whispering that he loved me, assuring me everything would be all right. I searched his face for some clue as to what he was thinking, but he was wearing his Indian face, and I could not penetrate that impassive mask.

Five days after I lost the baby I felt well enough to travel. Joshua was all gentle concern as he bundled me onto a travois rigged behind Sunny. It was rather pleasant, lying there in the pale sunlight, and I watched through heavy-lidded eyes as Josh's men packed their gear and saddled their mounts. Earlier in the day, the troopers had drawn lots to determine how to divide Shadow's few personal belongings. "The spoils of war," the men had said, laughing, though I saw little humor in the situation.

Shadow's rifle had gone to a young, freckle-faced private; his hunting knife went to a lantern-jawed sergeant. Over my protests, Shadow's sacred medicine bundle had gone to a hollow-cheeked veteran who had taken a quick look at the contents, dumped them out, and filled the deerskin pouch with tobacco. Not surprisingly, Josh decided to keep Shadow's beautifully wrought warbonnet for himself.

Red Wind had gone to Corporal Hopkins, who was even now saddling the big red stud. The stallion humped his back as Hopkins cinched his McClellan down tight and fought against the bit as Hopkins prepared to mount. But Red Wind, who was usually as docile as old Nellie unless there was another stallion around, refused to stand. Ears laid back, teeth bared, he fought Hopkins' hold on the reins, snorting and sidestepping each time the corporal reached for a stirrup.

Angry and impatient, Hopkins called for help, and two troopers sprang to his aid, only to retreat before the stallion's flashing hooves and snapping jaws. It took Hopkins the better part of fifteen minutes to get into the saddle, and when he finally made it, all hell broke loose.

Indian born and bred, Red Wind had never felt the weight of a saddle on his back nor tasted a bit between his teeth. Little wonder that he commenced pitching and bucking like a loco bronc. The watching troopers stomped and hollered like cowboys at a rodeo as the stallion exploded across the slushy ground. Hopkins cussed like a veteran muleskinner as he raked his spurs over the stud's sleek red flanks. Accustomed to the gentle touch of Shadow's moccasined heels, Red Wind screamed with pain and rage at this new indignity. Again and again Hopkins roweled the stallion's flanks until the animal's sides were flecked with blood and lather and he stood trembling in the sun, proud head hanging low, sides heaving.

Hopkins smiled as the troopers cheered him. He was still smiling when Red Wind reared straight up and pitched over backwards.

Hopkins hollered, "Oh, shit!" as he kicked

free of the stirrups and hurled himself from the saddle, barely managing to roll out of harm's way as eleven hundred pounds of twisting horseflesh crashed to the earth.

Man and beast scrambled to their feet simultaneously. Ears back, teeth bared, Red Wind hurtled toward Hopkins. A lot of men would have panicked at such a time, but Hopkins stood steady as a rock as he unholstered his service revolver and shot the enraged stallion between the eyes. Red Wind fell heavily, kicked once, and died.

"Damned outlaw!" Hopkins muttered, and turned away.

Shadow's face was as something carved from granite as he stared at Red Wind's blood-spattered carcass. Shadow and Red Wind—they had been inseparable. I remembered Shadow telling me how long it had taken to train the stallion to hand and heel and voice; I recalled the pride and affection in his eyes when he told me how Red Wind had once saved his life by dragging him from the field of battle when he was wounded and unable to ride.

Shadow's face remained inscrutable, but I knew he was seething inside and that, had his hands been free and unfettered, he would have killed Hopkins then and there. His eyes followed the corporal as Hopkins swaggered over to the remuda, and I was chilled by the implacable hatred I saw glittering in Shadow's black eyes as Hopkins quickly roped and saddled another mount.

It was a long arduous ride to Fort Apache. Joshua rode beside me, ever concerned for my welfare. I knew that, but for me, they would have reached the fort much sooner, but Josh called a halt to the day's travel whenever he thought I looked too weary to go on. I was grateful for his concern, for I was always tired, and riding was harder than I had thought it would be. Josh made sure that I was warm enough at night, insisting that my bedroll be spread close to the fire. He took great pains to see that I had plenty of good hot food, even though I had no appetite.

Christmas came, and that night a few of the troopers got together and sang Christmas carols. I wept softly as I thought of Mary giving birth to her Son in a lowly stable, and I wept for my own son, buried in an unmarked grave in a hostile land.

My arms ached to hold the child I had never held nor seen. Sometimes I wondered if I had really had a child. Perhaps I had imagined it all. Perhaps it was just a bad dream. Perhaps I was dreaming even now.

But it was not a dream, for my breasts were heavy, and the bodice of my doeskin dress was stained with milk.

Often, when Joshua spoke to me, I did not hear him. My baby was dead, and the man I loved more than my own life had no future but a rope. My whole world was falling apart, and all Joshua could talk about were his plans for the future and for us. I wondered how he could be so insensitive. How could he even think I would consider marrying him when Shadow was still very much alive?

Shadow. How my heart ached for him. His hands had been tightly bound behind his back for a week. Hopkins released Shadow twice a day so he could relieve himself. Other than that, he was tied up and under guard. I was sure his arms were sore from being restrained so long. His wrists were raw from the constant chafing of the rope. But his expression remained inscrutable. Head held high and proud, he rode between Hopkins and an unsavory looking trooper known as Shorty Barnes.

To make doubly sure Shadow did not try to make a run for it, Hopkins took to dropping a noose around Shadow's neck. The loose end was secured to the pommel of Hopkins' saddle. The corporal taunted Shadow continually.

"Best get used to the feel of that there

rope, redskin," he'd call, tugging on the rope that cut off Shadow's wind, "cause you're gonna swing high and dry when we reach the fort! Yes sir, I seen lots of Injuns dancin' at the end of a rope. Ain't a purty sight, no sir. Sometimes a man's neck don't break just right, and he strangles kinda slow like, eyes bulgin' and feet kickin'." Hopkins grinned wolfishly as he added, "That's how you'll go, Injun, if I get to tie the knot!"

I shuddered at the grotesque images the corporal's word painted across my mind. Sometimes at night, I dreamed of Shadow's execution. I saw him slowly climb the stairs to the gallows, his head high, his eyes blazing defiance. I saw the noose dropped over his head and pulled snug around his neck, with the heavy knot secured below his ear. I would wake, crying, just as the trap-door yawned beneath him.

Cruel as Hopkins' taunts were, they had no visible affect on Shadow. Indeed, he did not seem to hear them at all. It was as if he had withdrawn into a world all his own, some inner haven of refuge where nothing Hopkins said or did could touch him.

When we reached Fort Apache, Shadow was pulled off his horse and hustled toward the stockade. He did not go peacefully. Though his hands were bound behind his back, his feet were free, and he struck out viciously, catching one of the soldiers full in the groin. The man went down with a hoarse cry, clutching his battered manhood.

Twisting and turning, Shadow managed to elude the soldiers as he made a mad dash for the gates.

"Stop him!" Joshua hollered, a half-dozen troopers raced after Shadow.

One of them threw himself at Shadow in a flying tackle, his arms closing around Shadow's ankles. Both men crashed to the ground. Kicking violently, Shadow made it to his feet, but by then he was surrounded by five soldiers. I cringed as they beat him into submission and then dragged him into the stockade.

Joshua carried me to the infirmary and left me in the care of the Army Sawbones. Dr. Mitchell was tall and lanky. Despite his advanced years, he was a lively gentleman, his face smooth and virtually unlined. He had the merriest blue eyes I had ever seen, and as I glanced around the hospital, I wondered how he managed to maintain his sunny disposition. There were a dozen beds in the hospital, and they were all filled.

"Damned Apaches," the doctor muttered. "Attacked one of our patrols day before yesterday. No matter how many times we beat and run them back to the reservation, a few always manage to sneak off and cause trouble." He smiled and gave me a fatherly pat on the shoulder. "Enough of that. Let's take a look at you."

So saying, he took me into a small room adjoining the main building, and after I undressed, he gave me an embarrassingly thorough examination. Then he tucked me into bed and declared I would be fit as a fiddle after three weeks bed rest and some decent food that didn't come out of a can and hadn't been charred black over a campfire.

"Three weeks!" I complained. "Why so long?"

"You've been through a rough time, Miss Kincaid," he explained patiently. "You're considerably undernourished and underweight. Not only that, but you suffered a minor concussion when you went tumbling down that hill. Not to mention the fact that you seem to have had a difficult delivery, a long, bumpy ride to the fort, and no time to rest." He gave me another fatherly pat. "Trust me, my dear," he said kindly. "I know what I'm doing."

Three weeks, I fretted. Three weeks! I thought the days would never pass. There were bright spots, of course, the brightest of which was hot water. The first time I was allowed to take a tub bath, I thought I'd died and gone to Heaven. And there was the near-forgotten taste of fresh milk, the satisfying aroma of coffee, the fragrance of a real soap, and the comfort of a real bed with a real pillow. Yet I would gladly have traded all the wondrous comforts of civilization to be living wild and free with Shadow.

If only I could see him. If only the days did not pass so slowly. I was accustomed to riding from dawn to dark, to cooking and sewing, to being constantly on the move, and the enforced inactivity was frustrating, to say the least. I did not feel sick, only lost and alone.

Josh came to visit me morning and evening, sometimes bringing me candy or a ribbon for my hair, as well as the eastern newspapers which were usually several weeks old by the time they arrived at the fort.

I sincerely appreciated Joshua's thoughtful concern, but it was not Joshua I ached to see, and I begged him daily to let Shadow visit me. And daily he told me such a thing was impossible.

Shadow was behaving badly, Josh said. Had tried three times in as many days to escape from the guardhouse. Had broken Hopkins' nose in a scuffle. Had nearly killed Sergeant Warren with his bare hands. And when he wasn't attacking the guards, he could be seen pacing his cell like a wild animal, or standing at the window for hours on end, just staring at nothing. Sometimes the guards heard him beating on the walls with his fists. He was incorrigible, Josh said disdainfully, but then, what could you expect from a heathen savage?

Nettled, I wanted to cry out that Shadow was not a savage, that he was a fine decent man, proud and brave and honest—but I held my tongue. As long as there was a chance Josh could help Shadow—any chance at all—I could not afford to antagonize him by defending Shadow.

When I was finally released from the hospital, I went straight to Regimental Headquarters and demanded to see the Colonel.

Colonel Grant Crawford was a tall, austere man with close-cropped black hair and frigid green eyes. He was very cold and very polite. In short, clipped sentences he told me that he had received orders from Washington stating that the Cheyenne war chief known as Two Hawks Flying was to be executed February 1st. It was felt by certain parties in Washington that the Indian situation would be vastly improved if Two Hawks Flying was disposed of, permanently, before spring.

And then, as if he had just solved all my problems, Colonel Crawford smiled and said

I was welcome to remain at the fort as long as I wished.

Taking a deep breath, I thanked the Colonel for his hospitality and then asked if I might see Shadow, prepared to argue my case all day, if necessary. But the Colonel only shrugged and said I could see the prisoner immediately if I so desired.

Five minutes later I was standing in a dark, dank cell located in the bowels of the guardhouse. The cell was little bigger than an outhouse and smelled about the same. It contained no furniture and had no windows and no light save that provided by the candle in my hand. A ragged blanket was spread on the dirt floor. A foul-smelling slop jar occupied one corner of the room. The odor of sweat and excrement was very strong, and I shuddered with horror and disgust.

Shadow stood in the middle of the floor, blinking against the light. He looked thin and discouraged. His long black hair was dirty and unkempt; his clout and moccasins were filthy. Always having taken such pride in his appearance, I knew he must be humiliated—not only by his surroundings but by his own unwashed condition.

"You should not have come here, Hannah," he said flatly. "This is no place for a woman."

"This. . .this dungeon is no place for anyone," I said. "Why aren't you in one of the cells upstairs?"

"I am being punished for trying to escape once too often," he replied bitterly.

"How long have you been here?"

"I am not sure. Two weeks. . .three. I have lost track of the time."

He began to pace the length of his prison, his naturally long stride shortened by the heavy leg irons that rattled and clanged with every step he took. Leg irons, I thought angrily. Wasn't it bad enough to lock him up without shackling him, too? Oh, it was cruel. Shadow was accustomed to vast sunlit prairies and bold blue skies. He should not be locked up in this ugly little cell, away from all he loved.

He came to an abrupt halt and grabbed me by the shoulders. There was a look of quiet desperation in his eyes, and I could feel him shaking with pent-up rage and frustration as he said, "Hannah, tell them to hang me or shoot me or slit my throat, but for God's sake tell them to do it now!"

"No! You're all I have left in the world."

"Joshua will take care of you."

"I don't want Joshua," I wailed. "I want you."

Shadow let out a long breath, and I felt the

anger drain out of him as he pulled me close, murmuring my name. I melted into his arms, lifting my face for his kiss. His mouth was warm on mine, his hands gentle as they caressed my cheek and my hair. Our kisses grew more urgent as our bodies pressed together, and I needed him as never before. It had been five long weeks since the soldiers had found us, five weeks since I had felt his arms around me.

The dirt-packed floor was hard and cold, the blanket he used for a bed was smelly and damp and rough against my bare flesh, but I didn't care. Shadow was hesitant, afraid of hurting me, but only he could fill the emptiness in my heart and help me get over the loss of our child. Whispering his name, I pulled him down beside me. How I gloried in the feel of his naked flesh rubbing against my own! We held each other tight, straining together, as if we could never be close enough. I thrilled to the touch of his hands on my breasts and belly, felt my insides tingle with excitement as his throbbing manhood probed my quivering flesh.

With eager hands, I stroked the hard muscles in his back and shoulders, reveling in their strength and power. My eyes looked at him and were pleased with what they saw. He was perfect in every way, from his broad shoulders and flat belly to his long legs and arms that rippled with muscle. His nose and mouth were proud and strong, his eyes blackly beautiful. And his hands. . .Ah, there was magic in his touch and as his mouth descended on mine, the horrid little cell was swept away in a magical transformation. Suddenly it was spring in the high country. The world around us was fresh and clean instead of dark and musty; the cold floor became sweet grass, and the darkness gave way to sunlight as warm as vibrant as our love.

Gently, Shadow caressed my willing flesh, his fingers probing the secret places only he knew until I burned with a fire only he could quench. I moaned with pleasure in his arms, my fingernails digging lightly into his back as I drew him closer, closer. . . .

Later, we lay facing each other, our bodies still fused together. Shadow murmured my name, and I knew then that he needed me as never before. I was the only one who cared if he lived or died, the only one who could free him from his awful prison and from the sentence of death that hung over him like a dark cloud. Somehow, I would find a way, for I could not bear to think of him spending one more day in dreary darkness, living like some kind of wild beast, forced to suffer the indignity of captivity. He deserved better—much better—and I intended to see he got it.

I was allowed to spend thirty minutes a day with Shadow. Sometimes we made love, sometimes we talked, and sometimes we only sat side by side, holding hands, with no need for words.

Daily, I pleaded with Colonel Crawford to free Shadow from that dreadful cell, but the Colonel adamantly refused, insisting that Shadow was much too desperate a character to be treated like an ordinary prisoner.

When I wasn't arguing with Colonel Crawford or visiting Shadow, I was with Joshua, begging him to please, please think of a way to save Shadow from hanging. The date of his execution was only two days away, and I was half out of my mind with worry. Already, the gallows had been built and a hangman selected.

"Can't you think of some way to help Shadow?" I begged. "Please, Joshua, I'd be ever so grateful."

An odd look passed over Joshua's face as he said, "As a matter of fact, I have thought of a way that might work, but it depends entirely on you."

"On me? Oh, Josh, I'll do anything to save him. Anything!"

"Will you, Hannah?" Josh asked, and his eyes sparkled with an intense blue fire.

"Anything," I repeated firmly. "Just name it."

"I want you to marry me," came his unexpected reply. "Tonight."

"Marry you?" I exclaimed. "How will that help Shadow?"

"Once we're married, I'll arrange for him to escape."

"But that's blackmail!" I exclaimed, stunned that he would even suggest such a thing.

"Perhaps. But you said you'd do anything to save him. Here's your chance to prove it."

"How do I know you'll really set him free?"

"You've got my word on it. Once we're married, I'll see him safely out of the fort."

"And I suppose a dozen soldiers will be waiting outside, ready to cut him down."

Josh laughed softly as he took my hands in his. "Hannah, trust me. I'll see he gets safely out of the fort and into the woods. No gunshots, no soldiers waiting to ambush him."

"How?" I asked, wanting desperately to believe him. "How will you do it?"

Joshua shrugged. "It shouldn't be too difficult. There are a couple of men in my company I can trust. I'll see to it they're on guard duty tomorrow night—a lock accidentally left open, a horse waiting outside the back gate. All you have to do is marry me tonight, and the redskin goes free."

"I don't suppose you'd let me go with him?"

"Not a chance. We do things my way, or he hangs day after tomorrow at dawn."

Shadow would be lost to me either way, I thought ruefully, but if I agreed to marry Josh, at least he would be alive and free.

"All right, Josh. I'll marry you. But only after Shadow is safely out of the fort."

"I've waited for you this long," Joshua said cheerfully. "I guess I can wait one more day." He threw me a crooked grin. "You know, I never stopped thinking about you. I've met a lot of beautiful women since I left Bear Valley, but none of them ever meant a thing to me. Only you."

"I don't know what to say," I stammered. "I'm flattered."

"You said you'd be my wife, and that's enough." Joshua's hand was on the door knob when he said, "Just one more thing. When you see him tomorrow, I want you to tell him you're marrying me because you love me. You're not to mention our agreement in any way. Is that clear?"

Puzzled, I said, "Yes, but why? What difference does it make?"

"Just this. If he finds out you're marrying me to save his hide from the hangman, he's liable to stick around trying to get you back. Probably get himself killed after all. But if he thinks you're marrying me because you want to, he'll likely head back for Montana where he belongs."

Josh was right. Shadow would not try to get me back if he thought I was in love with Joshua. His pride would not let him interfere. No real warrior wasted his time with a woman who did not want him.

"You've thought of everything, haven't you?" I said bitterly.

"I try," Joshua answered curtly, and left me alone with my dismal thoughts.

In the morning, I went to see Shadow for the last time. I longed to run to him, to throw my arms around him and pour out my love. But to do so would be like putting the noose around his neck myself, and that I could never do.

Instead I said bluntly, "I've decided to marry Joshua."

"I know," Shadow replied quietly.

"You know?" I said, frowning. "How could you?"

"Berdeen came to see me last night. He loves you, Hannah. You will be better off

337

here, with him, than you ever were with me."

"Yes, that's true," I agreed, almost choking on the words. "He can give me a home and security."

Shadow's eyes probed mine. "Do you love him?"

"Yes," I lied. "I guess I always have."

Shadow nodded, his face impassive. I knew I was hurting him, and I wanted to die. He had always been able to read my thoughts. Why couldn't he read them now? Surely he knew I was lying, that I had never loved anyone else. Only him.

"I hope you will be happy in your new life," Shadow said coldly, and turned away from me as two heavily armed troopers opened the cell door and motioned for me to step outside.

I stared at Shadow's back, my heart breaking as I realized I would never see him again. He was lost to me forever now. Never again would I feel the strength of his arms around me, or know the joy of his touch, or hear his voice whisper my name.

I wanted to cry out that I loved him, that the only reason I was marrying Josh was to save him from the gallows, but I could not. Shadow's life was dearer to me than my own, and I could not let him hang when I could prevent it.

I whispered, "Good-bye, Shadow," and then one of the soldiers took me by the arm and led me away.

Chapter 17

Restless as a caged tiger, Two Hawks Flying prowled the narrow confines of his prison, feeling as if he'd explode if he had to spend one more day locked up, feeling as if he'd go mad if he had to spend one more hour in the rank darkness. After a lifetime of living wild and free, the constant confinement, coupled with the unending darkness and the weight of chains, was almost more than he could bear. He had not been allowed to bathe, and he found his own smell almost as disgusting as the foul odor rising from the slop jar overflowing in the corner. His empty belly rumbled for food—real food, not the stale bread and tepid water he was served once a day.

Dark thoughts tumbled through the corridor of his mind as he paced the tiny cell. Anger and rage burned through him like slow poison as he pictured Hannah in another man's arms. Not that he could fault her for marrying Berdeen. She should have married the arrogant paleface years ago and spared herself the miserable life he, Shadow, had given her. She had spent the better part of two years following him around the country, and what did she have to show for it? Nothing. Nothing but heartache and a dead child.

Grief welled in his breast as he thought of his son, a tiny corpse bundled into a dirty Army blanket and buried in a shallow grave on a lonely hillside.

Two years of fighting, and what had it accomplished? Perhaps nothing, he mused ruefully. And yet, had he known the ending from the start, he would have done it all again. He was part of the land, part of the sky and the rocks and the water. He could not have turned his back on all he loved and surrendered without a fight. Nor would he go peaceably to the gallows, or grovel before the hangman and beg for mercy. No, he would fight if given the chance. And if he did not take at least one white man with him, it would not be for lack of trying! And if there were no opportunity to resist, then he would go quietly, with dignity, and not like a dog with its tail between its legs.

Unbidden, the horse killer's words came to mind. "Eyes bulgin' and feet kickin'. . .that's how you'll go if I get to tie the knot!"

It was not a pretty picture.

Abruptly, he broke off his restless pacing and raised his arms in supplication.

"Hear me, Man Above," he prayed in a loud voice. "Grant me the courage to meet death bravely, as a warrior should."

He did not fear death itself, only the manner of his dying. The Cheyenne believed that the soul left the body with the last breath. But when a man was hanged, his soul was forever trapped in the body by the rope.

He scowled into the darkness. A warrior should die in battle with his weapons in his hand and a war cry in his lips. But hanging! It was a bad way to die, with hands bound and a rope around your neck. But even hanging would be better than spending another day in this awful place, and suddenly restless, he began to pace back and forth. Back and forth. Hour after hour. The heavy leg irons chafed his ankles; their infernal clanking wore on his nerves. But still he paced, choking back the urge to scream, to hurl himself against the door and beg for his freedom, to call the guard and ask if he could see Hannah one last time. But pride—the fierce arrogant pride that burned in the blood of every true warrior—stilled his tongue, and a great loneliness settled over him as he realized he would never see Hannah again.

Murmuring her name, he stretched out on the ground, clutching the ragged blanket they had so recently shared.

He was lying thus when the door swung open and a whey-faced trooper handed him a tin plate piled high with roast beef and potatoes. And a water glass filled with whiskey.

"Enjoy," the bluecoat muttered sardonically, and slammed the heavy iron door.

"The condemned man ate a hearty meal," Two Hawks Flying murmured, then quickly wolfed down the first real food he'd been given in nearly three weeks.

The whiskey was like liquid flame as it burned a fiery path to his belly. Much better than the cheap trade whiskey he was accustomed to, he wished for another glass. Glass, hell, he'd like the whole damn bottle!

A sudden weariness enveloped him as the last drops of amber liquid trickled down his throat, clouding his vision and stealing the strength from his limbs. The glass fell from a hand gone numb, and he pitched headlong into nothingness. . . .

* * *

He awoke, shivering. There was a sour taste in his mouth and a steady pounding, like two buffalo bulls colliding, inside his skull. Uncomprehending, he stared at the stars splashed across the sky for some time before he realized he was no longer locked in his cell, but outside in a wooded meadow.

It was when he tried to rise that he discovered, with some surprise, that he was spread-eagled between four stout wooden stakes, naked as the day he'd been born. Like an animal caught in the jaws of a trap, he struggled against the ropes that held him. But the ropes held fast, and his thrashing about only elicited pain from a new source as the ropes cut into his wrists.

Muffled footsteps sounded behind him. Seconds later two figures bundled in heavy coats materialized out of the darkness, and Two Hawks Flying grimaced as he recognized Hopkins, the horse killer, and the trooper known as Shorty.

"Looks like he finally came out of it," Hopkins drawled. "I was beginning to think you'd cashed him in."

"Naw, I didn't give him enough to kill him. Now he's awake, get on with it and let's go. This wind's colder than a whore's heart."

"Go on back if you want. I won't be long."

"I'll wait."

"Suit yourself," Hopkins muttered, and hunkered down on his heels alongside the prisoner. "Just thought I'd let you know what's goin' on, case you're wonderin'," he drawled. "Ya see, it's like this. The lieutenant, he promised Miz Hannah he'd help you escape. But then he got to thinkin' you might not high-tail it outta the territory like you should. He figured you might just take it into your head to stick around and try to get your woman back. So, he told me and Shorty to dust you off. We was gonna shoot ya, but the lieutenant promised Miz Hannah you wouldn't get hung, nor shot neither, so. . ." Hopkins shrugged elaborately. "Me and Shorty decided to carve you up a little and let the cold and the critters finish you off." Hopkins' face split in a malicious grin, much like that of a lobo wolf about to bring down a buffalo calf as he added, "Personally, I'd as soon be shot, but a promise is a promise."

Chuckling, the horse killer drew a long bladed knife from the sheath of his belt. His eyes were as cold and flat as the weapon in his hand as he rubbed his nose, permanently mishappen since Two Hawks Flying had broken it.

"Time to get down to business," Hopkins

murmured ominously, and smashed his left fist into the prisoner's face, bloodying his nose and mouth.

"Get on with it," Shorty whined. "I got a bottle stashed in my bunk, and I could use a couple snorts to ease the chill in my bones."

Grinning his shit-eating grin, Hopkins raised his knife. Two Hawks Flying tensed from head to heel as fear's clammy hand took hold on his insides, but his face remained smooth and impassive as Hopkins made the first cut. The blade was razor sharp, and tiny rivers of red appeared each time the corporal dragged the blade across the prisoner's broad chest and muscular thighs. A dozen times the knife met flesh, cutting just deep enough to draw blood.

With a grunt of satisfaction, Hopkins rose to his feet and sheathed his knife. "That ought to do it," he allowed. "Iffen the cold don't get him, the blood scent will draw the wolves down on him like ducks on a June bug."

"Yeah, he's finished," Shorty agreed, "so let's make tracks back to the fort."

Minutes later Two Hawks Flying was alone.

Shivering convulsively, body aching, wounds stinging from the cold wind, he stared into the darkness. The minutes crept by on broken feet. A pair of wolves howled in the distance, and he tried not to think of pink tongues dripping saliva and yellow teeth rending living flesh. A third lobo answered the call of the others—and then they were there, not three feet away, their hungry amber eyes glinting fiendishly in the frosty moonlight, their hot breath rank and tantalizingly warm on his naked flesh. Warily, they stepped closer, growling as the scent of fresh blood grew stronger, only to flee as the Cheyenne war cry split the wintry night.

Two Hawks Flying grinned wryly. What was the use in prolonging the inevitable? Why not let the wolves finish him off now? Why fight for one more hour, one more minute? The cold was painful, and his body was wracked with violent tremors as it sought to warm itself. His face ached from Hopkins' vicious blow, and there was a cut across his left thigh, deeper than the others, that throbbed with steady precision. He felt himself sinking into darkness; he fought against it, knowing if he slept now he would sleep forever. And he was not ready to die, not yet. Not until he had dipped his hands in Lieutenant Joshua Berdeen's blood. Not until he'd seen Hannah one last time. . . .

Sleep snared him in its net, and he dozed fitfully until a low-throated growl roused him. Startled, he loosed the tribal warwhoop again, though what emerged from his throat was not a bloodcurdling cry but a harsh, raspy wail. Still, it spooked the wolves, and they scuttled for cover.

Sluggishly, Two Hawks Flying moved his head from side to side. Unblinking yellow eyes stared back at him. They had not gone far this time. Next time they would not run. Summoning the last reserves of his strength, Two Hawks Flying raised his voice in prayer.

"Hear me, Man Above," he called hoarsely. "Give me strength to survive this night."

Again and again he whispered his plea, until his voice was gone and he only mouthed the words.

Stillness filled the night. Then a rush of mighty wings filled the air as a dark shadow crossed the moon and a pair of red-tailed hawks appeared out of the murky darkness.

Mighty wings outstretched, they floated lightly to the ground. Alighting on either side of the stricken warrior, they spread their wings over his body, warming him with their feathers and shielding him from the wind's icy breath.

"Be strong," the male admonished. "Be strong and you will yet conquor your enemies."

"Be brave," the female admonished. "Be brave and all you desire will yet be yours."

All you desire....Whispering Hannah's name, he slept.

He awoke to the sound of heavy wings beating the air. He opened his eyes to thank his special helpers, the hawks, and came face to face with an enormous black vulture. Wings extended, the ugly creature stared at him through unblinking black eyes, occasionally taking a clumsy hopping step toward him, its funereal clothed body awkward and ungainly on the ground. As it drew nearer, its hooked beak opened to tear at his bloodied face.

Frantically, Two Hawks Flying rolled his head from side to side, hoping to ward off the advancing bird, but to no avail. Like the shadow of death, the hulking creature loomed over him, poised to strike. The curved beak was darting forward when a gunshot flatted across the early morning stillness. The vulture toppled over backwards as if struck down by an invisible hand. Moments later two riders emerged from the trees.

They were white men. The one on the left was in his mid-thirties, with a handsome boyish face, blue eyes as cold and clear as a

349

mountain stream, a fine straight nose, and hair the color of new wheat.

The second man was older—perhaps forty, perhaps fifty—it was hard to tell. He had thinning brown hair, washed-out green eyes, and narrow sloping shoulders.

Both of the wasicuns smiled, as if they found it terribly amusing to come across a naked Indian spread-eagled in the middle of nowhere. The older man spoke first.

"Well, Clyde, what do you make of that?" he queried in a deep, resonant voice.

The man called Clyde shrugged. "Why, right off hand, Barney, I'd say he must have made an enemy of two somewhere along the line."

"Yeah, and they caught up with him!" Barney chortled.

Clyde's blue eyes glinted, and his mouth twisted into a mirthless grin. "Well, my ma always taught me that animals should be put out of their misery," he remarked, raising his rifle to his shoulder, "and this here beat-up buck looks as miserable as any I've seen."

"Hold on a minute," Barney said. "Let's see who he is and where he's from. Might be he's an Apache. Might be he could tell us where that there Apache gold mine is we heard tell of in Tucson."

Clyde grunted and lowered his rifle. "You, Injun, you an Apache?"

Almost imperceptibly, Two Hawks Flying shook his head.

Clyde's rifle thudded against his shoulder a second time. And again his companion stayed his hand.

"Don't be so all fired hasty to kill him," Barney admonished. To Shadow he said, "What's your name, Injun? What tribe you from?"

With as much pride as he could muster, the prisoner rasped, "I am Two Hawks Flying of the Cheyenne."

"Two Hawks Flying? There's something familiar about that name," the older man murmured thoughtfully, then slapped his thigh. "I've got it! Two Hawks Flying—one of the war chiefs at the Little Big Horn. The last fighting chief on the plains. Hot damn! Clyde, put that gun away. We're going to be rich!"

Clyde Stewart frowned. "Rich?" he asked irritably. "What the hell are you talking about?"

A faraway look spread over Barney McCall's weathered face. "I can see it now," he purred in a silky tone. "You—all dudded up in a fancy suit, billed as Clyde Stewart, Indian scout and plainsman, the man that captured Two Hawks Flying, the last fighting chief on the plains! Clyde, don't you see? It's a natural. If we take this redskin east, the dudes will come from miles around to get a look at him. Imagine, a live Indian! One of the chief's responsible for Custer's death. Why, those city slickers will pay a fortune to get a look at him."

At the mention of money, Stewart's eyes glittered like sapphires. "Yeah," he murmured. "Yeah, I think you're right."

Grinning now, he slid his rifle into the boot that hung forward of his saddle and hooked a coil of rope from the horn as he dismounted.

"Cover me while I cut him loose," he said tersely, stepping lightly to the ground.

Shadow had listened to McCall's plan with mounting horror. Appalled by their idea, it was in his mind to make a break for it as soon as Stewart freed him, but he was too stiff, too sore in every muscle and joint to offer more than a token show of resistance, and Stewart quickly overpowered him. In minutes, Shadow's hands were securely bound behind his back; a noose, fashioned from Stewart's rope, hung around his neck.

Swinging into the saddle, Stewart touched his spurs to his mount's flanks.

"Let's go, Injun," he growled over his shoulder and tugged, none too gently, on the rope.

As the noose closed around his throat, Two Hawks Flying lurched forward, gritting his teeth as his punished body protested every step by sending sharp pains through his arms, legs and torso. Feet dragging, body aching, chilled to the bone from spending the night on the damp ground, Two Hawks Flying stumbled along the path of Clyde Stewart's big black gelding. The country they traversed was laced with prickly cactus and spiny shrubs that scratched his face and tore at his naked flesh, while rocks, stones and sharp gravel made walking treacherous. Still, the first few miles were not too bad. The forced march stirred his blood and worked the stiffness from his limbs, even as the warm sun caressed his weary body with a delicious heat.

But then his feet began to bleed and his belly rumbled for food, reminding him he'd not eaten since the day before. By noon, it was an effort to put one foot in front of the other. A short time later, he fell.

With an oath, Stewart gave a savage jerk on the rope, and Shadow struggled to his feet to save himself from being dragged, choking, over the rocky ground.

Ahead of him, he could hear Stewart and McCall deciding how they'd spend all the money they intended to make by showing him off to the whites across the Big Muddy. The idea of being exhibited like a tiger in a cage stirred Shadow's anger, infusing him with strength, and he worked his hands back and forth in an effort to loosen his bonds, but the ropes held fast and struggling only caused the harsh fiber to cut into his flesh, wearing away his skin until his hands were sticky with blood.

In the next two hours he stumbled and fell a half dozen times as he trudged along in the dusty wake of Stewart's mount. And each time he reached down inside himself and found the strength to rise and stagger on.

It was nearing dusk when he fell again, and this time not all Stewart's impatient cursing as he tugged on the rope, or even McCall's cold-blooded threat to geld him on the spot could bring him to his feet. Even the strongest man could not walk twenty miles on an empty belly, not if his feet were bleeding and his body was throbbing with the pain of a dozen knife wounds. Not when he'd spent the previous three weeks in solitary confinement subsisting on stale bread and water.

"Looks like he's through for the day," Barney opined. "In fact, if we don't put some clothes on his back and shovel some food into him, I think he's through for good."

After a quick glance at the countryside Stewart swung out of the saddle, saying, "Yeah, I reckon you're right. See if you can round up some duds for the chief while I rustle up some grub."

Thirty minutes later Two Hawks Flying was clothed in McCall's extra shirt and a pair of stained levis. Warm now, with his hungry belly wrapped around a hot meal and his hands securely tied behind his back, he curled up on a patch of brown buffalo grass and slept.

Chapter 18

The cell was empty, the prisoner gone. Apache scouts went out at dawn, only to return empty-handed, reporting that Shadow's tracks had been thoroughly and expertly erased.

That afternoon Josh and I were married by the post chaplain. It was a short, simple ceremony attended by Colonel and Mrs. Crawford, Doctor Mitchell, and a dozen or so of Joshua's friends. The whole thing was unreal, a nightmare from which I could not awaken. Didn't these people realize I was already married? Why didn't they understand? Why didn't Josh understand that I was Shadow's wife in every way that mattered? What difference that we had never stood before a judge or a priest and exchanged vows? Our hearts and lives were bound as surely as if we had written our names on a license before a hundred solemn witnesses. I had slept at Shadow's side, tended his wounds, born his child. How could I marry Joshua while Shadow still lived?

And yet, in a matter of minutes, the deed was done and I was Mrs. Joshua Berdeen—for better or worse.

I closed my eyes as my husband kissed me, praying that our union would be a happy one. I told myself we had a good chance. After all, once I had been genuinely fond of him. Perhaps, in time, I would grow to love him.

There was cake and champagne at the Crawfords after the ceremony, along with handshakes and presents and good wishes from Joshua's friends, and a warm kiss from Doctor Mitchell. And then, all too soon, Josh and I were alone in his quarters.

Head spinning from too much champagne, I stood in the middle of the room, watching dumbly while Josh shrugged out of his uniform. Only then did the full impact of what I had done hit me. In bargaining for Shadow's freedom, I had completely surrendered my own. I belonged to Joshua now. And as he crossed the floor toward me, I knew he intended to claim what was his without further delay.

A rising tide of panic engulfed me as his arms closed around me and his mouth covered mine. Unable to help myself, I recoiled from his touch.

It was the wrong thing to do. Joshua's eyes burned with all the fierce intensity of a raging inferno as he grabbed a handful of my hair and gave a sharp tug, forcing my head up and back so that I was staring into his face.

"Forget him, Hannah," he said curtly. "You're mine now, all mine, and don't you ever forget it."

"Josh, you're hurting me. . ."

"Mine," he said huskily, and grasping the bodice of my wedding gown, he ripped it down the front.

I shrank from the unadulterated lust blazing in my husband's eyes and clenched my teeth to keep from crying out as his hands fondled my breasts.

"Mine, Hannah," he said again, and lifting me in his arms, he carried me to his bed.

And boldly made love to me—if indeed it could be called love. There was no tenderness or gentleness in his touch, only an angry urgency, as if I were another enemy to be conquered.

His hands were cruel as they explored my cringing flesh, his mouth hard and relentless as it ravaged mine. And as his knee forced my thighs apart, I made myself remember that, but for Joshua, Shadow would be dead now, hanging from the gallows behind the post guardhouse.

Shadow. . . . In my mind's eye I saw him astride Red Wind, a warrior as proud and free as the hawks whose name he bore. I saw him dressed for battle, warbonnet fluttering in the breeze, handsome face streaked with broad slashes of vermillon.

I saw him crawling across the floor of my father's house, determined to die rather than be crippled for life.

I saw him kneeling at my side, his dark eyes filled with love and compassion the day our baby died.

Shadow, my beloved. No matter that Josh's touch filled me with revulsion. No matter that I was repelled by his kisses.

Shadow was free!

Hansen's Traveling Tent Show proclaimed the gaudy red, yellow, and blue banner, and then went on to promise chills, thrills, and surprises. Adults and children alike oohed and aahed as they rushed from one gaily-colored tent to another. Eyes wide as saucers, they stared open-mouthed at a man wrestling a six-foot alligator and gaped at a two-headed snake and a six-legged goat. The women swooned over a handsome sword swallower and sighed over a daring highwire walker. The men whistled and cheered and stamped their feet as a raven-haired belly dancer displayed her voluptuous charms. The children fell down laughing at a dozen funny clowns dressed as firemen. There was a thin man and a fat lady, a mysterious gypsy fortune teller, a boxing kangaroo, and a dancing bear. And in the last tent there was a real live Indian.

"Hurry! Hurry! See Chief Two Hawks Flying. The last fighting chief on the plains. Hurry! Hurry! Come one, come all!"

Clyde Stewart's dazzling smile stretched from ear to ear as he watched a horde of city slickers rush down the midway, drawn by Barney's ballyhoo. Old Barney was grinning broadly as he sold the last ticket, closed the cash box, and hurried inside. It was a sell-out crowd.

Stewart chuckled. The eastern dudes shelled out a dollar a head to see the chief. On a good day, with three shows a day, they cleared over a hundred bucks, often more. It sure beat huntin' outlaws!

Still chuckling, Clyde hurried to the rear of the big, blue-striped tent and ducked inside.

Over in a corner, shackled to the wheel of their wagon, sat their gold mine.

"Get those feathers on, chief," Stewart ordered brusquely. He was changing clothes as he spoke, putting aside his natty pin-stripe suit and vest to don a flashy, all white cowboy outfit laden with yards of fringe and glittering spangles. It was a rig to curdle the stomach of any real westerner, but the city slickers ate it up. White boots and a huge white stetson came next. Lastly, he buckled on a fancy, hand-tooled gunbelt, complete with a matched set of pearl-handled Peace-makers in cutaway holsters. The guns, worn for the show only, were loaded with blanks.

Clyde glanced into a mirror hanging from a tent post and smiled at his reflection. "Handsome devil," he purred, then hollered, "Hey, Rudy, it's time!"

Smothering a mammoth yawn, Rudy Swenson rose, stretching, from behind a bale of hay where he'd been napping since the last show. A giant of a man, with tiny brown eyes and a shock of unruly wheat-colored hair, he stood six foot six in his stocking feet. Moving like a grizzly just rousted from his winter sleep, the Swede took up his rifle and lumbered toward Two Hawks Flying.

"Hit the dirt," Rudy growled, and Shadow bellied out on the ground, the Swede's cocked Winchester snug against his spine, while Stewart cuffed his hands and removed the heavy chain from his ankle.

Stepping back, Rudy muttered, "Let's go," and Shadow rose obediently to his feet and walked toward the stage located in the front half of the tent, keenly aware of the Swede's ready-cocked rifle tracking his every move.

There was a round of applause as Barney McCall stepped on stage. Tall, thin as a porch rail, with thinning brown hair and pale green eyes, McCall was a plain, homely man, unlikely to draw attention in a crowd of two—until he opened his mouth. As if to atone for his lack of physical beauty, Nature had endowed McCall with a rich, commanding voice, one that could hold an audience spellbound or bring them to tears. In earlier days, he had preached on street corners while his accomplice, an engaging young Negro boy, nimbly lifted the wallets of unsuspecting passers-by who stopped to hear the Gospel according to McCall.

Now, as the applause faded, Barney went into his spiel, recounting in vivid detail how Clyde Stewart, world famous buffalo hunter, trapper, Indian fighter, and Army scout, had singlehandedly and at great personal risk captured Two Hawks Flying, the last fighting chief on the Great Plains. Barney McCall was nothing if not silver-tongued, and the audience sat on the edge of their seats, totally mesmerized, as he wove his tale, relating in dramatic tones the atrocities Chief Two Hawks Flying had perpetrated against untold numbers of innocent whites, mostly women and children. His voice dropped to a reverent hush as he told of Clyde Stewart's unmatched bravery in tracking the heathen savage over miles of barren wilderness and sun-bleached desert, how he had risked his life in deadly hand to hand combat and defeated the chief in a knife fight unparalled in the annals of history for bloodletting and daring.

Barney paused, staring into the rapt, unturned faces of the crowd. "Suckers," he thought disdainfully, amused by their ready acceptance of what any cowhand worth his salt would recognize as nothing more than a long line of bullshit.

"And now!" he boomed, "here's Chief Two Hawks Flying, scourge of the West, and the heroic man that out-thought him and out-fought him, Clyde Stewart!"

Prodded by the Swede's rifle, Two Hawks Flying climbed the stairs and advanced toward center stage. Several elderly women gasped aloud, shocked by his appearance, for

he was clad in breechclout of black wolfskin
and high, Apache-style boot moccasins. An
elaborate warbonnet (of Crow origin and
purchased for the exorbitant price of ten
silver dollars from a shrewd brave of that
tribe) trailed down his back, the ends nearly
brushing the floor. Two scalps, which everyone assumed were fake but were, in fact,
quite authentic and had been purchased
from the same enterprising Crow warrior,
hung at his side. In the flickering lamplight,
his skin glistened like burnished copper.

There was a thunderous roar of applause
as Clyde Stewart appeared on stage, his
boyish smile as dazzlingly white as his
outfit.

Rudy remained out of sight in the wings,
covering Two Hawks Flying with his rifle.

Clyde bowed and waved, then bowed
again, thoroughly enjoying the rousing
cheers and unabashed admiration he saw
shining in the eyes of the crowd. He made an
impressive sight, and he knew it. Tall and
blond, with a sweeping Cavalry-style
moustache, vivid blue eyes and boyish smile,
he set many a feminine heart aflutter and
filled many a lesser man with envy.

When he could be heard above the
adulation of the crowd, Clyde asked the
audience if they had any questions. Thirty

hands shot into the air. It was going to be a good night.

While Stewart answered their queries, Two Hawks Flying stared straight ahead, his dark eyes focused on a narrow slice of deep cobalt blue sky visible through a ragged tear in the side of the tent. His face, dark and handsome, was inscrutable, causing several of the women in the audience to wonder what thoughts lay behind his impassive facade.

Standing there, he looked every bit as formidable as McCall had claimed, and quite capable of committing the atrocities of which he had been accused. Powerfully built, with broad shoulders and long muscular horseman's legs, he stood a good three inches over six feet. His hair, thick and black and parted in the middle, hung to his waist. To the easterners, he appeared to be the personification of evil and terror, just as Clyde Stewart appeared to be the personification of all that was good and wholesome.

"What'd you say, boy?" McCall asked, waving the crowd to silence.

"I said, where's his war paint? How come he ain't wearin' any?"

"That's a mighty observant boy," Barney informed the audience. "Come on up here, son," he invited, and smiled, encouraging the youth to come forward. Someone usually noticed the Indian's lack of paint. If they didn't, Clyde asked for a volunteer from the audience to come up and paint the chief. It was always a show stopper.

The boy reached the stage in nothing flat, turning to wave at his family. He was a small kid, painfully thin, with no more substance than a shadow on the wall. Sparse blond hair and a sallow complexion added to the boy's washed out appearance. Even the freckles liberally sprinkled over his cheeks and across the bridge of his nose seemed pale. But there was nothing pale about the boy's eyes. They were a bold, vibrant blue, and they sparkled with awe and excitement as he stared wide-eyed at Two Hawks Flying.

"What's your name, son?" Stewart asked, friendly-like.

"Jeremy Brown, sir," the boy answered politely, heeding his mother's advice to 'mind your manners, or else!'

"Well, Jeremy, how'd you like to remedy the situation?"

"Huh? I mean, I beg your pardon, sir?"

Clyde Stewart indicated the tray Barney had produced from the wings. It contained two pots of stage make-up.

"How'd you like to paint the chief—show us how they decorate themselves for war?"

Jeremy's eyes grew even wider. "Wow! Would I!"

"Well, go to it, son," Stewart prompted, grinning at the boy's exuberance.

Jeremy hesitated. "Could. . .could my cousin help me?"

"Sure," Clyde allowed. "Come on up, cousin."

There was a sudden flurry in the crowd as a young girl with flying pigtails ran up the steps to the stage. The two youngsters put their heads together for a moment, then picked up the brushes and began daubing paint on the Indian's broad chest. Several people in the audience guessed their intent and began to giggle. Then, as Jeremy and his cousin stepped aside, the crowd erupted into full-fledged hilarity, for there, clearly marked on the Indian's torso, was a red and yellow game of tic-tac-toe with X the winner.

Clyde and Barney exchanged amused glances, then joined in the hearty laughter as the two youngsters took elaborate bows before resuming their seats.

Through it all, Shadow's face remained impassive, betraying none of the rage and humiliation that burned within him. How many times, he wondered bitterly, had he endured the mocking laughter of a crowd?

* * *

On the way east, before joining up with Hansen's Tent Show, Clyde and Barney had exhibited him in bars, in schoolhouses, on street corners. Even at a church social. Always for a price, of course.

He had been poked, prodded, mocked, ridiculed, spat upon. And even shot at. Once by an eight year old brat with a toy bow and arrow, and once by an enraged father whose son and daughter had recently been killed and scalped by Apaches.

They had been in a little Iowa town at the time. Stewart and McCall had outdone themselves that night and sold tickets to just about every soul in the community. Barney had just started his spiel about Clyde's unequaled bravery in capturing Two Hawks Flying, the scourge of the west, when one of the men in the front row sprang to his feet and let go a round from a fancy derringer. The bullet plowed a shallow furrow the length of Shadow's left forearm.

Before the grief-stricken father could adjust his aim for a second shot, Two Hawks Flying whisked McCall's knife from its sheath and let it fly, and the would-be assassin squealed like a stuck pig as ten inches of solid steel bit deep into his right shoulder.

There was a moment of utter silence, and then all hell broke loose. Women and children screamed. Several men pulled concealed weapons. A matronly lady fainted dead away in the aisle, while another stood up, sobbing hysterically, until her husband slapped her face.

Unleasing a string of profanity, Stewart had hustled Two Hawks Flying out of the room, leaving Barney to handle the uproarious crowd. It had taken a lot of fast talking on McCall's part to get the audience calmed down again. And a fat bribe to soothe the local law. But for all that, it had taught Stewart and McCall a valuable lesson. Thereafter, they left their weapons off stage, and Stewart took to loading his Peacemakers with blanks, trusting Rudy's marksmanship to keep the chief in line.

One other incident stood out in Shadow's mind, and even now just thinking about it sent shivers down his spine. It, too, had taken place before they joined up with the tent show. This time they were in St. Joe, in a saloon. They were just leaving the stage when a high-pitched voice called, "You there! Hey, you in the big hat. Hold on a minute."

Clyde turned warily toward the bar. Rudy turned at the same time, the ready-cocked Winchester aimed in the general direction of the crowd at the rail.

The speaker displayed upturned hands in a

gesture of peace. He was a ruddy-faced individual, duded up in an expensive eastern style suit. He held a thick black cigar in his left hand.

"Whoa, now," he admonished the big Swede. "I ain't aimin' to start any trouble."

"Just what are you aimin' to start?" Clyde posed, noting the diamond stick pin in the man's silk cravat and the rings on his fat fingers.

"A friendly wager is all," the stranger assured him. "I was quite fascinated by your partner's tale, especially the part about the Indian's cunning and purported indifference to pain." He nodded at the bartender as he added, "Charlie, here, says you can whip a redskin to within an inch of his life and he'll never utter a sound. I say that's a lot of hogwash."

"So?"

"So I've got a thousand dollars says that there Injun will holler 'uncle' just like anybody else when he feels Charlie's blacksnake dancin' across his back."

A thousand dollars! Heads turned. The piano went silent. Rudy smiled greedily. Barney took a firmer hold on Shadow's arm.

Clyde grinned broadly. "Well, now, Mr. . . ?"

"Smith. Homer Kennsington Smith."

"Well, Mr. Smith, just how much of a lickin' do you have in mind?"

"Forty lashes seems fair," Smith suggested.

"Not to me," Stewart replied affably. "After all, this here Injun is my livelihood. I can't take a chance on seeing him killed, or permanently tore up. You understand?"

"To be sure, to be sure. Shall we say thirty?"

"Shall we say fifteen?" Clyde countered, his eyes wandering from Smith's face to the solid gold watch fob that spanned the fat man's belly.

"Shall we say twenty?" Smith posed in the same agreeable tone.

"Done!" Stewart said with a grin and held out his hand.

Shadow's face had remained impassive while the two men haggled over how many strokes would be a fair test of his courage under the lash. Now, as Stewart and Smith shook hands, he felt his stomach knot with dread. Damn Stewart's greedy black soul to hell! He really meant to go ahead with it.

A rolling gasp moved through the saloon as Charlie the bartender dropped an eight-foot rawhide whip on the bar top. It was a formidable weapon. Even coiled and at rest the thing looked deadly, and Shadow knew a

371

moment of genuine gut-wrenching fear. A whip like that, wielded by an expert, could gently tap the ash from a cigarette, or cut a man's back to ribbons.

Shadow's initial panic settled into a hard cold lump in his belly as he glanced surreptiously around the room, looking for a way out. Stewart and Smith were discussing the terms of their agreement, trying to decide whether a groan from the Indian would be considered a cry of pain, thereby signaling defeat for Stewart. Rudy was standing beside the swinging doors, the rifle cradled lovingly in the crook of his arm. So the door was out. The side window then, he decided, and twisting out of McCall's grasp, he sprinted for the open window and freedom.

"Stop him!" Barney screamed, and four men jumped up from their seats and tackled the fleeing warrior.

Shadow struggled briefly, but to no avail. The four men obligingly held him immobile while the last bets were made and the terms of the deal agreed upon. That done, the four men holding Shadow wrestled him outside and spread his arms along the crossbar of the hitch rack in front of the saloon.

Using rope supplied by a couple of cowhands, who had stopped to see what was going on, Barney and Stewart secured

Shadow's wrists to the rough wooden pole.

Under pretense of checking the ropes, Stewart bent down near Shadow's head. "Not a sound, Injun, if you value your hide," Clyde warned ominously. "If I lose this bet, I'll carve you up an inch at a time."

Rising, Stewart joined Barney on the sidelines. "Remember, no blows to the face," Stewart reminded Smith, and the dude nodded as he shook out the whip.

Shadow felt the sweat bead across his brow, felt every muscle in his body grow taut as he waited for the first blow.

The crowd counted out loud. "One. . ."

It was worse that he expected, and before he recovered from the first stinging kiss of the whip, the second and third were already striking home.

"Four. . .five. . .six. . ."

The force of the last drove the breath from Shadow's body, searing his flesh like liquid fire.

"Eight. . .nine. . .ten. . ."

His back was a solid sheet of flame. Blood and sweat coursed down his shoulders and back, dripping onto the dusty, sun-baked ground at his feet.

"Eleven. . ."

"Hold on there!"

Lash in midair, Smith pivoted on his heel, his face an angry frown as he snapped,

"Mind your own business!" then added, sheepishly, "Oh, sorry, padre."

"What is going on here?" Father Senteno demanded. "Why is this man being flogged."

"To, uh, settle a bet."

"A bet!" the priest exclaimed incredulously. "I insist you cut that poor man loose at once. A bet, indeed! I have never heard of anything so barbaric!"

"Sorry, padre," Smith replied. "But I've got a thousand bucks at stake here, and I don't aim to quit now."

"A thousand dollars? Surely a man's life is worth more than that."

"A man's, maybe," Smith allowed with a crooked grin. "But not a redskin's."

"We are all the same in the eyes of God," Father Senteno said with quiet dignity.

"This is none of your business," Stewart said, taking his place beside Smith. "This is between Mr. Smith and myself, and I suggest you stand aside. I ain't never hit a preacher man yet, but if you don't step aside, you'll likely be the first."

The priest was a small man, barely tall enough to reach Stewart's shoulders, but there was no fear in his face. He swelled up like an enraged rooster, ready to launch an attack if necessary, but before he could make a move, two burly men in bowler hats stepped out of the crowd and strong-armed the indignant priest out of the way.

The ensuing silence warned Shadow that his would-be rescuer had failed, and he sucked in his breath as the whip whistled through the air.

"Twelve. . .thirteen. . ."

Breathing was suddenly painful, and his chest heaved with the effort required to draw air into his lungs.

"Fourteen. . .fifteen. . ."

Shadow's legs refused to hold him upright any longer, and he went to his knees. The wood of the hitch rack was cool against his burning cheek as he rested his head on the crossbar and closed his eyes. His throat ached with the strain of holding back any cry of rage and pain that pleaded for release.

It would have been a pleasure to give voice to his agony and see Stewart lose the bet. For a moment he considered it and then put the thought away. Stewart's threat meant nothing, but the strong, stubborn, arrogant pride of the Cheyenne warrior ran hot in his veins—stronger than his hatred, stronger that his contempt for the growing circle of bystanders, stronger than his fear of Stewart's retaliation.

He would show them how a Cheyenne warrior withstood pain. He would show them all! And summoning every ounce of his strength, he struggled to his feet, fighting the urge to vomit as the whip seared his flesh like a relentless flame.

"Twenty!"

Smith put his whole arm behind the last blow, and it landed with the sharp crack of a gunshot, gouging a fair-sized hunk of meat out of Shadow's tortured back. Blood sprayed from the cruel wound, glinting like tiny red jewels in the sun's harsh glare.

There was a long silence as Smith dropped his arm to his side. The men in the crowd stared at Shadow's back. A few felt sick to their stomachs. A couple made jokes to cover their embarrassment at participating in such cruelty. Now that the fun was over, they were ashamed.

Turning away, they quickly forgot about their revulsion as bets were paid off and they returned to the saloon.

Smith paid Stewart with a sickly smile. Tossing the whip to the bartender, he stormed into the saloon to mourn his depleted bankroll.

Clyde Stewart was grinning with satisfaction as he cut Shadow free. The Injun's back was pretty messed up, he mused. Not so bad he would have to stay in bed, or miss the next show, but he'd be sleeping on his belly for some time to come. But what the hell—he was strong and healthy and would soon heal. And in the meantime, they were a thousand dollars richer.

A polite cough drew Stewart's attention, and he glanced over his shoulder to find the padre standing at his elbow.

"If you'll permit me, I have some herbs and bandages at the parish house," Father Senteno offered.

"Forget it, padre. I'll take care of him."

"Yes, you're doing a good job of that," the priest retorted with uncharitable sarcasm. "Of course, if infection sets in, you won't have to care for him much longer."

Stewart's brow furrowed as he considered the priest's words. "Say, padre, on second thought, maybe I could use a little help. . ."

Remembering, Shadow sighed. Thanks to the little man's excellent medical attention, his back had healed beautifully, though he still bore the scars of the whip. Since then, Stewart had treated him pretty decently, all things considered. But that didn't make captivity any easier to bear.

At last the show was over, and he was alone in the tent, his leg iron securely locked to one of the heavy, iron-rimmed wheels. Stretched out on his back on a pile of straw, he lay motionless, his thoughts bleak. There had to be a way out, he mused bitterly, and if he hadn't found it yet, it wasn't for lack of trying.

Again and again he had tried to escape. Of necessity, all his attempts had been made during performances, since that was the only time Rudy wasn't breathing down the back of his neck, the only time he was free of the restricting leg iron. And even then his hands were shackled and the Swede's long gun was leveled at his gut, tracking his every move.

Nevertheless, he had made a dozen, ill-fated bids for freedom, gambling that Rudy would not shoot to kill. The first time he'd tried to run, he'd made it out of the tent, only to be apprehended by a policeman who happened to be patrolling the midway at the time. Another night, McCall roped him from the stage. More than once, men in the audience had cheerfully blocked his path.

He had tried again just last week. Would have made it but for some fool dude in a white suit and spats who tripped him just before he made it through the doorway.

Enraged by his repeated attempts to escape, Stewart had threatened to ham-string him the next time he bolted from the stage. But all the threats in the world would not stop him. He would try again and again and again, until he gained his freedom or perished in the attempt.

He scowled into the darkness. He had been Stewart's meal ticket for the better part of three months, he thought bitterly, though it seemed longer. Much longer.

The sound of someone crawling under the heavy canvas reached his ears. Curious, he swung his head toward the noise and frowned as a young girl slipped under the back of the tent. Dusting off her long blue skirt, she stood still for several moments, letting her eyes adjust to the tent's gloomy interior.

She was about sixteen, with long brown hair and light eyes. Her mouth was wide and red, and her figure was well-rounded and pleasing to the eye.

Spying Shadow lying under the wagon, she took a tentative step forward. "Hello, there," she said nervously. "My friends and I were at the show tonight." She took another step toward the wagon. "They dared me to sneak in here."

Shadow stared at her quizzically as she closed the distance between them.

"I'm supposed to bring them a feather from that thing to prove I was here," she explained, pointing at the warbonnet hanging from a nail on the side of the wagon.

There was a faint rustle and a clatter of chains as Two Hawks Flying rolled to his feet. His sudden movement startled the girl, and she took a hasty step backward.

"You scared me!" she accused, then giggled when she saw he was chained to the wagon and could not reach her. "My!" she exclaimed. "You're even bigger than I thought."

The faintest trace of amusement flickered in Shadow's dark eyes as he turned and plucked one of the snowy white feathers from the warbonnet. Twirling it between his thumb and forefinger, he held it out to the girl, daring her to come closer.

With some trepidation, she stepped forward and accepted the feather and smiled her thanks. For a moment they stood facing each other, then she reached out an inquisitive hand and touched his naked shoulder. Bolder now, she let her hand slide down his arm, caressing the thick muscles that swelled beneath her fingers.

"I wonder if Indians kiss?" she mused aloud, and foolishly closed her eyes, imagining herself caught up in the warrior's strong arms and carried forceably away to his wickiup where she would be compelled to submit to his savage embrace.

Her eyes flew open as fantasy became reality and she found herself imprisoned in his arms—arms as solid and unyielding as steel bands. Fear's icy hand throttled the scream that rose in her throat. She trembled with terror as his dark head descended over her own, blotting everything from her vision but the desire smoldering in his eyes. All the awful stories she had ever heard, all the atrocities Indians reportedly inflicted on white women tumbled through her mind, making her heart pound and her knees weak.

Expecting to be brutally assaulted, she was taken aback when, ever so gently, he kissed her. His mouth was warm as it traveled from her lips to her cheek to the pale curve of her throat, awaking passions that lay dormant within her.

He had not had a woman for longer than he cared to remember, and he thought fleetingly of pulling her under the wagon and satisfying the hunger her nearness had triggered. But she was little more than a child and he could not bring himself to take her and so, reluctantly, he released her.

The girl swayed against him, face upturned, ripe red mouth tacitly asking for more, and he willingly obliged her.

"Wow, you're really something," she murmured breathlessly. "None of the boys at home kiss like that."

For the first time in months Two Hawks Flying laughed. Still grinning, he pulled the warbonnet from its hook and handed it to the girl.

"Here," he said softly. "You deserve the whole damn thing!"

Chapter 19

I was all alone atop a high mountain. All around me the world was dark and cold and I was afraid. Shivering, frightened of the unfriendly darkness that shrouded me, I fell to my knees, buried my face in my hands, and began to cry. There was an emptiness inside me, a growing ache that took the joy and color from life and made all the world sad and gray.

Suddenly a familiar voice called my name. Could it be...? Not daring a hope, I raised my head and brushed the tears from my eyes. And he was there. Tall and dark, eyes black as midnight, he stood before me, arms outstretched. Crying with joy, I hurled myself into his arms, and as I did, the darkness melted away, taking with it all the sorrow and fear that had made life unbearable. Happiness as I had never known filled my breast.

"Shadow!" I cried, and awoke with his name on my lips. "Shadow," I whispered, and heaved a great sigh of disappointment as I realized it had all been a dream.

Beside me, Joshua was snoring softly. Not wanting to wake him, I eased out of bed, slipped on my robe, and padded barefoot into the parlor. Taking a chair by the window, I felt the tears come as I stared out into the darkness. Strange, how quickly the days had passed when Shadow had been with me. Now they dragged, and it seemed like five years had passed since I last saw him, instead of only five months.

Sighing, I leaned back and closed my eyes. I had thought to make the best of my marriage to Josh. We had made a bargain, Josh and I, and I had fully intended to keep my part. But try as I might, I could not make myself love Joshua. I didn't even like him anymore. He was hard and cold, and his implacable hatred for Indians tarnished his feelings for everything else. I had seen that poisonous hatred in action more than once, and it left me with a cold lump in the pit of my stomach. Just last week he had hung three Apaches caught stealing a stray calf.

The cow thieves were only boys, the oldest not more than fourteen or fifteen. Just skinny, scared kids driven by hunger. I had watched my husband's face as he gave the order that sent three young boys to their deaths. I saw him smile, pleased, each time the trap door was sprung.

The only bright spot in our marriage was the baby I carried under my heart. I think we were both hoping the child would work a miracle and create a bond of love between us. Personally, I knew such a hope was futile, but I had to cling to something, for there was a terrible tension between us, a strained, bitter feeling of failure that grew harder and harder to bear as the days went by.

I thought often of Shadow. How I envied him his freedom. I had never realized how much I'd grown to love the Indian way of life until I found myself confined to four walls again. Somehow, I felt like I was smothering. I could understand now why Shadow's people had fought so hard to stay free. I, too, longed to ride the high plains again, to lie on a curly buffalo robe inside the snug cocoon of a hide lodge. I longed to follow the buffalo, to see them moving across the vast sea of grass, to hear the thunder of their passing. I was homesick for the smell of woodsmoke and roasting meat, for the warm friendliness of the Cheyenne people, for the sight of painted ponies grazing in the tall grass. Often I thought of Black Owl and Fawn and New Leaf, of Elk Dreamer and Tall Horse and Calf Running. And of a tiny grave beside a snow-covered hill.

I did not like my new life—or my new clothes. Joshua had burned my doeskin dress and moccasins the day we were married and had bought me several colorful cotton frocks for everyday wear, as well as a lovely blue silk gown for parties. I knew I was being ungrateful, but I found my new clothes stifling; the corsets and voluminous petticoats were burdensome after the loose-fitting comfort of my Indian garb. And after wearing moccasins for nearly two years, high button shoes and stockings were a torment beyond belief.

I was plagued by boredom. I spent long hours at the corral with Sunny. I brushed her so often, her chestnut coat shone like smooth satin, and her mane and tail were like silk. She was fat and sassy now, and I longed to ride her outside the fort, to see open spaces and rolling hills, to hear the song of the forest and the gentle whisper of rushing water, but riding outside the fort was forbidden.

Sunny was my last link with Shadow, and

as I watched her prance around her corral, I remembered other happier days when I had ridden at Shadow's side, content just to be near him. Content to suffer any hardship so long as I could feel the warmth of his love and the touch of his hands.

Living with Shadow had never been easy, but it had been satisfying and exciting. And I had always had plenty of work to occupy my time. Now I had little to do once the house was clean and the day's meals planned and prepared, and that took less than no time at all.

In an effort to pass the time, I decided to redecorate Josh's quarters. I ordered some paint from back east—light blue for our bedroom, yellow for the kitchen, pale green for the parlor. Josh wanted to have one of the enlisted men do the painting, but I refused help. I had to feel useful again. I needed to feel like I was accomplishing something worthwhile, so every day for a week I painted, until our little house looked new.

When the painting was done, I began to sew new curtains for each room. Josh was pleased by my domestic efforts. He thought that I was blissfully happy and that I was sewing and cooking to please him, never dreaming that I worked myself to exhaustion in a vain effort to forget Shadow.

Only by keeping busy could I shut his memory from my mind and pretend that I was where I wanted to be.

When the curtains were made, I quilted a bedspread for our bed.

In June, three Apache warriors were brought into the fort. I knew them all from the days when I had ridden the war trail with Shadow. Hands and feet securely shackled, they were hustled into the stockade.

Knowing they would not eat Army food, I made a big pot of stew and carried it to the jail after Josh left on patrol.

The soldier guarding the prisoners was reluctant to let me pass, but he was young and inexperienced, and I finally persuaded him to let me inside the cell by implying that I had Joshua's permission.

The three warriors glared at me, hate and distrust evident in their black eyes as I offered them each a bowl of stew, which they all refused.

"Take it," I said. "It will give you strength."

"Usen will give us strength," the warrior called Gray Wolf retorted.

"Usen cannot feed your empty bellies," I said, offering him the bowl again. "Nor yours, Yellow Crow."

Yellow Crow regarded me with curious eyes. "How do you know my name?"

"Do you not recognize me? I am the woman of Two Hawks Flying."

"How come you to be in this place?" Gray Wolf asked. "Are you a prisoner?"

"No, I am not a prisoner," I said, sighing. "Here, eat quickly."

At ease now, the warriors accepted the food, emptying their bowls several times.

I was glad when Josh did not return to the fort that night. He would have been angry when he learned I had taken food to the prisoners, and I was in no mood for a fight.

I took breakfast to the Indians in the morning. "Have you seen Calf Running?" I asked. "Or Tall Horse?"

"Tall Horse is dead," Yellow Crow said stonily. "We have not seen Calf Running since the time of new grass."

"Have you seen Two Hawks Flying?"

"No," Gray Wolf answered. "We have heard nothing of him. Why are you not with him?"

"It's a long story," I said, collecting their dishes. "There is no time to tell it now."

Pensive, I left the stockade and went to see Doctor Mitchell. I told him, convincingly, that I was having trouble sleeping, and he prescribed a mild sedative.

Thanking him, I returned to the house, praying that Joshua would not return from his patrol that night. Apparently, Man Above heard my prayers.

At dinnertime, I made my way to the stockade with a tray for the prisoners. I had also brought a cup of coffee for the guard, generously laced with brandy, and the sedative Doctor Mitchel had given me.

The guard thanked me so profusely for the coffee, I felt a little guilty, but I could not sit idly by and see three of my friends hanged without trying to save them.

When I left the stockade thirty minutes later, the guard was sleeping peacefully. His gun and the keys to the jail cell were in Gray Wolf's capable hands.

I slept little that night. In the morning, I felt a warm sense of peace and satisfaction when I heard the prisoners had escaped without a trace. Colonel Crawford was furious. Twice now, prisoners had escaped from the stockade. The guard on duty was stripped of his rank and given ten days at hard labor. I felt terribly guilty about that, but his punishment seemed a small thing compared to three lives.

Josh returned to the fort that afternoon. He threw me a hard, probing look when he heard about the Indians and their escape, but for once he did not question me, and our reunion was relatively peaceful.

Their patrol, which had started out as a routine check of the area, had flushed out a dozen young Apache and Comanche youths who had raided a small farm some fifty miles to the west. They had trailed the culprits for two days, found them hiding in a dry wash, and executed them on the spot.

Josh was all aglow with the thrill of victory. He considered the deaths of the Indian boys quite a coup and talked about it all through dinner.

That night, when he took me in his arms, I wondered if I would ever learn to enjoy his touch. He was my husband, legally and officially. Once, I had cared for him a great deal. Why couldn't I respond to his caresses? Why did his touch leave me cold? Why, oh why, couldn't I forget Shadow?

As Joshua's hands fondled my breasts, I wondered where Shadow was now, and what he was doing. Had he found someone else to warm his blankets? Was he making some other woman his, possessing her even as Josh was now possessing me? The very thought filled me with pain.

At least once a week Josh and I were invited to Colonel Crawford's house for dinner. Naturally, we always accepted. There were usually several other officers present and they invariably began to talk about old campaigns. The battle of the Little Bighorn came up most often. Usually, Colonel Crawford started it by saying, "If only Custer hadn't split his forces. . ."

Which prompted Major Callaghan to remark, "If only Reno had had some experience fighting Indians. . ."

Which led Lieutenant Broadhead to mutter, "If only George had waited for Terry and Gibbon. . ."

And then the others would chime in.

"If only Custer had listened to Varnum. . ."

"If only Crook hadn't been whipped at the Rosebud. . ."

"If only Custer hadn't been so cocksure of himself. . ."

"If he hadn't been so greedy for glory. . ."

"If Grant had only kept Custer in Washington a little longer. . ."

Certain names were repeated again and again whenever anybody talked of Custer. The Powder River. The Tongue. The Yellowstone. The Rosebud, named for the rosebushes that grew wild along its banks. Medicine Tail Coulee. Sundance Creek. The Crow's Nest.

Lonesome Charlie Reynolds. Mitch Bouyer. Varnum. Bloody Knife, the Arikara scout—the only friendly Indian who didn't turn tail and run when the fighting started.

The steamer, "Far West." Captain Keogh's horse, Comanche. The newspaper reporter, Mark Kellog. Isaiah Dorman, the Negro interpreter.

Names. Benteen, Reno, Crook, Gibbon, Terry, Weir, Tom Custer—and the general. Always the general.

Why had Custer divided his regiment? Why had he refused to believe his own scouts when they told him there were thousands of Indians camped in the valley? Had he wantonly risked the lives of his men? Or had he really believed the Seventh was unbeatable?

I never joined in these discussions or in any others that involved Indians. My love for Shadow and my affection for the Cheyenne made me an alien among my own people.

As the days went on, I grew increasingly grateful for my friendship with Doctor Mitchell. We had gotten well acquainted during my stay in the hospital, and I began to seek his company more and more. He was the one person I could talk to about Shadow without fear of reproof, the one person I could be totally honest with. Early in our relationship he had asked me, bluntly, how I could love an Indian when Indians had killed my family and friends. In reply, I had explained how Shadow had saved me when the Sioux attacked the trading post, and how, from that night on, Shadow was not an Indian and I was not a white. We were simply two people in love.

Doctor Mitchell had smiled at my answer and then remarked, "Of course. That's the only way it could work."

After Josh and I were married, I invited Ed Mitchell to dinner often. He was never at a loss for words and his presence at our table brightened many a strained evening.

I grew increasingly lonely for Fawn and New Leaf as the days passed, wondering often if Fawn had ever regained her health. I missed the laughter of the Cheyenne women and the warm closeness we had shared while working side by side.

There were women at the fort, of course. Five of them besides myself. Outstanding among these was Margaret Crawford, the colonel's wife. She was a tall, angular woman, with graying brown hair and sharp brown eyes, every bit as cool and self-assured as her husband. Margaret Crawford had been an Army wife for twenty years and she had definite opinions about every phase of Army life, which she aired freely and often.

Mabel Brinkerman was the sutler's wife. She was about my age, with delicate skin, a mane of black hair, and mischievous brown eyes. She openly adored her husband, Tom, and frequently said so.

Sylvia Wallace was married to Jake Wallace, the chief of the Army scouts. She was a timid, mousy creature, hardly the type you'd expect to be married to a hardy frontiersman.

Emily Morton was married to the colonel's aide. She rarely had two words to say for herself and dutifully agreed with the colonel's wife on everything.

Stella MacDonald was married to Sergeant Major Carl MacDonald. Their marriage was not a happy one, and I had the distinct impression that if a stray arrow found its way into Carl's rotund flesh Stella would not grieve hard or long. She hated everything about the west—the heat, the Apaches, the scorpions, the snakes, the dust—and she complained long and loud about them all.

As the colonel's wife, Margaret Crawford felt it was her duty to invite the ladies to her home once a week. Sometimes we played cards. More often we quilted, or rolled bandages for the hospital. I would have preferred to avoid these little get-togethers but Josh insisted I attend. I did not feel comfortable at these gatherings. The good ladies of the fort were nice enough, I suppose, but in their eyes I could see a hundred questions they dared not ask. They thought it scandalous that I had willingly lived with an Indian, and even worse that I had done so without the blessings of the church or benefit of clergy. But what shocked them right down to their socks was the fact that I had crossed half the country with seventy warriors. I could look into their eyes and see them wondering if I had slept with all seventy!

The subject of Indians came up at our weekly get-togethers as often as it did everywhere else, which was practically every minute of every day. Geronimo and his bronco Apaches were raising hell on both sides of the border, and the women constantly lamented the fact that the West wouldn't be a fit place to live until the Indians were completely subdued. It galled me to hear them talk about the Apache as if they were less than human and infuriated me even more when Mrs. Crawford said they should all be exterminated, as if they were bugs or spiders, fit only to be crushed under the heels of white men. Sometimes I thought

I'd scream if I had to listen to Mabel Brinkerman tell how her brother had been burned alive by the Comanche in Texas, or sit through another accounting of how scared Sylvia Wallace had been to cross the plains to join her husband here at the fort.

"Why, those Indians are just like mad dogs," Sylvia said breathlessly. "Biting and snapping at anything that moves!"

"Yes," Margaret Crawford readily agreed. "And ungrateful dogs at that. Why don't they stay on the reservation where they belong? My goodness, we give them food and clothing and blankets. What more do they want?"

"Perhaps they want their freedom," I suggested quietly. "Perhaps they want their land back. And the buffalo. And the right to live and hunt in the old way." I heard my voice rising as I went boldly on. "Perhaps they don't want charity from the hands of their enemies. Perhaps they just want to be treated as human beings capable of taking care of themselves and making their own decisions!"

As I had never entered into any conversation concerning Indians before, or expressed any opinions or sentiments in their behalf, my outburst took the good ladies of the fort completely by surprise.

Mrs. Crawford could not have been more shocked if I had suddenly disrobed and thrown myself naked across her table.

"Human beings!" she exclaimed, aghast. "Mrs. Berdeen, do you know what you're saying?"

"I think so," I replied calmly. "After all, I did live with the Cheyenne for nearly two years."

I was immediately sorry I had ever opened my mouth. Five pairs of eyes swung in my direction, and I felt exactly like a bug under a microscope as Margaret Crawford said, ever so sweetly, "Yes, I'd forgotten that. Tell me, my dear, what's it like to live with savages?"

"I don't know," I replied in the same cloying tone. "I didn't live with any savages. I lived with the Cheyenne, and for the most part I found them to be decent human beings, just like everybody else."

"Come now, my dear. Everyone knows the Indians are totally uncivilized. Why, they're nothing but barbarians, totally lacking in honor and human dignity."

"Is that so!" I snapped, incensed by her patronizing tone. "I suppose you call the Camp Grant Massacre the act of a civilized people? And how about Sand Creek? Was Chivington acting like a civilized human being when he opened fire on all those helpless women and children? And as for our race being honorable, why we haven't kept one treaty we've made with the Indians. Not one!"

An uncomfortable silence fell over the parlor. Mrs. Crawford's face was crimson, not from embarrassment but from shock that the wife of a junior officer would dare speak to her in such a tone. I knew I had committed a terrible breach of post etiquette, and before anyone could speak, I mumbled a brief farewell and hurried out of the room and out of the house.

Later that day, Joshua caught hell from Colonel Crawford and that night I caught hell from Josh. Eyes blazing, my husband reminded me that I was no longer a squaw but a soldier's wife and I was not to forget it again. Not only that, he told me in no uncertain terms that I was never again to defend the Indians, publicly or privately. Further, I was to apologize to the colonel's wife for my outburst before the day was through, and then I was to forget I had ever even seen an Indian, let alone been so misguided as to live with one.

Forget, I thought. I would never forget. Not if I lived to be a hundred. Living with Shadow had never been easy but I would gladly have suffered the cold, fatigue, and gut-wrenching hunger all over again for one night in his arms.

Shadow, my heart, my life. Shadow, my strength, my love. Where was he now, when I needed him more than ever?

Chapter 20

Summer came and with it a wave of home-sickness. Lying beneath the equipment wagon late at night, Two Hawks Flying dreamed of home and freedom, hungry for the sight of broad grassy plains and curly-haired buffalo, for the sight of friendly Indian faces and sleek pinto ponies. He yearned for the sound of rushing rivers and the wind sighing over the prairie. He longed to see majestic waterfalls cascading over snow-capped mountains. His mouth watered for the taste of roast buffalo hump and boudins.

But more than this he dreamed of revenge. Night after night, in a hundred ways, he killed the three men who held him in captivity.

And always, invariably, he dreamed of Hannah. He remembered her merry laughter as they tumbled in the tall grass beside the river. Remembered the warm radiance of her smile, the sweet taste of her lips, and the good clean smell that was hers alone. He remembered, too, how she had ridden the war trail at his side, never complaining. She had endured hunger, thirst, and bone-chilling cold and fatigue as stoically as any warrior. She had nursed the wounded, comforted the dying, and grieved for the dead. No Cheyenne squaw could have done more. Her image danced before him, now fresh and pink with the first blush of womanhood, then swollen with the bloom of new life she had carried beneath her heart. He recalled how eagerly she had molded her lovely golden body to his own, and a wild animal-like cry of outrage rumbled low in his throat as he thought of her lying in another man's arms. And his hatred for Clyde Stewart and Barney McCall and Rudy dwindled to nothingness in the face of his hatred for Joshua Berdeen.

And so the days passed. Long lonely days, and each one the same as the last. Long lonely nights, and nothing but his own dismal thoughts to fill them, until the thought of another day in captivity was more than he could bear. He became increasingly hostile and surly as the weeks went by. Five times in as many days he tried to escape and failed. The sixth day, on stage, as a pasty-faced dude slapped bright yellow paint across his face, the anger burning inside him burst into flame. Yelping the Cheyenne warcry, he knocked the startled man aside and hurled himself at Stewart.

Pandemonium broke loose in the tent as the Indian's shackled hands closed like steel jaws around the throat of the great white scout.

Moving with incredible speed for one so big, Rudy exploded out of the wings and clubbed Two Hawks Flying into submission while Barney McCall soothed the hysterical crowd.

Thereafter, the Indian's hands were shackled behind his back before the first show and remained that way until the last show of the night was over.

And still he fought them, determined to cause Stewart and his two pals so much trouble they would either free him and find another meal ticket, or kill him. Obsessed with the need to be free, he did not care which course they chose, so long as it ended once and for all the misery of his captivity.

That summer, Hansen's Traveling Tent Show toured New York, Pennsylvania, and

Virginia. In each town, they raised their tents and sideshows, and people came from miles around to see the funny, the strange, the unusual. Clyde Stewart and his wild Indian were always the biggest draw in any town. There were Indians in the East, of course — Huron, Delaware, Shawnee, Cayuga, Iroquois, Onondaga, Seneca, Seminole. But they had been subdued long ago; they had either been expelled from their native homeland by the intrusion of the white man or restricted to cramped reservations where they were virtually forgotten.

But here, live on stage, was a Cheyenne warrior who had actually participated in the Custer massacre. It was thrilling to see him standing on the stage, only a few feet away, clad in a skimpy clout and moccasins. Why, he was a piece of history!

For Two Hawks Flying, it was an endless nightmare. Sometimes he felt as if every white man in the world had gawked at him, eyes filled with curiosity or loathing or bitter contempt. Some spoke with peculiar accents; some had skins of yellow or black. He saw women dressed in calico and gingham, and women dressed in silks and satin and plumed hats. And yet, despite race or sex or position in life, they all stared at him as if he were something less than human.

* * *

In August, the show took a three week vacation. They were in Philadelphia at the time. Stewart puzzled over what to do with Two Hawks Flying. They could not keep him in the hotel, nor did Stewart want to spend his vacation babysitting the Indian. There were saloons and whores that cried out for his attention, and Stewart fully intended to sample all the delights the city of brotherly love had to offer.

He was strolling casually through the town, pondering his problem, when he happened upon an old jail near the outskirts of town. It was a small square cell; the back wall was made of stone, the two side walls were made of iron bars, and the door was constructed of iron bars set in three-inch oak.

The local constable readily agreed to let Stewart house the Indian in the abandoned jail for the time needed, and Stewart grinned with satisfaction. His problem was solved.

Two Hawks Flying shuddered visibly as the heavy door slammed shut behind him. There were no furnishings of any kind in the cell. The floor was a slab of cement, the roof was tin, and the building was small—so very small. Three long strides carried him from one wall to the other.

It was the longest three weeks of his life. There was no privacy inside the cell. People came to stare at him at all hours of the day and night. Sometimes he woke in the morning to find a dozen kids staring at him, making jokes.

At night, men who were feeling the effects of a little too much liquor stood around the cage taunting him, boasting about how they would beat the devil out of his red hide if they could just get their hands on him.

Occasionally, women would pass by, careful not to get too close. They talked among themselves as if he were an animal who could not understand their words. It surprised him—the way supposedly well-bred white women speculated about his masculinity.

Stewart brought him a bucket to relieve himself in and a blanket to ward off the chill of the night. Rudy brought him three meals a day. Food was one thing Clyde Stewart did not skimp on, knowing no one would pay a dime to see a skinny, undernourished Indian who didn't look strong enough or fit enough to have done the deeds he was accused of.

It was humiliating to have to eat and sleep and urinate while white men and women stared at him like he was some kind of freak. The first two weeks it seemed as though there were always at least two or three dozen people standing around, pointing and laughing, trying to make him laugh or get angry. Only his iron control kept him from screaming with fury.

He had been locked in the tiny cell for about two and a half weeks when he lost his temper.

It was a Sunday, and a number of people had gathered around the cage. Most were dressed in their Sunday best, having just left church. One man, dressed in work clothes and smelling of sour whiskey, began to brag about how many Indians he had killed when he rode shotgun for the Deadwood stage line. He was, he boasted, a better shot than Buffalo Bill or Hickock or any of them so-called fancy gun artists.

Abruptly, the man's topic turned from the number of Indians he had killed to the number of squaws he had lived with.

"Them Apache women," he mused, "they're mostly fat and ugly. The Comanche, too. But them Cheyenne women—now they're something else. Handsome women, they are. Right handsome. But feisty." He pointed to a long scar on his left cheek. "Cheyenne woman give me that. Come at me with a knife, she did. But hell, once I tamed her, she was a real pussy cat. Good beneath the buffler robes, once you tame 'em down a mite. Ain't that right, Injun? Hell," he said, grinning and strutting before the cage, "it might have been one of this here Red John's relatives what gave me this scar!"

The crowd laughed, some in genuine amusement, some in embarrassment.

The white man stepped closer to the cage, his face almost touching the bars. "What do you think, redskin? Think it might have been one of your kin tried to kill ole Pete with that knife?"

"I think you are full of shit," Two Hawks Flying retorted, and then, taking a step back, he grabbed the slop bucket from the corner and hurled the foul-smelling contents into the man's face.

The crowd gasped and hurriedly backed away as the vile contents sailed through the bars. A few of the men snickered, and then there was a deadly silence as the urine-drenched Pete pulled a derringer out of his coat pocket.

"You dirty redskin bastard," he hissed. "I'll kill you for that!"

He was raising the deadly little gun when Barney McCall slammed into him, knocking him flat.

"What the hell's going on here?" McCall demanded, wresting the gun from the man's grasp.

"That Injun of yours threw piss all over me!"

"Yeah," Barney said, wrinkling his nose

with distaste. "I can see that. And from what I heard, maybe you deserved it."

"Why you. . ."

"Come on," Barney cut in, his tone conciliatory, "let's go over to the barber shop and get you a bath, and then I'll stand you to a bottle at the Velvet Palace. What do you say?"

The man known as Pete started to shake his head, but the prospect of a bottle was too good to pass up. Pasting a grin on his face, he said, "Sure. Sounds good to me. But only if you'll throw in a new set of clothes. These are purely ruint."

"You've got yourself a deal," Barney said. Rising, he gave the man a hand up, and the two walked away down the street, talking and laughing like they were old friends.

The crowd drifted away after that, leaving Two Hawks Flying blessedly alone. With a sigh, he sank down on the floor and stared up at the bright blue sky. He wondered, absently, what punishment he would receive for his rash act. Whatever it was, it would be worth it. Stupid, loud-mouthed white man. He hated them all.

But no punishment was forthcoming, and four days later they left Philadelphia.

They were in a little West Virginia town when Barney voiced the opinion that the act needed a little something extra, a little touch of added color and excitement.

"Just one more stunt," McCall said, thinking out loud. "Just one more gimmick, and we could raise the ante two bits a head."

As always, the thought of more money put a gleam in Stewart's hard blue eyes, and after careful consideration, he decided Two Hawks Flying should do more than merely stand on stage—perhaps do a rain dance, or better yet, a real Cheyenne war dance.

"Why not both?" Barney posed. "And maybe chant a couple of their heathen medicine songs, too."

Clyde nodded. "Not a bad idea," he drawled, stroking his jaw. "In fact, it's a hell of an idea. A performing Injun will draw the people like flies!"

But Two Hawks Flying refused.

"What do you mean, you won't do it?" Stewart exclaimed incredulously. "I'm not asking you. I'm *telling* you!"

"And I am telling you to forget it," Two Hawks Flying snapped. "Because I will not do it."

"And just why the hell not?" Stewart demanded angrily.

Two Hawks Flying remained mute. Rain dances and war dances were sacred to the Indians, not to be taken lightly or made sport of. But you couldn't explain that to a

410

white man, especially a white man of Stewart's ilk. And why should he have to explain anything to Clyde Stewart anyway? Let Stewart rant and rave all he liked; he, Two Hawk Flying, would not perform any of the ceremonial dances or chants of his people before the mocking, disbelieving eyes of the whites. And if Stewart threatened to kill him, which was likely, so be it. Better to die than bring shame and dishonor to his people.

"I asked you a question!" Clyde snarled. "Answer me!"

Two Hawks Flying shrugged negligently. "I am tired of being made a fool," he replied tonelessly. "If you want a Cheyenne war dance, do it yourself."

The quietly spoken words sparked Stewart's volitile temper. Anger flared in the blue eyes, making them glitter like chips of glass, as he bellowed, "Rudy! Barney! Hold him."

Here it comes, Shadow thought dispassionately. And while Stewart rolled up his sleeves, McCall and the Swede grabbed Shadow's arms, pinning him neatly between them. Scowling, Clyde planted himself squarely in front of Two Flying Hawks, flexing his hands and cracking his knuckles, his whole attitude one of impending doom.

"You gonna dance, Injun?" he asked softly.

Stubbornly, Shadow shook his head, adding fuel to the rage already blazing in Stewart's eyes. With a snarl, Clyde unleased a barrage of short hard punches to Shadow's midsection.

"How about it, Injun? Wanna change your mind?"

"No."

Livid now, Stewart attacked again, driving his knotted fists deep in the Indian's belly and throat. The last blow smashed into Shadow's face, bloodying his nose and mouth.

"You had best change your mind," Stewart warned, "or I'll beat the shit outta ya with my bare hands."

It was like Bear Valley all over again, Shadow mused ruefully. Only this time there was only one man attacking him instead of a handful of angry settlers.

"You do not scare me," Shadow retorted recklessly. "I have been worked over by experts."

Clyde Stewart uttered a vile oath. "I'm the boss here, you damned redskin!" he roared. "And you had damned well better know it!"

And so saying, he snatched Rudy's knife from his belt and drove it into Shadow's left shoulder.

"Clyde. . ."

"Shut up, Barney. This is your last chance,

Injun," Stewart growled. "Are you gonna dance or die?"

Shadow's eyes narrowed under Stewart's threatening gaze. He had no doubt that Clyde meant what he said, but he no longer cared. He was tired of captivity, tired of the long empty nights and endless days, tired of being laughed at and stared at. Damn it, if he couldn't be free, he'd as soon be dead.

"Get yourself another Indian," he said wearily. "I quit!"

It was the last straw. Clyde Stewart's face went purple with rage, and before Barney or the Swede could stop him, he plunged the knife into Shadow's side. The Indian grunted and went limp as John Hansen entered the tent.

"What the hell's going on in here?" the carny owner demanded. "We can hear you yelling and screaming down at the other end of the midway."

"None of your business, Hansen!" Clyde snarled.

"This is my tent and that makes it my business," Hansen retorted, "and I'll not see a man cut to ribbons in my carny. Not even a godless savage."

"Then don't watch!" Stewart snapped.

"Now see here," Hansen protested. "I don't have to. . ."

"Shut up, old man!" Stewart bellowed,

413

and taking a step forward, backhanded Hansen across the jaw.

The force of the blow sent the old man reeling. Unbalanced, he tripped on a stool and fell sideways. There was a sickening thud as his head struck the corner of an iron-bound wardrobe trunk; a taut silence ensued as McCall, Stewart, and the Swede exchanged uneasy glances.

Releasing his hold on Two Hawks Flying, Barney scrambled toward Hansen. His face turned ashen as he noticed the unnatural angle of the old man's neck and the thin trickle of blood seeping through colorless lips. Taking a deep breath, McCall felt for Hansen's pulse. There was none.

"Not you've done it," Barney hissed. "The old man's dead."

"Let's get out of here," Rudy whispered. "The Injun's dead, too."

Stewart swore. "Let's make tracks!"

Working swiftly, the three men collected their trail gear and slipped under the rear of the tent. Outside, they mingled with the thinning crowd, then faded into the shadows. They were arguing which way to go when Rudy suddenly remembered he'd left his bankroll under the seat of the equipment wagon.

"Forget it!" Stewart advised crossly. "Let's move."

"Forget it, hell," Rudy retorted. "I got better than two grand back there. You two go on ahead, round up some horses. I'll meet you behind Fremont's hash house."

"You've got ten minutes," Stewart warned. "You take one minute longer, you're on your own."

For all his bulk, the Swede moved like a dark, silent shadow as he skulked along the deserted midway and bellied under the big blue and white striped tent. The two bodies lay as before, still and ugly in death. An eerie stillness hung in the air, and Rudy shivered superstitiously as he stepped over the Indian's inert form and rummaged under the wagon seat.

One of the bodies stirred slightly, turning just his head as he watched the Swede. Teeth clenched against the pain and nausea that threatened to render him helpless, Two Hawks Flying pulled the knife out of his side and stood up.

At the wagon, Rudy grunted with satisfaction as his searching fingers closed over his money pouch.

"California, here I come," he muttered under his breath, and then froze as he felt the unmistakable prick of a knife just behind his left ear. A warm trickle of blood spilled down his neck as the blade nicked his flesh.

"Do not move," warned a voice behind him.

"No. No, I won't," Rudy said quickly. "Listen, mister, if it's money you want, I got plenty. You can have it all."

"I do not want your money. I want the keys to these irons."

"Injun?" Rudy gasped. "I thought you were dead."

"Not yet. Give me the key."

"Sure, sure," Rudy said, delving into his pants pocket. "Here, take it."

"Stewart," Shadow rasped, taking the key in his free hand. "Where is he?"

"I don't know," Rudy said, and yelped as he felt the knife bite deeper into his flesh. "Wait!" he croaked. "I'll talk. He's in the alley behind Fremont's Hash House. Him and Barney both."

"You talking straight tongue?"

"I swear it!"

The Swede knew a moment of sweet relief as the blade was withdrawn, but it proved to be shortlived and he roared like a wounded bull buffalo as Shadow drove the blood-stained knife through his back. A great rush of blood jetted from the Swede's mouth as he collapsed against the side of the wagon, still clutching his money pouch.

"One down and three to go," Shadow murmured, and with one hand pressed against his bleeding side, he bent down and removed the chain from his ankle, then slipped under the back of the tent. Feeling lightheaded, he glided silently down a dark alleyway. He had not gone far when he spotted Stewart and McCall outlined in the darkness ahead.

"He's late," Stewart was saying.

"Let's give him another minute or two," Barney urged.

"Not me," Clyde said, swinging aboard his black gelding. "I'm leavin'. You want me, you'll find me in Abilene."

McCall gazed uncertainly after Stewart. "Oh, hell," he muttered, and started for his horse.

He never made it. Shadow's knife swished through the air, silent as the finger of death as it caught Barney McCall high in the back, just left of center. With a grunt, McCall fell face down in the alley, hands clawing for the blade that was slowly stealing the life from his body.

The warrior's moccasined feet made no sound as he approached the dying man and callously yanked the knife from his back.

Fighting to stay conscious, Two Hawks Flying lifted McCalls gun from the holster and then, with teeth clenched and great beads of sweat pouring from his brow, he hauled himself into the saddle of Barney McCall's dun gelding and urged the animal down the alley after Stewart.

It was after midnight when he found Clyde Stewart sleeping peacefully beside a babbling brook. Leaving the dun ground-reined out of sight and downwind of Stewart's mount, Two Hawks Flying moved soundlessly toward his quarry. The black gelding blew softly and pawed the earth as Two Hawks Flying materialized out of the darkness.

Stewart woke instantly, automatically reaching for the Winchester rifle that lay close beside him. He shrieked with pain as Shadow's knife drove through the back of his hand, pinning it to the ground. In desperation, Stewart made a clumsy grab for his six-gun with his left hand, then hollered again as Two Hawks Flying kicked the gun from his grasp. He swallowed hard as he found imself staring into the unblinking eye of McCall's Colt .44.

"If you know any prayers, you had better say them," Two Hawks Flying suggested coldly.

"You!" Stewart breathed. "You're supposed to be dead."

"I will be, before too long," the warrior allowed. "But not until I finish with you."

"You can't kill me!" Stewart cried shrilly, the pain in his hand forgotten as he gazed into the Cheyenne's flat black eyes. "I saved your life. You would have died in the desert if me and Barney hadn't come along when we did."

There was no change in the Indian's fathomless black eyes, and Stewart whined, "Injun, wait! Can't we talk this over?"

Two Hawks Flying pressed his hand over the wound in his side. A warm sticky wetness coated his palm. Slowly, he shook his head.

"No time for talk," he said thickly.

A tiny flicker of hope sparked in Clyde Stewart's blue eyes as he noticed the dark stain that was rapidly spreading down the Indian's side. If he could just stall for a few more minutes, the redskin would be dead at his feet.

The warrior's lips curled back in a wolfish grin as he read the thoughts scudding across the white man's mind. Slowly, he thumbed back the hammer to full cock.

"You will die before I do," Two Hawks Flying promised, and as Stewart's face began to blur, he squeezed the trigger.

Clyde Stewart's last terrified scream was swallowed up in the roar of the gunshot. The bullet took him squarely between the eyes, and his handsome face dissolved in a torrent of bright blood and bone fragments.

Two Hawk Flying knew a fleeting moment of satisfaction as he stared at the yawning maw that had once been a man's face. He smiled faintly as he dipped his hands in the warm blood of his enemy.

And then there was only darkness as he pitched headlong into oblivion. . . .

Chapter 21

He regained consciousness a layer at a time, vaguely aware that he was not alone, that he was lying on a bed, that his hands were tied to the bedposts. A cool cloth covered his eyes, blinding him to his surroundings. His throat felt tight and it was an effort to swallow, even to breathe. The faint fragrance of wildflowers hung in the air, mingling pleasantly with the aroma of fresh perked coffee. Fragments of a hushed conversation penetrated the mists of pain that held him fast, like a wolf in a trap.

". . .pretty bad."

"Good thing we found him when we did. . ."

"Lucky to be alive. . ."

". . .so much blood."

Exploring hands touched his side, and he flinched involuntarily as scorching fingers of flame lanced through his right side.

"Mother, be careful!" a young voice admonished.

"I'm being as careful as I can, Beth," Rebecca Matthews answered, "but I've got to see how bad he's hurt. Bring that light closer, child. And hand me that bandage. And that roll of tape."

Two Hawks Flying groaned as a thick wad of dressing was laid over the knife wound in his side and taped in place, then shuddered convulsively as his unseen benefactor sponged the dried blood from the shallow gash in his shoulder. Someone—the young girl?—wiped the sweat from his brow with a gentle hand.

"Well, that does it," the woman said matter-of-factly. "He's lost a powerful amount of blood but he looks strong and healthy. I reckon he'll make it."

"Can't we untie him now?" Beth asked. "He looks awfully uncomfortable trussed up like that."

"No, Beth, not until we find out who he is, and what he was doing lying out in the road."

"But it seems a shame to keep him tied up when he's hurt, like he was a criminal," the girl argued.

"It would be a bigger shame if he up and

killed us while we slept," her mother replied dryly. "And for all we know, he might indeed be a criminal of some kind. You keep an eye on him now, while I go rinse the blood out of these rags."

"Yes, Mother."

There was the sound of footsteps leaving the room, then a faint squeak of springs as the girl sat on the edge of the bed.

Two Hawks Flying moistened his dry lips and rasped, "Girl?" in a barely audible whisper.

"Oh, you're awake," Beth observed, taking the cloth from his eyes. "How do you feel?"

"Like hell," he croaked. "Where am I?"

"In my room," Beth said, smiling. "Mother and I were on our way home from town when we found you lying beside the road." Head tilted to one side, the girl stared at him curiously. "You're an Indian, aren't you? What are you doing so far from home?"

"It is a long story."

"Oh. Well, maybe you'd better save it for later, when you're feeling better. Why don't you get some sleep now?"

"Could I. . .have some water?"

"Sure," she said, and quickly poured him a tall glass of water and held his head up while he drank.

"Sleep now," Beth suggested.

And he did.

When he woke again, it was night. A woman clad in a long cotton nightgown stood silhouetted against the window, facing out. Sensing his gaze, she turned toward him. The moonlight streaming through the parted curtains cast a fainty silvery glow around her, giving her a ghostly appearance as she padded barefoot toward him.

"Are you in pain?" she asked. "Can I get you anything?"

"Water," he husked, and she poured him a glass from a bedside pitcher, carefully raising his head.

"Drink it slowly," she cautioned. "Would you care for anything else? Some broth, perhaps?"

"No."

In a gesture much like her daughter's, Rebecca Matthews tilted her head to one side, took a step backward as she exclaimed, "You're the Indian from the tent show! The one that killed Custer! And Beth wanted to cut you free. Oh my," she murmured, and sank down in the rocker next to the bed.

"Listen, white lady, before you work yourself into a sweat, I did not kill Custer. And I do not go around murdering women and little girls either."

"Surely you don't expect me to believe

that," she retorted. "I read the papers. Two Hawks Flying was mentioned in the local paper as one of the chiefs at the Custer massacre."

Two Hawks Flying smiled wryly. "I did not say I was not there. I said I did not kill him."

"That's a mere technicality," the woman countered.

"Maybe. But if Custer had stayed home where he belonged, he would be alive today."

"Perhaps, but what about all the other people you've killed. Mr. McCall said you were responsible for killing hundreds of white settlers who had done you no harm."

"McCall was a liar," Shadow said flatly.

"Well, it doesn't matter one way or the other. Tomorrow I'll send word to the tent show that you're here."

"No."

"I beg your pardon?"

"Do not tell them I am here."

"Why shouldn't I?" the woman snapped, piqued by his impertinent attitude.

"Because I am tired of being stared at like I was some kind of freak."

"Oh?" she replied coolly, but her expression mellowed somewhat as a hint of compassion rose in her eyes. "Just what should I do with you, then?"

"Let me go home," he said quietly. "Or kill

me if you are afraid to turn me loose, but do not send me back to that circus."

Rebecca stared at him quizzically for a long time. He did not seem like the ferocious savage McCall and Stewart claimed he was, nor did he speak the way she had supposed an Indian would. In fact, he spoke better English than many of her neighbors. Still, he had admitted to being at the Little Bighorn, and even at this late date she could recall the horror she had felt when she read of the Custer massacre. Over two hundred men had died that day, scalped and mutilated by thousands of Indians.

"I'll have to think about it," she murmured, and left the room.

In the morning, Rebecca was still undecided. She warned Beth to stay away from the man, afraid that he might persuade the child to turn him loose. A soft-hearted child, Beth was easily moved by a sad tale or a wistful glance.

After Beth left for school and the Indian's wounds tended, Rebecca went into the parlor and picked up her mending, only to sit staring into the fireplace.

The Indian had again asked her to free him or kill him. Since she could do neither, he had asked her, with quiet dignity, not to notify the tent show of his whereabouts until his wounds were healed. Reluctantly, she had agreed.

"But you'll have to stay tied up the whole time," she warned.

"I do not care," he had replied wearily. "Even this is better than being chained to a wagon."

Now, much to her dismay, she found herself feeling sorry for him. He was a proud man. Anyone could see that. Captivity would have been unbearable, she mused, but not as bad as being made sport of. He seemed like such a quiet, soft-spoken man, she was hard-pressed to believe he was really the cold-blooded killer McCall had said he was. But then, looks were deceiving. . . .

At noon, she took him his lunch. After a moment of indecision, she untied his right hand so he could sit up and feed himself. Then, taking a derringer from the dresser drawer, she sat in a chair at the foot of the bed, the gun lined on his chest while he ate.

Two Hawks Flying studied her surreptitiously as he sipped a cup of coffee. She was a pretty woman, with a mass of wavy brown hair and placid brown eyes. Her features were soft and even; her figure was trim and pleasing to the eye. She was so lovely, so feminine, the derringer looked ludicrous in her hand. Yet he was quite certain she'd pull the trigger if he made the slightest move in her direction.

"You do not have to be afraid of me," he assured her as he finished the meal. "I will not bite you."

"I'm not afraid of being bit," she replied tartly.

"What then?"

"I don't know," she lied, avoiding his gaze. "I only know I don't feel safe with you in the house."

"Why? Because I am an Indian?"

"I don't know!" she snapped crossly, and taking the tray from his lap, she quickly tied his hand to the bedpost again.

His black eyes probed her own, bringing a flush to her cheeks. "Could it be you are afraid of me because I am a man?" he asked softly.

He had ventured too near the truth. With a wordless cry, she slapped him, then fled the room.

Later that night, after Beth was safely tucked into bed and the house was dark and quiet, Rebecca paced the living room floor. Her cheeks burned with shame at the sinful thoughts tumbling through her mind. She had been a widow for three years and she had not been with a man 'that way' in all that time. Had not even wanted one.

Until now. She had been on fire for Shadow's touch since she first saw him lying in the road. Even unconscious, there had been something vital and sensual about him, something coarse and earthy that aroused her as no other man ever had. It was a hard thing for a preacher's daughter to admit—harder still because he was a heathen Indian, but true nonetheless. And though she might burn in hell for her thoughts—thoughts no lady should entertain—she could not put them from her.

There was a faint creak as Beth's bedroom door opened. Filled with dread, Rebecca whirled around and blanched when she saw him outlined in the doorway. Frightened as never before, she cast about for a weapon, wishing she had kept her derringer close at hand.

"Easy, white lady," he admonished quietly.

"What do you want?" she whispered hoarsely.

"Nothing."

She did not believe him. There were too many stories of white women raped by savages, too many tales of treachery and bloodshed.

"Look," Shadow said, "if I sit over there and behave myself, would you make me a cup of coffee?"

"Yes," she said, and fled the room.

Moving slowly, Shadow took a place on the sofa, winching a little as he sat down. The wound in his shoulder ached only a little, but the knife wound in his side remained a constant, throbbing pain.

Glancing around, he saw that the parlor was clean and neat. There was a piano in the corner, a couple of uncomfortable looking chairs, and the sofa on which he sat. A braided rug covered most of the wooden floor. There was a picture of the white man's god on one wall, a pot of flowers on a shelf, and a worn Bible on a low table.

The woman was gone for quite a while—so long, in fact, he began to wonder if she'd slipped out the back door and gone to one of her neighbors for help. He hoped not. He was in no fit condition to fight, but fight he would. Because now, with Stewart and the others dead by his hand, he knew there was a rope waiting for him.

He looked up sharply as Rebecca entered the room carrying the tray laden with a blue enamel coffee pot and two china cups.

"I thought maybe you had run off to get the sheriff or something," he remarked.

"I thought about it," she admitted as she

poured him a cup of coffee, then took a seat in the chair furthest from the couch.

"You really are afraid of me, aren't you?" he mused aloud. "Well, relax, white lady. Even a heathen savage does not attack someone who saved his life."

"Where did you learn to speak English so well?" she asked, curious in spite of her fears.

"From a trapper, when I was a child. He married one of our women and my father decided it would be wise for us to learn the white man's tongue. He said it would be harder for the whites to cheat us if we understood their language. It was harder," he added bitterly. "But it did not stop them."

"How did you get hurt?"

"The great white scout got mad because I would not dance for the people," he answered flatly.

"I'm surprised Mr. Stewart hasn't come looking for you. In fact, no one seems to be looking very hard."

"Stewart will not come," Two Hawks Flying muttered.

"Oh? Why not?"

"Because he is dead. His friends, also."

"You killed them, didn't you?"

"Yes."

"I suppose I can't blame you. Not after the way they treated you."

"You do not sound very sure about that," Shadow remarked dryly.

"I'm not. You talk about it as if it were nothing. Does killing come so easy to you?"

"Believe me, it was not easy. Now, if you will give me another cup of that coffee, I will go."

"No," she said quickly. "I mean, you're in no fit condition to travel."

"I will be all right."

"Please don't go," she whispered hoarsely, and lowered her eyes before his penetrating gaze, ashamed of the hunger she knew was shining in her eyes.

Two Hawks Flying frowned, wondering if the signals he was receiving were the ones she meant to send.

A week later he was up and around. Beth was thrilled by his presence and she dogged his footsteps, asking endless questions about Indian life and love, pestering him to teach her to speak Cheyenne.

Once she overcame her fear of him, Rebecca, too, was glad for his company. It was nice to have a man to do for. She found herself taking greater pains with her appearance, baking more often and singing as she worked. He did not behave at all as she had supposed an Indian would. He knew how to read and write, he spoke English better than some of her neighbors, and his table manners were impeccable. In fact, dressed in one of her husband's shirts and a pair of pants, he looked pretty much like any other man, except for his long hair and coppery skin.

As she got to know him better, she realized he possessed many of the qualitities she had admired in her late husband—virtues like honesty, pride, tenderness, and a strong sense of right and wrong.

For Two Hawks Flying, the days were peaceful and serene. Plenty of rest and Rebecca's good cooking soon had him feeling better than ever, and he began to think about moving on. But then, late one night, Rebecca came to his room. She stood in the doorway, her cheeks flushed and desire shining in her eyes.

He knew what it had cost her, coming to his room. A woman's pride was a fragile thing. She wanted him, and he could not refuse her. She had saved his life, and he had no other way to repay her kindness. She uttered a small sigh of joy and relief when he held out his arms. . . .

The days that followed were the best Rebecca had ever known. All her inhibitions seemed to have vanished like smoke in a high wind, and every night she went eagerly to

Shadow's bed, finding in his arms a joy and fulfillment she had never known. Each day was better than the last, each night a time of blissful delight.

Only on Sundays, in church, did her conscience bother her. Out of his arms, in the harsh light of day, she was forced to admit she was living in sin with a heathen savage. She knew her neighbors would shun her if they knew, and yet, each Sunday night, she shut the door on her conscience and went once more to taste the forbidden fruit.

The days passed, growing longer and warmer. And Shadow grew increasingly more and more restless. Though he had the run of the house, he dared not go outside except late at night for fear of discovery. It was like being in prison again, he mused—a velvet prison this time, but a prison nonetheless.

His temper grew short; often he was silent and brooding. Rebecca was not unaware of his inner restlessness.

"You're thinking of leaving, aren't you?" she asked late one evening.

Two Hawks Flying continued to stare out the bedroom window, his back toward her. "Yes."

"Why?"

"I miss the plains," he answered honestly. "I feel trapped within these walls."

434

"Take us with you."

With a sigh, he turned to face her. "I cannot," he said quietly.

"There's someone else, isn't there?"

"Yes."

"An Indian girl?"

"No. She is white, like you."

"I hate her!" Rebecca cried petulantly.

"Do not waste your anger," Two Hawks Flying chided gently. "She belongs to another."

"Then why must you go? Why can't you take us?"

"I am sorry," he said sincerely, "but I cannot stay. And I cannot take you with me."

"When are you going?"

"In a day or two. Unless you want me to go now?"

"I don't want you to go at all," Rebecca sobbed, and hurled herself into his arms. How would she live without him? He had become important to her. With him, she felt safe and protected. It would be unbearable, to be alone again after knowing the warmth of his arms.

Two Hawks Flying held her while she cried. He did not want to hurt her; in the last few weeks he had grown very fond of her. But it was Hannah who held his heart, Hannah who he yearned for even more than the sun-swept hills and valleys of home.

It still hurt, even after all this time, to think of her in another man's arms. Hannah—soft, honeyed flesh, with a spirit as sweet as life itself. If only he could forget her, but try as he might, she was ever in his thoughts.

With a strangled cry, he carried Rebecca to the bed they had shared, hoping to ease his desire for one woman in the caring arms of another. It was a futile hope, and he knew he would yearn for Hannah even in the After World.

When Rebecca woke the next morning, Two Hawks Flying was gone. Rising, she went to the window and stared into the distance, toward the west. The house seemed unusually quiet, empty without his virile presence.

"You might at least have said good-bye," she murmured brokenly, and then the tears came.

Chapter 22

Two Hawks Flying traveled stealthily across the night-shrouded countryside. In his white man's garb and hat, he knew he could pass as a farmer, but only from a distance, and so he moved with caution. Afoot and unarmed, he would be no match for a mob of blood-hungry whites, and he had no desire to experience again the abuse he had once suffered at the hands of the men in Bear Valley.

He had gone about ten miles when he spied a farmhouse situated atop a small crest. The windows were dark. No smoke rose from the chimney, but still he watched the place for a full thirty minutes before he padded noiselessly up the hill toward the barn, stopping only once to pick up a large rock.

He was opening the barn door when a low

growl sounded behind him. He turned in time to see a large white dog launch itself from the ground, teeth bared in a vicious snarl.

With smooth precision, Two Hawks Flying twisted sideways so that his left shoulder took the brunt of the dog's attack. His right arm was moving too, swinging high and then crashing down as he struck the dog's skull, killing it instantly.

The interior of the barn was dark and smelled of horses and hay and manure. There were three horses housed in the building—two Clydesdale geldings and a chestnut Quarter Horse mare.

A search of the tack hanging on one wall produced a bridle for the chestnut. The mare snorted and backed away as Two Hawks Flying entered her stall. For a moment he stood unmoving, letting the animal get accustomed to his smell and the sound of his voice.

Then, talking gently, he patted the mare's shoulder, gradually moving his hand up her neck to scratch her ears.

The mare rolled her eyes as he slipped the bridle over her head but followed docilely enough as he led her out of the stall.

"Easy, girl," he murmured, and swung effortlessly aboard her back.

Once clear of the farm yard, he put the

mare into a gallop. It was exhilarating to be astride a horse again, to be riding free across open ground. The wind was cold against his face, but it was a good feeling and he threw back his head and laughed aloud. He was free! Free at last!

He rode until dawn, then took shelter in a sandy wash until nightfall. Two nights later, he raided a store in a small town, helping himself to a rifle, ammunition, and a sack of beef jerky.

In the weeks that followed, he rode at night and holed up during the day until he was well away from civilization, and then he rode hard day and night, resting only when the chestnut mare needed time to rest or graze.

A deep need for vengeance against Joshua Berdeen burned hot in his blood, and he knew he would never be content until Berdeen was dead. He felt a twinge of guilt because Berdeen was Hannah's husband, but that fact would not save Berdeen. Two Hawks Flying had suffered much because of the white man's treachery, and the proud warrior blood in his veins cried out for vengeance.

In the land of the Comanche, he traded his weary chestnut mare for a spotted stallion. He was well treated in the Comanche lodges, and he stayed with them for three days, eating and sleeping. He threw away his white man's clothes and again donned clout and moccasins.

The morning of the fourth day, he bid the Comanche farewell and headed west, through the arid plains of Texas and New Mexico.

Three weeks later he reached the Arizona border.

Chapter 23

My baby was a boy. Healthy and strong, he entered the world October 29th, red-faced and howling at the top of his lungs, sounding for all the world like an enraged Indian on the warpath. I wept tears of joy and happiness as Doctor Mitchell laid him in my eager arms. Oh, but he was beautiful, from the top of his black-thatched head right down to the tips of his pudgy little feet.

Doctor Mitchell looked grave as he washed his hands in the basin beside my bed. "You'll never pass that child off as white," he remarked. "You know that, don't you?"

"Why should I want to?" I replied. "I'm not ashamed of him."

"Josh will be," the good doctor stated flatly, and his face was lined with worry as he closed his bag and slipped into his coat. "Do you want me to tell him?"

"Would you, Ed?"

"Sure, honey. Call me if you need me," he said succinctly. "For any reason. Any time." And with a last glance at my son, he left the room.

His words had taken the edge from my happiness. No one knew better than I how angry Josh was going to be when he discovered he was not the baby's father. But there was nothing he could do about it, and after the first explosive burst of fury, he would just have to accept the baby. Josh and I could always have another child—several, if he so desired, though I knew this child, fathered by the man I loved, would always hold a special place in my heart.

Childbirth was hard work and I was on the brink of sleep when I heard Josh's footsteps in the hall. Instinctively, I held my son closer. Josh crossed the room in long strides, and his blue eyes were like pools of glacier ice as he glared down at us.

"So you slept with that red nigger when he was in the hole!" Joshua flung at me. "You dirty little tramp. Rutting in the dirt like a damn squaw!"

I flinched before the disgust in his frosty gaze, but my chin came up and my voice was strong and clear as I said, "Yes, Josh, just like a damn squaw."

Eyes blazing, my husband leaned over me until his face was only inches from my own. "Let me tell you something, Hannah Berdeen. You're not a squaw anymore. You're my wife. And I don't intend to have any little half-breed bastard running around clinging to your skirts."

"Joshua. . ."

"Shut up, you slut! I sent Hopkins out to the Apache reservation to find a squaw to look after your brat, and as soon as he gets back, the kid goes. We'll say it died. I've already discussed it with Mitchell."

"You can't be serious!"

"But I am," Josh replied coldly.

For a moment I could only stare at him, unable to believe my ears. Unable to believe I had once cared for him, that once, long ago, I had fancied myself in love with him.

"Joshua, please don't do this," I begged, "Please! I can't bear to lose another child."

"Stop whining!" he snapped. "You think I want my men whispering behind my back about you and that redskin? You think I want people to know you slept with him right up to the day you married me?"

"Josh, please let me keep the baby. I'll be ever so grateful."

Joshua's eyes pierced mine like daggers. "Shut up, Hannah, or I'll take the bastard out and drown it!"

He wasn't bluffing and we both knew it, just as I knew that nothing I could say would change his mind.

Choking back my tears, I asked, "How soon will Hopkins be back?"

"Tomorrow morning, early," Josh said, going to the door. "And don't worry, I'll see to it that you have another child. One whose skin is the right color."

I stared at the ceiling long after Josh was gone, hearing his voice over and over again as he promised to give me a child who was the 'right color.' I thought of my son growing up on the Apache reservation, raised by strangers, and I went cold all over, as if my blood had suddenly turned to ice. The baby stirred in my arms. My baby. Mine and Shadow's. I couldn't let him be raised on the reservation. Shadow's son should grow up where men were free, where warriors lived and died in the old way. I wanted Shadow's son to know the thrill of chasing down his first buffalo, wanted him to see the prairie in bloom when all the world was green and new, wanted him to experience the wondrous quiet of a midsummer night in the high country.

I had seen San Carlos, the Apache reservation, and been appalled at the poverty in which the Indians lived. Warriors, once proud and free as the wind, sat idly before their lodges day after day, their eyes empty of hope and their spirits broken. The women, even the young ones, looked old and tired. Many of them sold themselves to the soldiers in exchange for food to feed their families. And the children. . .hollow-eyed, gaunt, listless. Their once bright black eyes were dull, their merry laughter stilled. They did not sing, or play, or laugh. No, I could not send Shadow's child to the living hell of life on the reservation.

"I'll think of something," I promised as I kissed my son's downy cheek. "Don't worry. . ."

It was late when I awoke. Tired as I was, there was no time to waste. Dragging myself out of bed, I dressed quickly, threw some food into a sack, and grabbed a canteen from Joshua's field kit. Bundling my son in a heavy blanket, I tiptoed out of the house.

Sunny nickered softly as I led her from the corral, hurriedly slipping a bridle over her head. It was a struggle to swing the heavy saddle in place. That accomplished, I made my way to the gates. There were two sentries patrolling the catwalk, and I was pleased to see they were both standing at the far end, talking quietly as they shared a cigarette. Moving swiftly, I wrestled the heavy bar from the big gate, opening it just enough to allow the horse and myself to pass through. Then, with my son cradled in my right arm and Sunny's reins held tight in my left hand, I disappeared into the shadows. Well away from sight and sound of the fort, I hauled myself into the saddle and lashed Sunny into a gallop.

The wind was cold and damp, and I turned up the collar of my coat, drawing the blanket tighter around my son. In the distance, a coyote raised a lonely lament to the moon. There was menace in the darkness, but the unseen creatures lurking there were not half so frightening as the thought of losing the baby I held in my arms, and I whipped Sunny's flank, demanding more speed.

With the stars to guide me, I headed for the Dakotas. The things I wanted for my son no longer existed. Not here, in Arizona. Not anywhere. The great herds of buffalo were gone. The old days were gone. And if my son was destined to live out his life on a reservation, then so would I. But it would be the Cheyenne reservation, where he could learn the ways of his people.

His people. I thought of Fawn and New Leaf and Black Owl, and a weight seemed to lift from my heart. If they were still alive, I would not be alone. Shadow's father would welcome his son's wife and child. We would be loved and cared for. Black Owl would teach his grandson the things a warrior should know. My son would grow up listening to the old men tell stories of Dull Knife and Black Kettle, of White Antelope and Two Moons. He would hear stories of the great chiefs and thrill to the heroic tales of Sitting Bull and Crazy Horse, of Gall and Hump. He would hear the warriors boast of Two Hawks Flying, the last fighting chief on the plains.

Shadow. Despite the weariness that weighed me down, I suddenly felt much better. I knew Shadow would never live on a reservation under the white man's thumb, but perhaps Black Owl would know where he was.

Joshua swore softly as he saw the rumpled bed and Hannah's nightgown on the floor. So she had taken the brat and run away. Damn her! He'd be the laughing stock of the fort now. And damn that Indian, too—even dead and buried, he still held Hannah tight in his grasp.

Jealousy burned in Joshua's heart. It seemed he had loved Hannah all his life. He still loved her, but she couldn't see him for dust. He wanted to be nice to her, to spoil and pamper her, but every time he looked into her eyes, he knew she still loved the Indian. Would always love the Indian. No matter what he, Joshua, did, he knew she was comparing him to Shadow and finding him wanting.

Indians! How he hated them. They had been the cause of all the unhappiness he had ever known. He had happily killed dozens, perhaps even hundreds, since joining the Army. Once, he had thought that the shedding of Indian blood would somehow atone for the loss of Hannah's love and for the deaths of his parents and his brother. And it had helped a little, but killing had not cooled the hatred in his heart. No, if anything, his hatred for the whole red race burned brighter and hotter than ever.

Shoulders sagging, he sat on the edge of the bed and stared at the nightgown lying in a heap on the floor. The gown was soft and feminine, like Hannah herself. She was so beautiful, so desirable. Yet even in the privacy of their marriage bed, he knew she was comparing him to Shadow and finding him a poor second. If only he could wipe the Indian's memory from her mind once and for all. If only he could win Hannah's love. There had to be a way.

Muttering an oath, Joshua stomped out of the bedroom and made his way to the parlor. Pouring himself a tall glass of rye whiskey, he downed it in two swallows. He would not let Hannah go without a fight. No, by damn, he would not!

In the morning, he would find her trail and bring her back.

Chapter 24

Dawn was flooding the horizon with color when I drew rein in a dry wash. I fed my son, and then fell into a deep sleep. Hours later, his crying awakened me. I fed him again, dug some bread and cheese out of my pack for myself, and drank sparingly of the water. Then, tired and aching, I climbed into the saddle, more certain than ever that I was doing the right thing.

I rode all that day, stopping only to nurse my son. That night, as he stared up at me out of solemn, midnight blue eyes, I gave him his name, as was my right according to Cheyenne custom. And the name I choose was Heecha, meaning Owl.

I rode day and night for a week, and at the end of that time, I was out of food. More rational now that I was out of Joshua's reach, I realized how foolish I had been to act so impetuously.

Looking back, I realized I should have let Josh send the baby to the San Carlos Reservation. Then, when I was stronger, I could have followed him. At the reservation, I could have hired an Apache warrior to guide us to Pine Ridge. But it was too late for that now.

In despair, I realized that my son and I would probably perish out here in the wilderness. I had no gun to hunt with, and in any case, I had seen no game. The next day I ran out of water.

Ahead lay the cave where Shadow and I once had stayed—the same cave where Joshua had found us. Leading Sunny, I trudged up the hill. There was no sign of the tiny grave where my firstborn son was buried.

Inside the cave, I used the last of my strength to spread a blanket on the ground. Then, cradling Heecha to my breast, I closed my eyes and fell asleep. And sleeping, began to dream. . . .

I was home again, back in Bear Valley. It was spring, and the world was in bloom, fragrant with the scent of wildflowers. My son slept peacefully in his cradle beneath an open window while I turned out a loaf of fresh bread. I was happy, so happy, and I sang as I worked. At noon, Shadow came in for lunch, and I flew to his arms, lifting my face for his kiss.

"Hannah," he whispered, and the sound of his voice thrilled my soul even as it filled my heart with peace and love.

"Hannah. . .Hannah!"

I woke, and still the voice called me. A loud, insistent voice, heavy with impatience and anger. Josh's voice.

"You little fool," he scolded. "Where the hell do you think you're going?"

"Home," I said wearily. "Home to the Cheyenne."

Muttering an oath, Josh slapped me, hard. So hard, my ears rang and tears scalded my eyes.

"Get up!" he demanded.

I hugged my son closer as I shook my head. "No, Josh. I'm not going back. Tell people I died. Tell them anything you want, but leave me alone. Please, just leave me alone."

Josh swore as he pulled me to my feet. Face contorted with rage, he grabbed Heecha from my arms and shoved me outside. Corporal Hopkins was waiting at the foot of the hill, and the way he looked at me made me shiver with apprehension. His eyes were as cold and yellow as those of a hunting lobo; he glanced at me and then, with a gesture I could not misunderstand, he drew his forefinger across his throat. I knew then, with crystal clarity, that Josh intended to kill my son before we started back for the post.

With a strangled sob, I whirled around and made a grab for Joshua's pistol. He pushed me away, and I fell to my hands and knees on the rocky ground. I scraped both my shins, but I was unaware of the pain as I sprang at Josh again, my hands clawing at his face.

Suddenly, from below, came the shrill cry of a man in terrible agony. Startled, I glanced over my shoulder in time to see Hopkins fall face down in the dust. A single arrow protruded from his back.

"Indians!" Josh muttered.

Grabbing a handful of my hair, he yanked me back into the protective shelter of the cave.

"It's not Indians!" I cried exultantly. "It's Shadow!"

"Impossible," Josh scoffed. "He's dead."

"Dead?" I stared at Joshua blankly. "When? Where? Who told you that?"

"No one, you little fool. Did you really think I'd let him go?" Joshua's hollow laughter echoed eerily in the dim cavern. "I had Hopkins kill him. He's been dead all along."

"No!" I shrieked. "No, he can't be!"

He can't be, I said to myself. The arrow lodged in Hopkins' back belonged to Shadow. I knew it did, because I had seen dozens of similar shafts when we rode the war trail together. Every warrior made his own arrows, and each arrow bore the mark of its maker. Shadow's feathers were always black, the shafts striped with red and black, exactly like the one that had killed Hopkins. I could not be mistaken.

Joshua thrust Heecha into my arms. "Here, take the kid."

Dropping to his knees, Joshua crawled to the entrance of the cave. "Damn," he muttered irritably. "I can't see a thing."

An hour passed, and nothing moved on the desert floor. High overhead, a lone black buzzard hovered in the air. Soon another joined it, and then another. With easy grace, they floated lightly to the ground, to become the awkward, ugly birds of prey they were. With clumsy hopping steps, they made their way to the corpse. Soon hooked beaks and long curved talons were rending the Corporal's flesh. Sickened, I pleaded with Joshua to shoot the birds—to do something, anything, to scare them away.

"Don't be a fool," Joshua snapped. "Hopkins is beyond caring, and I'm not wasting good ammunition on a bunch of vultures."

Another hour passed. I nursed Heecha, silently praying that Man Above would help us get safely away from Josh. I feared Joshua's hatred for Indians had destroyed his reason, and I feared greatly for my son's life and for my own.

My hands were shaking with nervous tension as I changed Heecha's clout. Joshua remained at the cave entrance, his gun drawn, his eyes restlessly searching for Hopkins' killer.

Another hour crawled into history. The birds had gorged themselves and left long ago. The stench of Hopkins' mutilated corpse drifted up the hill, as did the sound of the hundreds of flies that were swarming over what was left of his corpse. The two cavalry mounts stood at the foot of the hill, heads drooping, tails swishing lazily. Nothing else moved.

Finally, about five o'clock, Joshua decided it was safe to venture outside. Setting his hat on his head, he gestured at Heecha with his gun barrel.

"Leave the brat here," he said curtly.

Clutching Heecha to my breast, I took a step backward. "No, Josh. I won't leave him."

My heart began to pound heavily as Joshua started toward me. Closing the short distance between us, he unsheathed his knife and laid the finely-honed blade against my son's tiny throat.

"Put him down, Hannah, or I'll kill him."

Woodenly, I laid my son down on the rough ground and lovingly covered him with a blanket against the night's chill. I knew Heecha would die soon enough, with no one to care for him, but I could not bear to see him killed before my eyes.

"Let's go," Josh growled, and forcibly propelled me out of the cave.

Gun in hand, eyes darting warily from side to side, Josh followed me down the hill. We were almost to the bottom when I felt a warm rush of wind past my cheek, heard the quiet swish of an arrow, and then the dull thud as the shaft pierced Joshua's right arm, just below the elbow.

Josh grunted with pain and surprise as his arm went numb and his gun fell from nerveless fingers. A soft oath escaped his lips as a lone warrior rose up from the dusty brown earth.

It was Shadow. Hard and lean, naked save for a wolfskin clout, he moved catlike toward us as my hungry eyes lovingly devoured every inch of his lithe copper-hued frame.

Excitement fluttered in my stomach as I waited for Shadow to take me in his arms and hold me close, but he made no move in my direction, and when he did look at me, his eyes were hard and cold.

Joshua's face went white, as if he had seen a ghost. "You!" he hissed. "You're supposed to be dead!"

"Before the sun sets, you will wish *you* were dead," Shadow remarked flatly. Without warning, he loosed a second arrow. "You will wish it many times."

Josh groaned as the shaft pierced his left arm. Drops of bright red blood dripped from his wounds, staining the ground at his feet.

"Shadow, don't," I whispered.

"Keep out of this, Hannah," Shadow said brusquely. "It is between Berdeen and myself. You have no part in it."

Feeling as though I were talking to a stranger, I crossed the distance between us and laid my hand on Shadow's arm. "Please don't kill him. It isn't right."

"You love this man so much you would beg me for his life?" Shadow demanded scornfully. "You are a foolish woman, if you think I would spare your lover after all he has done."

"He's not my lover! I've never loved anyone but you."

"You lie!"

"No, it is the truth. I only married Josh because he said he would let you go free."

"None of it matters now, Hannah," Shadow said tonelessly.

"What do you mean, it doesn't matter? I love you, Shadow. I've never loved anyone else. Only you. You must believe me!"

Something that might have been joy flickered in the depths of Shadow's fathomless black eyes as he read the truth in my face; then it was quickly gone.

"He must die," Shadow said.

I knew better than to argue with that hard cruel tone of voice. It was not Shadow speaking now, but the warrior Two Hawks Flying, and I knew nothing I could say or do would deter him from killing Josh. It was a matter of pride, of honor. The same sense of honor that had taken him away from me once before, when he left me to fight with his people.

Joshua screamed as Shadow callously ripped the arrow from his left arm. He fainted when Shadow jerked the shaft from his right arm.

Face impassive, Shadow staked Joshua out where he had fallen and stood there, unmoving, until Joshua regained consciousness. I stood beside Shadow, wondering what he was thinking. Was he remembering that day long ago at this same place? Was he remembering a tiny baby and an unmarked grave? Was he remembering Red Wind? Or was he remembering the long ride to Fort Apache, and the days he spent in a tiny cell?

With a low moan, Joshua opened his eyes. He glared defiantly at Shadow, his expression filled with pain and hatred, nothing more, until he realized what was in store for him. Then, and only then, did I see fear in his eyes.

"I leave you the death you once planned for me," Shadow said tonelessly. "And I take back what is rightfully mine."

"Hannah, for God's sake, stop him," Josh croaked. "I'll do anything you say. Anything."

I turned away then. Much as I had grown to hate Joshua Berdeen, it grieved me to see him in pain. I shuddered to think of the agony he would suffer before he died, and yet I could not help feeling that he had brought it all on himself. All the pain and hatred he had so callously meted out was coming home to roost at last.

While Shadow stripped the rigging from the two cavalry mounts and turned them loose, I ran up the hill to the cave.

Inside, I scooped Heecha into my arms and hugged him close before scurrying back down the brush-covered slope.

Shadow's expression turned sour when he saw the blanket-wrapped bundle in my arms, and I could not help grinning when I thought how surprised he would be when he learned the child was not Joshua's, as he supposed, but his.

Shadow had stripped Josh of his clothing and boots. Blood continued to ooze from Josh's wounds, and I hoped he would bleed to death before the animals came. Sweat stood out on Joshua's brow, caused more by pain and fear than the heat of the day. Great clouds of black flies had deserted Hopkins' stiffening corpse to swarm on the fresh blood dripping from Joshua's wounds.

A wolf howled in the distance, and its predatory cry sent a shiver down my spine. The scent of blood would draw them to Joshua, and he would be powerless to fight them off. A horrible picture loomed in my mind of yellow fangs rending still-living flesh. I could hear Joshua's screams of agony, taste the fear in his mouth as the wolves closed in, see his wild struggles, feel his helpless despair. It would be a cruel death, and even though I realized Josh had planned a similar fate for Shadow, I was appalled at the prospect.

I turned pleading eyes toward Shadow, but he shook his head. "Berdeen dies, Hannah," he declared sharply. "I know you do not approve, but it is the way it must be."

Shadow lifted me into the saddle, handed me Sunny's reins, and then swung aboard his own horse. It was a tall spotted stallion, the kind favored by the Nez Perce Indians.

Side by side, we rode away from the hill. I did not look back.

The cave, and Joshua, lay far behind us when Heecha began to whimper. Wordlessly, Shadow reined up in the lee of a high yellow bluff. His handsome face was shut against me as he helped me dismount, and I could not help smiling as I anticipated how surprised he was going to be when I told him the baby in my arms was his.

Just then Heecha let out a long hungry wail, and I crooned, "Don't cry, little one. See? Your Father is here, and everything is all right at last."

Shadow's dark eyes searched mine and then, ever so slowly, he reached out and took Heecha from my arms.

It took but one look to see that Heecha carried the proud blood of the Cheyenne nation in his veins, and I murmured, "Is he not beautiful, my husband?" and then laughed aloud at the look of wondrous joy and astonishment that swept over Shadow's face.

Moved beyond words, Shadow nodded as

he examined the baby from head to foot. "A son," he murmured at last. "My heart soars like the hawk."

He kissed me then, long and hard, and I sighed with contentment. At last, I was back where I belonged. I nursed Heecha beneath Shadow's loving gaze, and at that moment, I would have asked for nothing more.

Later that night, camped alongside a shallow stream, Shadow told me everything that had happened since we parted. He told me of Joshua's treachery, of Clyde Stewart and Barney McCall and the awful months he had spent with Hansen's Traveling Tent Show. It filled me with bitter sorrow to think of the pain and humiliation he had endured, to think of him being exhibited before mocking crowds. How his pride must have suffered! I wept unashamedly when I saw the ugly scars that cross-crossed his broad back and shoulders; I murmured a silent prayer when he told me of the white woman who had taken him in. I did not begrudge her the hours she had spent with my man. But for her, Shadow might have died, and I would never have seen his beloved face again.

Lying content in the circle of his arms, with our son sleeping peacefully between us, I asked Shadow where we were going.

"I do not know," he answered. "There is

no place left where an Indian can be free."

"We could go back to Bear Valley," I ventured.

And suddenly I was homesick. Oh, to go home, I thought. To see the plains and swim in the river again. To ride the trails I had ridden as a child. To see Rabbit's Head Rock and walk in the woods.

"We could rebuild the house," I went on eagerly. "It would be a good place to raise our son."

"We can try, if you like," Shadow agreed, but there was no enthusiasm in his voice.

Home. How good the word sounded in my ears. There would be painful memories there, but in time, they would fade, and we would replace the sad times with happy ones as we watched our children grow.

Excited by the prospect, I sat up, hugging my knees to my chest. In my mind's eye, I saw a small two bedroom cabin, and me in the kitchen baking bread. I had a sudden mental image of Shadow behind a plow, and I began to laugh. Might as well try to change the spots on a leopard as try to make a farmer out of a warrior, I thought, and laughed the harder as I remembered how I had once tried to imagine Shadow in a suit and tie, strolling down a lamplit street in New York City.

"What is so funny?" Shadow asked,

baffled by my laughter.

"Oh, nothing," I said, wiping the tears from my eyes. "Forget about Bear Valley. It would never work. Listen, Shadow, what about Mexico? I hear Geronimo is on the warpath again."

"No. It would be too hard on you and the little one," he answered dully, but I saw a gleam of excitement flicker deep in his eyes.

"But better than the reservation," I countered stubbornly. "And that's all that's left to us now."

Shadow made a sound of disgust low in his throat that eloquently summed up his feelings about living on the reservation.

"Mexico," I mused pensively. "Perhaps Calf Running is there."

"Perhaps."

"I should like to see Calf Running again."

"Mexico, then," Shadow agreed.

I had a glimpse of the future then—of running and hiding, of being always on the move. Shadow was right. It would not be easy, especially now that we had Heecha. But it would be better than life on the reservation and depending on greedy Indian agents for food and clothing.

We made love the whole night long, eagerly getting reacquainted with each other. What bliss to be in Shadow's arms again and hear his voice huskily murmur my name. The touch of his mouth on mine and the way his hands caressed my willing flesh—all combined to carry me into a wondrous world where nothing else existed but the man rising over me.

How I loved to look at him! I held him close, drinking in the scent of his flesh, relishing the touch of his sweat-sheened skin beneath my hands. My fingers kneaded the powerful muscles in his arms and back and gloried in their strength.

I looked into my past, and it seemed he had always been there. Friend, lover, companion, a tower of strength to lean on. He was a part of my life, deeply woven into the fabric of my past and my future.

Ecstasy followed ecstasy as the passion between us burned brighter and hotter than the sun at noonday. Higher and higher we climbed, until we reached that glorious moment when two became one.

Never had our love seemed so sweet as it did that night under the stars, and I knew I could face anything the world had to offer so long as I had Shadow at my side.

Chapter 25
Fall 1878 - Spring 1879

In the morning, we packed our few belongings and began the journey to Mexico. We rode close together, our legs almost touching. Shadow frequently reached out to stroke my arm, as if he couldn't quite believe I was really there. I felt the same. We had been apart for so long, I was afraid I would wake up to find him gone.

Despite our joy at being together again, we traveled warily across the desert, fearful of running into one of the patrols from the fort. I knew if Shadow were caught, he would be hanged, and the thought weighed heavily on my mind, for I could not bear to lose him again.

The sun was hot, the land dry and arid, unfriendly as we made our way across the sandy wasteland. For miles, there was little more than sun and sky and spiny cactus. Water was scarce and though our rations often ran short, we never had to do without, for Shadow knew every tank and waterhole.

Heecha was a good little traveler. He slept most of the time, lulled to sleep by the rocking motion of my horse.

Shadow often watched me nurse the baby, and I could feel his love for us and see it in his eyes.

Moving ever southward, I had the feeling that we were the last two people on earth, for we never saw another soul, red or white. In fact, the only living thing we saw was a wild pig. When I expressed a desire for pork, Shadow put his spotted stallion after the grizzled sow, and the chase was on.

I watched, laughing with delight, as the harried pig cut back and forth across the desert, trying to elude the man on horseback. But no matter how fast the sow ran, or how adroitly she zigzagged back and forth, the spotted stallion stayed close on her heels.

Shadow cut loose with the Cheyenne war cry as he drew an arrow from the quiver slung across his back. It did my heart good to see him having fun for a change. Looking back, I could not recall too many times when he had been carefree and happy. It seemed he had always been weighed down with responsibility—first for his people, then for me. Later, he had our little band of renegades to worry about. And now he had a baby to think of.

At length, when both horse and sow were getting winded, Shadow put the arrow to his bow and killed the pig.

He was grinning with triumph when he reined his stallion to a halt. Dismounting, he landed lightly on his feet beside me.

"I have done my work," he said, handing me his knife. "Now you must do yours."

"Yes, master," I said with mock submissiveness. "Anything you say, master."

"Be still, woman," he said, his voice as mockingly grave as mine had been docile. "Or I shall be forced to show you just how masterful I can be."

"Spare me, milord," I said, pressing myself against him. "I will do anything to avoid your anger."

"Anything?" Shadow posed wickedly.

"Anything but skin that carcass. Do it for me, please."

He laughed at that. Taking the knife from my hand, he butchered the pig while I nursed the baby and changed his clout. Soon, the sweet scent of roasting pork filled the air, and my mouth watered as I sliced the succulent meat and served it.

* * *

Day by day, we made our way toward Mexico. My original attitude about joining Geronimo changed from enthusiasm to trepidation as the miles passed by.

Geronimo was a name to strike terror into the heart of any white man or woman. Born in 1829, he was a Bedonkohe Apache. Originally, he was called Goyanthlay, meaning One Who Yawns. As a young warrior, he married and lived in peace, but when his family was murdered by Mexican troops some twelve years later, he turned into a man of vengeance. It was the Mexicans who gave him the name Geronimo. In the 1860's, he married a Chiricahua woman and lived with her people, according to Apache custom. When Cochise decided to walk the path of peace, Geronimo left the Chiricahuas and continued to ride the war path, raiding Mexico and Arizona.

Perhaps we were being foolish to ride into his war camp deep in the heart of Mexico. Perhaps he had never heard of Two Hawks Flying. The Cheyenne and Apache had never been allies. There was a good chance we would be shot on sight.

I held Heecha closer. What had I gotten us into?

It was a cool fall day when we crossed the shallow Rio Grande and entered Mexico. I was suddenly tense all over, and I noticed Shadow rode even more warily than usual, his sharp eyes and ears attuned for anything that might mean trouble.

We made no fire that night. I slept fitfully. Shadow did not sleep at all.

We had been south of the border three days when Geronimo found us. One minute we were alone in the desert, the next we were surrounded by twenty Apache warriors armed and painted for battle.

I searched their faces, seeking for a trace of welcome or a familiar face. I found neither.

Geronimo was a stocky warrior, with a flat Indian face, a wide mouth, a high forehead, and unfriendly eyes.

"What are you doing here, Cheyenne?" he asked in a deep voice.

"I have come to fight with Geronimo and his warriors."

Geronimo looked skeptical. "Does your woman fight also?"

"She has ridden with me into battle in the past," Shadow boasted proudly. "If need be, she will ride with me again."

What might have passed for a smile flitted briefly across the old warrior's face. "And the little one?"

"He will learn."

"Calf Running has told me often of Two

Hawks Flying and his warrior woman. Come, our camp is not far from here."

The Apache rancheria was located in a canyon that had only one narrow entrance. I saw immediately that it would be a good place to hold against invaders, for a handful of warriors, strategically placed atop the rocky canyon walls, could easily discourage anyone who sought to enter.

Only a handful of Geronimo's people were here; the rest of the warriors and most of the women were in the mountain stronghold farther south.

The women in camp were all young and strong. They eyed me curiously as I stepped from my horse. One of them stared hard at Shadow, her expression indicating she found him desirable.

Lifting my chin, I laid my hand possessively on Shadow's arm. My gesture clearly said, "He is mine." The Apache woman understood. With a friendly grin, she shrugged and turned away.

Our reunion with Calf Running brought tears to my eyes. His left arm hung useless at his side, shattered by a bullet during a run-in with Mexican soldiers.

"Do not be sad, Hannah," he said. "An arm is a small price to pay for freedom."

The next few days were busy ones. The

women helped me erect a wickiup, and I was grateful for their help, for I did not relish the thought of living in the open, as did some of the warriors. Nor did I have any desire to nurse my son in public. I knew many Indian women had no compulsion about such things, but I felt shy among strangers.

In a week, it seemed as if we had been living with the Apaches all our lives. The women were friendly, and they all fussed over Heecha, who was the only child in camp.

We spent many evenings with Calf Running and his woman, catching up on the past. Calf Running told us how, in 1877, Geronimo and his followers had been arrested by United States authorities and confined to the San Carlos reservation, a place so awful it had been nicknamed Hell's Forty Acres. They had tried to farm the land, but the Apaches were warriors not farmers, and they had run away and were even now being hunted by the American military and the Mexican rurales.

We spent two months with the Apache. Shadow joined them in many raids on both sides of the border, and once again I knew the awful gut-wrenching fear every woman knows when her man is at war.

One day they raided a Mexican rancho, and that night they returned with a treasure of clothing and blankets, sugar, coffee, salt, clay jars of milk, and a half-dozen mules and horses.

It was a rare treat to have coffee generously laced with sugar and milk, and yet I felt guilty as I drank it, for I knew people had been killed in the raid.

My days were busy ones. Shadow killed a large buck, and I worked hard at tanning the hide to make new clothes for the three of us.

Heecha was growing every day, it seemed, and I loved him beyond words. He was a happy, healthy baby, and I thanked God daily that I had been blessed with such a son.

Late that fall, our peaceful existence was shattered when a troop of Mexican soldiers found our hideaway. There was a brief skirmish in which four Mexicans and seven Apaches were killed, then the Mexicans drew back out of rifle range. They did not attack again. They did not try to enter the canyon. They simply took a position and held it, so that the warriors could not leave the canyon.

As the days passed, food grew scarce. A week earlier, the balance of Geronimo's people had come to the valley from the mountains, so that there were now many more mouths to feed. In a month, most of our food was gone.

Shadow did without, insisting that I eat what little we had. And I did not argue, because I had Heecha to think of. It was touching, when some of the women brought me the last of their food.

"For the little one," they said.

With the coming of winter, conditions went from bad to worse. All the mules and horses had been killed, save a handful of war horses. I had wept when Sunny was killed, but I could not insist she remain alive when people were starving. It seemed odd to spare some of the horses, but I knew they would be needed if we got a chance to make a run for it. If that time came, the young men and women would try to escape. The old and infirm would stay behind.

And then, when it seemed we would perish, the soldiers mysteriously withdrew.

Hunting and raiding were never good in the winter, and with that in mind, Geronimo and his people decided to return to the reservation until spring. It was a tactic many of the Indians practiced—raid and fight in the spring and summer, return to the reservation for food and blankets in the winter.

Naturally, Shadow refused to go. Calf Running and Flower Woman also decided to stay behind.

"I will fight no more" Shadow said as he

watched the Apaches ride out of the canyon. "Life is too sweet to risk in a war that can never be won. There is a small valley four day's ride from here. There is water, and grass for the horses. There is game and fish. I think five people could live there in peace for a long time. What say you?"

Calf Running and Flower Woman agreed, and Shadow glanced at me.

"Do you think there will be room enough in the valley for six?" I asked.

For a moment, Shadow looked puzzled. Then his eyes darted from my face to my stomach and back again.

I nodded slowly, wondering if he would be pleased with the news that I was pregnant.

"Six will not be too many," he said happily, and lifting me up, he twirled me round and round until we were all laughing.

The little valley was beautiful. There were trees for shade, a winding blue river filled with fat fish, berry bushes, and tall grass that was now brown but would be green again in the spring.

As we set up our wickiup, I felt as if I were home at last. The valley, uninhabited for years, seemed to welcome us. Winter that year was short and mild. We had food enough and plenty of water, and setting up housekeeping was, for once, more of a pleasure than a chore. Flower Woman and I became good friends, and when she announced that she, too, was pregnant, life seemed perfect.

Spring came overnight. Flowers bloomed, the grass turned a brilliant green, and the trees sprouted leaves. Sometimes, in the evening, we saw a doe at the river, a spotted fawn at her side.

The days passed in sweet contentment. The past, so full of trouble and heartache, seemed far behind us now. And the nights. . . ah, they were glorious, for Shadow was ever beside me, his dark eyes ablaze with love and desire.

Tonight was no different, and as he whispered my name, I was flooded with a sense of peace and happiness. I went eagerly into his open arms. His mouth was warm on mine as he drew me close, igniting the fire that smoldered always between us, welding our bodies together.

I closed my eyes as he drew me close, and the past and the future were forgotten in the breathless wonder of now and the timeless magic of our love.

FORBIDDEN LOVE

Karen Robards

PASSION, TENDERNESS AND WIT

Justin Brant, Earl of Weston, had prided himself on meticulously fulfilling his obligations as guardian to his dead brother's adopted daughter, though he regarded the rebellious child as a nuisance. On her part, Megan considered him a stern figure, cold and distant.

Now, at seventeen, Megan had blossomed into a breathtaking beauty. For Justin, Megan was forbidden fruit dangling temptingly within his grasp. But Megan knew that in spite of everything, she must give herself to the one man in the world whose bride she could never be.

LEISURE BOOKS

PRICE: $3.50 US/$3.95 CAN
0-8439-2024-6

UNDER CRIMSON SAILS

Lynna Lawton

Beautiful, spirited Janielle Patterson had heard of the reckless way pirate Ryan Deverel treated his women. He seduced them with the same abandon with which he plundered ships. To the handsome pirate, women were prizes to be won, used, and tossed away.

Ryan intrigued and repelled Janielle—and when they finally met, she was shocked to discover that her own nature was as passionate as the pirate's!

But while he was driven by desire, she was driven by a fierce hatred. Yet she knew neither of them would rest until she had surrendered to him fully.

LEISURE BOOKS   **2002-5/$3.50**

Make the Most of Your
Leisure Time
with
LEISURE BOOKS

Please send me the following titles:

Quantity	Book Number	Price
_____	_____	_____
_____	_____	_____
_____	_____	_____
_____	_____	_____
_____	_____	_____

If out of stock on any of the above titles, please send me the alternate title(s) listed below:

_____	_____	_____
_____	_____	_____
_____	_____	_____
_____	_____	_____

Postage & Handling _____

Total Enclosed $_____

☐ Please send me a free catalog.

NAME _____
(please print)

ADDRESS _____

CITY _____ STATE _____ ZIP _____

Please include $1.00 shipping and handling for the first book ordered and 25¢ for each book thereafter in the same order. All orders are shipped within approximately 4 weeks via postal service book rate. PAYMENT MUST ACCOMPANY ALL ORDERS.*

*Canadian orders must be paid in US dollars payable through a New York banking facility.

Mail coupon to: **Dorchester Publishing Co., Inc.**
6 East 39 Street, Suite 900
New York, NY 10016
Att: ORDER DEPT.